WE ARE BUT A MOMENT

WE ARE BUT A MOMENT

ULRICH BAER

Warbler Press

ISBN 978-1-7347353-9-0 (paperback)
ISBN 978-1-7348526-2-2 (ebook)

warblerpress.com

Printed in the United States of America. This edition is printed with chlorine-free ink on acid-free interior paper made from 30% post-consumer waste recycled material.

JACKET AND BOOK DESIGN BY STEPHEN DOYLE

Why see the world, when you got the beach.

—FRANK OCEAN, "Sweet Life"

We are these transformers of the Earth. Our entire existence, the flights and sudden plunges of our love, everything qualifies us for this task (beside which there exists, essentially, no other).

—RAINER MARIA RILKE, Letter to Witold Hulewicz, November 13, 1925

I thought that my species was in danger, that we are in the end, that we deserve to live. But today it's not important if you die, if you don't die; if you live, if you don't live. What's important is the planet.

—SEBASTIÃO SALGADO, "Climate Change: Genesis - A Call to Arms," International Center for Photography, New York City, September 20, 2014

CHAPTERS

Day 1

You make the bed you lie in, they say, but in this case, it's Zaha Hadid who made the bed. I'm prone on the floor in front of Hadid's curvy creation, slight ripples pressing into my butt and back. The room's floor, walls, and ceiling are all molded out of a plastic that feels like a cat's tongue. The bed is curved like everything else in this room. Walls, door frames, a fixed table, a chair. Instead of windows, display screens all around. An opening for medical staff to reach into the pod. The surfaces are probably coated with something so that bacteria won't stick. It's not a big room, for sure, but the bed and table flip up so I have space to exercise. Like a college dorm room, or a cheap hotel. No sharp edges, to avoid injury, and to discourage those in quarantine — I'm one of *those* for the time being — from getting any funny ideas about how to cut short the incubation period by their own doing. It feels like being in a spaceship, or as if I am a seed expected to sprout.

I arrived yesterday and slept for a couple of hours. I am exhausted from the processing that followed the determination that I had been exposed by one of the doctors who'd come to see me at the White House for debriefing from a hot spot. "Positive," a technician had mumbled without so much as looking up at me from the monitor he was holding in front of him like a medieval shield. It was a whirlwind after that, getting checked by the White House doctor, rushed by ambulance to a better hospital in Maryland, and from there deposited here. It all worked well, under the circumstances, just as we had designed. RWS, we call what I'm going through now: *real world scenario*. Just funny that I'm the one out of all of the people on our team who has to test drive the whole thing. Not really funny. Ironic.

I have been issued hospital clothes made of the same fabric as the sheets. Soft as cashmere but they are, of course, a synthetic bacteria-eating fiber. Someone in a hazmat suit with a long tube coming out the back led me to my pod in a warehouse-type building with long, hospital-bright hallways. The quarantine carpets glowed when I stepped on them and more people in suits with infection-sniffing dogs peered at me from behind their masks before moving out of the way. Seth had funded the prototype for Hadid's design of this pod. After the med engineers tweaked her design, he got IKEA to finance and take over global production. If I searched my tablet, I could find out exactly how much each unit costs and how many of them have been produced so far. Probably even the exact measurements, airflow, and the nanotechnology that makes the walls feel like they're alive. The units were designed to be lightweight, collapsible, and pretty much indestructible once set up, and they can be so thoroughly cleaned that they can be used over and over again.

The air is being sucked out and filtered, and the small drains on the floor will also suck out any fluids. The toilet, even with Hadid's genius design, has no lid and looks like something you'd see in prison. The small windows on the door can be closed on my side, but it's easy to spot the tiny recessed lenses in the ceiling and walls, so I know I'm never quite alone. Well, it's not supposed to be a vacation. What we developed here is something to protect the population at large if there's a risk of contagion. I will be in here for exactly six days. Then I'll be released, free to go. Unless symptoms appear, but I don't want to think about what happens then. The rate of developing symptoms hovers near 60 percent. So, I have one in three chances of getting out of here. I haven't exactly been a model of health, but I'm thirty-four, obviously haven't eaten meat in a long while, don't smoke, don't drink much, take edibles only occasionally, consume a pretty good amount of sea minerals (thank you, Keon), take all of my boosters, and have no major health problems. That takes me out of the high-risk group.

And to think that it was I who had helped come up with all these rules in the staff meetings, with Seth, the reps from State, the UN, the WHO, the other geeks, the Joints' medical team, and our own scientific and medical advisors. To think it was I who presented to the group — right when we were first tasked by Lucia after the Inauguration — a draft of the protocol for minimizing risk while retaining some patients' rights. I posted an overview of every public health threat throughout history, including plague, influenza, tuberculosis, HIV, cancer, bird flu, SARS, and Ebola 2r. Didn't know about whatever it was the doctor brought back from his assignment.

I remember the planning meetings in a large conference room at State. We didn't meet in the White House since everyone assumed an outbreak would start abroad and be brought here on a plane, or in a container of pork from China. We all thought a dude in Arizona frying some bacon would start sweating and retching, and suddenly we would act to isolate a community, with military backup, domes, choppers, and all. The medical researchers waged a campaign against the word "if" and insisted that a large pandemic hitting the US was not a matter of "if," but "when."

I've made the bed. Now I'm lying in it.

Some of the rules we came up with:

- No VIP treatment for anyone, not even senior administration. "The priority of quarantine is to protect the general population, and also to care for the affected individual," the head medical guy explained to us.
- Borderline cases get quarantined. That means anyone who's been in contact with contagious people will be locked up and observed until symptoms show, or don't.

- "Humanitarian concerns require the temporary suspension of movement and restriction of access to the rest of the population," our legal folks explained. "Putting people in quarantine — including foreign nationals — is compatible with UN charters."
- No right to opt out of quarantine unless completely cleared and authorized by government-approved doctors. This was intended so that you couldn't bribe your way out.
- The same treatment protocol for everyone, based on maximizing outcomes for the public good. (That pretty much means I'll have to swallow whatever pills they'll give me, unless I want to be tied to the bed for six days so they can inject the stuff.)

A lot of medical rules, of course.

I couldn't take any personal belongings in here besides the tablet. Thank God for Apple's *Pachyderm* product line. They would've dunked this thing in an acid bath if they followed all the protocols we had developed. It looks as good as new, and the disinfectant finally took off the glue from the stickers Asturias's team put on each time they scrub the tablet for spyware.

Weirdly, though, I cannot get online. I can place the tablet on the table or against the wall to charge the battery, but there's no connectivity. They seem to have strong firewalls — I've thought of all possible password combinations, used a few older VPNs, tricked it by impersonating an outside break-in to activate the tablet's system to get online help, but I cannot jump on the network. "No outside contact during quarantine, so as not to alarm the population, and to make it more difficult for rumors to arise," Seth had proposed in his typically grandiose way. But why keep people off-line?

I didn't have a chance to speak to Lucia before they checked me out and brought me here. There were quite a few people in that meeting and now I wonder whether others are here in the same unit right now. I forwarded the files for the next couple of days when I was already in the ambulance, but everything was such a rush that I'm worried I missed something.

"Sending good energy/ you'll b fine," she had messaged from her private line right before I got checked in. That's the last message I got. I know she wrote it herself: it had the little checkmark. With the exception of her few days on Nantucket, and one or two trips to Montana, today is then one of the first days we haven't directly communicated, probably since the first campaign events. They must have told her where I was headed. But once protocol for health stuff kicks in, even POTUS gets only partial updates. It sure isn't going to work to have me out of contact for days.

The time's displayed in the wall. Five hours have passed since I arrived. I didn't think I would have slept that much. Someone must have been in the room because everything looks sort of straightened up, although there are so few objects here, and they've pulled down screens on the walls. Or maybe a robot does that. I'll have to stay awake so I don't miss the next visit. They project stuff onto the screens to make you feel like you're looking at the outside. I am surprised that it doesn't bother me all that much — that I'm locked inside a gleaming white and curvy pod with a door that does not have a handle or lock on the inside. I should be panicked. Did I get a shot to calm me down? Who knows what they're putting in the water or the air. It's the first time I've slept more than four hours at a stretch, except on a plane, since the first campaign.

Still no connectivity.

The time display comes on only when I move, like an ad in the mirror of a hotel lobby. I wonder about my watch. You would think that they could disinfect it, like the tablet, from whatever it is that's making people sick. A gift from Keon. It was expensive, and he bought it for me right after the election.

We had been celebrating all night, and even he had been drinking. In the morning, we slept for a few hours and then walked to a fancy jewelry shop in D.C. where the only other customers were two women in headscarves trying on insanely big diamond necklaces. It was surprisingly cold for November, and parts of the city were still blocked off due to the damage from the second hurricane. Lucia was in Montana with the family, and I had two or three days to myself. Keon asked the sales guy a million questions about who manufactured the watches, under what conditions, how the company disposed of waste, what green certification they had, and whether the luminescent dots on the dial were toxic.

We watched promo videos of an Italian company that gives back to the regions where the metals are mined, and Keon pretended not to be happy with their sourcing. It was a ruse. Then another sales guy came out and presented a gaudy box with white silk orchids on top: I loved it. The watch has a blue face with the moon phases. On the back, he had engraved the stars above New Orleans on the day, or rather the night, when we met. Very Keon. The watch is beautiful and also pretty much indestructible, and I always wear it. A few weeks after Keon gave it to me I accidentally left it at the shed, and we had to drive back for nearly an hour to retrieve it, me already on a conference call, Keon racing like a madman down the forest road. This was when we hadn't even yet bought the shed, since we couldn't really figure out who owned it between the two guys who claimed to have the deed. Keon had talked to one of them, who turned out to be more or less a squatter, into giving him the keys before the whole sale was settled. We had spent two glorious, quiet days there during which we noticed how the squatter had turned what had been a logger's shed into a really clever little house. Smart windows, smart roof, smart ceiling: a lot of it glass and all of it quite beautiful. The kitchen and living room looked like an amazingly well-lit cave until you pulled some levers, and then, when the panels retracted, it felt like you were standing right in the forest, since pretty much one whole side of the little house is transparent. Keon's ex-girlfriend, who is now married to the guy who manages the soccer stadium where I saw the Mexico game with Lucia, had left us a couple of amazing wool blankets that are thick enough to use as rugs. It wasn't one of our first trips, but the first one after the election, and the two days we spent there really brought us closer together. The nights were magical, with the tall trees surrounding the cabin awash in silvery moonlight, and the only sounds made by the wind and some birds and critters. We slept on the floor back then, since Keon had not yet built the bed he wanted, and just looked up at the trees and stars above. In the mornings the sun inched across the floor when it cleared the treetops, and we got up after only a few hours of sleep to sit outside despite the chill, sipping coffee and just being still. Keon talked a lot about his childhood in New Orleans, about his mother and his grandparents, about his ex, and why they had broken up. I remember making mental notes during that conversation so we wouldn't end up in the same place ("not a worry!" Keon said and laughed his infectious laugh when he noticed that my face had tensed up), but for most of those two days I was carefree. I dug up a weedy section right by the house that may once have served as a tiny pasture, maybe for goats or chicken, picking out rocks and preparing beds, even though we hadn't been able to put money down for the place. Today that part has gotten bigger, and it's where I've put some really big blue-leaved hostas, big ferns, hellebores, and asters. We were on a bit of a high from the election, of course, but we made a point not to talk about work, about the change that was going to happen in our lives with the move.

I realized on the drive back that I didn't have the watch.

"It's fine to get it next time," I said. "It's safe there, and we have to get back."

Keon nodded and I thought we had settled the matter. Then, he braked quite suddenly, and spun the car around in a U-turn. "I gave you that watch, and I want you to wear it," he said. "Especially now, when you'll be at work pretty much all of the time. It'll make you think of me when you'll be too busy to do anything else."

We raced back. It takes about ten minutes to properly lock everything at the shed, and so we spent about a half an hour total to get into the house, look for the watch (hanging from a nail by the shower), and then barricade it again. I felt bad we had to go back, since it meant I would be on a call for most of the drive home. "I'm so stupid not to check whether I had it . . ." I started, but Keon wouldn't have any of it.

"No worries. I liked the look on your face when you first opened the box, and the point of a present is to make someone happy. What's so important about a half an hour of sleep?"

"I had that look because you must have spent a ton of money," I said.

"No, you had tears in your eyes because it's so romantic," Keon said and laughed again. "And because, if I do say so myself, it's quite inspired to have the stars engraved on it."

"True," I said, and rested my hand on his leg.

We drove back with my phone mounted on a small stand on the dashboard for my conference call. Keon raced down the road like a squirrel chased by a hawk, and just smiled when I gestured with my hand out of the camera's view for him to slow down.

The bamboo that I planted when we first got the place now blocks the view from the the service road to the shed. The only giveaway is the patches of berries, and in spring and then again in the fall, the fruit trees that at least to my eye stand out like scarecrows amidst the spindly pine and brush on the side where the forest has been cleared. Some heritage guys in Ohio breed these old cultivars that are strong enough not to get choked by the weeds and brush.

Natural Negotiation: Tokyo

I woke up to the sounds of howling winds and driving rain. I looked around. Nothing had changed inside the room. I lay there for a while under the astronaut-type blanket. I banged on the door, tried to get the attention of the medics who checked my vitals from the other side of the screen, even wrote a message on my tablet, "Please turn off sound!" and held it up to the screens. The medics nodded, but I couldn't see their expressions behind the masks. They moved along. Then suddenly the sound died down.

I listened intently. I powered down the tablet since it seemed to be humming even in sleep mode. Nothing. No wind, no patter of rain. Complete silence, punctuated with the occasional banging of someone working outside the unit. No rolling thunder. Nothing. As if the vents had suddenly sucked the sound out of the room along with the used air.

It reminds me of Tokyo, the day after Typhoon Michio. I have never been in a place of such silence before or since. I've never been in a place where the silence seems to fill your lungs.

We had landed at Narita at dawn after a long flight that had chased the sun, a golden glow always just ahead of us, and out of sight, below the horizon. From the plane, the edge of the earth had looked like the rim of a vast soup bowl set on a dark blue velvet cloth. Even though Air Force One is an official Global Alliance plane, we sat at Narita for a good hour for disinfection and on-board temp screenings. I'd been to Tokyo once before, when there was no crisis, with Keon, and even then we had been struck by the length of the arrival corridors with disinfectant carpets, the rows upon rows of security gates to check the passengers' temperature, and the number of medics standing by with clipboards, cameras, and dogs. "I think we're being timed," Keon had said, "like runners on the steeple chase," but from his voice I knew that he wanted to pass through this gauntlet quickly without getting stopped.

Stepping off AF1 onto the tarmac, I noticed the absence of any greeting committee. No ceremony. Domineek had prepared a memo on how to properly interact with our Japanese counterparts since Lucia was the first US president to visit to Japan in a while. But instead of the phalanx of officials we had been told to expect, only a small handful of people bowed deeply to Lucia and quickly ushered her into the first car lined up on the tarmac. I got in with her, and everyone else hurried to the other cars. We drove past big airport parking lots filled with what looked like thousands of buses, many with their doors open but nobody in sight. There were a lot of empty cars lined up along the roads leading out of the airport, too.

Typhoon Michio had made landfall in the morning three days before. No trains were running. All private transportation had been suspended so that emergency vehicles could use the roads. As we drove along the empty highway in the small motorcade, I watched long treks of people march past the military guarding the road. Only a few people carried anything.

"These are people who don't want to wait for buses to take them back to their homes," the woman next to me said. "People can move freely, of course, but we don't provide services yet in this region for non-emergency use."

We drove past heaps of cars piled on the highway's opposite lane. They were packed tight against the guardrail, like toy cars jumbled in a moving box. There were no cleanup crews, no tow trucks, no cranes. The motorcade slowed down; we stopped a few times. When we moved again, we crossed a pontoon bridge where part of the highway had been ripped out. We exited our cars and from a spot just past the bridge lined with soldiers, we looked over a vast lake dotted with floating trees, parts of buildings, rooftops, walls, smashed furniture, pieces of wood, small cars, dead cattle. The water shimmered in all directions, with occasional islands made of flotsam bunched around a tree or post, where you could sometimes spot people in neon-colored jackets. Small orange-and-white boats maneuvered the watery plane. Bigger, flat inflatables with armed soldiers on patrol plowed along the water right next to the highway.

We got back into the car, and I sat in the row behind Lucia and the Japanese prime minister, next to another official. The prime minister pointed out things and talked to Lucia in a soft voice. It was hard to hear anything. First, I thought it was crackling on the driver's radio, which was audible even in the back. But it was the silence that swallowed everything up, as if we ourselves were underwater.

The prime minister quietly described the estimated death tolls. It had been the worst storm to hit Japan in living memory, and the worst ever to hit Tokyo.

"We are lucky that so many people could evacuate beforehand," he said, "but many have no place to go. We stationed the army in strategic areas to prevent people from returning to homes in the reclamation zone. People want to go back and retrieve things, but it's not safe yet. There have been some problems with those trying to force their way past our men."

I watched the soldiers on the side of the highway, and the patrol boats. Several smaller vessels picked up those stranded on the islands. It was strangely peaceful, and in spite of the little boats going to and from the islands, loading passengers in bright orange-and-red vests, and the clouds passing above, the whole blue-and-white scene struck me as immobile, chiseled in time like Hokusai's *Wave*.

We got out of the car again. I had expected to hear the sounds of outboard motors, but then remembered that Japan had banned diesel engines in 2018. The water lay flat and satiny in all directions, as if pressed down by the silence around us. It felt as if you would have to make an effort to push through it.

"Much of this area will become part of 'natural negotiation,'" the woman next to me said. "We are letting the water carve out its needs."

Like everyone in the Japanese delegation, she wore a dark suit. Around her neck she had a bunch of official ID cards with biometric pictures of her, and as she pointed at something in the distance, the little portrait gallery on her chest fanned out like a deck of cards.

"Shinagawa, Minato, and the whole southern area around Haneda Airport will be restored," she said. "This means that townships will not be rebuilt, and homeowners will not be permitted to move back. Many people refused to evacuate. For the moment, our forces only assist those who request help to retrieve essentials and leave for good. The area from Shinagawa to Haneda has been condemned and will be fully restored even after the water recedes."

"So no rebuilding there?" I asked.

"Correct, no rebuilding. Here is a map of the flood zones that had been established before the storm. So anything in this area will be left uninhabited."

Lucia gave me a look when we got back into the car. The scene seemed peaceful, but there was something off. We studied a map that the woman projected on the inside screen. It was hard to see what she was referring to since everything outside was just placid blue. She swiped the screen for another map. It showed Tokyo Bay all the way down to Yokohama. The woman pointed her hand at the screen, and the town names switched to English.

"The Tokaido Shinkansen train line has been reclaimed north of Hirama," she said while zooming in on the map.

"This means we will not rebuild that line," the prime minister said. "We have studies that had predicted this kind of impact during a big storm. You know these studies, of course. The expense of rebuilding will be wasted when the next storm hits, and we have considered just about every option to protect these areas from water. Seawalls, draining docks, floating towns. Look at the devastation one storm was able to do here in the last two days."

The process of "natural negotiation," had been in discussion for years. But this was our first experience of putting the policy into place.

We had started moving again, and now we looked out at rows and rows of small buildings flooded up to the second floor.

"All of this was supposed to be safe, protected by walls engineered to withstand severe storms," the prime minister said.

"Storms of the century?"

"But they were broken — " He hesitated for a moment. "You say 'breached,'" he corrected himself. He was silent.

"They were breached almost an hour before the storm made landfall. Many people did not make it. They thought their homes would be safe — that the wall would protect them. There was supposed to be more time still before the storm hit. A lot of people died because they started to flee when it was too late."

We looked out at the placid waters surrounding the row of homes.

"What about that peninsula?" Lucia asked, pointing to the map at a piece of land that sheltered Tokyo Bay from the Pacific.

"The prefectures in the south will give up large tracts of land, including from the Kinugawa peninsula to the ocean," the woman said.

She spoke English like someone who had grown up in the United States.

"What does 'giving up' mean?" I whispered to Lucia.

"Exactly," she whispered back but kept her eyes on the map.

The map changed colors now. Parts of the coastal areas first turned to red, then blue. I thought of the times when I played Risk as a child with my cousins, when their wooden blocks had invaded my countries, and I had been forced to let someone's colored blocks pile up in the areas I had controlled before.

After the tsunami killed nearly 16,000 in 2011 and rendered a swath of Okuma uninhabitable for centuries, and after the far worse 2018 disaster had killed over 800,000 people in Indonesia and around the Indian Ocean, "natural negotiation" had been introduced as a way of managing such disasters. But this was not a matter of an invading army conquering land and turning it to their color à la Risk. Here, no one surrendered to marauding groups of soldiers and voracious settlers who pillaged and plundered. Instead of fighting and killing each other over scarce resources, here, in Tokyo, for the first time, a national government, in accordance with guidelines developed by HEPP, the UN Climate Committee, and others, let nature reclaim what was hers. With the help of their army, the Japan Self-Defense Force, the Japanese government would allow the ocean to negotiate a new shoreline, even if most of the water ultimately receded after the storm.

"The new shoreline will be the buffer for other storms," I said to Lucia.

"Looks like a lot of land to give up," she whispered back.

"This is how far the water could come inland from now on," the woman pointed at the map although she couldn't have heard Lucia.

"It's not a matter of just saving money," the prime minister said, "although currently the expenditures of protecting land from storms nearly exceeds our military budget. It's a matter of not repeating past mistakes, and putting all of these people at risk again."

"There are so many more people living here than only fifty years ago," the woman said. "Each storm takes a greater prize."

I had crunched the numbers pretty carefully myself. Malibu, Normandy, M'bour in Senegal, Chittagong, Rio, Venice, Tokyo, New Orleans, Miami — monstrous money had been spent to secure these areas against the regular and inevitable ebb and flow of seawater fluctuations. With the kinds of storms people were now predicting, it was a whole different matter. People bickered about the reasons for superstorms, but they agreed that these storms took heavy tolls on people living by the coastlines in recent years. Nobody could deny the numbers. Maintaining the status quo in these coastal areas was too expensive. And when storms hit, the money that was spent to fix those regions went mostly to the rich in beachfront homes rather than businesses or those who couldn't afford to rebuild.

Once M'bour in Senegal and Chittagong in Bangladesh had been renegotiated by the ocean, the regions settled into a different but more sustainable economy. "Sustainable," here as everywhere, meant "fundable," which is something I learned in Washington. Without money, nothing is sustainable, but what's not sustainable cannot always be made so with money. In M'bour, new and integrated infrastructure projects had resulted in big construction jobs. People had to give up their homes, but the local government was also no longer overwhelmed with the upkeep and rebuilding of roads, sewers, and pipes that had been too close to the water. Keon and I had visited Senegal about a year before I started on the campaign, when I was as a consultant and had a flexible schedule. We had spent two days in a colorful seaside hotel in Dakar, with round windows and the names of celebrity guests from Muhammad Ali and President Obama to Destiny's Child set in tiles on the seashell-decorated walls. On our first morning we had breakfast in the room overlooking the sparkling sea, and then spent the day walking around local markets. Keon bought me a little ostrich-shaped bird made of a polished driftwood and bits of metal that I still have on my desk at home. We drove down the coast to M'bour to visit one of Keon's professors from graduate school, a pretty well-known poet, and her husband.

"These houses were built by Dakar's middle class a few years ago," the poet explained while we walked along the ocean. "Every few weeks the tide washes over them, so they are slowly sinking into the sand."

It looked like an elephant graveyard, with huge abandoned concrete structures bleached white in the sun and surf, with curved rooflines, small turrets, Juliet balconies, and arched, square, and rectangular hollow window openings staring mutely toward the sea. It had been a hot and clear day, and small white crowns topped the waves of the sparkling blue Atlantic lapping at the little walls bordering the terraces in front of the big houses. In many places, those walls had been broken up by the seawater, which now pooled in what had been tiled patios. Thousands of houses had to yield to the ocean's steady, impassive force.

"They tried to block the sea with concrete barriers, seawalls, you name it. A lot of people sued the developers, the township, even each other for deception and misleading information. But it's just a fact that the sea is now a tiny bit higher than when they first developed this part."

We had lunch on the terrace of a small seaside restaurant run by an expat Frenchman who had pinned up posters of his homeland's forests and some castles in the Rhône and Loire valleys. We shared a large plate of fresh fish, and I was the only one who went into the water after we ate. Everyone had had some beers, and the mood was peaceful but a bit sad. From the water I could look up and down the shore for miles at the houses, stripped of paint and stucco to bare cement walls, that stared out to sea from dark windowless openings like cracked shells abandoned by hermit crabs.

Here, in Tokyo, the silence was different: fresher, palpable, and vivid, like a recent wound. In M'bour, the water had taken its toll over the course of several years, with each tide chipping away tiny bits of foundation, and people had fought back for a while. The sea had inched up on them in full view, gently and quietly, and for a while people had thought that their intentions could stop this indifferent, shapeless force. But in spite of the concrete and rocks put in its way and the ingenuity and hope marshaled by humans, it proved unstoppable. In Tokyo, Typhoon Michio had come overnight and with shocking violence that seemed nothing like the incremental erosion of the shores of Senegal. In M'bour the Atlantic looked placid. But with the same indifference that had roiled the Pacific and hurled it ashore in Japan, in Senegal the water had shaved off a bit of sand where people had built their homes.

Our little motorcade had arrived at a small lookout secured by armed guards wearing military vests or jackets, but many wore jeans or civilian pants and sneakers. They stood at attention when we got out of our cars, but went back to their tasks as soon as they were dismissed.

The Tokyo skyline rose in the distance. One or two helicopters hovered over a cluster of rooftops and bigger structures sticking out of the water, but very few vehicles moved on the roads. The city looked like an island in a shimmering sea. The sky above had turned a pale blue, tiny silver sparkles dancing on the water below. A few clouds, thin and stringy like blanched seaweed, were the only remnant of the devastating typhoon. Though people had been aware of the potential threat, they had convinced themselves that the walls they had built were stronger. It had been a particularly unlikely scenario, with the brunt of the storm bearing down on Tokyo Bay. The water had been pushed from the Pacific into the bay where it had nowhere to go but past the seawalls, docks, and fortifications. Sea barriers had burst in so many places that the entire bay had expanded briefly by a third, crushing in its swell most man-made structures, some of which were centuries old.

"We are assisting only those who wish to be resettled in secure spots," the woman with the IDs around her neck said. "We are not permitting people to return to their homes in natural negotiation areas. None of the highways or homes here, or in another area closer to the shore, will be rebuilt. All of this will be left to the sea. It would be flooded again by the next storm." She pointed at the partly submerged road below.

"What will the people do?" Lucia asked. "Who will pay for them to resettle?"

"We are working on that," the prime minister responded. "We know that long-term costs for resettlement are less than rebuilding the seawalls, but people are not so happy here."

We could see small boats trawling between houses standing in the water.

"Ho has been selected to become the new port, based on the plans we drew up after the Tohuku earthquake," the woman said. She did not refer to Fukushima. Domineek had instructed us to not refer to the Tohuku earthquake by name in meetings with Japanese counterparts. All of the names seemed pretty pointless to me, in any case. I had studied and discussed so many color-coded maps of coastal regions from the East Coast to Bangladesh, Indonesia, the Philippines, and China, with rings of different colors marking the sea level during various-level storms that I had come to not pay all that much attention to national boundaries. And names. What did it matter whether it was Pakistan or India that governed the Keti Bandar area once that region was underwater? No military in the world and no ingenious storm-adaptation plan of water-preserving plazas, sponging buildings, and active sewers would be able to defend Rotterdam, or parts of Venice, when it went the way of the sea. Nor would the Army Corps of Engineers be able to protect Miami from being soaked in salt water every few years.

The political wrangling after those events had been fierce at times. But the numbers spoke for themselves. Fighting nature was a losing proposition; it cost too much. After parts of Miami were trashed during a big storm, it had been a bit easier for Lucia to enlist some developers to start thinking about locating new communities farther away from the shore.

"The sea level rises naturally once a century during a big storm," her opponents had insisted. Lucia never engaged in debates about the causes for rising tides. "People will deny science if it's convenient for them to do so," she said when we presented her with evidence of long-term temperature changes detected in ice cores, tree rings, and deep sea sediments. "I want to ignore, as a matter of principle, the topics of aerosol, soot, and greenhouse emissions," she said to me when we first started thinking about shoreline policies. "People band together when they have a common cause. And that cause is the risk to our country's safety and security by spending exorbitant sums on a futile and unwinnable battle against the elements."

She joined a few senators during a press conference when they rolled out old studies that explained rising sea levels due to solar and volcanic variation.

"Our greatest mistake would be to build seawalls at the expense of upgrading our military. These are tough choices. But thankfully there are ways to work with nature, and to protect our country at the same time."

I had walked back from the Senate after that meeting with her.

"Their world is like a goddamn children's picture book, isn't it," she said. "We have to encourage buyers to sue the developers for fraud, for willfully ignoring available information. That's the way to get their attention. And we have to play up the military angle, how protecting the shoreline is a risk we cannot take given our security needs."

Japan had been pressured into natural negotiation policies with the same argument. Lucia had made onetime aid guarantees to resettle the negotiated regions. Hence her questions about money. But, more importantly, she had kept US bases open on the condition that Tokyo sign the natural negotiation regulations.

The threat of withholding aid packages was not big enough to force Japan to participate. The threat of losing our military presence was. Once you signed on, the United States would no longer step in to help rebuild after a storm, and recently passed bills prevented American NGOs from helping when a future storm affected the regions left for natural negotiation.

Japan adopted natural negotiation rules soon after Rotterdam. There would be no further funding to secure and expand new shorelines, no further land reclamation projects. Instead, policy dictated the gradual and intentional abandonment of most seawalls and dykes, the adoption of wetland buffer zones instead of marked land/water borders, and an end of residential construction near the coast.

We spent the afternoon touring what was left of Kashima port. Parts of buildings, whole walls, metal roofing, smashed windows, and large doors pulled off their hinges, bloated drywall spread like white fungus around a huge dock strewn with shipping containers. A barge had been left on top of one of the piers like a beached whale, and there were massive cranes dangling their innards into the water as if they had lost a bloody fight. There were cables everywhere, and the remnants of engines and computers. We had studied images of similar scenes from Chittagong and Rotterdam. In Bangladesh and the Netherlands, the United States, along with everyone else, had sent aid, in several huge ships and a lot of planes: containers of food, millions of water packs, sealed bags of clothing, and an emergency hospital or two. The difference to Tokyo was that now the United States and the UN would not help with engineers and shovels to rebuild Japan's port.

After about twenty minutes, we got into the cars to return to Narita. We drove alongside an elevated highway that seemed untouched by the storm until it suddenly disappeared in the water below. We crossed another pontoon bridge in silence.

I tracked the flight of a few gulls over the smashed container port. The birds settled on a bent crane that would definitely not be put to use again, and would probably never be removed. But these white-plumed birds were not vultures, and this was not a sign of defeat. We were leaving Kashima port and some of the smaller towns around Tokyo to another future, but we were not giving up. We were preparing a better, healthier, saner destiny for us and the planet by adjusting ourselves to the claims of the ocean.

At the airport, our Japanese hosts bid us farewell. The prime minister, who had been so confident in his military-looking parka when explaining their strategies throughout the visit, now seemed subdued. I watched him while he said something in a low voice to Lucia, and then bowed deeply. They had the difficult work ahead. They had to redraw a map that had proudly defied the oceans for centuries.

We flew toward the east and looked down on Haneda Airport, located only some twenty kilometers outside of Tokyo near the Pacific. I think almost everyone took some edibles right away, just to help process what we had seen. I remember that deep silence, even though the engines were droning, when our plane banked into the sun and we left behind the debris-ridden waters for the Pacific's open blue. I remember that silence more vividly than anything that was said on the long flight home.

Day 2: Early Morning

I am sleeping a lot. Probably just catching up, or perhaps they are putting something in my water or in the air. This morning they put me on IVs. Not one IV, not two IVs, not three IVs. Four bags of liquid in a row. Flush out the system. Drip. Drip. Drip. Drip. My arm was hooked into a sling that allows them to put the IV in through a kind of porthole in the wall. I lay there, watching the fluid drip into me, although I don't feel sick in the least. Finally they had to unhook me so I could go and pee. Then back for another IV. Over four hours. Drip, drip, drip.

I discovered a display by the door that lists my vitals, along with notes that explain in lay language what normal levels should be.

Still no connectivity. Very frustrating. After the IVs, I felt calmer, though. I am telling myself to be methodical. I don't remember approving a rule about no connectivity. I remember only Seth: "No outside contact during quarantine to make it more difficult for rumors to arise." He cited studies, as was his wont, that proved his point. It's likely that I won't be online for six days. Another four days, after today. I felt a wave of panic, but it passed, similar to the way you feel when you have to throw up, but then don't.

I sat by the table, tracing its circular patterns with my index finger, struggling to be rational. I'm not in touch with anybody, and whatever Lucia is doing now she is doing without me. She's probably thought of contacting me, breaking the rules, but then someone might leak it to the press that POTUS flouts the rules when her staff is concerned. Not a good idea. We usually talk for a minute or so after official meetings, and even that's raised a lot of eyebrows. Which senator might back us, whether State is cooperating, that kind of stuff. But sometimes, Lucia just gossips with me. A brief, unscripted moment like during the first months of the campaign, when we would travel together a lot, spend time in cars, makeshift green rooms, on the plane. "What's the mood in the East Wing like? Why is the media so obsessed with this story? Why do people care? What actors can we invite for the Fourth of July who won't embarrass us totally, like that one who got piss-drunk? Tell me that the Chinese ambassador isn't gay." We often laughed briefly about some off-color comment she would throw in, and I would be the one with the daggers from the rest of the staff. "It's time, Madam President," Domineek would say, and she would look at me conspiratorially, which I relished of course, even though it cost me with everyone else, who wanted the same access. But we have a history. We've been through the campaign, and when she first made the environment into a major plank on her platform, I was one of the very few who could really tell her the mood of the people. "Check with Keon," she'd say after we had gotton all the polls and data. "He has a good sense of things."

They must have briefed her on my status, and she's probably made sure I get the best care. But she can't contact me — it would get out and turn into a story. Then there would be questions about her health, how this doctor got to the White House without having been cleared, all sorts of stuff. Major distraction. She can't risk that.

I had talked with Keon briefly from the ambulance. He said he'd do anything to get me out, and I had to remind him that quarantine rules apply to everyone. He was very worried, and I could hear that he was upset but trying to be calm. Everything happened so fast that I didn't know what to say, but I felt I had to reassure him. "I'll be okay," I had said. "It's just a precaution." I tell myself that they must be giving him updates about my status, as next of kin.

Worrying over things I cannot control is "not useful," as Keon likes to say. "Worrying keeps you stuck in the loop," he tells me when I am obsessing. Keon. I wonder what he's doing now. He's probably tried calling a few people in the Administration to find out more. I wonder whether he's called Mom, or anyone else in my family. He would not want to alarm them, if they hadn't been told. And it's likely that he was told to say to everyone that I was traveling, classified but no risk. I feel stupid that I haven't given him my passwords so he could check my messages. But it's always felt weird to me to share my phone. As if there's nothing left for myself.

"The worst you're gonna find is a drunk text from my ex, saying that the one thing she's mad about is that I don't have a brother," he once said, laughing, when he told me that his phone code is his grandmother's first name. But I'm not sure he would laugh off my messages in the same way. It's not really anything bad, but it's also not so easy to understand. When we first started dating, he had just broken up with his girlfriend, but they still talked a lot. Then we gradually got closer, fell in love, I moved in. But we never had the major talk where we agreed on how to treat our former relationships. Probably because of me, because I hate that kind of reckoning, where people are sorted into categories because you've met someone. But I would feel terrible if I made Keon unhappy. So my phone and tablets are locked.

Is he frantic? What are they telling him?

There is nothing I can do to shorten my stay here. I don't want to start counting the hours and days, sitting here like an idiot and trying to get online over and over, staring at the IV drip, harassing the medics. They examined me this morning, through a part of the wall that is made of a strong, rubbery membrane. I have a hard time remembering it since I was so sleepy. I was told to stand on spots marked on the floor, and they scanned me for my vitals. They remained unimpressed when I complained about the lack of connectivity. One of them shrugged his shoulders behind the panel.

Not even "No, we won't help you," or "Sorry, dude." Not even "It's not our responsibility to get you online." More like, "We have our priorities, and for the time being you are nothing but a risk factor."

I've decided to do something useful, and to focus only on things I can control. Exercise. Sleep. Assess honestly how much we have accomplished, domestically but more so on a global scale and with HEPP. Take stock of the amazing things we've been able to do for the planet, the specific ways Lucia has been able to focus people on the environment and leverage those victories for the next challenge, since now there's more proof on hand as to how much can be done when we work together. Look at the ways in which so many people have finally started to see how urgent our situation is, and the need for large-scale cooperation. How exciting it's been to see people come together over this. The tally of all of those efforts explains how Lucia became the global champion for the planet that she is today. I'll use the time here to outline our successes, so they can be useful in the next campaign. Also good to have a record of what I've done. "You gotta promote yourself more," Keon always eggs me on. "That's what most people spend their time on, promoting themselves."

I think the work should speak for itself. Obviously, there were key events during the first campaign. Silicon Valley. The two hurricanes. But I want to focus on what we have been able to do for America and for the planet since we have become the administration. China. The garbage wars. The typhoon in Tokyo. Eco brigades. The fact that we passed Restore the Shore. That we brought Australia into the fold. India. Mata Ganga. Opt-outs. Ha'areti. How we made the Middle East listen up. How we galvanized Europe's lethargic leaders.

The setbacks, too.

Mbtembo. The cattle industries.

But mainly the way Lucia's been able to put the planet above everything without hurting American interests. Why people started to believe in Lucia, Why they have started to care. Why you can buy lucky charms with her portrait in Delhi and watches with her image in Beijing.

It's all on my tablet. The stuff we accomplished; and also the things *I* worked on.

The things *I* deserve credit for.

Lucia's global role started with the creation of HEPP. It started with a war over water. With subterranean canals gushing clear, cool water from up north, and with blood flowing in Mexico.

Mexico

The bodies had been burned. The heads had been placed atop crude wooden spikes all along the town's main road. Some of them still wore baseball caps with the Global Alliance insignia; most of the women's heads still had their hair tied back in ponytails or tucked under bandanas. If there was an expression on their mutilated faces, it was of great surprise — as if they still could not believe that they were stuck on tall poles. *Our* faces wore expressions of shock, not surprise. We had regular briefings about the narco-gangs' beheadings of Mexican students, hotel workers, civil servants, local officials, bus drivers, and teachers as retribution for governmental action. State alerted us each time US citizens were among the victims, which was often the case.

None of us had been prepared for the stench. The smell was sweet, but also sharp, as if tiny insects had invaded your nose and throat.

We walked along in silence. Lucia stopped before each head and looked intently into the open eyes, a handkerchief pressed against her mouth. Judging from the open gashes, crows and turkey vultures had pecked at the heads before we arrived. The officials had left them up for us to see. At the last spike, Lucia bent down and placed a bouquet of origami flowers at its base. She tied a green paper ribbon around the stake. She stood there for a few long and eerie moments, while everyone else waited in the heat. It felt wrong not to pay these people our respect, but it was also grotesque to look directly into their wide-open eyes.

Our plane had landed after military convoys had already brought several battalions to the region. The severed heads, as gruesome as they were, had been only a small part of the reason for our presence there.

Heads had been displayed in Mexican towns for a while since the narco-wars started. Bodies strung on lampposts and from bridges, charred corpses buried by the dozens in shallow ditches or left helter-skelter on manicured lawns in front of fancy hotels and colonial-era city halls after being dumped from pickup trucks in the soft light of dawn. A dozen or so flayed hands arranged into a horrid mandala on the conference table of Mexico City's mayor one Monday morning. The methods were medieval but the message was wholly timeless: we run this place. *Gobernamos Este País. GEP.* You could see the acronym graffitied everywhere: on highway overpasses, on columns, and on walls, emblazoned on the sides of buses and delivery trucks, and even inside restaurants, on bathroom walls and doors. The victims of the narco-wars, the world was told. Each time another batch of bodies was discovered, the hand-wringing, the social media campaigns, the political blame games started up again.

We touched down near Mexico City a bit after noon. In a heavily secured room crowded with computer terminals, we stared at several large screens displaying rows of numbers. Large numbers, in the billions, that then fanned out to smaller amounts, all headed by generic North American names that I can still recall. Scott Cosgun. Liz Apel. Derek Sands. Also on display were graphs and numbers that spelled out much of the narco-empire's banking practices, which our team of cyber warriors, led by Asturias and Malang, had hacked. The rows of numbers cascading down the screen represented the enormous drug profits of the Mexico-based cartels. They all flowed in one direction, into US accounts, from everywhere around the globe where drugs were sold: Cairo, Lagos, São Paolo, Hong Kong, Mumbai, New York, Bangkok, all of the European capitals. Our geeks had used cybermarkings to trace those accounts directly to dummy accounts set up by the campaign offices of the governors of Texas and California, one from each of the two major parties.

"I want to see the canals," Lucia said, pointing at the screen displaying the money that had gone to California. "I want to know how much water we are talking about here," she said.

In exchange for the narco-dollars that ended up in the campaign coffers and private offshore accounts of California and Texas politicians, the two governors had turned a blind eye to the many networks of underground pipes — the "canals" that Lucia had wanted to see — that siphoned water from California and Texas underneath the fortified border to the Mexican peninsula. The scheme was simple but clever, and it had taken years to uncover. Bank points and dollars flowed to Mexico, while the authorities used the severed heads and mutilated bodies provided by the drug cartels as a way to control the news and public political priorities. A distraction — nothing more, nothing less.

"Atrocities in Mexico!" the headlines screamed, especially when rich first-worlders got snagged. "Young American Couple Executed by Gang," kept CNN busy for days. "How can these thugs be stopped?" an earnest-looking Justin Valdez had asked on his channel when they had discovered another mass killing of students.

Two of the screens now showed live footage of the interior of a round sewer pipe. The bottom half of the image was filled with running water.

"The water pipes all run parallel to the sewers," Asturias explained while pulling up different clips on the screens. "Indestructible water pipes, placed inside the sewage. That's why nobody discovered them. They were maintained by the garbage companies, all working on public contracts."

Asturias pushed a few keys and a satellite shot of the Baja

California Peninsula appeared on the screen.

"The blue lines are water being shipped south," he added. "The parts of the Central Valley that are completely dry are yellow."

Lucia studied the maps for a few moments. "How long have these pipes been used?" she asked, leaning forward.

"About ten years or so," one of the EPA guys said. "But we think that the whole network became so vast only in the last two years. They probably doubled the volume of water going south in that time."

"Water for drugs," Lucia said. "Years ago they traded weapons for drugs. My father would have cried if he had seen this. Hell, it makes me cry."

She turned back to Asturias. "Let's look at the money now."

We had visited Mexico twice during Lucia's first months in office. It had been her intention to signal a new era of cooperation with Mexico after the construction of La Gran Valla.

"We will work with you to stop this senseless violence," she had declared on all of the major Mexican web platforms. "We grieve with you over the innocent lives lost here," she had said in Seattle when news of the Mexico City Sheraton massacre broke. "Addiction fuels this violence, and we will work together to stop it."

I had been the only staffer from her original team, or at least the only one outside full security clearance, to know about our team of cyber warriors who were uncovering the CalTex water connection at that time.

"Can you put tracers on all transactions in a way that will not be detected?" Lucia had asked Asturias in that first meeting. "We need hard proof that narco-dollars are used to finance the water theft draining the southwest."

One early June morning, following Lucia's directive, EPA swat teams had raided the offices of the governors of Texas and California. The governor of California had attended Lucia's inauguration and even hosted an inaugural ball for her, the only governor to do so. He had considered Lucia a close friend, and she had campaigned with him during many visits to the Golden State.

"This is a political ambush based on lies, which will swiftly be brought to light," he said on camera, while in the background federal officers hauled boxes from his offices in Sacramento. He looked calm, collected, and not in the least bit perturbed. But while he was responding to reporters' questions, Asturias hacked into his sites and posted a resignation letter.

On official letterhead, "I have failed the State of California," appeared in large print above a picture of the governor, taken seconds before he stepped into the press conference. "My actions have been shortsighted and selfish, and I have risked the future of our state. My office will cooperate fully with President Jackson to stop the transfer of water to Mexico." It was signed with his official seal. Courtesy of Asturias and his team.

Of course he denied the resignation, decried it as false, a hack, and his team worked hard to walk back the statement that he hadn't even made. But the damage had been done. They sounded defensive, irritated, confused.

"We will cooperate," "the governor is cooperating with the authorities," "these are baseless accusations," and so forth. They couldn't beat Asturias. After he had seeded the web with the governor's fake resignation letter, he fed the governor's social media with more admissions of guilt. The spark caught on and was fanned into a firestorm by the governor's own team when they kept fueling our story in their attempts at denial. "I didn't know," "we are investigating this," "we will get to the bottom of this." It wasn't even hacking; it was a full-scale takeover of the governor's persona on all media that turned the "resignation" into a fait accompli.

A stream of carefully staged California drought images in *The New Yorker* trended big. The black-and-white photographs were made to look like WPA-era dustbowl shots by Walker Evans, Dorothea Lange, and Margaret Bourke-White. A picture of an Asian-American mother clutching two kids on a parched lawn in front of a suburban house in L.A., with dead shrubs as a backdrop, became the *Migrant Mother* for our era. "Our Water Sold for Ca$h," a caption read. #narcodrought trended. We had tested these images with focus groups for months, and tweaked them to get responses of pity mixed with anger: shot from below, with people, and especially families staring into vast, colorless skies, as if searching for hope and rain. Our cyber team flooded the web with these pictures, making them appear in people's personal feeds with randomized comments of concern and outrage. They then seeded the same feeds with shots of victims of drug cartels in Mexico to link those two events in people's screen experience.

Crowds gathered in L.A., San Diego, San Francisco, Fresno, San Antonio, Austin, and Dallas to demand answers, calling for the governors to resign. We had waited for that moment.

"Our actions have consequences," Lucia said in a speech when the protests in California and Texas grew big. "*Sabemos desde hace tiempo que nuestras acciones tienen consecuencias para la tierra.* When we disregard nature, we pay a price," she continued. "When we refuse to look past the horizon," Lucia said, "we fail ourselves. We fail the planet. In California and Texas, we've failed everyone."

I had gone over the speech with her several times and was curious whether she would express anger toward California's governor. Lucia's cadence shifted, and she briefly opened her eyes more widely, and took a deep breath.

"My administration is taking action in California and Texas to protect our own interests," she said. "Water is more than a national resource. While we help the people of California and Texas to regain the rights to their water, we are working closely with our Mexican partners to develop sustainable water practices in the Southwest." She paused for a moment, and the screen cut away to small images of water gushing from a concrete pipeline into irrigation canals under a bright sun.

"My father worked on California farms when I was young," Lucia continued. "He picked fruit on fields that are long gone. Drug money siphoned off that water from California to Mexico."

Behind her, Asturias let roll pictures of desiccated orchards before cutting very briefly to shots of bodies strung from a bridge, and then corpses lying in a park. The pictures quickly returned to the black-and-white shots of the California drought. It was risky to show Lucia in front of the violent images in terms of PR, but it worked.

Lucia finished her speech while behind her on the screen a leafless tree appeared against a sky, the cross on Golgotha, washed out by the merciless white sun.

"In 1916, US troops entered Mexican territory in pursuit of Pancho Villa. It was a time of shortsighted goals. For two decades, a US-Mexican cooperative project has failed to stem drug violence. Today, it is time for Mexicans and Americans to work together to stop the theft of our shared resources. Today, we come together to secure a healthy and sustainable planet. It is time to understand that we are in this together."

A few hours later, we landed near the irrigated fields of Chihuahua. Lucia pointed at the workmen in the lush fields before us.

"My father always reminded me that the Mayan calendar was more accurate than the Roman calendar. He loved that fact — that they had figured something out that the Europeans couldn't."

We had all heard the stories about her father many times, about his years of following the water to find work as a fruit picker, about his shame for being too poor to provide for his family, and his pride in being a descendant of the great civilization of Mesoamerica. How the Mayans had built a vast empire on clever canal systems and high-yield crops. What her father never understood was one of Lucia's primary motivations — how the Mayan empire collapsed, like the Sumerians in Mesopotamia, or in the region of today's Iraq, and the Roman Empire in the fourth century, because unsustainable progress had led to the depletion of resources.

I had spent two days at Tikal when I was barely sixteen. Mom and Dad couldn't decide with whom I ought to spend the summer, so I'd signed up for a language course near Tulum, where I met three Canadian kids at a party. Together we traveled to Chichen Itza and sneaked past two dozing guards to see the ruins early in the morning. I liked the Canadians a lot. They seemed less burdened by the fact that even us regular, middle-class *norteamericano* kids were incredibly wealthy compared to the locals. I especially liked one of the group, a really pretty girl with dark curly hair who knew the name of every bird, bug, and butterfly, wore armfuls of painted resin bracelets, and, without much of a lead-up, made out with me for a long while on the bus to Chichen Itza. Bryella. The Canadians had no problems with bribing guards and policemen when necessary, and somehow laughed those moments off as it were all routine for them.

I was a bit rattled after our make-out session when we got off the bus, hot and bothered not only from the heat, and Bryella seemed to think we were now something of a couple, at least for now, holding my hand, laughing. We walked around the silent stone buildings while the sky was already getting brighter and then settled down on the huge stone steps of the central pyramid, not far from a few other tourists who must have had the same idea and were waiting for sunrise. Like an orchestra tuning their instruments before a concert, the forest slowly came to life.

There were flocks of small, brown, quail-like birds pecking in the dust at the foot of the pyramid. They made little nasal cries as if from a clarinet, and I imagined these birds scurrying in the middle of a great Mayan market filled with peasants offering all sorts of things to the priests and city dwellers some two thousand years earlier. I stared out over the treetops at the dawn sky for a while, and then again at the bottom of the pyramid where I imagined people bringing baskets filled with maize, squash, and fish to the square below. The sky above us turned from an inky black to the grey of dawn. Then I *saw* priests with feather headdresses and feather necklaces walk through a crowd. I saw women with babies slung across their chests, and men with feather cuffs on their wrists and ankles, squatting over a game played on the dusty ground. I saw people sitting behind large baskets, and monkeys or dogs running underneath. I explained what I saw, in a very low voice, to Bryella. I babbled on about floating vegetable beds and the Mayan calendar and baskets of fruits and trade and drained swamps until Bryella shifted the leg against which I had rested my head, and got up.

We all scrambled to our feet. I laughed and pretended to be a bit embarrassed at having gotten so carried away with my guidebook knowledge of the Mayan ruins. But I was shaken. I *had* seen lots and lots of people below me, not working as tour guides or security guards but on a busy market day, and I knew it wasn't the edible I had taken before climbing up the steps.

The sun had risen, and I explained to the Canadians why the temples were sited exactly in this way— stuff I'd read about for weeks when I was young, and then had re-read before the trip on an app.

The Canadians and I drove back to the hedonistic hell of Cancún later that morning. We blasted Mexican hip hop and did not speak much. Bryella's interest in me had waned, or she was just tired. I also tried to sleep. Soon screams of "Shots! Shots! Shots!" turned the two Canadians guys into rude idiots, and I left all of them, even though Bryella was seeming to show interest in me again. That early morning in Chichen Itza has stayed with me as a moment in my life when "morning" really meant awakening.

"The people of Mexico have revived the great Mayan experiments by bringing water from the north," Lucia said while we walked through mile-long rows of tall, plastic tubes with punched-in holes out of which poked strawberry vines. "And like the Mayans before them, their plan is shortsighted. We have to work with the environment, not against it," she said and shook her head. "The entire region needs to shift its water economy. American companies can help."

In the car back to the airport, Lucia used the secure line to speak to HEPP headquarters.

“Mexico will join HEPP,” she said. “Mexican military and police will report to you as Chief Command.”

“I want to meet the candidates for your direct report in Mexico,” she said and gave me a sign. “Aleks will schedule us,” and with that she clicked off, gave me a nod, and closed her eyes. I was proud to be part of this effort, and proud that she asked me to coordinate it. “It’s okay for you to stay,” she said. “I’ll just sleep for a few minutes.” I got busy immediately with scheduling, and made sure that HEPP realized that Lucia had entrusted me with that task. I checked with Asturias to confirm that all of our sites were current in Spanish, Nahuatl, and Yucatec Maya. HEPP had just gained control of over 760,000 square miles, bordered by the Atlantic and the Gulf, and inhabited by 124 million people, plus a complex network of irrigation tunnels running from the United States into Mexican territories, and a critically important agricultural zone dependent on water stolen from California.

It was going to be a busy few months ahead. I looked at Lucia asleep, and then got back on my tasks. I was going to make her proud. I felt important. My Spanish was going to come in handy.

Water Wars

From Wikipedia, the free encyclopedia

[This article is about the definition of the specific military and political conflict between the United States, the United Mexican States, and Canada during the 2010s that resulted in the creation of HEPP, Hemispheric Environmental Protection Pact. For other conflicts related to water shortages, see specific countries and regions; or List of water conflicts. For other uses, see Water War (disambiguation). For the book and movie with the same name see Kiran Khajooei's author's page]

Water Wars refers to the drug money–financed large-scale scheme by Mexican criminal gangs to secretly purchase large quantities of water siphoned from Texas and California in the 2000s and 2010s. Some experts attribute the severe droughts in California during those decades to the Mexican water theft.[1citation needed] The "Water Wars" ploy was uncovered by US special forces during a joint US-Mexican investigation into the murder of a group of US and other non-Mexican tourists in Tulum, Mexico, in 2018. [2] During a months-long investigation the illegal sale of water was traced to the governors of Texas and California, who resigned under pressure from the public and the federal government. US forces were deployed by President Lucia Jackson to halt water theft from US territories. A period of political instability in Mexico led to the incorporation of Mexico into the Hemispheric Environmental Protection Pact (see also: HEPP). The term "Water Wars" refers to a conflict with limited military engagement but political and paramilitary strategies that exposed the drug violence in Mexico as a ploy to distract the authorities from the water-siphoning scheme that included corruption at the highest level in Texas and California.

The integration of Mexico into HEPP has prompted a long series of legal challenges in Mexico's Supreme Court (Suprema Corte de Justicia de la Nación).[3] Experts expect the Court to rule in favor of Mexican independence advocates and void the emergency decrees that permit US or HEPP forces to control part of Mexico, and place parts of the Mexican Armed Forces (Fuerzas Armadas de México) under US command.[4,5] The Court has not issued a decision on a number of these challenges to date.

There have been incidents of armed resistance to the presence of US forces on Mexican soil, and reports of tension between Mexico's president, Enrique Costas, as commander-in-chief of the armed forces of HEPP, and US President Lucia Jackson.

Part of a series about

War

History

Battlespace

Weapons

Tactics

Operational

Strategy

Grand Strategy

Organization

Logistics

Related Entries

Environmental Conflict

Droughts

Water

Environmental Justice

Keon's Grandma, Lucia's Dad

Lucia pulled the sound curtain closed for privacy to take a call. She had woken up after about thirty minutes, smiled at me, and then called Domineek. For an instant, I saw her the way most people see the president of the United States: focused but also detached, thinking many steps ahead.

"What happened with the president's dad?" Seth whispered to me even though everyone around us was wearing headphones.

"You don't remember that?" I wondered whether he could be serious. "It was a huge thing in the media, when her father" — I looked over at Lucia to be sure she couldn't hear — "her father chose to die," I said.

"Yes, I know, but what was the big deal? Wasn't it legal then?" Seth asked. "I mean, what state did he do it in?"

"It was legal, yes, but the media was harsh on Lucia. The evangelicals didn't like it, even if it was legal. The story was everywhere. You didn't see it? Everyone was talking about it. Pictures, clips that Lucia's family hadn't authorized. The opposition used her father's 'death with dignity' to paint her as a callous bitch who sacrificed her father so she could focus on her career." I had lowered my voice and put air quotes around "bitch."

"I remember, but it always seemed like a stupid issue," Seth said.

"Not stupid as far as the opposition was concerned."

On the tablet, I have a lot of clips of Lucia during that time. Also some with her dad. He looks serious in most of them, with a wrinkled face that you don't see so much these days, with almost every lens on self-correct. On some cameras you can't even turn that feature off. We all want the truth in our images, but we also want the truth to look good. Then there are the notorious clips of Lucia's father with the white horse, and the clip of the forest trail where they found his body. I didn't know that I had saved those.

It still makes me more angry than sad, the way his passing had been handled. "Death with dignity" was legal only in some states at that point. What wasn't legal anywhere was to steal images of the dying and then post them as part of a political agenda. In the long run, the fact that the media was so merciless in publishing those pictures against the family's will, and that a couple of bigger sites lost in court when the family challenged them on that, probably did Lucia a lot of good. Politically speaking, I mean. Not emotionally, but politically.

"Jackson Farms Dad Out to Death Farm," the headlines went. "Kind to Planet, Cruel to Papa." Some of that got to her. It was probably one of the few times I saw her angry, with the exception of the elephants. When they published pictures of Lucia's dad's dead body, Asturias went on the offensive. He flooded the media with images of Lucia and her family in mourning at the funeral. One of the kids, it must have been Isabella, who was pretty young then, broke down in tears online. Our bloggers made that moment the focal point, which created a lot of sympathy for the family.

Lucia's father had checked himself into a rest home somewhere in Montana. Like a number of others, the home operated just within the law at that time. But there were several court cases against these places. There were doctors and nurses, but something about the patients' legal status in Montana versus their home states was an issue. Whether the laws of one state could apply to patients who came from another state. Today, of course, a lot of people choose such places. Aunt Christine did, both of Keon's grandparents went together, the Vietnamese guy who used to live next to us when I was a kid moved to some place in Colorado to die on his own terms. Lucia's dad hadn't wanted to be poked and prodded, after his diagnosis and when there was little hope of recovery. When his condition got worse, Lucia flew back to Montana and spent two days consulting with medical experts. Several teams with different approaches advised Lucia while her father lay in an induced coma. Lucia had to learn the benefits and drawbacks of the different kinds of treatments and make an immediate decision. He pulled through, felt better, and checked out of the hospital.

Based on the clips and on what I have heard from Lucia over the years, he must have been a determined person. One day he simply announced to his family that it was time to go. They were free to visit, but he did not permit anybody who showed up to cry and be sad and try to change his mind.

Horses played a big role at the place he chose. From the clips, the place looked like a fancy ski resort in summer, with wide green lawns and trees and mountains in the distance, and people lounging in soft slanting sunlight. But horses have become quite popular now. Even Keon's grandparents, who had lived in Europe with the army in the 1980s and then in New Orleans and never spent time in the countryside, had horses around them at the end. Something about overcoming innate fear and being guided. Apparently it works. According to the media and whoever leaked the clip to them, Lucia's dad took his medication that morning, asked for a white horse at the stables, and guided it down a path with the reins in his hand, into the forest. The people at the stables said he was talking to the horse, chatting quite happily, but since none of the staff are officially permitted to speak to the media in these places, it might not be true. It never became clear who took the video, and why.

The horse returned from the forest in the evening by itself. The staff found Lucia's dad next to a creek. There is a picture of his body in one of the clips, and Lucia spent quite a bit of money to bring down the person who had taken that image and posted it. If people went so peacefully in those places, and if they all made their own decisions, then why didn't they die sitting under a tree? Or in a meadow of flowers? The body was lying at an angle to the creek, with one arm bent back under his back, in a muddy spot filled with rocks, fallen branches and dead leaves, and all but hidden by tall, feathery reeds. It looked more like a crime scene than a dignified death.

Aunt Christine opted not for a farm with horses, but for pools and a pretty wooden bench next to a bed of purple asters. The morning she died, she took some kind of medication that affected her heart rate. Then she went for a swim. She got out of the pool, punched in her code at the little dispensary, took another dose and sat in the garden, still in her bathing suit and wrapped in a hyper-absorbent towel that clung to her body. They found her next to the bench in the clump of asters.

Keon's grandparents died together, in their living room in the condo where they had lived for a little while. It was part of a compound that looked like any gated community, except that it was much more heavily secured, and meant for people who chose to make their own decision about end-of-life care. They had told Keon in advance, so we both went to visit them for the last time. I remember that they asked us to dance. Keon's grandmother was 82, with beautiful milk chocolate skin and a cabinet full of page-boy wigs in all sorts of colors. Keon's granddad, who was 80 at the time, was wearing a vintage Hornets shirt and shorts. "Can't get him out of his uniform even on a day like today," Keon's grandma said, and his granddad just laughed. He put on his playlist and we danced for quite a while — long enough for me to feel exhausted, so it must have really worn his grandparents out. They laughed at my dancing, and Keon danced with his grandmother for a bit longer while his grandfather and I just sat and watched. The two of them looked so happy; she was beaming while Keon clowned around in a low crouch, shimmying back, shoulder walking, doing all sorts of moves that had been big in her day. Then we sat around their small living room, full of white and cream minimalist furniture, with dark wooden low tables from the early 2000s. They served us wine and chicken, and Keon's grandfather teased me for being a vegetarian.

"Denying yourself meat won't help this chicken now," he said, and put a piece on my plate.

I couldn't say no, obviously, though Keon finished most of it for me when grandpa wasn't looking. After dinner, we watched clips of Keon as a young boy with his grandparents: in a soccer uniform, with a Mohawk and silver studs in his ears, fishing off the piers in Key West with his granddad, all buck teeth cuteness.

His grandmother then sent us on our way.

"You're going to take care of my baby now," she said to me, and then hugged us both. She held me by the shoulders and smiled with her lips pressed together. "And he will take care of you. You both can do great things. You be sure to keep our president on track!"

"I want you to listen to our playlist on the way home," Keon's grandfather instructed me. "And don't let K check his phone tonight. I'm sure you'll find something else to do," and he laughed.

"William!" Keon's grandmother said in a mock tone of shock.

"He's right," she added. "Have fun tonight, you two. It's important that K is happy tonight."

Keon was crying at this point, silently, with his cheeks wet and the front of his blue shirt spotted from the tears. His chest was heaving but he controlled himself enough not to sob.

"Hush, baby," his grandmother said, and reached for him. "Don't cry. Don't you cry." She hugged him, and he let out a soft moan against her shoulder.

"No need to cry, K," his grandfather said. "Show me your goofy smile."

Keon forced a smile through his tears, and we all sort of tried to laugh. His grandmother took a napkin and wiped his face, and then kissed him on the forehead.

"It'll be all right." She handed him an envelope. "Don't let Aleks see any of that," she stage-whispered. "All of this is probably sort of illegal, or at least being reviewed by some court, and if they find out in Washington that you both were here and I gave you this, he'd have to resign."

I half-smiled to keep from crying. They both walked us to the door. Keon's grandfather kissed both of us on the forehead, and his grandmother slapped me on the butt.

"Go!" she said and turned away from the door. "I love you! Now go!"

Keon's grandfather waited by the door till the elevator came. I can still see him today, tall and lanky, with the purple and white jersey, waving us goodbye. In the elevator I hugged Keon while he sobbed into my neck.

We drove along the paved narrow roads of their small compound, lined with pretty plantings and past the mini town square.

"Some people obviously stay here for a while," Keon said, and wiped his face.

"There's a time limit, though," I said. I had read up on the facility's policies. "If people stay past a specific date, they are required to move out."

"You mean if they change their minds and don't want to die yet," Keon said.

I looked over at him, but he stared straight ahead.

"It's strange to think of all these people here looking for parking spots and buying the newspaper, and groceries and ice cream. Look at this guy," Keon said and lowered his voice, even though the car windows were rolled up. "He looks like he's in his early forties. He's actually kind of cute," Keon said, and forced a laugh.

"Maybe he's visiting someone, like we are," I said, but Keon interrupted me.

"No, he's got a bracelet. Just like grandma has. Had. Fuck!" He banged his hand against the side of the door. "Fuck!"

We drove out of the little town area in silence.

"It's supposed to be easy!" Keon said right before we reached the gates. "I knew in advance, had time to prepare. But this. . . ."

"It's so hard, baby," I said as I put one hand on his leg. "It's so hard."

I really didn't want to cry so I focused on the checkpoint ahead.

"There are people protesting outside," the woman at the booth said when I had handed her our passes. "But our guards are keeping the road open. You should lock your doors, and not stop, please." She bent down to look through my window past me at Keon, and her deep red hair spilled from underneath her cap to cover her forehead and part of her face.

"Sweetie," she said and with two fingers gently tucked her hair back under the cap. "You go take care of yourself, baby. You know your grandma wouldn't want you to be sad."

Keon sobbed quietly. I rolled up my window and nodded at the security guard. It looked like she also had tears in her eyes. I wondered how she handled her job, saying goodbye to bereft relatives every day. Seconds later the gate was open, we left the compound, and then the car was surrounded by a screaming mob armed with placards, huge crosses, funeral wreaths, and megaphones.

"Death Is a Divine Matter." "Heaven Cant be Scheduled." "Its HIS Perogative." The signs were waved at us. I remember being angered by the bad spelling, as if that mattered. The crowd had apparently just finished harassing another car ahead. Children in long white robes carrying plastic flowers and electric candles stood in the front row, right behind the metal barrier and the security guys, and there were people dressed as priests, or rabbis, or imams — maybe they were real priests and real rabbis, maybe real imams. They were chanting and shaking their fists at our car. I turned up the music — something from Keon's granddad's playlist that was very dancy, with a rapper and a big chorus. Something island-style. Keon turned the sound back down. People waved huge crosses and yelled at us.

"Murderers!" a woman shrieked loud enough for us to hear,

although it was mostly her gaping mouth and twisted face that alarmed me.

"Suicide is evil," a young man shouted, pointing at us. "Who made you God?"

"Life is precious!" people screamed. "You have no right to end it!"

There were a lot of people outside the gates, many more than I had expected. The uniformed guards were lined up along the road to keep the people behind the barriers, but people shoved and pushed to get past them and toward us. I wasn't exactly afraid but wondered briefly what these people would have done to us if they could have reached the car. Pulled us out and killed us, in the spirit of protecting the sanctity of life?

I was glad I had rented this ridiculously big hydro Jeep, which put us eye-level with the protesters.

"Goddamn motherfuckers!" Keon said. "As if it's easy to decide to end your life."

He gave the people the finger. I checked that the doors were locked. "Leave us alone!" he screamed. "Fucking idiots! Get the fuck away!"

We had nearly cleared the pack. In the rearview mirror I saw a car follow us out of the heavily guarded gates, between the pretty hedges spilling flowers to the left and right that concealed the high-security walls around the compound. The gate closed right behind them. There had been "rescue missions," where evangelicals had broken into end-homes and kidnapped people who had scheduled their own deaths.

It had happened a few times. I recalled a media story about someone's grandmother being held hostage inside a barricaded church — a white storefront in a strip mall, next to the obligatory Chinese restaurant, maybe a donut shop, and the liquor store, with a hologram of "Life is Sacred" above. A little disheveled lady escorted by police out of the darkened church. There had been organized assaults on other dignity communities, and doctors and staffers had been killed in ambush attacks on their way home from work.

Many of the homes were located in really secluded spots after that, with the kind of security you usually saw only for politicians or the very rich, and even direct relatives were vetted in order to visit.

Up ahead, the people thinned out. We saw a few makeshift chapels adorned with plastic flowers, sparkling lights, plastic angels on top, big glowing signs announcing: "Treasure Life!" "Honor Life!" In the rear screen, I saw that a woman, or maybe some shaman, in a long white robe had jumped the metal fence into the roadway. Two uniformed guards chased her for a moment while she ran toward the car. They caught her and carried her back to the side. The road in front of us was clear.

"Goodbye, Granma and Granpa," Keon said quietly.

We drove for a few minutes with an Alicia Keys oldie on the playlist.

"My grandmother was married three times," Keon said. "To two men, and, before it was legal, to Aunt Phyllis. She never allowed anybody to tell her how to live her life. She certainly wasn't going to let some self-righteous religious nut tell her the best way to die. I can't even imagine how many people are held hostage by their nice religious families."

I kept the playlist going, just as Keon's grandfather had instructed me. It shuffled through Mariah, The Wu-Tang Clan, Drake. Keon closed his eyes, and we were quiet for a while. When we got home, I turned off the messaging system and put dinner in the steamer. I did my best to keep Keon busy that night. We watched a few episodes of a show, then slept for a while, and later he hugged me so hard and long that for a moment I couldn't breathe. He cried a little, and we talked about his grandparents. He fell asleep again.

I got up and sat in the living room for a while, without getting dressed, just looking out the window. There were several bouquets of silk roses on the table — faint yellow blossoms that shed the occasional biodegradable petal. They were the expensive kind that start to wilt in a week or so. I watched our security lights graze the building opposite our house. It flickered like something out of an old movie, and for a little while I must have drifted to sleep. When I woke up, Keon stood in the doorway, also staring out the windows. He looked at me for a minute and then went into the kitchen. He got wine and ice cream, and then we watched some shows on the small screen in the bedroom, all in 2D. Keon fell asleep in my arms while I quietly, without waking him, checked my phone. It was dawn.

His grandparents' community had sent the log-in so I could access their memorial site. It was not terribly big or complicated, the way some people archive their entire lives, but it was clear that Keon's grandparents had hired a professional. It started with blueish water gurgling next to mustard yellow and ochre walls. Someone repeatedly called out a brief word, which I couldn't understand. Then the water faded and there were images of Keon's mother as a young girl, clips of her and her brothers as children. Clips of the day Keon's uncle died immediately after having visited his doctor for a routine checkup where nothing unusual had been detected, and of his grandparents at the funeral in front of a large wreath and the coffin draped in silk flowers. There were photographs of a legal ruling that determined that the death was caused by medical malpractice, edited like someone leafing quickly through an old paper file. More images of that uncle, when he was younger. These pictures faded out and gave way to images of Keon as his uncle's spitting image: playing baseball as a kid, basketball, singing at a family event, goofing off. I gently put my hand on Keon's head. Shots of Keon's mother and other uncles, then of him and his sisters. There were clips of Keon's grandparents on their trips, with big smiles and matching hats, sometimes waving from the front steps of a hotel, or from the top of a sightseeing boat or bus. They looked happy, as if their whole life had been one big discovery trip around the world. The images of Keon's uncle and mother faded to black until the screen was filled by the eddying waters against the yellow walls again. The whole clip moved very slowly, except for the court-ruling sequence, with no music and no quick cuts. The only sound had been the sharply called-out, melancholy word.

I watched it a few more times before Keon woke up. I went to the kitchen to let him watch it by himself. He was crying silently when I came back into the room. I sat in the bed next to him, kissed his face and then his ears, which made him laugh through his tears. Then we watched the clip again, together.

It took us several more viewings, and a bit of searching some other stuff on Keon's grandparents' site, until we had figured that the word was a gondolier's call in Venice before they turn a corner in a canal. Keon's grandparents had gone to Venice nearly every fall for many years. All of the water shots were of Venice, probably taken with a camera held over the edge while riding in the vaporetto. The sound that echoed throughout the film, like a bird-call, was a gondolier's voice bouncing off the low bridges and ochre walls without a response.

By the time the lifers had screamed at us and waved their fists and placards at our car and Keon had screamed back at them through our rolled-up windows, his grandparents had posted the clip on their site. By the time we had returned the rental car, the time stamp showed, they were gone.

Keon had taken leave from work in preparation of his grandparents' "departure." I could take three days off, and we spent one day at the shed, where Keon chopped wood for hours while I put in clumps of dandelion that had arrived a week earlier and nearly died while sitting in a box in our apartment in the city.

It had finally gotten too dark for me to continue. Keon was asleep on the couch, with his feet on one of the kitchen chairs. I did not wake him until the shed was prepped for our departure, and he slept more on the ride back. We hadn't talked much that day, but once or twice we had hugged, or I'd touched his cheek. I drove carefully along the service roads in the forest for the first few miles, worried about a deer or fox jumping into the lane. Then we rode along the heavily secured mining area, most of which is screened by tall fences and rows of dense, huge pines. You wouldn't know it's a mining site unless, well, you care about those things. I drove straight to the airport where we caught a late flight to New Orleans, me with dirt under my fingernails and still smelling of garden, and Keon with tree sap in his hair that didn't come out for days.

At his grandparents' former bar, much later that night in New Orleans, the manager refused to let us pay for dinner once he had figured out who we were. People kept buying rounds of drinks to toast Keon's grandparents. On the wall was a picture of them standing behind the bar, with his grandfather in a white shirt and floppy bow tie and his grandmother in a beaded black-and-silver dress, wearing a silvery wig. The picture was decorated with strings of twinkling lights that turned on only when a live act was playing. We stayed at the club till two or three, and then returned to Keon's aunt and uncle's house, where we talked in the living room, spread out on several couches and the carpeted floor, till dawn. I may not have remembered it right, but in my mind, people were at the house without interruption until someone arrived early in the morning with coffee and doughnuts.

They came by to check in on "K." People wanted to know how that last day had gone, exactly what Beverly and Will had said. A few people were still upset at Keon's mother for not telling them about his grandparents' decision to depart. There were sharp words between his mother and a cousin or friend who loudly complained how "selfish" his grandparents had been.

"Shame on you!" Keon's mother cut the woman off. "They had no obligation to tell you when they were going to die. It was her life to live and her death to die. Nobody else's. She was clear about that."

Someone took the woman aside and talked to her. It was a cousin. After a while she came over, hugged Keon and me, and just sat with us.

"Death remains mysterious to us," the minister said at the service that afternoon. He was young, with a British-style goatee and a neatly shaved part that made him look like a star athlete. The family's portly minister, who was also at the service, wore a three-piece suit, with a silver tie and a pocket square. He had declined to speak.

He still did not accept departure choice, even though more and more of his congregation's relatives had opted to die with dignity, and not in a hospital hooked up to machines and a morphine drip.

"And even when we know that we are ready to leave our earthly existence, we are filled with wonder and awe," the young minister said, to the room's *amens*. "There is guidance for us, even here. God gave us his Son to relieve our suffering and to deliver us from our sins."

There were more *amens*.

"Heaven is open to all souls, and Heaven welcomes everyone at any moment." Many of the people at the service nodded.

"Death is a chance for redemption, and God welcomes everyone into His kingdom." He had put the emphasis on *everyone*. More *amens* from the crowd.

"Mom set this up months ago," Keon said after the service, in the room filled with flowers and mourners, and put his arm around his mother's shoulders.

"Nana told me about a year ago," his mom said. Her eyes sparkled with tears, but she laughed. "She picked out the caterer, the flowers, the minister, the place," she said. "Well, she actually got into a fight with our minister, which is why we got this young guy here, and our minister just sitting there. He couldn't stay away, but he also couldn't bring himself to speak, even though he had known Nana since she was a teenager!"

"The young guy was fine, Mom," Keon said.

"'Don't let my memorial service be some slapdash affair, Pamela,' Mom told me. I had to book and reserve everything, make sure she approved, and at the same time keep the date secret from most of these folks here." She glanced at the big room filled with people eating and talking. "They are just upset they weren't told beforehand. But it was necessary. They would have called and harassed Grandpa and Grandma to change their minds."

"Nana would be happy," Keon said, and kissed his mom on the forehead. "She would have liked the service. And Grandpa would have been happy that you didn't play some easy-listening jazz. You know they made Aleks and me dance that last day," he added.

"I saw the clips," Keon's mom said. She laughed and added, "You were cute, but you gotta practice your moves!"

Ultimately, Keon's mom took the footage of our dancing during her parents' last hour offline. Seeing last moments filled with joy seems blasphemous to some people. I have heard from other people who also faced the religious crowds after visiting relatives in one of the homes. After Aunt Christine had gone through with her decision, Mom became a bit of an activist. She posted a brief essay in two columns, like an old-fashioned bank ledger, listing the pros and cons of her sister's decision to "take charge of her death," as she put it. In the left column, as the "pros," was everything from Socrates and Bible quotes to John Stuart Mill on freedom, to Rilke's lines on having to work for a lifetime to learn how to die properly. Mom has those lines framed on her wall.

On the "pro" side, Mom also put Christine's final letter, in which she explains what dignity and freedom meant to her, and why having courage in the face of death was for her a sign of character. Aunt Christine was a proud Republican and Christian who disagreed with me and Mom on some political issues, but she listed all of these ultra-conservative values as reasons why she would choose "her way to go." On the "con" side, Mom had put PAIN in block letters, which she has always considered senseless, dumb, and not an occasion for learning, in addition to "pleasing relatives and people who put doctrine above life," "bankruptcy while the cancer eats me from the inside," and the religious arguments that life is sacred and not ours to take. The "con" side ended with a simple phrase: "I love life."

Mom prefaced the list with a short piece about their childhoods, how her sister had taken care of her from an early age, and how desperately she missed her. She wrote about the sense of security she had felt as long as she knew Christine had been in her world, even long after they moved to different cities and countries as adults. The piece received so much attention that I helped Mom with changing her online profile. With Asturias's assistance, we buried her address under false data. Although the piece accounted for the pros and cons, people in the lifer movement were enraged.

The issue blew up in the media. It had been legal in Europe for a while, of course. But here in America, the debate was heated. Businesses were way ahead. There's something reassuring about American business in those debates, when commerce trumps belief. Keon has a college friend whose law firm specializes in end-of-life provisions. It's a huge industry already even though a lot of people are still skeptical about dignified death and hush up their relatives' decisions.

And there are travel and entertainment options for senior citizens that exist entirely for folks who want to go out with a bang, and have money to do it. Although it's mostly older people who choose these options, Keon and I have had a few friends of friends who have ended their own lives that way, with doctors and families in attendance for a final party, often at a beautiful destination before they doze off. Those are the hard-to-diagnose cases, especially the autoimmune conditions that have so many forms that they're not even called diseases, just syndromes.

After the media storm around Lucia's dad, the campaign released all sorts of statistics. How people in induced comas experience great pain although they look like they're peacefully asleep, how decisions in end-of-life situations are driven by doctors beholden to the insurance giants, how big pharma makes more money off the last few weeks of a person's life than during their entire lifetime. Stuff like that. There were the crazy death-feeds also. People posted their end-of-life moments, farewells, final words of wisdom. Offering themselves one more time live on camera, aside from coffin-cams, which people set up for fear of being buried alive and which have proven creepily popular live-feeds, or really dead-feeds.

I ended up telling Seth quite a bit of all of this on the plane ride — about Aunt Christine, about Keon's grandparents. I was rambling. He seemed to care, but looking back at it now, I don't really remember his reaction. What if he had been a lifer? What if he had only heard the horror stories of kids putting their parents into an end-home so they could inherit a fortune? Thinking back, I can't quite believe that I didn't ask about his experience. I must have still been shaken by the memory of Keon's grandparents. And it had probably been a relief to talk about it.

Today, when the topic comes up, I shut up and listen. I don't think I've talked about Lucia's dad or Keon's grandparents much at all since that conversation with Seth. I've seen other people go on about it. Once you mention dignified death people can't stop talking. As if they want to top everyone else's story with their tale of woe. I think we should leave it to individuals how they wish to die, like Plato recommends in the *Republic*. If the government has a responsibility, it's to make sure that all people have access to the same kind of proper end-of-life care, and that a dignified death isn't only available to the rich. Like the right to an education, or the right to bear arms. The right to love.

Phnom Penh

Another wave of panic came over me when I recalled today's schedule for Lucia, the letters that I need Domineek to get signed, who had to be invited to what meetings, the speech. I was nauseous, like being seasick, and sat down on the floor for a few moments for the feeling to subside. I banged on the door and the walls and screamed through the slimy membrane, hollered and yelled to get them to let me go online. It's been almost 48 hours now since I was brought here. This isn't going to work, to be out of touch with the Oval for a week.

Punching the walls felt like hitting a mattress. A loony bin, that's where I am. And to think that I served on the Global Health Committee that approved the rules to which I'm now subjected.

After some more screaming, a part of the wall receded to reveal another screen where a face appeared behind a protective bug-like mask and hazmat hood. I explained that I needed to be online, that I am the president's advisor on the environment, that it is imperative for national security to grant me access. I reached for the White House pass around my neck but didn't have it. My fumbling must have looked strange, but through the mask it's hard to see whether the medic reacted. I tried to sound professional and authoritative. Not let the panic creep into my voice.

"All communication is restricted when under observation," the person in the suit said. I couldn't even tell if it was a man or a woman. "Your loved ones and place of employment have been informed that you are undergoing voluntary observation and, if needed, treatment."

"Who?" I blurted out, "Who did you inform?"

The hooded person said nothing.

"I absolutely need to be online," I explained again. "I am aware of the rules — I wrote most of them — but this is a special situation."

The hooded face nodded slightly.

"It's not possible to have connectivity while in a q-unit," the voice said, robot-like. "Even if we could make exceptions, which we cannot, there is no connectivity here."

"That may be, or not. Look, I work in the White House. I have high-level clearance. I work for President Jackson. I need to communicate with her immediately!"

"I understand, sir," the person said in the same staccato voice. Maybe it was just the mask. "We are aware of your status, but, I repeat, in the units there is no connectivity."

For a moment, I thought of charging the mesh screen, bursting through it with my head and shoulders to collar the medic and get a response.

Of course I didn't.

Of course I'm being reasonable.

Lucia would be horrified if she learned that I tried to break out of quarantine, especially after she had put me in charge of convening the Global Public Health Committee. "White House Special Advisor on the Environment Goes Berserk in Quarantine and Puts Others at Risk!" "White House Staff Breaks Their Rules!" The Republicans would have a field day with that one.

So I sat down to show the medic that I am a reasonable person. For a moment, while I was thinking how to get through the screen to the other side, I had forgotten *why* I even wanted to be online. I wanted to communicate with Keon, with Lucia. Find out what was going on outside this bubble. I realized I must have the rules on the tablet. The worst thing for me would be to lose my security clearance by attempting a break out. I vowed to stay calm until my discharge.

I pulled up a file with a big mosaic of PDFs attached, all studies about medical outcomes of pandemics when individuals' behavior choices are factored in. In a video summary presented by Seth, he asserts that the spread of fear is most effectively contained when quarantined individuals do not communicate with the outside, and when families receive only official medical updates.

"The fight in a pandemic is always simultaneously a fight against fear, rumors, myths, and misperceptions," Seth says in the clip. He's dressed up, for once, but his boyish face and the unfamiliar suit and tie made him look like he's at his own bar mitzvah. "Rumors can greatly hinder public health efforts and even hurt medical teams. The elimination of subjective messages is an effective and critical effort in controlling the spread of contagious disease."

So here it is.

Rules for Quarantine Units, Section 3: "Under quarantine, patients will have no connectivity in order to minimize the dissemination of subjective and non-scientific information that can counteract public health efforts."

But no clips of any vote.

There are not many files from the Global Public Health Committee on my tablet. Pandemics had not been the only focus of our agenda. We had several other goals: to increase global awareness of the environment in order to reach agreements on toxins, on GMOs, on micro-plastics, to build a multinational coalition on water and energy. The clips on my tablets did not include many details of crisis prevention.

"We must not be motivated by fear," Lucia often says. "There is a way out even in the worst crisis. I expect the experts to chart this path for us."

Thinking of Lucia I wonder if she's concerned about me, whether she will contact me. Then I remind myself that POTUS would have other, bigger things to deal with in the midst of a pandemic, if that is what is going on. Still, some part of me felt, what, disappointed? Slighted? Overlooked? Not even a message. A heaviness came over me, a headache wrapped in fatigue. I shook my head, splashed water on my face. Drank two glasses of electrolytes. I'm being silly. I've been instrumental to her for years. She can't break the rules in this case, although she's done it before.

I recalled going on a trip to southeast Asia early in her presidency, before we had formulated our global agenda. Before Canada. Before Mexico and China. Before HEPP.

A small team was in Cambodia to scout a location for APEC's big climate summit.

Lucia joined us on the last day to meet with Cambodia's newly elected prime minister. This was before Lucia had succeeded in inviting India to join APEC, before Mata Ganga.

There had been a local outbreak of avian flu, and on the way to the airport, the motorcade had passed a vigil outside of a makeshift hospital. Traffic in Phnom Penh had all but stopped. Since all the roads near the hotel had been closed to civilian traffic, food had to be helicoptered in from outside of the city, and the hotel workers were ordered to stay in the hotel's extra rooms rather than return home after their shifts. We didn't see much of the city besides the empty streets around the hotel guarded by military. The hotel employees and our hosts tried to carry on as if everything was normal, despite the deafening noises from the choppers landing on the hotel tennis courts and the armed guards posted on each floor.

Our motorcade merged onto a highway. We passed a few hundred people surrounding what looked like a school with boarded-up windows. Armed guards stood in front of the building.

"Stop the car," Lucia ordered. The driver hesitated, glancing at her in the rearview mirror.

"Stop now!" she said more loudly and banged on the back of his seat. The driver slowed the car, then stopped. While he was speaking into his headpiece, Lucia had already opened the door.

Hot air rushed in. I scrambled out of the car into the blinding sun. From across a few railings and a concrete ramp of the highway, we faced a crowd that now looked back at us, with the blue flashes of the parked motorcade washing over them. Lucia pushed past her agents toward the railing, while the Cambodian officials and our guys struggled to get organized. I was right next to Lucia when she climbed on top of a concrete block and waved both arms, like someone lost at sea trying to get help.

"Hello!" she shouted. "Hello! I am here for you. I worry with you. I am waiting for good news, like you!"

Lucia gestured impatiently for Domineek to hand her the phone, which she used as a mic. She spoke into the phone and her voice boomed from speakers mounted atop the SUVs. "I pray for you! We will not forget you. I worry for your loved ones!"

It was eerie to have her voice come at us from behind. The people on the other side of the highway looked at us, pointing and talking, holding up their phones to take pictures.

"You are strong! I know you are strong! Your love and resilience are strong!"

A Cambodian official had climbed on the concrete block next to Lucia. She handed him the phone-turned-mic and he translated her words into Khmer.

The crowd was silent now, listening closely. Some had picked up children and put them on their shoulders.

Lucia turned and swept her hand toward us, toward the SUVs, the armed guards, the police escorts standing with their motorcycles.

People put their hands up and yelled out. I was worried for a moment when I sensed the soldiers around moving closer and changing the grip on their guns. Lucia gestured with her right hand back to the security around her, signaling them to stand down.

"We are sending the best doctors and the best equipment. We will defeat this!"

With the last sentence Lucia swung up her arms. The crowd

yelled and clapped.

These people were camped outside the makeshift hospital, waiting to find out how their family members were doing, desperate for good news. There were older women among them, and young mothers with children. Not a lot of men, I noticed, but groups of teenagers holding up signs.

Now Lucia pointed past the crowed, at the large building behind them with the sealed-off windows and guarded doors. She put her hands together, prayer-like, and bowed slightly to the crowd. Then she stepped off the concrete block and slipped into the SUV. I barely had time to climb into the massive car before the motorcade took off again.

We were silent. Lucia sat with her hands folded in her lap, her head bent down and her eyes closed. I wondered whether she was thinking about the people quarantined in the building, or about the mothers and wives waiting in the beating sun for news of loved ones. Or something else altogether. I knew better than to ask.

When we were airborne and high over the clouds she started the next meeting as if nothing had happened.

Silicon Valley

The ambient sounds are getting to me. I know that nature's sounds are proven to be calming (we're apparently hardwired that way), and I was on the committee that approved this design element. But I don't remember making rain, thunder, rustling wind, and birdcalls from around the world a mandatory feature of quarantine stays. Our committee had focused on maximum efficiency in a tiny space and on minimizing the risk of exposure while protecting the patients' fundamental rights, needs, and comforts. Except for the right not to be locked up against your will.

"Your work is important. More important than any one individual," Lucia had said when we briefed her on the committee's progress.

In these briefings she wasn't big on details. That had become clear during the first debate.

"You can outwonk me but you can't outsmart me, Mr. Senator," she had famously quipped live on national media when Hart had blasted her with some arcane numbers. I was backstage watching it on a monitor, and we heard the audience break into raucous cheers and applause. It was one of the moments that gave us hope that she had a chance of winning, that we could turn her lack of experience into an asset. Her no-nonsense, non-technical approach to things played well with voters, especially with people who felt that the data contradicted their experience. "Big data, little dick," was a common saying.

That quote directed at Senator Hart was Lucia's first big viral moment, and we made sure to keep it going.

I have a suspicion that the birdcalls were Seth's idea, and that he sneaked in hooting owls, chirping buntings, warblers and robins, and a woodpecker that annoys the heck out of me, without our approval. I love birds. Really do. I had two absolutely tame parakeets when I was a kid, named Billie and Lena, who'd fly around my room when I got home after school. But this piped-in bird racket is getting on my nerves.

"There'll be time for sanding the edges," Lucia said the first time I lost my cool with Seth. That was during our first trip to Silicon Valley, when the techies were still on the fence about Lucia's platform. Seth had arranged the meeting for us, and it was my first time seeing him in person. Not very tall, a wiry build. Back then he still had closely cropped hair, with a receding hairline. Like a lot tech guys always on some weird diet. Okay, he's in shape. He wore a dark gray hoodie and the kind of pants popular on the West Coast, made of high-tech fabrics, loose but cuffed in a different color high up on the calf. The standard uniform of wealthy younger tech guys, I discovered. Seth was rich enough to get most of the other CEOs to come to the meeting. He had developed the first commercially viable computers to be directed by brain waves.

"So you're the eco guy of the operation," he said to me quietly after he had greeted Lucia. "It's good to see someone serious on the team. I was worried we'd get a bunch of Washington nerds who don't understand the West Coast's ways of getting things done."

I was flattered. I'll admit to that.

"I've spent some time in Seattle," I said.

Seth smiled and said, "I know. Me too. I got my PhD at UW."

"These meetings are about ideas above all else," he said to me still in a bit of a whisper. We were driving from the airport to our meeting, and Lucia and her husband sat in the front of the car.

"People out here really care about what the senator has to say about the environment. They loved her during the debate. We need new ideas, and we need to think about the big issues facing us all. The fact that she's made water scarcity a campaign issue is huge around here."

"That was my idea," I said. I immediately regretted it.

Seth looked at me for a moment.

"Good for you. Well, I guess you understand since you've been out here a lot."

"The senator is really the one who connects with the water issue," I quickly corrected myself. "Her father . . ."

"Yes," Seth interrupted me, still in a whisper. "It's the main reason we are all here today to meet with her."

I was worried that I had taken too much credit, or told him too much about our strategy, but Seth seemed okay. He leaned forward to chat with Lucia, and I looked out at the endless rows of shiny new vehicles zooming past. Mostly hydrogen cars, of course, since they had passed legislation to phase out gas-powered vehicles in California. On Sundays people with special, very expensive permits could drive oldtimers, which made the weekends on California freeways loud and stinky affairs. I stole a glance at Seth's watch, which probably cost more than I made in two years. I'm sure that, in spite of his environmental commitment, he also had a garage full of vintage Mercedes, Bentleys, Jags, and Porsches — the kinds of cars that had never gone hydro.

At the company headquarters, a woman in a long flowing outfit that looked like a cross between Buddhist robes and a track suit led us to a large conference room. On one side of the room there was a curved and super-modern window, and on the other side, a Balinese-looking sideboard with a California array of juices in glass jars, small pots of wheatgrass, wooden boxes with edibles, and tiny obsidian cups next to a shiny large espresso machine that probably had been shipped from a two-hundred-year-old café in Naples or Rome.

Lucia started out the meeting. "To think bigger remains our greatest challenge." "Computers, planes, nanotechnology, space probes, and drones have afforded us a more nuanced view and new perspectives of our planet. Silicon Valley has led much of that revolution. But even after millennia of evolution, and even with all of those technologies that have remade the world, we humans have changed very little. We still see and hear mostly what is in front of us. We see, sense and perceive the world pretty much the same way we always have."

"We certainly know what you mean," Seth interrupted Lucia. "We have changed the world, but now every day we look out at miles of fancy Astroturf, at desiccated but supposedly drought-resistant plants, at scorched and dusty playing fields for our kids. And we have not found a way to change that."

"Silicon Valley was once orchards and fields," Vicki Chang, head of Coinster, said. "Over the past ten years, since the new water laws, this place has become a desert."

"So, what we need to do," Lucia said pointedly, clearly not happy about being interrupted or lectured, "is to use our eyes and ears and look again." She waited for a moment. "You are ahead of the rest of the country in many aspects. In fact, you are in many ways ahead of most of the world."

I felt the mood in the room change with the compliment.

"You can see where everyone is headed. Silicon Valley has been shaping the world's future for four decades now."

She glanced at the executives in the room, all of whom led companies that directly impacted all those among the planet's seven billion people who counted as consumers, and indirectly had an effect on all human lives.

"And you have done so by thinking about human beings as part of greater networks, greater systems, bigger grids."

"With respect, Senator, your platform restricts growth and interferes with most industries," Winnie Samuels said. "At WorldWide, we are not in favor of governments telling us what to do. The UN,

Delhi with its trade embargoes, Beijing, which runs practically a parallel system, Washington, the EU with its obsession about privacy, carbon regulations, now Russia with energy. Governments are the most bureaucratic and non-thinking entities we know!"

"Look outside, Winnie," Lucia said and turned toward the conference room's huge, curved window. She had her back toward the room now, and was silhouetted against the glass. "What do you see?"

Frank Tan spoke up, apparently eager to show up Winnie and WorldWide. "I see fake grass, fake trees, fake ponds, and a bunch of plastic that is made to look like timber," he said. "I see a world that needs some big thinking to get fixed. And I see a situation that has not been helped by fewer regulations, Winnie."

"So how will more red tape turn this place green?" Winnie responded sharply. "How will more regulation from Washington bring water back?"

When WorldWide had still been Facebook, Frank had developed a touch-based operating system poised to hit it big. Facebook's merger with Winnie Samuels' Company, which already had sensory recognition software, had obsolesced that project before it got launched. Seth explained all of that to me later. At that time, all I picked up was tension. I glanced at Lucia, who seemed unperturbed.

"Nothing is going to turn California green anytime soon," Frank said curtly. "But if we keep on worrying about Washington getting it wrong, your kids won't even play on grass when they visit other states," he added. "Look at what's happened over the past twenty years here! We all knew what the problems were, and they passed incremental laws to fine me for washing my car, for watering my lawn. No wonder people got mad. So the state imposed some quotas on big farming. That didn't help. Big thinking! That is what we need, and fast."

Lucia stood by the window, her arms folded. She did not say anything.

"Frank's right," one of the younger guys said. "We need good ideas. We need good people. We need to stop sitting around debating whether or not we care about plants and grass. I personally don't care very much for grass; I have terrible allergies. I don't even think about trees all that much, but that's not the point. I'm interested in doing something big to keep this state going."

"This is your state," Lucia said. "Some of you remember a green California, when driving from here to L.A. involved passing miles of lush fields dewy with the spray of massive sprinklers. When there were lakes south of here where people sailed and fished. My father worked in these fields, picking avocados, strawberries, asparagus, you name it. That was until the water dried up, and he was forced to leave the state."

She looked out of the window.

"You have the power to change the world for the better. You have the power to reboot Washington. Your kids live can in a world where people don't have to abandon their homes because their elected leaders were so shortsighted."

Lucia glanced in my direction. I pressed a button on the keyboard projected onto the table. The huge curved window instantly darkened. A map of the United States appeared.

"The red areas show consumption of water that exceeds average rainfall, groundwater, or reservoir capacity," Lucia said. Large swaths of the American West, much of the middle, and parts of the South turned red. "You can see what is just ahead of us."

The continent behind Lucia grew increasingly red, and soon pulsed in hues from maroon to magenta and crimson, like a bloated and misshapen heart.

"We will soon have water issues in most states," Lucia said. "I don't need to tell you that groundwater pollution, salinization of soil, and flooding have become a permanent infrastructure threat. People will attack water trucks and sue to get big farming out of their state. We do not want another Phoenix, with mobs attacking people who own pools. You of all people know that we can change the way these things unfold."

She had everyone's attention now, which was not easy in a room filled with billionaire geeks.

"You have changed the way we write, how we communicate, how we treat disease. You have made big data the way we govern. Now I ask you, I appeal to you, in the name of the planet and of a future that contains us all, to change the way we act."

I pushed the button again. Lucia was now darkly silhouetted against the glaringly bright, green park, as in an early Cindy Sherman print.

"I'll do whatever I can," Seth said, to which Lucia nodded. "Greenery doesn't necessarily interest me. Disrupting ingrained patterns, and changing our destructive ways, does."

We had known about Seth's commitment in advance, since he had arranged this meeting and sent a plane to get us there. He also connected the old Valley guys — those who had made their fortunes when computers still had keyboards and screens, when we still used money and credit cards — to the younger guys.

"I personally don't wish to see the hippies take over," Winnie said. "I don't like people who think they're superior because they grow their own tomatoes. And I sure as hell don't like Big Government telling us what to do. But I can also see that all of our individual efforts, all of our charities, can't do enough without some coordination. We are all going in the same direction, but not on the same track." She swept her hand in the direction of the window behind Lucia. "Senator Jackson, to be frank, you seem to be the best option. And will you please dim the windows again."

I pushed a button and the room instantly returned to a pleasant soft glow.

"I'll support you, Lucia," B. K. Adeyemi from Microsoft said quietly.

I mentally made a note. B.K.'s contribution meant huge funding. But more important, he was an idol for many people after he had hit it big with holograms. He had loads of money, was married to a famous actress, and his apps were on most of the world's phones.

"I've seen much of my country destroyed by Big Oil," B.K. said.

"And since I've arrived in the United States, I've seen this valley sucked dry by Big Water. It's time we support someone who understands that we are guests on this planet. Someone who can unite out efforts. We are custodians! We are custodians at best, and we are screwing it up."

We debriefed in one of WorldWide's courtyards, lush like a Henri Rousseau canvas with replicas of tropical plants and a hologram pond so real I nearly threw in bits of granola to feed the fake koi. It was only Lucia, us staffers, plus Seth and Frank.

"It's not about the money," Lucia said.

"Well the money won't hurt," Domineek said with a smile. "There is so much of it here, and we sure will need it."

The opposition had a lot of money coming their way: Big Energy, Big Agriculture, Big Pharma, Big Waste. Some of them Lucia had only reached once she'd arrived at the White House, and she could threaten legislation that would hurt them. Domineek projected a seating chart of the meeting from her phone onto a rickety marble-topped table that probably came from the same Italian café where they had found the espresso machine. The chart was titled "Silicon Leads," with each person's net worth in a small window above their head.

"Our hologram campaign alone will cost hundreds," Asturias said, and I wasn't sure whether he meant thousands or millions. I can never keep track on tech pricing, and which technology has suddenly dropped in cost while some other thing remains ultra-expensive. "B.K.'s support could be critical here."

Lucia pulled on a branch sprouting clusters of red bougainvillea blooms and let it flip back. All of the blossoms stayed in place.

"This is about who we are as a species on this planet. We are one species of maybe eight million total, but we're the one that's taken up most of the planet's resources, by far. And we're the one species that can stop the downward spiral into environmental collapse."

"You know how to think across platforms and silos," Lucia said to Seth and Frank. She ran her fingers over the tabletop with the seating chart display. "You and your friends can help us bring together all of the competing conservation and grassroots movements in a united, clear cause. Even all of the charities, all of which pursue their particular vision of doing good. Talk about herding cats."

"Let's focus on how to fund this," Domineek said. "Asturias is right: we need a lot of money to produce holograms in time for the primaries. B.K. seems to be pretty excited. Am I right?"

"Absolutely!" I said. I was about to give my assessment of everyone's level of enthusiasm, the way I saw it.

"Getting Winnie to participate will take work," Seth preempted me. "But if we can, a lot of folks will pay attention and follow suit."

"When," Lucia said. "*When,* not *if* she joins us. Winnie's family has been important in California politics for four generations," she added. "They care about our issues. One brother has been involved in sustainable harvesting in South America for years, and he was instrumental in getting the first round of water laws passed here in the West. Another brother has had some drug problems, and she's been taking care of him lately. Her mother is big in the anti-zoo movement. She only wants everyone to know that she came to this decision by herself."

"And *before* anyone else," Seth added. Lucia nodded. I had a whole plan for getting Winnie involved, and I wanted to present it.

"We want to be cautious," I said quickly. "We will insist on regulation to achieve the country's environmental targets."

Seth jumped in again. "She will object to more stringent government controls."

"We cannot compromise on this issue. Our platform is not open for debate."

Lucia looked at me, then at Seth. He had leaned back with his head titled up, as if he were waiting for things to be decided in his favor.

"Let's work together here," Lucia said. "Aleks, make sure Winnie has briefing materials by this afternoon. When she understands that our policies make both economic and environmental sense, she'll come around."

"I've already posted our data to her site," I responded quickly. "Next week you are speaking at the School for Earth Sciences at Stanford. Winnie endowed it. We'll be sure you'll get an hour with her that day," I added.

I was a bit flustered, with everyone weighing in on things that were really in my purview.

We ended the meeting and Lucia asked me to follow up on some details. I appreciated the gesture of scheduling my one-on-one with her right then and there. While the other guys scattered or checked their tablets, we moved to another table in the courtyard with its fake plants, koi pond, and grass.

"There'll be time to sand the edges, Aleks," Lucia said again. "These tech guys aren't exactly known for their interpersonal skills, but Seth will be a good partner for us." She laughed and I joined in.

That afternoon, we flew to Los Angeles on Seth's plane to visit Mark Zuylen's home. We had accepted the invitation because no politician says no to the head of Connectr, and Lucia was speaking at the Los Angeles Earth Day celebration that evening.

"We have pissed our way into a desert," Zuylen said right after we had said hello, as if just continuing a conversation that had been going on in his head for a while, and we were just late to join. We were at his beach house, sitting on deep white couches around a huge round wooden table made of some ancient tree, with a big hole in the center. The rim was wide enough to hold glasses and dishes, and in the cavity of the wooden block, a small galaxy of gleaming seashells, slowly spun in space.

Zuylen brushed a hand over his neatly tonsured head. He was wearing flowing robes and was sipping juice from a black obsidian cup with red and gold speckles, made from compacted ash, I guessed.

"We live on imported water and project greenery all around us. This will be the next Dust Bowl in no time at all." A kid ran through the room, followed by a large Airedale terrier and two women dressed like Buddhist nuns. Zuylen didn't look up. He kept his focus on the large windows facing the ocean, as if searching for his next insight.

"All of us here in California have known about environmental degradation longer than we care to admit. Or at least long before we started to start things in earnest, on a grand scale. We have committed huge resources, and it's all — or almost all — been too little, too late, Senator Jackson," he said. "We've known before most others that we're pretty much fucked," he added, quite un-monkishly. "We know that if an issue don't bite you in the ass, it ain't your problem. So it seems a bit like you're jumping on a bandwagon here."

"I know that California has led the country in the fight for environmental legislation," Lucia said a bit archly. "I'm only sorry the wake-up call had to be so dramatic. And I'm glad you were able to move back on your campus."

Zuylen looked at her but did not respond immediately.

"Senator Jackson," he finally said. "As you know, my company lost four people in the ecoterrorist fires. Four good colleagues and personal friends. It galls me to appear to be swayed by them."

"I was very sorry to hear about the fires," Lucia said. "We appreciate that your company is a leader in looking at development as an interconnected set of issues, from water and native plants to building materials, roads, and energy."

"We are trying our best," Zuylen said. "Most of the tech world understands that things will not take care of themselves any longer. The whole state will soon be dry. But we are global companies, and we realize that your platform goes beyond local concerns."

"I am in complete agreement," Lucia said. "There are no local solutions to the water problem."

Nobody in that room could have known how prescient his remarks, made before our takeover of Mexico, had been. Maybe

Zuylen's whole Buddhist routine wasn't just an act. Maybe he was seeing the connectedness of things.

We sat zazen with him for about thirty minutes. The space did not look very different from his living room, except that the windows were tinted. It was filled with natural objects: sea shells, driftwood, rocks. I tried to clear my head but ended up going over our schedule for the evening instead. The *gotta gotta gotta* mind won out. Lucia, who's always been a better meditator, nonetheless surprised me when she joined Zuylen's chant. I only knew *Om Mani Padme Hum,* the most basic Buddhist mantra.

I asked Lucia afterward how she knew the chant. She smiled. "Long story. I've been to India a few times, and I have friends there who hang out with monks and nuns."

That evening Lucia addressed several hundred thousand people at Earth Day. Security had been extremely tight even though Lucia had not been announced yet as a speaker. The organizers were worried about ecoterrorists, who had destroyed new developments in parts of the southwest, taken the San Diego Zoo off the grid several times, and successfully shut down LAX twice in the last year. People also blamed them for sabotaging tankers coming up from Panama, and for deliberately setting fires that had killed scores in California alone.

We flew back to Washington in Seth's plane. I ended up in a seat next to him while Lucia slept in the back. I quizzed him about every one of the tech tycoons, how likely they would be to donate, and told him about some of the challenges we had with getting the DNC to back Lucia's platform. I confided my worries about the party forcing Lucia to replace her campaign team with their people, not all of whom thought the environmental issue would play past the elections, when the poetry became prose. He knew all of the key party leaders and assured me that he would keep an ear to the ground. When I think back to that moment, I cringe.

Eventually every single person from that first Silicon Valley meeting signed on and donated, even though most of them also supported our opponents. The Valley was dry. Grant's solution was to pipe in more water from even farther away, which hadn't worked for two decades. There were droughts now in regions where rain had always been plentiful.

The birdsong has given way to the steady patter of rain and distant thunder. On the tablet, I can look at files from our health-planning meetings on ambient sounds for the quarantine pods. It had been authored by Seth, of course.

"Certain sounds are good, others are bad," he says in a clip I've pulled up. This must have been later, after the election, when we had used the techies' money and expertise to make sure that Lucia visited every last community in America via hologram.

"The act of listening to sound is a world-making activity. We create and live in sonic environments." Seth turned full-on academic in a lot of those meetings. I thought it was a waste of time since we all had the same data, but most of the other White House staffers ate it up.

"There are studies that show health gains directly linked to certain ambient sounds," he said. "We can use the sounds in the libraries of Cornell and Taipei as ambient treatment for patients everywhere."

So I have to thank Professor Steven Feld, PhD, who invented the field of acoustemology, and Seth, for the cicadas, the warblers, and the rain and distant thunder that rumble through my room right now.

There's more thunder now. It sounds like I'm in the center of a huge rainstorm, with howling winds. I try to ignore it, but I feel a chill.

The Atlantic

Why Canada Joined the Alliance

By BAOQI WEN, OCT. 12, 2021, POLITICS

The road that leads out of the town of Bigfork, Montana, runs alongside the Flathead River, a green band of still water lined by majestic Lodgepole pines. All the trees along the Flathead are new growth planted in the early twentieth century. Most of Montana's virgin forest had been consumed by the prospectors' run for mining rights in the 1890s. Upstream is Columbia Falls, a kind of medium-sized Niagara that attracts a good number of ecotourists in the summer but usually slows to a trickle by late fall. Toward the south, Flathead Lake can be spotted through thick brush and a dense ring of willow trees, none of which were native to the region when Europeans first settled there in the mid-1800s.

Since the Integration and the reversal of upstream pollution, the Flathead Basin has seen a spike in waterfowl. The secretive American bittern has been spotted along the shore, although in July there was no sign of this native species, with its distinct brown and beige speckled plumage. It was reported that on a recent, unexpectedly cool July evening, the lakeshore was lined by immobile long-necked snowy egrets spaced out as if on duty. The people of Somers, a town of about twelve hundred off the north shore of Flathead Lake, wedged between three national forests and Glacier National Park, had made the more stately great egret the symbol of the Integration. Now when you drive along Flathead River into the Greater Region formerly known as Canada, there are flags with egrets on virtually every passing car. Not that it's busy up there. The Flathead Basin, where the border between Canada and the United States was first breached in dramatic fashion, seemed quiet now.

In the spring following Lucia Jackson's inauguration as the forty-fifth president of the United States, a spike in fatal skin infections in the towns of Coeur d'Alene and Whitefish around the Flathead Basin led to renewed requests for the Canadian government to release data on major pollutants that could affect Montana groundwater and freshwater. Jackson flew first to Ottawa and then, with Canada's premier, to Banff National Park near Calgary. An agreement was provided for US inspectors from the EPA to visit sites in the Canadian Rockies.

On July 12, 2021, the group requested access to an abandoned mining complex in Banff. Canadian officials cited security and military concerns to prevent the US inspectors access, but eventually relented. Accounts of what happened on the evening of July 16, 2021, differ widely. The undisputed fact is that twelve US inspectors were found dead in the charred remains of their EPA vehicles.

Jackson sent investigators, of course. Canadian officials first claimed it had been an accident, and then blamed a group of local men for carrying out an attack. When a recovered cellphone video showed that Canadian paramilitary personnel staged a direct attack, a few senior heads in Canada's ruling party rolled. It was soon discovered that the attackers were financed by large companies who had assumed control over water in the region.

"I have come here with feelings of grief over the deaths our agents and sorrow for their families. These people were working to keep the world safe and clean," Jackson said at a press conference in Calgary after the video of the attack had gone viral. "My concern now extends to all the families living in the Northern Rockies and in the run-off regions of water to the south and east. You and your children deserve clean and safe water, and you deserve to be protected from short-term practices that harm the planet." Jackson had declined to let Canadian officials join her onstage. She gestured toward the trees behind her.

"These vast forests were first protected in 1886 as points of Canadian significance. In 1891, the United States followed this wise example and established similar protective zones." Jackson pointed over the heads of the assembled press. "Although we enjoy them, National Parks were not created for tourism alone. They are our insurance policy for survival. These forests have global significance."

"Water is not American; the sky is not Canadian. No tree has ever held a passport, but this is true as well for toxic sludge. I have asked a small number of American forces to stop the toxic dumping into the Kikomun Creek catchment area. These dedicated men and women will work for all of us. But is this enough? We need to protect creeks and streams, trees and valleys, parks and rivers. I speak to you not as president of one country, and not out of anger. I speak with concern for our shared future on this planet. I am working with the Canadian parliament—with those leaders who remain committed to this great nation—to ensure the safety of this region."

A series of leaked videos showed exclusive deals between the country's largest polluters and government. Families who had been awarded large sums to keep quiet about sick children came forward, and judges threw out the government's efforts to enforce confidentiality agreements (atlantic.com/legalmatterscanada). But it was not the legal decisions or revelations of hanky-panky between politicians and big businesses that concerned President Jackson.

"We have forgotten that we share a world. These men and women, Canadian and US citizens, will secure our future."

A group of people in Global Alliance uniforms waved at the camera.

"We will work alongside of all of you to achieve small victories locally. We will plant trees, bring in solar power, clean rivers, build wildlife corridors. And jointly, we will protect ourselves from the threats of toxins fed into groundwater, and pollutants carried by the wind."

The crowd cheered and chanted, waving small flags with the white egret bordered by the starred stripes and the maple leaf. At that moment, the bracelets on everyone's wrists lit up a deep emerald green. President Jackson raised her arm to display her band.

"Green is not a national color," she said. "But green brings us all together. Together we can turn the tide."

Thousands of hands were raised, and the wristbands now changed colors. They were red, white, and blue, a tapestry of the American and Canadian national colors, then everything turned a lush green again.

"This is our moment to put differences behind and to think about that which connects us all," President Jackson said. Behind her on a Jumbotron screen, the camera tracked along a canal bordered by cement walls and industrial areas on both sides.

The screen changed and now the camera flew above a blue river bordered by lush pines on both sides. In rapid succession, it displayed large stacks of freshly cut timber in front of deep forests, elk and eagles, and workers in the Global Alliance uniform with various tools and machines nearby.

"We live in a time for large-scale action," President Jackson said while behind Global Alliance flags unfurled on flag posts, which had just risen out of the platform. The crowd broke into applause again, and now balloons with the Global Alliance logo floated up from the strategically placed hutches in the aisles.

HEPP

From Wikipedia, the free encyclopedia

[This article is about a political alliance called HEPP. For the French food brand, see HEPP.]

The *Hemispheric Environmental Protection Pact* (HEPP) [French: Pacte du Protection Écologique de l'Hémisphère (PPEH)], also called the *All Americas Alliance,* is an inter-governmental environmental alliance based on the Hemispheric Environmental Treaty, which was signed by representatives of the governments of the United States of America, Canada, Mexico, Haiti, Jamaica, Barbados, Panama, Nicaragua, Costa Rica, and Curaçao, in Mexico City, on August 27, 2021[1]. The pact constitutes a collective defense system of natural areas of local and transnational significance whereby its members agree to mutual defense against major dangers to the environment by any party. HEPP's headquarters are in Victoria, Canada, and Seattle, USA, the founding member states of the 16-member alliance in North and South America[2].

HEPP directs national governments on major environmental policies ranging from payments for ecosystem services (following the rationale of the Coase Theorem[3]). As a supranational body, it has an integrated armed defense structure under the direction of two US Supreme Commanders. It has occasionally used these forces to enforce compliance with climate treaties or "trade-off" deals between nations. HEPP's member states commit to at least 4 percent of GDP to "green" spending with much of the funds used for postindustrial cleanup, rewilding of landscapes, species protection, natural negotiation measures, and subsidies for green and non-carbon based industries.

US president Lucia Jackson ordered US troops to Banff National Park in Canada after 12 US agents from the E.P.A. died under unresolved circumstances.[5] Jackson continues to send US troops there annually, under an agreement reached with then Canadian Prime Minister Kevin Coates, to integrate US and Canadian troops into HEPP's armed defense forces.

The Banff incident revealed high-level corruption in the Canadian government, which shortly thereafter collapsed.[6]

The organization's standing has been a source of several legal challenges in various jurisdictions since its founding in 2021.[4] Coates's authority in forming an alliance that supersedes Canadian national interest has been challenged several times in the Supreme Court of Canada.

The Supreme Court of Canada has struck down various provisions of the HEPP agreement. The Canadian government has failed to comply with these rulings, prompting a crisis in the legislative branch that has not been resolved.[7] To date, the United States has refused to remove HEPP forces from Canadian soil.

When Canada's Environmental Party gained a majority in Parliament in 2021, the HEPP organization was strengthened, and many of its policies aligned with national Canadian Law. Debates about the legitimacy of HEPP continue, especially among the country's other parties, along with doubts over the credibility of the United States as an environmental leader.[8] President Lucia Jackson is credited with convincing large parts of the Canadian electorate of the benefits of remaining a member state of HEPP.[9] After the widely documented disappearance of polar bears from Manitoba, and an economic boom in green industries proved beneficial for Canadian companies, HEPP has become part of the political landscape of Canada. Jackson regularly visits Canada as a "guest of honor"[10] who is formally invited by members of Parliament, and recent speeches and appearances have placed her squarely within the field of Canadian politics.[11

Jackson has led a campaign for HEPP member states to increase green spending and deploy HEPP forces outside of the North American hemisphere.

Garbage Wars I

I've tried a few tricks that Asturias taught me, but I cannot jump onto their network — it really looks like the firewalls are strong. We had made it a quarantine policy that there would be no VIP treatment, no special privileges, even for bigwigs. We weren't expecting to have to enforce the rule. The truly rich, the flashy CEOs, the quiet guys in the back who ran the bigger global companies, the celebrities — those people quickly vanished when there was a health crisis.

Asturias taught me to organize my files "like you would your kitchen drawers," as he said with his Eastern European accent. "You want to know instinctively where the spoons are and where the knives are, even when it's pitch black and someone's breaking down your door. You don't want to reach for a knife and come up with a spoon."

The tablet is the only personal item they let me bring in here, and I am glad it's indestructible.

I miss the fake suede cover that they had probably incinerated right away; a gift from Keon. Gone up in smoke that's been filtered 50 times at least. Along with my suit, shirt, tie, shoes, socks, belt, wallet, duffel bag, and the underwear I had bought in a London hotel shop.

"Extra baggage, Aleks?" Lucia had asked when I met up with her in the lobby of our hotel in London with a small shopping bag.

"Don't you know the less we have, the more we give?" Lucia said with a half-smile as we rode up in the elevator to our rooms.

We were in London for the Garbage War meetings. Trash was the underlying dispute, of course. I have footage of those discussions from the same hotel where I had bought the underwear. The Canadians had insisted on holding these meetings in London, perhaps because they felt that being close to Westminster Palace would impress the Chinese.

"China has unleashed a war on our waters," the Canadian prime minister said in the opening round. "The coastline of British Columbia from Prince Wales Island to Vancouver has been covered in a carpet of garbage that we know originates from the South China Sea. No other current could have pushed it this far north, and we demand that this assault on our country be stopped."

He pushed a button on a small screen to pull up a video on the wall behind him.

"What you are seeing is the coast of British Columbia. This is Vancouver Island — one of the most successful re-wildings of landscape achieved in the world to date: a model for the planet. We have reintroduced a number of species and revived local fishing in the region. But for the past nine months, most of the western coast of Vancouver Island has been littered with Chinese garbage that we believe they intentionally steered toward our shores."

The video zoomed in on what looked like a sea of colorful and shiny crystals marbled with pale, white lines. A gigantic, gently swaying carpet of glistening crystals that slowly and almost tenderly lapped at the shore. When the camera zoomed in, the sparkling island turned into an incredibly large amount of plastic. Bottles, bags, toys, packaging, boxes, string, shoes, tubing, containers were packed so closely that it looked, even though this was the temperate climate of the northern Pacific, as if the Arctic Ocean's white and sparkling waves had frozen in place. Everyone stared at the screen, mesmerized by the strange beauty of the glistening crystal sea that undulated in all directions. Finally, the camera found a place of dark blue ocean at the carpet's edge. But even there, tiny plastic parts glistened in the sunlight when the camera dove under the surface, and small bits of Styrofoam floated like ice cubes in a drink. The camera pulled back and up, quickly. The sparkling extended for miles and miles into the open sea.

"This rubbish slick has killed thousands of shorebirds and two colonies of otters protected by international agreements. Vancouver's tourism has decreased by 70 percent this season alone."

The clip homed in on several large birds that squatted and hopped along a narrow strip of rocky beach, with necks and wings entangled in plastic filaments. Then the camera showed a small group of sea otters rolling in the surf. They were floating on their backs, with their paws holding shells and other objects like swimmers doing a drill. Several of them were entangled in plastic netting that had cut through their fur to expose strips of raw flesh.

"This is direct retaliation for our tariffs on non-green goods, which have hurt Chinese companies," the Canadian prime minister concluded.

Lucia turned to face the Chinese delegation.

"We are as concerned as our Canadian friends are about the plastic-waste site in the Pacific Ocean," the leader of the Chinese delegation said. She had been introduced as Chen Minghua, vice president of the People's Republic, but I remember some disagreement in the White House over her real title and role.

"China has been a responsible and conscientious steward of the oceans for centuries. In fact, one of China's illustrious sons, Admiral Zheng He, first arrived in the Americas in 1421 by sailing across the Pacific. From the courageous voyage of Zheng He till today, China has regarded the ocean as the great connector between nations."

The Chinese vice president, her hair pulled into a tight ponytail and her outfit a blinding azure, stood with her fingers gently resting on the table before her. She hardly moved while she spoke.

"China has been developing technologies to produce

hydro-degradable plastics," she said, as if explaining something to a somewhat dimwitted person. "The People's Republic has also fought the accumulation of plastic waste in the Pacific's dead zones. It is absurd to think China would intentionally destroy the ocean that touches our shores, or that we could move this vast mass of material."

A picture behind her showed a map of the Pacific with two long, amoeba-shaped blotches.

"Those are still vortices," the vice president said, enunciating the last two words carefully in her precise British accent. "China has worked for years to contain and remove these floating rubbish heaps before they do further harm."

The next image showed a huge ship sucking up a rubbish patch with what looked like a big flat vacuum tube. The vessel was bright white, like a cruise ship, and it was sailing under a splendid blue sky. In front of it the ocean sparkled turquoise, but behind it the plastic patch shimmered in many different colors fanning out in the wake of the ship.

"What Canada accuses us of is impossible on a natural and institutional level. We cannot control the currents and over the past two years, more than four million Chinese school children have volunteered to clean the shoreline from Shanwei to Fuzhou, and all of the beaches of the Hong Kong peninsula."

Images of people in bright yellow T-shirts and plastic gloves working on a beach flashed across the screen. There were hundreds of them, and along the shore sat lines of large yellow trucks, toward which the people rode bags on small, fat-tired carts.

"China has reduced the use of plastic bottles by 37 percent in the last two years."

The woman held up an angular metal thermos with two bamboo handles to prove she did not drink from plastic.

"The People's Republic regards Canada's assertions as baseless and injurious to our role as a global environmental leader. Remember that China alone has led the effort to pass fishing restrictions that have been blocked by HEPP member states. We are very concerned with the Canadian government's refusal to stop mobs from carrying on in front of our embassy, threatening our ambassador and her staff."

Here, China was veering off-script, but then so had the Canadian prime minister. I pause the clips because I think I've heard a knock. Something being turned on? Nothing.

I have to develop a routine, I think, like those prisoners in Russian novels, or the guy in Oriana Fallaci's books, or Edward Snowden during the years in his Moscow hotel. When we presented Snowden with a National Medal of Honor and an official apology on behalf of the US government for triggering what would result in the OITO, the Office of Information Transparency and Oversight, Snowden had at first refused to show up for a ceremony at 11:30 a.m. in the Rose Garden because he would not alter the routine he had developed in Russia and Ecuador. I don't want to end up like Snowden, trapped in a pattern that keeps me fit and alert but also inflexible, with the crazed look and roving eyes of a cat stalking an imaginary mouse. But then, Snowden was stuck in Russia for years. Depressing guy, that Snowden, even if he sacrificed his freedom for the greater good.

Back to the clip.

China now rolled out waves of data, kind of like the flotsam on the seas, while the Canadian prime minister glared from his seat and small beads of perspiration glistened on his forehead.

Finally, Lucia stepped in.

"Prime Minister Daly, Vice President Chen," she said. "Why are we here today? We are here to find a solution to the Pacific garbage patch. China is an important ally in this effort that affects us all. We are all here to work together to eliminate these heaps of plastic that kill marine life and slowly poison the rest of us." Lucia paused for a moment. "An ally as great as Japan, Korea, and Australia."

The members of the Chinese delegation, seated next to the vice president in her bright blue outfit, stared straight ahead.

Next came Canada's fiery rebuttal, China's equally fiery counter statement, then the moment when Lucia "brought the issue home," as she likes to say.

"Canada's green tariffs on all imports will become standard HEPP policy this spring, and APAC and EVEC are considering similar measures."

I pause to study the Chinese delegation absorb this fact. Lucia knew all along but had not told them in our pre-meetings that the green tariffs would become widespread among China's trading partners. Chen Minghua's face was tight, but she did not blink.

"In the Pacific, we are not fighting against one another. Canada will agree to increase its HEPP contributions to build eco barriers to protect its shores from the garbage threatening us all."

Now it was the Canadian prime minister's turn to seethe. He was compact but imposing, like a bantamweight raring to get out of his corner. He knew this part of Lucia's plan — we had told him during briefings — but he did not like it one bit.

"China will agree to the electronic monitoring of large vessels in the area north of the Eastern Garbage Patch during the Northern Hemisphere's summer months. China will also allow HEPP to release drifters to track the Eastern Patch's movement throughout the summer."

Ms. Chen sat with her fingertips hovering just above the surface, while Kevin Daly leaned across the table with his arms slightly raised.

I chuckled at this scene of diplomatic theater, although it was not really funny. We had already begun building up the HEPP's position in the Pacific. Lucia had pressured Canada to impose greater tariffs on Chinese but not American imports to force this showdown over the garbage patch. All sensible and reasonable tactics, and all in the service for the planet's greater good. The clip ends with a formal handshake ceremony, where the Chinese and Canadian delegations pass each other like two soccer teams who somehow both lost the championship game.

Garbage Wars II

When I put my finger over Vice President Chen's face, a couple of clips come up on the tablet. I've also found some clips Yanfen sent to me in private chat. I randomly touch one of the hovering icons, and up comes a clip of Chen in Hawai'i, at the Environmental Summit for APAC nations after Lucia's election. Until the last minute, it hadn't been certain China would show up. The Summit was Lucia's first big international event, if you didn't count the creation of HEPP. It had been China's political strategy for the past few years to simply not accept US invitations, or to communicate in advance that they wouldn't accept an invitation before it had even been issued. We needed China at the Hawai'i Summit for Lucia to be taken seriously on the international stage. It's strange to think how quickly we had started to view all HEPP issues, including the meetings in Mexico City and Ottawa, as domestic.

"Given the threat to America's health, safety, and prosperity by environmental issues, we cannot leave the security of our country's resources, which includes clean air and water, to other nations," Lucia had told Congress when it became clear that we would not withdraw the troops from Canada, and after the Mexican Water Crisis.

There had been loud applause. The murdered EPA agents had become heroes in the media, and Lucia's swift deployment of our troops sated the public's desire, fanned by social media campaigns, not only for justice, but revenge.

"We are working for the greater good through this partnership with our neighbors to the north and south in the form of HEPP."

Our senators were not pleased that the opposition celebrated HEPP like a military victory over Canada and Mexico. Lucia was undeterred.

"Let congress roar," she told me more than once. "The art of politics is aligning someone else's self-interest with your goals."

Congress had roared; Lucia's approval ratings soared. Who knew that ruling over Canada and Mexico had been the Republicans' wet dream? Which allowed more Mexicans to enter the United States legally than ever before? After they had spent billions to build La Gran Valla? But China was different. China aimed at aligning our interests with theirs, not the other way around.

"I don't want to appear to be begging Beijing," Lucia said. "It was the only piece of good advice I received from the previous administration. 'Don't let the Chinese dictate the terms of any deal.'"

But without China, the whole idea of a summit would have been hollow. State was adamant about not having the White House extend an invitation until they had resolved some cyber issues with Beijing. But there were cyber issues all the time. Finally, we sent a personalized invitation from the Oval. Lucia even said a few words in Chinese, and her pronunciation wasn't half bad.

"A nice shindig in Hawai'i to talk about the weather and the oceans is not going to get them on board," Derek from the Asia Desk at State told me. "The Chinese don't care about your planet, Aleks. Our planet, excuse me. Your Chinese friends want to rule the world, on their terms. And we can't let that happen."

I ignored Derek and called Seth. We needed a viral strategy.

"It's been done before," Seth said. "Companies place their stuff on Chinese social media all the time. The Chinese find it and scrub it off. The companies move somewhere else. It's an endless game of hide and seek. But there are a couple of different ways."

It may have been the only time Lucia joined the meeting in Asturias's tech cave. There were screens on all of the walls and a few simple keyboards and data balls that controlled whatever Asturias and his team did.

"We want to put pressure on the Chinese leadership from the inside," Lucia said. "Of course, nothing can be traced to us. We want them to feel that their own people consider this a big topic, and that they should join our meeting in Hawai'i."

"China cares about the environment," I said.

"But Beijing has not responded to my invitation, Aleks," Lucia said. "My office is upset; State is upset. Our ambassador has basically locked himself in his bedroom, since he cannot be seen in public until Beijing responds. The invitation is out there, so we look like idiots if the Chinese ignore us. Seth, what have you got?"

"Flood Chinese social media with clips of the rubbish in the oceans, and of shorelines," Seth instructed Asturias and his geek squad. "Yes, like that!" He pointed at one of the screens in front of Malang. Beautiful white-capped waves rolled in from a sparkling, otherwise calm blue ocean before breaking steadily over a coastal highway. On another screen a huge net emptied its content of wriggling, silvery fish onto a ship's deck. When the camera moved in, we could see that there were as many plastic items as fish, and that most of the fish had weirdly bulging heads and eyes.

"People have to make the connection between an issue and their lives all by themselves. You can't force it. The fate of the oceans? Not relevant for people who live inland. Droughts? Not an issue if you're hit by floods every spring."

"We have to seed Chinese social media with images that will instinctively feel like this is happening in China," Seth continued. "Use local markers so people understand right away that this is local stuff."

"I'm not interested in changing China's mind," Lucia interrupted him. "First off, because I can't. And second, because people don't do anything unless they want it for themselves. Chinese leaders may bow to our pressure when they're in a room with us. But like everyone else, when we're not looking, they'll walk right around all of our agreements and pacts."

Asturias and his team worked the keyboards like kids at a high school hackathon.

"I've seen the Chinese in my country," Malang said. "They don't care much about the environment."

Lucia looked at him.

"It's easy to blame them," she said. "It's easy to blame the world's largest economy because they are powerful."

Malang nodded. "On some level the Chinese have given us a better deal," he said. "The Europeans quite literally really bled our countries dry."

"There is a way to make a deal with China," Lucia changed course.

For a moment Asturias and Seth looked away from the screens.

"The impulse for China to fight for the environment cannot come from some 'neo-colonial' power, as people like to call it, like HEPP." She had put air quotes around the word, and smiled at quoting her own detractors.

"They are more aware of the ocean's significance than we are. More than half of their trade depends on open shipping lines, and a good two-thirds of their fish consumption on healthy marine habitats."

"Yeah, but they are still the biggest polluters of the oceans!" said Cecily. "I've seen it myself, the way some Chinese factories dump their toxins into the sea and get away with a slap on the wrist."

"That's what our country was doing for a few centuries," I said.

"No history lesson on first world polluters, please," Cecily said, shooting me a glance, but smiling. Then she looked at Lucia. She is a good head taller than Lucia, a striking beauty with long, black hair usually put up in a carefully wound bun. Lucia really likes her, has invited her to two women's tech events, but it was good that she was sitting down so as not to tower over the president. I like Cecily, and we occasionally hang out in some divey bar to talk about the pretentious losers she tends to date, all of whom have radical leftist politics but kind of expect her to clean the bathroom and the kitchen. She grew up in Taiwan and Australia, and has her doubts about China.

"Let's focus on the present," Lucia said, and I didn't know whether this was directed toward me.

"China ignores much of what we all know about the impact of industrialization on the environment," I added.

"I know, but we won't get anywhere with them by talking at them," Lucia responded.

I quietly switched on "record" on my tablet. Lucia often develops ideas in sidebar conversations with our team, and I relied on these points to brief our staff.

"I understand your frustration, but for too long, our politics have been, us versus China, local versus global. We've been in a cyber war with China and entered into a tacit arms race with Beijing. We have alienated the Chinese at just about every turn. But without China, all of our environmental efforts are pointless. China is part of a greater solution, not a problem to be solved."

I glanced at Asturias, Cecily, and Seth to gauge their reaction. I knew my face had turned red. I have loved my time in China dearly and, before I joined the first campaign and when I first met Yanfen, I had briefly considered settling there for a few years. But in the Garbage Wars, China had never looked like part of the solution. I was close to the American mainstream position of blaming China, and I had indicated as much in front of Lucia, even if I always ended up defending China in my arguments with Cecily. China had looked like the problem, the polluting villain who dumped toxins into the ocean and the air, and sold everyone else the junk that now floated around in big patches.

When I had watched Asturias and Seth begin their hacking session, I'd been excited to see them slip the Chinese our Trojan horse via social media. *Us versus them!* I had thought. *Beat the mighty dragon at his own game!* I had thought Lucia would take this course as well, to manipulate the Chinese via a stealth campaign.

"It's a matter of working together," she said instead. "There's little point in trying to clean the Pacific when China isn't on board."

"It's a matter of persistence, of seeding the Chinese sites with more images each time the censors shut them down," Seth said. Lucia was silent. "But above all it's a time of engaging people on the ground," Seth continued. "The campaign has to be driven from within China."

"In a way that does not blame them!" Lucia said. "We need engagement, not defensiveness."

I wondered whether Seth had made his money this way, by infiltrating social networks and making people share with friends what was in reality corporate fluff. Asturias keyed in strings of commands on several keyboards, as if he were playing a church organ. I watched a fleet of clips race across some of the screens, while others went completely blank for seconds at a time. It was like watching storm clouds or flocks of birds form and dissipate quickly as if filmed in time-lapse. The images chased one another across the screens, and for a moment we all stared at the lights without saying anything, in the knowledge that Asturias's keystrokes sent them to hundreds of millions of little screens halfway around the world.

"This cannot be traced back?" I finally asked, glancing at Lucia.

"Effectively we are somewhere in the Middle East right now," Asturias said. "Probably a university server that's not well protected. Maybe a local media station or maybe a reality show, maybe somewhere in South America with lots of people tuned in. From there it moves on until it reaches Chinese servers. That's what you are seeing—every screen here uploads from those servers. It changes every few minutes, though."

"We've started with Chinese students studying over here in the United States right now," Seth said. "That's a bit over a million kids. And then we have a few more million Chinese with American phone contracts, who've gone to college or grad school in the United States."

"We follow all of them," Asturias said, grinning.

"Me and my buddies," Victor said, smiling from under his knit cap. "Every Chinese student in the States on a visa is logged and tracked," he explained. "We can access their profiles right here— " He pointed at one of the screens. "And none of it can be traced to us."

"I assume the Chinese got my info as well," I said.

I thought of the glass-walled arrivals hall at Pudong Airport with the dusty plastic plants and slightly worn carpets. Sensors in the glass walls screened all arriving passengers for explosives, but everyone knew that they also siphoned data from incoming visitors. We did the same, after all.

"No," said Asturias when he saw me looking at my tablet. "I wiped that clean."

"But with Apple?" I ventured.

"Doesn't matter," Asturias said. "As long as we get to your tablet every few days, and as long as you leave it with us before and after you travel, you'll be okay." He smiled as if he was telling his kid brother that there was no monster under the bed.

"We gotta get to work," Seth said. "We've started posting pictures on Chinese users' social media. They won't stick unless someone forwards them. But once they do, the whole chain should be viral within a few hours."

Asturias and Seth now had the look of two nerds in an online war game, their eyes fixated on screens and their hands doing an ever-faster dance on keyboards and controls.

Lucia was right. Blaming China for the Garbage Wars was easy, convincing, and completely self-serving. We could fault the Big Bad Dragon for what they were doing, and feel righteous and superior to boot. It was also an easy way to deny our complicity with China, our addiction to products made in factories cooled by burning fossil fuel, which were then loaded onto huge container ships powered by cheap diesel, shipped through the Panama Canal, our ports, and then transported by trucks and vans and drones to our homes, where we ripped off the wrapping to handle the next shiny toy, only for it to end up in a landfill where it would rot for centuries, while we debated policies about how to make our towns and cities more sustainable. Faulting China would deny our craving for new things, and our willingness to overlook all of these problems as long as we could get our hands on Chinese software and Chinese drugs.

Lucia had left the room. For a few more minutes I watched Asturias, Victor, Malang, Cecily, and Seth.

"We're placing clips of environmental problems into the social media feeds of millions of people," Asturias explained to me. "Cecily is posting random comments that applaud the government for taking action. It's all very patriotic, and very pro-Chinese."

Cecily did not look up, and I felt a bit left out.

"I'm singing the praises of the Chinese leadership," she said after a minute. "So even if the censors find it, they'll let it pass. My favorites are old slogans from the Mao era." She made a face.

"But will people know they have been hacked?" I asked.

"We don't use that word around here, Aleks, in the White House," Victor said with a mock serious tone. "You should know that. We are disseminating tailored information to a wider public."

"We're not reading anybody's private messages," Seth said. "All we are doing is placing our messages directly onto their feed. Think of it like a private message slipped under your door, sent by a stranger who's pretending to be your best friend."

"Room service," Victor said. "We should get that around here."

Everyone laughed, but it was clear that I was distracting them. I left the boys and Cecily to do their work.

Then I called a staff meeting for the APAC Hawai'i planning group and threw half the people off the team.

"You've done great work," I said, "and I really thank you for your service."

They were stunned.

"We need more Mandarin speakers," I said. "POTUS has made it clear that we need people who understand China from the inside."

People got up and walked out without so much as looking at me.

I was in charge of the agenda, but none of these people were direct reports. I had just canceled their vacation in Hawai'i. They would go to Domineek, to their bosses, to State to complain, but there was little they could do to make their case. I had invited them to the meeting, and I could disinvite them. A few of them would try to get to Lucia. It would cost me, but I felt it was the right thing to do.

I called in Royce and Graham to help Asturias's team with content. Royce is a big Latino guy with curly hair that spills over his shirt collar embroidered with tiny skulls. I'd met his parents in Los Angeles when Lucia spoke at Earth Day. His mother is a high-powered corporate attorney; his father a massively built high school teacher sporting an impressive set of tats running up both arms and around his neck.

"I hate the government, but I love Lucia Jackson," Royce Sr. had told me when we met. "She's the only one that made me care about politics in years. We have dealt with environmental issues here in California for decades, since the big drought years. But until now everyone has simply made the poor folks pay for it. And you won't find a smarter guy than Royce for your team. He's got my looks, but his mother's brains."

Royce's sidekick, Graham, is blond, skinny, and has a Wildean sense of irony. He wears black-rimmed glasses, and majored in Chinese and some kind of bio-engineering.

"We have very little time," I told them. "Asturias's team is putting clips out to engender Chinese concern in such a way that they won't immediately be taken down by the censors."

"We gotta have pictures that are patriotic, nationalistic. That make the oceans look relevant to China's self-understanding," Royce said.

"Let's bring up Zheng He, China's 'global citizen,'" Graham said. "All Chinese students are taught how Zheng He first connected China with the world."

"I studied at the Zheng He campus in Nanjing," Cecily said.

"I thought you went to the Hopkins program?" Royce said.

"They renamed it when they nationalized foreign campuses, but it's still the same program," Graham said. "Just a change in name, like when we changed the name of King's College to Columbia University after the American Revolution."

"The Chinese students definitely care that universities are named after Chinese heroes," Graham said. "But Yale had a total fit when the Chinese renamed one of their programs, claiming intellectual property theft and betrayal."

"So now that you've established that you went to such fine schools," I said, interrupting them, "how do we use Zheng He's name? Isn't that like referring to Columbus?"

"We're on it, sir," Malang said, and grinned. "Didn't know you've become the expert on cyber strategy all of a sudden."

"I mean . . ."

"It's all right," he said. "Just kidding."

If China didn't show up in Hawai'i, the guys from State would back burner our strategy on the environment. Domineek would have to cut Lucia's trip short with a made-up crisis so we wouldn't lose face. If that had happened, I would have lost more than face.

For State, HEPP was a boon, of course, but they were furious that Canada and Mexico had been integrated because of the environment. They wanted to set the agenda, and the environment didn't overlap with enough of their portfolio.

"The three greatest issues for most Chinese are family, money, and travel. The environmental movement ranks fourth or fifth, but it is not connected to anything outside of China," Graham said.

"We gotta link Zheng He to the environment," Royce said. "Beijing's greatest political crisis has been the travel bans during Avian Flu II. It was the one time people got so mad when they couldn't travel anymore that they nearly shut down the government."

"My grandma was stuck in China for months!" Cecily interjected. "It was ridiculous. They put everyone on the plane in quarantine in a hotel by the airport, totally locked down, because someone had had a fever. We couldn't figure out where my grandma was for two days, and then we couldn't get her out for another week. She's refused to travel to the mainland ever since."

"So let's create images that link pollution of the oceans to travel," Royce continued, undeterred. "Let's link Zheng He to environmental issues."

"We have to make garbage into something interesting, and above all, manageable," I said. "Like upcycling, and new sources of energy."

"Upcycling yes, energy, no," Cecily said.

"Going full geek on us!" Graham laughed, and both Royce and Cecily joined in. "The thrills of alternative energy!"

"Nobody wants to think about power plants that burn your trash," Cecily explained. "But I've been to Reborn, in North Carolina. Been twice, actually. Biggest upcycle event in the world. It was awesome — all these people creating cool stuff from things they found just lying around."

"Those are awesome pics!" Royce chimed in. "And the Chinese have created their own festivals after that! I went to one near Shenzhen."

I left them to it. They are only about five years younger than me, but already a world apart. They wear FY clothing, don't really own much, and have no problem sharing their apartments, travel, even their pets with like-minded folk. I'm sure Royce had embroidered the skulls on his shirts himself, and Cecily's elegant jackets were definitely sewn by her and her friends, from a few parts ordered from some fancy store but put together with self-spun yarn, all of it deliberately visible in tiny tufts along the seams. Keon makes some of his own stuff, and I have a great FY jacket that he put together. But for these kids "finish yourself" is a religion.

A few hours later I messaged Derek at the Asia Desk with the news that the Chinese would come to Hawai'i. He knew already.

"State assumes White H handles protocol," he messaged back instantly. "ST still concerned about China military role in region. ST doesn't think POTUS's participation helps strategy of containment."

Domineek showed Derek's message to Lucia.

"They don't get it," she said. "State wants to have their boogeyman, and China fits the bill. You'd think they were the Pentagon. Our purpose in Hawai'i is to find common ground with the Chinese. We have to make them care about the oceans as much as Canada does. I want a plan that will end the Garbage Wars once and for all."

I felt vindicated at having gotten the Chinese to come. It lasted only a moment.

The Canadians were furious when we scheduled the Chinese delegation to present first.

"China is the greatest polluter in the Pacific," someone from Daly's office yelled through the screen. "Allowing China to open this conference is like letting Japan set policy on whale hunting!"

"China is part of the solution," I tried saying, but he interrupted me.

"China is deliberately polluting our coast!" He still shouted. "You were there in London, when they denied all responsibility! If anything, the garbage patches have gotten bigger in the meantime!"

The Canadians lobbied Lucia directly, trying to cut me out. It was stupid, as if they really believed I would not be given their messages to handle.

"Stick to your guns, Aleks," Lucia said. "Let the Canadians yell at you. Politics is not about making people feel good. It's about making people do the right thing. Demonizing China plays domestically in Canada, but it gets us zip. The kind of thinking that blames everyone else is exactly why we created HEPP, instead of letting three separate countries fight about how to keep the water safe."

The conference in Hawai'i opened in a huge room, on the top floor of a hotel, with a bank of windows facing the ocean. We sat at a horseshoe-shaped table, with Lucia presiding in the middle like Moses parting the seas between China on one side, and Canada and the rest of the APAC nations on the other. She was serious, very formal, not showing her cards. The only geek warrior who had come with us to Hawai'i was Victor, but he wasn't in the room. His role was to monitor POTUS's tech case and to keep our communication open and bug-free. But when the Chinese delegation used clips that we had put on their servers to make their case during their official presentation, I wished that Asturias's team could have enjoyed that moment live.

"Full circle," I whispered to Seth without moving my lips, and kept my eyes directed toward the front.

"The Chinese people are deeply concerned about the environment," Vice President Chen said while the screen behind her flashed Chinese social media threads about the ocean cleanup. "Beijing is eager to push the efforts to clean our oceans. We are here to present our country's intention to partner in this effort."

Seth quietly pumped his fist, as if we had just scored a touchdown. When we walked out of the room, even Domineek was upbeat.

"Good one, Aleks," she whispered. "I didn't think you could have pulled this off. POTUS is quite happy."

I just nodded, but on the inside I was beaming. Lucia had scored a major victory, and I had been a part of it.

At the formal dinner later that evening, Vice President Chen toasted the HEPP delegations. Lucia then toasted China, using some of the Mandarin she had studied again on the plane, and then the HEPP countries together, making sure to give Canada credit. She and the Chinese VP spoke of a new era for our oceans.

Right before dinner was formally over, I caught Lucia's eye. She gave me an ever so subtle smile and slightly lifted her glass. It was the briefest of moments, but I felt as if the two of us had for an instant arrested the proceedings, silenced the din, and without getting up actually clinked our glasses across the space of the vast, chandeliered and high-ceilinged dining room. Ding! I was proud, even elated. Even though I've spent hours next to Lucia during campaign events, have had private meetings in the Oval, and have been upstairs a few times with the kids, this brief glance across the incredibly busy room filled with hundreds of politicians, VIP guests, waiters, and security, was one of the moments where I've felt most connected to her so far.

On the way back from Honolulu, we had a bunch of signed agreements in the bag, with China paying the bulk for some serious cleanup.

"Hand people their own rope," Seth said in the plane headed back to the mainland. "Give Beijing the tools to dismantle their own house."

"That's not what the Chinese are doing," Lucia said. "Not at all. All we did was galvanize something that had already been there. Beijing fears nothing more than political unrest. We use that fear by giving a jolt to their home-grown environmental movement, and allowing Beijing to look like they initiated that. It's their safety valve to relieve political pressure! Beijing gains domestic peace; the world gains cleaner oceans."

Seth nodded.

"Hand them the rope," he mumbled, but Lucia had already plugged in to her briefing audio.

Bringing Bison Back

I've pulled up my finances on the tablet. Stupid mistake. No savings, paltry government income, a few loans. Unclaimed medical benefits. A car that Keon bought that's also in my name. Keon's much better with money. I always felt anxious about it, probably because of a childhood spent listening to Mom and Dad argue about who should pay for what. Hate doing my taxes, looking at my bills. Keon is much better. He's the one who negotiated and ultimately got us the shed. He actually likes that stuff. "Doesn't it make you feel good to organize these things?" More recently I've let him look at my finances, even though we still have separate accounts. Long-term, though, there's no way I can stay in government. Not when we'll have kids. Lucia did it right before going into politics: corporate law for a while, a media career, and only then a run for office, and finally the presidency.

"I'm an immigrant's daughter," she says frequently. "I've never expected anyone to pay for me."

Keon jokes that I'm expected to wear good suits to work but they don't pay me enough to buy even a decent tie. I do what I do because I believe in it — because there is so much potential for this administration to make an impact, globally.

But money is still critical.

"Without cash, we're dead," Lucia often said when we met with donors. When Seth joined us, after our first visit to Silicon Valley, Lucia wanted a sign of his commitment. He had bundled a huge amount for the campaign, but she wanted something else.

"They want to feel good about themselves," she said when we had left the meeting. "I don't have a problem with being used so they look good to others. But I'm expensive. I want them to really pony up if they claim they support us."

I was not part of the follow-up conversations with Seth, and I don't know how much of his thinking was influenced by Lucia. But he clearly wanted to impress her, and impress us he did. Money! Points! It makes the world go round.

A few weeks after our first meeting in California, Seth invited us to visit "something we would find interesting" in Texas. Lucia had to cancel at the last minute. I found myself with about a dozen senators on Seth's plane on a three-hour flight to Texas. Not all of the senators knew who I was and treated me accordingly, like a staffer on the Hill. Like someone made of air. Or maybe they did know, but wanted me to feel that it didn't impress them.

"That's why you gotta wear expensive suits and have a big watch," says Keon when I complain about having to dress up every day. "So they take you seriously."

Domineek also ignored me during the flight. She was busy chatting with the senators, all of whom were sucking up to get an in with Lucia.

I researched the senators' voting records on the plane: a few of them were big anti-environmentalists. They had voted no on carbon offsets, on restore the shore, on research into pesticides, on regulation of hog farming, wildlife trade enforcements, regulation of antibiotics, tax breaks for eco brigades, on fishing caps, and reducing greenhouse emissions. The more I read, the more upset I got. Those were not just a dozen random senators with power. They were the dirty dozen who had done more to roll back or stop green legislation than the lobbies of the coal and mining industries combined. By the time we landed, I didn't care any longer that nobody seemed to even acknowledge me.

"If you want to ignore me, let me help you," as Keon's grandmother used to say. I waited in my seat till the last and fattest senator had heaved himself off the plane.

On the tarmac, I thought for a moment that the SUVs were going to leave without me, but then one of Seth's peons pointed me toward the last empty seat. Everyone in the car was in a good mood, almost giddy. I guess Seth had promised them something exciting. I didn't care. Was it going to be a big museum with his name up top? A hospital where they researched autoimmune disorders? A lab for self-pollinating, edible weeds that would feed the world? Guys like Seth loved science incubators. They were also convinced that private money would solve the world's problems, as did these senators, whose aim was to privatize both transportation and education. Bit I'd spent enough time in college around supergeeks to no longer get excited.

"We can intervene at the molecular level," my college teaching assistants had proclaimed with great excitement. "There are ways to guide nature to protect itself from massive, man-made change." And then we would spend hours tearing apart and putting back together the molecules of some basic plant, which we then observed in real hothouses over a semester or so.

"Aleks!"

Seth leaned in the SUV's door. "Aleks! Wake up! You don't want to miss this!" I scrambled out of the car. The air was warm and humid, and for a moment I looked around to get my bearings. The cars had stopped on a grassy hill surrounded by forest. I looked around and saw a narrow path leading back into the trees. On the other side of the hill was an open area, but I couldn't really see below. The senators were some fifty feet ahead, near some rocks, and were looking at something.

"Do you think this patch of land can support a few hundred thousand bison to migrate through here every year?" Seth pointed toward the side without trees.

"Where are we?" I said, and instantly realized how stupid I sounded.

"Jurassic Park," Seth said and laughed. "I've cloned dinosaurs."

"How big is this area?" I asked while we caught up with the senators. I was acutely aware that I had missed some explanation of what we were looking at.

"It's about a quarter million acres of woodlands that we will revert back to a reforested area. I thought you, especially, would care to see it."

I took a few steps toward the point where the grassy area where we had parked gave way to small shrubs, and then spindly pines that stretched into something that I assumed looked like prairie, bordered by forest. I was half-expecting the whole scene to shift as I moved, the way 3-D games add space when you advance. We walked across the grass closer to the forest. Behind us, the cars gleamed in the speckled sunlight, but it was hard to pick out the road on which we had arrived.

"We have some major species that migrate through this area to other states. What's important is that all of this land has been bought through several private trusts, and that we've endowed an operating budget that will pay for forest maintenance for perpetuity," Seth said.

"How do you keep the animals in the park?" one of the senators asked.

"It's not quite a park," Seth said. "It's a corridor for big animals to get to areas that are more protected. Let's go to the center where this can be explained briefly, and then I'll fly you back over part of the reserve. If you're lucky, we'll see some bison. We have a herd of about sixty thousand."

"You'll be back in Washington by mid-afternoon," one of Seth's assistants said.

"And I just received a message that President Jackson will join you for a reception," Domineek said. The senators visibly cheered up. They liked being with big donors, but they also cared about face time with POTUS.

The Biodiversity Center had Seth's name tastefully engraved on the eaves, of course. But I couldn't really be cynical. We looked at a 3-D display and holos of black bears, bison, all sorts of turtles, an eagle, big antelope, alligators, lots of birds, swans. The senators asked Seth about the price of the land, how much it would have been worth for timber, for development, how he got people to sell it to him.

"You offer good money, and then people will sell," Seth said. "And you give them tax benefits by selling to a nonprofit, and you help them find another deal somewhere else."

Seth had hired the best people. They knew what they had created here. Invisible fencing kept the animals from getting close to the real fence, and chips tracked the movement of everything. The corridor connected protected land to the east and northwest of Florida, and to where Alabama had established bio sanctuaries in the 2010s.

"Let's use the plane before I sell it to pay for the bison," Seth said when he corralled us all back to the cars to drive to the airport.

"He's spending his way down to live like us mortals," Domineek whispered to me during takeoff. "He's committed to spending most of his fortune on this project. Seriously."

I glanced at Seth in his super-expensive sneakers, the high-tech cotton pants and sweater, the custom watch. Sitting in his own jet.

"I don't think he'll be broke soon," I said, and looked out the window.

Below us, the forest changed to swamp or drier ground dotted by tiny eco-lodges reached only on foot; it was hard to tell. The plane was too high to see individual animals, but I still hoped to catch a glimpse of the herd of bison. As a child, I'd put myself to sleep imagining I was running with herds of animals, the great bodies swaying like boats on water across the plains. Or just looking at miles and miles of the brown backs of buffalo from a train, during the period when the first Europeans arrived, after native people had cleared the forest so that the bison could take over. I've never lived anywhere close to the middle of the continent, or in one of the northern states, but I'd always liked the vision of a mass of great heaving bodies. Seth's corridor down there was only a drop in that long-gone ocean, and the bison he owned were less than half of 1 percent of the animals that had roamed North America only two hundred years ago.

"It's not a matter of bringing anything back," Seth said, as if I had spoken out loud. "Remember when we privatized Amtrak? We didn't bring back the old, creaky, overpriced system that depended on government handouts to keep the trains running. We changed the entire system. Same with this wildlife corridor. It tolerates some human presence, and we actually breed most of the big animals, or at least monitor them to achieve the greatest diversity."

"Why are you doing this?" the senator from Oklahoma asked. "Why not build big game parks where the animals are safe, like in Africa?"

I leaned forward a bit for Seth's answer.

"Probably everyone here has visited Yellowstone, Yosemite, or one of our other great national parks. Perhaps even Vieques. Those parks were visionary in setting aside land so your kids can know the greatness of our country. I'm doing this to preserve this land for Americans to enjoy in the future. And I'm not interested in game parks because I believe that most things, like software and water, should be open and free."

"He's put his money where his mouth is," I told Lucia when we had landed in Washington.

"It's the real deal?" she whispered while smiling at the group of reporters who had gathered to cover the reception, and leaning forward to shake another senator's hand. "How did you like it?" she asked him. "We think such partnerships could be a great project on the federal level, too." She turned back to me and whispered, "They're doing it right? I mean in terms of biodiversity, best practices, etcetera?"

"Yes," I whispered back. "He's really created something important here in terms of land management."

I didn't want to sound too enthusiastic. It was a great project, to be sure, but I didn't like how Seth's ideas now became the reference point for all our efforts. Of course he could do great things, with all of that money. But how did that get people engaged?

Lucia had turned her attention back to the senators and donors. After that, the Roosevelt Project became a key talking point in Lucia's speeches about private land stewardship. I probably have footage from the corridors on the tablet, but I'm not going to watch it. Stuff Seth would send me, always with an invitation to come along and visit out there.

"Don't be so resistant to him," Keon often says. "Of course he's a bit of a dick. Otherwise he wouldn't have made that much money so quickly. But he's had some good ideas, and you yourself say that the projects are the real thing."

"It's just hard to see everyone fawn all over him because he's been able to buy some land," I said. "Other people have worked for years on smaller projects, and have literally changed their states, but nobody sees them on the news."

"What counts at the end of the day is whether he's been able to protect that land forever," Keon says. "To think that they can find ways to allow herds of bison to migrate to other states again is amazing."

"We'll take small victories," Lucia often says when people want more drastic, wholesale changes. "I'm a farmworker's daughter, and as an American, I believe in changing things on the ground. But I became president because things also need to change on a global, planetary scale. My job is to connect those efforts."

With his fortune, Seth was able to do something just big enough to become a model for governments. Lucia had blessed the privatization of a public issue, specifically, the environment, by bringing Seth into her Cabinet as an unpaid advisor. "Unpaid," of course, means something else when you are a billionaire to start with.

"Let it go, Aleks," I admonish myself. It's a worthwhile project, and Seth donates enormous amounts to the right causes. Without him and his California friends, Lucia's campaign wouldn't have worked. But something about his role in environmental issues annoys me. The fact that he owns the biggest herd of bison in the world and is still able to keep a plane doesn't help.

Daffodils

This morning, I woke up in a field of daffodils worthy of Wordsworth. I opened my eyes and then just lay there staring at the gently fluttering trumpet-shaped, yellow blossoms on all of the unit's walls.

When I was young, Mom used to always get fresh flowers, even when she didn't have a lot of money after the divorce.

"You cannot exhaust the beauty of a flower," she'd say, and make me smell a white hyacinth, or some freesias, or the enormous lilies that I've always found too sweet to keep inside a room. Every night, she would take her flowers out of the vase, clip the stems, put them in fresh water, and then put the whole thing in the refrigerator for the night. For many years, when I was in high school, I got up before her and would take the vase out of the refrigerator so she would see the bouquet first thing in the morning. For a few weeks each spring, there would be bunches of cheerful yellow daffodils imported directly from Ireland in our house.

That was before people started blaming pollen for the autoimmune syndromes.

Mom considered it bunk science, but it caught on.

"It's the stupidest thing I've ever heard," she said in frustration when our markets stopped carrying flowers. "It's not like you'd eat the flowers, and there are so many worse things around us all day."

Almost overnight, it became difficult to buy fresh flowers. There was no law against it. But after a few media reports and a short, viral doc, *Flowers of Evil,* people just stopped buying them. The flower shop in our town, which had always been a labor of love and not a moneymaking business, closed within weeks, and the supermarkets stopped selling even local flowers that hadn't been inside a hothouse. Only in some small, twenty-four-hour bodegas was it still possible to get fresh flowers, stiff carnations and bunches of tea roses wrapped tight in plastic. A lot of people refused to eat in restaurants that kept bouquets on the tables, or those huge, tree-sized arrangements that used to burst in seasonal glory behind every maître d's desk. When I arrived at the White House, they had already switched to artificial flowers. They looked deceivingly real, and the expensive ones actually wilted and lost petals. But real, fragrant, and truly fragile lilies, daffodils, tulips, peonies, roses — they all vanished from most homes and virtually all commercial venues within the span of a year or so.

Mom posted a lot of studies that disproved a link between fresh flowers and the autoimmune syndromes, and I dutifully reposted them. In defense of daffodils!

"Another stupid overreaction by anxious people," she said when our city council passed an ordinance against flowers in hospitals and schools. "Let's blame tulips! After air travel, cellphones, and sleeping pills. But everyone keeps eating hothouse tomatoes. 'It's the roses that are making you sick'! Total nonsense."

But with more and more autoimmune cases, people looked for something to blame. And unlike Mom, most people found it pretty easy to switch to silk flowers. The studies had only considered hothouse flowers, but how was anyone going to tell the difference between local and imported roses?

Mom sent me clips of burning fields in Peru set ablaze by eco-terrorists, and smashed flower stores all over the United States. In one case, the masked attackers sprayed some kind of chemical that turned all blossoms into a black, slimy mush while a woman stood to the side, her mouth covered with a cloth, shaking and in tears. In Holland, black plumes of smoke rose from vast fields of fire-red and bright yellow tulips while police fought with masked protesters on motor trikes.

Similar scenes happened in countries from Israel to Ireland and Brazil. It was disconcerting to see people take out their fury on flowers, even when the scientific evidence about their risk was flimsy.

There were campaigns to disprove the danger posed by flowers, with images of beaming children handing their moms delicate bouquets of daisies and baby's-breath. But how do you prove that something does *not* cause an autoimmune syndrome? It looked like a corporate cover-up.

"People somehow think that hothouse flowers are unnatural, and therefore toxic," Keon said when Mom told us that workers had refused to unload containers of flowers from Chile.

"But how does that make a tulip dangerous to anyone?" Mom asked without expecting an answer. "The fact that for centuries people have selected strains of tulips? That's supposed to make people sick?"

"It's a feeling people have," Keon said. "A meme. Replacing real flowers with artificial ones makes them feel in control."

"But why don't these people let everyone decide for themselves? All of these lunatics blaming flowers for the illnesses we don't understand, and now even passing laws against them."

Needless to say, Mom's side did not prevail.

Today, it's unimaginable to give fresh flowers as a gift, especially when there are older people in the house. It's funny to watch old movies where people seem to put flowers everywhere. Might as well pull a slaughtered whole rabbit out of your bag for a dinner party, or a still wriggling, slithering fish. It's inconceivable to use real flowers at funerals, where there are usually older people, and hospitals and schools won't let you bring them in.

Mom has kept her potted plants, but most people we know have thrown out every green thing. There is a deep fear of waking up paralyzed: there have been so many stories of people, athletes and businessmen, totally active one day, who wake up unable to move a limb and sometimes have to be hooked to breathing machines for weeks. If hothouse flowers may be the cause, nobody wants to take the risk.

I look at the sparkling waves of daffodils on the walls and think how much I miss real flowers. I miss clipping the green, hollow stems, miss how quickly they open up their blossoms, miss refilling the vase, miss putting it in the refrigerator overnight. Once or twice, during the last few years, I've woken up and stumbled half-asleep to the refrigerator and reached for a vase, which of course is not there. "How Miss Dalloway of you," Keon said when I told him about it, but he understands. I miss having something that is fragile, alive, and pointlessly beautiful.

In the summer, Keon often brings home small bouquets of local wildflowers — very pretty but slightly anemic bunches that wilt quickly even when you change the water and keep them in the fridge at night. Blue cornflowers mostly, and yellow *Echinacea*. "Bachelor's buttons," Keon calls the cornflowers. "So you don't go off marrying somebody else and instead stay a confirmed bachelor with me." I usually keep the blue, yellow, and orange bouquets until their petals drop when you so much as look at them. Once or twice, guests have left our place as soon as they had spotted a bouquet, even when we assured them that the flowers are non-cultivars from a local organic garden. Now we hide any live flowers in a closet when we expect guests.

The crowd, a host, of golden daffodils on my walls has stopped as abruptly as it appeared. Just as abruptly as fresh flowers vanished from our stores and then from most people's lives. Perhaps even the projection here on these walls was only a memory when I was still half asleep, flashing upon my inward eye a time before the change.

Restore the Shore

I've found a box of imitation wood blocks in the unit. They are like Lincoln Logs, but with more design possibilities. Not small enough to swallow and not big enough to use as a tool or a weapon. I recalled the psychologist on our quarantine planning team, Suad, a Lebanese woman with dark, kohl-lined eyes who had grown up in California. She told dirty jokes that were usually too complicated for me to get, and is the global expert on how people behave when kept in confinement. For a moment I thought it weird to find these toys here. I thought I'd searched every inch of the pod, which isn't big to start with, so, it still feels as if this box had simply materialized out of the HEPA-filtered air. Then I remembered Suad explaining that the experience of hunt and discovery must be built into quarantine units. Keeps you healthy. Probably also keeps you from going mad.

"The possibility of discovery must be included," she insisted in our meetings. "No matter how small or confined the space. Dopamine is essential for the immune system, and it's what the body releases when one discovers something unexpected."

"'The dopamine queen,' they call her," Seth whispered. He sent me an article where Suad's work on dopamine was described as pathbreaking for self-healing. "She believes that with the correct dopamine levels, we can conquer major diseases. They also say she herself is always good for a surprise." Then he actually winked at me, like we were frat brothers.

When I was little, I used to construct towers out of Legos that Uncle Antoine gave me. I would rebuild famous modernist structures from pictures, anything with clean lines, like Wright, Pei, Kahn, and Ando, that was put up long before the 'new sensuality' that's made this pod look like a birthing room. Now, instead of re-creating famous works with the blocks, I'm setting up a row of houses on stilts underneath the curved side of the bed. Like the houses they built after big storms, like the house Uncle Wynn and Aunt Sophia built.

Lucia had toured the shoreline in North Carolina and Virginia after the two big hurricanes of 2019, when those states and Washington got slammed twice in the span of about a week. A lot of people considered it a sign. *Erika* and *Fernando* became synonymous with really, really bad luck. Or, for some, with God being really, really angry and singling us out. Or, for others, with the planet exacting its revenge on us for trampling on it for so long. Lightning isn't supposed to strike twice, but those two storms made landfall within a mile of the same spot.

Before *Erika* hit D.C., there were already so many uprooted trees, fallen branches, and damaged buildings that the Metro Police had declared a state of emergency. Then, when *Erika* roared into town in earnest, like an invading army, a few fancy apartment buildings had their glass balconies sheared off as if someone had run an eraser over a pencil drawing. That happened to Cecily from the tech team: her balcony just got ripped from the side of her building while she sat in her living room, in the dark. And she was lucky. Nothing fell on her, nothing slammed into her window, and she was not trapped in a tunnel like all those poor people on that train, when a few got electrocuted during the rescue when the power came back on. Sewage did not seep into the basement of her building. She wasn't stuck on top of her car with little kids in the raging river that had been a highway exit ramp, after having followed police orders to evacuate a low-lying area. She wasn't part of the group who had been evacuated in a police chopper that crashed after the worst of the storm was supposed to have passed. And that was only D.C.

All of those things, as terrible as they were, didn't compare to what happened farther south. In North Carolina and Virginia, entire beach communities were washed away. Houses ripped off their foundations, cars pulled out to sea and then slammed into piers when the tide rolled back in, and a lot of casualties.

During the week that followed, people mourned. Shock, disbelief, anger, sadness, acceptance, forgiveness. The media ran the cycle fast. Then our American "can do" spirit began to take over.

"We will recover," the good people of Virginia, among them Uncle Wynn and Aunt Sophia, said. "We can bring our communities back to life."

"We won't be cowed by a storm," the brave people of North Carolina said.

Then *Fernando* hit. Only ten days later, landfall again at night—and far more devastation. One in a million chances this could happen. Storm of the millennium. People lost the remnants of homes that had just been dug out of the debris. They lost their loaner cars. The shelters were wiped out, and all of the construction equipment. Bulldozers, trucks, containers, all toppled and smashed to bits. Many people were hit while still sleeping on the floors of schools and churches. People were monitoring *Fernando,* of course, but their attitude had been one of defiance and strength, also mild disbelief in another storm of equal magnitude. The media didn't want to be accused of crying wolf or stirring up panic.

After *Fernando,* the army was brought in to police neighborhoods. Entire towns were declared unsafe for habitation, so they set up barricades to keep people from returning to their destroyed homes. Debris from houses had been bulldozed into special areas. A lot of those things had blown back into streets and towns, destroying cars that looked like they had been hit by projectiles from a

Mad Max tribe. In several towns, the overflow sewage and drowned livestock led to diseases not seen before in America.

New Orleans had been re-engineered and the Jersey shore had been rebuilt after the big storms in the early twenty-first century. Hundred-year walls were built, shorelines restored. The Army Corps of Engineers dredged up several billion tons of sand to create beaches or to keep existing ones from washing into the sea. The effect was a shoreline that looked pretty much unchanged to people who had been there for decades, but was as artificial as an eco-hotel on a steel-anchored reef in the South Pacific. Those earlier storms had been wake-up calls, too: once-in-a-century affairs. Now we had had two or three of them in the span of a few decades.

After the big storms earlier in the century, the federal government spent billions to put in better drainage systems, and to drive fifteen-foot pilings into the sand on which the drenched houses, once dried, cleaned, repainted, and repaired, now perched. Pretty, pastel two-story colonials looked down from ugly concrete stilts like eighteenth-century society ladies tottering on high heels through muddy streets. Wooden stairs descended like gangplanks off a pirate ship down to concrete driveways lined with neatly spaced tufts of dune grass to hold down the sand.

All along the shore from Jersey down south, houses had been raised onto those stilts by an immense flood of federal emergency funds that gushed even higher than *Sandy*, *Erika*, and *Fernando* had.

When Hurricane *Theodore* rode in, Uncle Wynn had triumphantly watched the raging ocean roll right under their home.

"We've built our own Venice," Uncle Wynn joked as he filed insurance claims and received tax breaks for his water-damaged car. New pilings were poured to shore up driveways. More dune grass was trucked in, along with salt-resistant bamboo flooring. Even when I was still in college and hadn't yet studied storm damage and had never heard of natural negotiation, I thought there was something not just silly but downright wrong about this.

"Are you sure you want to stay here, surrounded by all this

water?" Mom asked Uncle Wynn when we visited them after the storm. "Wouldn't it make more sense to relocate to a place closer to town?"

"You don't understand how much the shore means to us," Aunt Sophia said curtly. "People here are more connected to nature than you city people. We wake up looking at the ocean, and we fall asleep to its sounds. For us, this is home, not a vacation destination."

"But there are going to be more storms," Mom said. "It's going to cost a fortune to rebuild these roads. . . ."

"We've improved our drainage systems, and each homeowner here has contributed money, too, to make the area flood-proof," Uncle Wynn said. "It's expensive, but we can preserve our homes and our way of life."

"You just don't understand how much we love the ocean," Aunt Sophia repeated several times in these discussions as if we had questioned whether she was fundamentally a good person. "We see it as something greater than us, and it makes us feel alive."

"Of course, of course," Mom said and turned back to her tablet.

Mom rarely engages in conversation with Sophia. She hates that Sophia always and exclusively refers to herself as "we" and "us," and basically never uses the pronoun "I," as if she and Uncle Wynn experienced all of their feelings jointly as one person. I think Mom takes it as a dig for divorcing my dad when I was eight and having remained single. Dad, of course, also hasn't remarried, but that hasn't really been a surprise to anyone. With his schedule and the traveling. And his other issues. The fact that Mom didn't remarry is, of course, one of the reasons for our visits to Uncle Wynn's beach house, since after the divorce there is no way we could afford a shore vacation otherwise.

I realize that right now, right here on the floor, I am using the Lincoln Logs to rebuild Uncle Wynn's street when they still lived right near the shore.

I've constructed a village of stilt-houses along the curved edge of the bed.

I imagine crashing waves and whipping winds on a pier, and webcasters reporting in neon vests with wet hair glued to their foreheads.

When *Erika* and *Fernando* hit, Uncle Wynn and Aunt Sophia's house survived. Several houses near them did not, and the storm eroded so much of the beach that parts of the road leading up to their place just sank into the sea. Mom and I had watched Uncle Wynn's house online, on grainy satellite footage, sitting on its concrete stilts above the raging sea like a Louise Bourgeois sculpture scared stiff by the storm. Methodically, gradually, obstinately, the storm ripped off part of the porch, then the stairs, the flagpole, the garage. Like a pack of wild dogs attacking a moaning water buffalo, over and over, until it collapses. It no longer looked anything like the home where I had spent a few summers lounging on the deck, drinking white wine, and eating bluefish and tomatoes from a local market.

"The goddamn government won't rebuild the road," Uncle Wynn railed once the storm had passed, and all through the winter of that year. The house had survived, maimed but ultimately intact. "They've decided to give up on the shore, 'restore the shore,' or some such bull crap. What does it mean, to restore, when you're giving up? What does that mean, to re-naturalize my home? People have lived here for hundreds of years, even the Indians were here, before the settlers came! And now these sissies in Washington want to cut this town off, just because their cherry trees got knocked over."

"I just think they don't want to rebuild it when the next storm will surely wipe it out again," Mom ventured.

"What do they know about a next storm? This was the storm of the century. There isn't gonna be another one like it too soon," Aunt Sophia said. "How would you feel if the government cut off the road in front of your house? How would you feel if some jerk in the Senate decided you had to leave your home?"

Uncle Wynn's road was not rebuilt. The government claimed there wasn't enough money. This dragged on and on. A lot of politicians visited the Virginia shore several times –swing state! – and promised to rebuild it as soon as they won. Wealthy homeowners protested alongside poor people, demanding that their shore towns receive emergency funding. There were counter-demonstrations, too. The issue brought out environmentalists who argued that rebuilding those towns not only wasted billions but also put others at greater risk. And that rebuilding efforts ignored protection for shorebirds and plants.

After the election, we pretty quickly held a budget presentation for federal relief slated for the shore.

"Rebuilding the infrastructure for the Virginia shore towns will not break the bank," the EPA officials said. "But it will break the bank when the next storm hits somewhere else. Then those people will want their roads restored, and then, after them, another town. The situation is made worse because there are many more houses on the shore today than in the past," the official said, flicking off her tablet. "It's just a matter of statistics. Lots of development, lots of roads, lots of storms. The two storms in a row, of course. . . . Nobody could have guessed that. But if you look at it in the past hundred-year intervals, no town had ever really lasted all that long. People regularly resettled, moved their homes."

"We must consider the effects of climate change and rising sea levels in our planning," Lucia said. The room fell silent. Staffers who had been scrolling through messages looked up, sat up straighter, got ready.

"President Jackson, I cannot conclusively point to one factor," the EPA official said. She was a stout, short woman with a no-nonsense haircut and old-fashioned, thick-lensed glasses without a chip. A holdover from the previous administration: one of the political appointments who was going to be thanked and fired within the next few weeks, to be replaced by one of ours in our round of spoils. She had been a fierce opponent of the Climate Coalition folks, but she was also from North Carolina. Her home state had suffered a lot.

"I don't have enough data to identify rising sea levels as a factor," she said. One of my interns, Martyn, a lean, athletic guy with big ears and the face of a depression-era farmer, leaned forward as if to interrupt her.

"But I can say with absolute certainty that most of what we rebuild now will be wiped out again within a few decades," the woman said. "The erosion of the coast requires deeper pilings with each round, and there is really no way from stopping the sea from where it wants to go. The seawalls in Louisiana? Florida? Much of that will be underwater in a few decades. Shorelines always change, and have always done so."

Lucia stayed silent for a moment.

"Do you recommend a fund to rebuild these towns?" she finally asked the woman. It was an odd question to ask of someone whose job would be gone within weeks, perhaps days.

"Madam President, I do not recommend an increase in spending on these projects," the woman responded. "I actually believe that any funding allocated there is irresponsible."

Nobody said a word.

"Thank you, Mrs. Shaughnessy," Lucia said. "I value your professional opinion, and I appreciate your willingness to be so clear."

Mrs. Shaughnessy sat down on the extra-high chair that had been reserved for her. She had balls, I thought. Her response was like a tacit endorsement of some fairly extreme positions, which would eliminate her from some of the consulting gigs that awaited her and her colleagues after we threw them out.

A few weekends after that, we rolled out the "Restore the Shore" plan, which allocated only existing resources for storm restoration, and authorized no rebuilding of broken roads and infrastructure in flood-prone areas. Limited compensation was provided for displaced residents.

Mrs. Shaughnessy was duly thanked and swiftly replaced by our own Jason Abigdor. But in a surprise move that infuriated Uncle Wynn and scores of people like him, Lucia appointed Shaughnessy to manage the federal payouts for storm victims.

"She used to be on our side," Uncle Wynn snarled when Shaughnessy's reappointment was announced. "She wasn't one of the kooks. And now, after screwing all the towns along the shore, she's handing out peanuts."

I've draped more layers of wet toilet paper over the Lincoln logs, and set the sticks from the frozen fruit bars on top like spikes. It's the kind of wall Uncle Wynn had wanted, that would last longer than the tank ramparts put up by the Nazis along the Normandy coast before D-Day, and be taller than the Great Wall of China. Our own pyramids. The epitome of human ingenuity, with materials that rebuild themselves under stress. Strong enough to let Uncle Wynn live within spitting distance of the ocean. Under Lucia, no such wall has been built. When you visit the shore in Virginia today, abandoned houses are visible at low tide. The EPA has sued the owners to take down those houses, but most have refused. Instead, they attached large, wind-resistant protest banners, silently screaming into the sky above the sea: "Abandoned by America," and "Homeless by Decree." In the summers, people find their way to the abandoned houses to party.

Uncle Wynn and Aunt Sophia have moved to the Florida Gulf Coast. They bought something cheap at a former navy base. When I visited last year in the spring, I admired the beautiful view of the beach from their porch. They despise Lucia, whom they make a point to always call "your" – as opposed to our – president; so we tacitly agree not to talk about my work in the White House.

I fling the remaining water against my wall so that the logs tumble down. The water pools on the floor. "There's no cleanup fund," I say out loud. "Restore the shore!" I add with a laugh and look at my destroyed wall, no longer rigid and defiant, but now truly in harmony with the sea.

Opt-Outs

This morning, there is no birdsong, no swaying daffodils, no lightning storm, no eerie silence. It just sounds like a regular day in a regular hospital. The whirring of fans and ventilators, and some clanging noises. One of the nurses told me through the intercom that the pod will go completely dark tonight, including reading and bathroom lights, as part of an effort to regulate my sleep patterns. These days, of course, shutting off the lights is standard practice in some communities. Opt-outs, they call it. It's become really big in Europe and in some of the Western US states. Less so in Latin America, with the exception of Chile. Towns near Valparaiso have taken it on big-time, apparently. Opt-outs are not popular in Asia, for some reason.

We were on a trip to Berlin to visit European leaders, and, oddly, we found ourselves with a nearly unscheduled evening before heading to Paris. Opt-outs had started in Germany and Poland, where the Green parties had struck deals with local unions to invest in renewables. Germany had become a leader in those industries. All of it heavily subsidized, and part of our trip's agenda had been to convince the Germans to open up their markets. But after the *Unglückswoche* in October 2020, when quite a few German companies were almost wiped out and the port security in Hamburg was breached, Germany had tried to force legislation in Brussels that would have shut down almost all except German-made solar and wind technology.

"In our view, the market should be pushed by consumers, not regulators, to provide the right thing," Lucia explained.

"Our citizens certainly do push the market," a German official had responded. "In some towns, 80 percent of energy, mostly solar and wind, is covered by private sources. And these people demand efficient products that meet our safety standards."

We had planned our visit to Berlin very carefully, given the sensitivities of an American president making announcements from inside the Reichstag. Once we were off duty, I had looked forward to a simple meal, but not in one of those German cook-it-yourself places. I wanted to sit down, be served a plate of locally grown food, and keep my phone off.

A really nice Brazilian guy at the front desk with a flattop and green eyes wrote the names of a few places in cursive script on a piece of paper. Old-fashioned pens and paper were a selling point of this hotel, along with actual, metal keys attached to chunky lumps of amber. Free edibles at night, and rainwater showers. I wasn't sure whether the guy had smiled at me, meaning *me,* or whether he was just being reception-desk friendly. He knew I was part of POTUS's detail, but he was also probably used to fancy visitors. I thanked him, took the paper, and set off into the balmy Berlin night to find the restaurant whose name he'd written down. It was nearly ten p.m., but only just now getting dark, the way northern European summer days fade slowly. I walked under the plane trees on the median of a wide street and watched the Germans with their fancy, well-behaved dogs, their gold and silver bikes, and the hippie clothes that were either meant to be ugly or an ironic critique of fashion. The phone buzzed before I had covered a block.

"Driving to Paris instead," Domineek texted. "Departure in 15 garage level."

Fifteen minutes later I was sitting next to Lucia in a Tesla SUV. For a moment I had been disappointed not to have my night out, but now I felt proud to be the only staffer, besides Domineek and the detail, to come along.

"We're not actually driving to Paris, Aleks," Lucia said when the car pulled out of the underground garage. "That's more than ten hours, and we all need sleep. But there's an opt-out town not too far from here, one of the first. I want to see it."

The driver had floppy hair over a buzz cut in the back, a small tattoo on one temple, and wore a vest over a priestly looking, high-collared shirt. I looked out the window as we drove through a long tunnel and then merged into fast-moving traffic on the Autobahn. I woke up as the car slowed down. Large signs above the highway flashed "opt-out" next to unintelligible German words.

"Solar powered," the driver said while pointing at the signs.

The car turned off the highway, and I spotted four motorcycles just ahead of us. Lucia put away her tablet.

"Let's see what this is really about."

We drove onto a smaller road without streetlights. Within minutes, the car's high beams picked out trees on both sides. Thick pines lined up neatly, with a bit of undergrowth just at the edge of the road. It reminded me of roads in Vermont and Massachusetts, also lined with daunting, second-chance forests that had been planted there over the past fifty years.

The driver seemed to sense my thoughts.

"These forests were originally planted for timber," he said. "But today's laws don't allow trees over a certain size to be cut down. And with the better artificial wood and bamboo, there's no real money in it. So the owners sold the forests to the government, which now manages these places. Kind of like your national parks. I've been to Yellowstone, and Yosemite!"

He pronounced it "*J*osemite." Lucia did not say anything. I just nodded and thought how these planted rows of skinny, ramrod pines compared with the immeasurable grandeur of our parks.

We slowed down at a checkpoint. Like fish emerging from the depths, a few guards in fluorescent uniforms came into the cone of light cast by the car's headlights. The driver exchanged a few words with them, and they saluted.

"Just regular police to make sure people don't drive with their lights past this point," the driver said. "Anybody can come in or out. They just watch out for everyone's safety."

We drove more slowly now with the lights off, the driver wearing night goggles. It was a bit disorienting. I did not yet have the feeling of entering a warm and welcoming place, the kind of comforting ur-womb that people have talked about when describing opt-outs.

But gradually it felt as if my mind was getting sharper while my eyes adjusted to the darkness. Lucia gently touched my arm and gestured to her side of the car, where the darkness seemed to have more shape. We were peering out of the windows as if we were on safari, trying to spot something, but there was little to see: the vague outlines of things, a few pockets of deeper shadows, then complete darkness. Then I saw it. We had driven from the country road, along what I assumed to be fields or just forest, straight into a town. I was staring at a wall.

The vehicle came to a stop and we carefully opened the doors. Lucia's detail donned night goggles and stayed close. We glimpsed a few feet of cobblestone road, but it was impossible to see where it led. I only needed to take a step and stretch out my hand to feel the rough surface of the wall.

We heard sounds. Footsteps, a bike's tires on the cobblestones, the sound of metal scraping on stone, doors opening and closing, some guttural German words here and there. The sky started to look a bit brighter but I could not tell whether that was due to my eyes adjusting.

"This town has opted out of fluorescent markers along the road," the driver said. "That's why we're required to park here. They go off the grid two nights per week in the summers. And you've picked a good night: *Neumond*. They call it 'true dark,' although there's still ambient light from the highway and other towns."

A few people walked past us, steering clear of the car without any apparent difficulty. I heard them approach but could hardly see their silhouettes until they were right beside me. Did they wear night goggles? I couldn't tell.

"Do most people stay inside when it's dark?"

"Most people get around without goggles," the driver said. "It's a matter of pride, and it's proven to be really good for you to learn to see in the dark. We don't even realize how much light pollution we're subjected to."

"Leave it to the Germans," I whispered to Lucia.

Lucia ignored my comment. "What about those who don't want to participate? Who don't feel safe?"

"Our fear of the dark is a modern invention," the driver said. "And in this town everyone participates. People encourage their neighbors to join."

"What about emergencies? If someone needs an ambulance, or the fire department?"

"Lights can be used in emergencies. There are designated emergency switches and pick-up points," the driver explained. "The town is divided by blocks, and no one's farther than five minutes from a safe spot."

Around us I sensed movement. People talked quietly.

"It's like Yom HaShoah in Israel," I remarked. "Or like Washington after the twin storms."

Lucia did not respond but reached for my hand.

"Let's take a look," she said and briefly laughed at her own joke.

As part of our energy strategy, we had studied real-time satellite maps of nighttime Europe in briefing rooms — spots from Portugal to Belarus going dark, as if the lights strung on a Christmas tree had blown out one by one. At first, people had dismissed opt-outs as a fad for wealthy towns. But the statistics showed that a large number of the newer European towns, filled mostly with people born in northern Africa, also opted out. Overall, the reduction of electricity consumption was negligible. But Lucia wasn't interested in opt-outs to reduce consumption. She was fascinated by ground-up initiatives, about people taking action without government incentives or threats.

"There's no hope for the planet if we rely on governments alone," she said repeatedly. "Unless we change our behavior as individuals, we stand no chance."

"Individuals also happen to be the ones who vote," Dominek said to me. "Engagement is the number one factor in voter participation."

The mayor of Amsterdam was a leader in the opt-out movement, and Amsterdam was one of the few big cities where whole neighborhoods opted out of electricity a few nights each summer. He was very tall, with a young face and a great shock of mad-scientist white hair. He had visited the White House once and showed up in jeans and a sweater that Keon identified, when I showed him clips later that night, as one of the top French DY brands. He'd probably finished it himself.

During one of the sessions, in a room full of fidgety dignitaries, the Dutch mayor presented studies that showed how opt-out towns had better metrics across the board. Improved school performance, especially on truancy, better overall productivity, and better major health indices for all age groups.

"We don't quite know the reasons, but fewer people use the emergency rooms during opt-outs," he explained while running his long fingers through his white hair. "This includes heart attacks, strokes, that sort of thing. But also cuts, wounds, injuries from fights. There are also fewer accidents."

"What about crime?" the mayor of Kuala Lumpur asked. "How can you police a town in the dark?"

She was petite and elegant and spoke Malay. "We've spent the last few decades putting in a reliable grid. During power outages, crimes spike in our city."

"Planned darkness, as it turns out, is a tonic for the stressors of our lives. It's very different from a blackout, which feels violent and like an attack. Scheduled opt-outs are like holidays. They restore the senses. We have seen great reduction in crimes for towns that have gone on opt-out three times a week."

"Like Shabbos," Mike Bloomberg had remarked wryly. "It isn't such a new idea." Bloomberg, the guru of urban renewal, still attended all of the conferences, dressed to the nines. He had taken a liking to Lucia and supported the campaign.

"But opting out is voluntary," the Malaysian mayor had said. "What about the people who keep their lights on?"

"Voluntary," Bloomberg laughed. "So is Shabbos. 'Voluntary' is a flexible term in most opt-out towns. They have citizen brigades that help the people to shut off their lights."

In the town that Lucia and I had gingerly stepped into, there seemed to be no holdouts. I couldn't make out a single lit window or even a glow stick. The balmy summer air felt as if we had crawled headfirst into a sleeping bag. We walked along the wall, and Lucia's security detail had fanned out just far enough that I couldn't see them. We moved tentatively so as not to knock into anything. We hardly spoke.

I could see about four to five feet in front of me. Lucia and I holding hands was awkward. I tried to keep my grip natural, and hoped my palm would not get sweaty. But then something inside of me expanded, and I relaxed. I physically felt my chest and lungs widen with each intake of the soft night air. Lucia let go of my hand as I sensed her also relaxing.

The air felt thicker, richer. Perhaps it was more humid than it had been in Berlin, but it also felt as if the darkness had made it more clean.

Lucia moved a bit faster, and I had to step up not to be left behind.

"Doesn't it just make sense?" Lucia whispered, but I knew she didn't expect an answer. "Opting out to reconnect," she continued. "Changing your situation to do something huge."

I could hear her inhale.

"It's as if opting out reconnects us to something primal."

I was taken in by what she said. From the various mayors' presentations at the Big Cities Meetings I knew of other visionaries who knew the night again as night, the day again as day. They made a small and local commitment to do something on a great scale. The colonization of foreign territory, the Industrial Revolution, electrification had some of the worst effects in history that would never be reversed. I'd heard that this re-synching of our biorhythms changed something within us on a basic level. But hearing Lucia say it while we walked through the velvety country night made me hear it differently, more acutely, for the first time. I felt calm and also exhilarated.

"Like a yoga high," Keon said later when I tried to describe it to him. "Or that mellow feeling right after sex?"

"Not quite that," I laughed then.

"I get it now," Lucia said. "You can feel why people are so excited by this. You feel more connected to your surroundings; you're doing something good, and it becomes a ritual."

"And it gets to the root of some of our problems," I added. "It gives people a way to stop draining the planet."

"Yes, empowers them to feel that they are making a difference," Lucia said.

We spoke quietly and had now reached what appeared like the town square or an open area between tall buildings. The light was different here, or I should say the darkness, since there were no lights. I assumed that there must be a church or city hall somewhere near. After a minute or so, I could make out the outlines of rustling trees and some stalls in a row in the middle of the square, but it was still not easy to interpret all of the details. We carefully crossed the open square. People were chatting around us, and we could hear the clinking of glasses. Suddenly we were next to our car again. The driver must have brought it around in silent mode while we were walking.

The ink-black darkness above had given way to the velvety extension of space dotted by stars. I thought I heard the call of some bird, maybe an owl. I felt, more than I actually saw, bats cycling through the air above in pursuit of bugs. Without a word, Lucia and I got into the car.

"In this darkness I see possibility," Lucia said in the car. I had hit Record on the tablet. Even the tablet's night screen seemed weirdly wrong now, its sickly pale glow like that of a deep-sea dwelling worm. I turned it down as much as possible. "This movement will be big."

The car rolled slowly out of the square and then, it seemed, onto a road away from the town. Soon the neon-vested guards swam into view again, and after the checkpoint the driver turned the body-glow back on, and then the headlights.

"People can do huge things," Lucia said. "These opt-outs may not affect energy consumption much, but I can see how they inspire people. It's a step toward taking control of the environment in a positive way, and participating in a solution. It makes people realize that they have a choice."

We were now driving again on some kind of cobblestone or rutted road.

"How often do they have these opt-out nights here?" Lucia asked the driver.

"They are like festivals," he responded. "Some towns hold them twice a week in the summer, and people come from all over to stay here and experience 'true dark,' as they call it."

"'True dark,'" Lucia repeated. "I like it. It's critical for people to take the initiative. They have to *feel* a connection, *feel* how they can make a difference."

I recorded everything Lucia said.

Soon we were back on the Autobahn. Headlights sliced through the darkness, and the huge lights above cast a pallid glow on the asphalt in front of us. After the quiet mood in that town, it seemed manic.

Soon we would be back at the hotel, ensconced in the glow of millions of watts and hundreds of lightbulbs, screens, lamps, and displays.

"Makes it all seem kind of silly, eh?" the driver said and glanced in the rearview mirror. "That we need to move around so much when nature intended for us to be quiet when it's dark."

Neither Lucia nor I responded, lost in our own thoughts.

We had visited a small European town. But in a few minutes of walking through the darkness, we had entered another, primally familiar realm that much of the planet had tried to banish with electricity for a century or more. The possibility to reconnect to this realm was right here, in the middle of densely populated Europe. It was the possibility of experiencing who we really are — or were.

The Guardian

Opt-Outs for Different Reasons in Eastern Europe

GMT morning edition

By PATRICIA GERGES

Monday, 22 June, 2021

CEPAUSK, HUNGARY - The small town of Cepausk is nestled in the green Carpathian Mountains that separate Hungary from Romania. Cepausk is famous for its residents' love of elaborate Christmas decorations that illuminate the cobblestone streets and eight-hundred-year-old stone façades during the long Hungarian winters, and stay on for much of the year. But on a recent opt-out date, Cepausk was almost entirely dark.

When Hungary was still under Soviet rule during the second half of the twentieth century, Cepausk was dark most of the time. Government-imposed, rolling black-outs rationed electricity use to military installations and urban centers but kept most smaller towns and the countryside without power. Before 1990, only 40 percent of rural houses in the region were connected to the grid.

After the collapse of the Soviet Empire in the final decade of the last century, Cepausk's residents adopted the yearlong, twinkling lights to show their newfound freedom. But now the town is shutting down its gaudy decorations. In a raucous town hall last spring, when the issue of opt-outs was debated, opponents had threatened to "light-blast" the mayor and other "opt-outers" who favor regularly scheduled shutdowns of all but emergency lighting electricity. These opt-outs have been popular in Germany and France for a while, where towns that shut off electricity for nights at a time attract tourists during the summer months. In the town meeting last spring, the opt-outers won. That is why on a recent night, the dark in Cepausk's town square was thick as the black bean soup for which the region is also famous. Only a faint glow here and there marked "safety spots."

"We fought to opt out and reclaim the night," Radu, 22, a burly business student in a blue peacoat said as he patrolled his neighborhood with three others to check for renegade "electrics," those rejecting the night-long ban.

With four scheduled opt-outs this past summer, and several "wild" events where people shut off their lights without any directive from the mayor's office, the town has reduced electricity usage by an estimated 17 percent. The number has surprised even skeptics, including some of the "electrics."

"It's another silly fad that won't change a thing," said Myria, a 43-year-old dental assistant. "But it's nice sometimes not to be bombarded by all the stuff that's run on electricity and that's taken over our lives," she conceded. "My kids look forward to opt-outs like school holidays, and my husband and I find private time in the dark," she added with a laugh.

What decided the vote in the town hall was a combination of the younger generation's environmental concern with their parents' longing for a simpler time.

Myria's husband, Slavok, a retired train operator, said, "After the Soviet Union fell, our jobs went to the immigrants. Our kids grow up in a wasteland of violence and obscenity produced in Hollywood and Germany. Opt-outs are another fad, that's right. But at least it lets us determine, even if only for a few nights a year, how we live our lives."

Environmental and energy experts say there is little evidence of the opt-outs' significant financial or environmental benefits.

"Consumer consumption is only about 10 percent of overall energy consumption in Europe. So a few towns turning off their lights doesn't change much. But it's a move in the right direction," explained Amir Zilbers, a professor of environmental science and engineering at King Abdullah II

School of Economics, and an expert on the opt-out movement. "Opting out gives smaller communities in regions outside of Europe some independence from multinational energy providers."

Voluntary opt-outs by whole towns have caught on in Europe, North America, and Australia. But their popularity in Eastern Europe is fueled equally by the desire to break free of Western influence and return to an era that many had consigned to the dustbin of history, and by the wish to conserve energy. They have also connected the local population with recently arrived immigrants, who tend to hold more conservative views.

"The night is the part of our lives we have been denied for too long," Radu said. He wears his close-cropped hair in the zigzag pattern popular among nationalists in Europe. "The West wants us to forget tradition. They have blinded us with all of their shiny, dirty stuff. Opt-outs create quiet in this madness."

The four young men had just completed their round through their assigned district. Radu signaled to his comrades to resume their patrol.

"We've just heard about an electric who doesn't want to comply," he said and tapped his earpiece once. All four of them adjusted their armbands and took out what looked like wooden clubs with a few blinking buttons. Then they marched into the night, presumably to compel a resister to turn off his light.

Lu-ci-a!

All evening, I've tried to get the medics to tell me the score, but either they are too dense or didn't really watch the game. Hard to believe. We're playing Brazil today in qualifiers. I'm not too worried, but still.

The first time I saw our guys live was when I went with Lucia to her box at Eon Stadium for an exhibition game against Mexico. Capacity crowd, insane traffic, tons of security everywhere. We first took a motorcade to the Department of Energy. In their garage, straight out of a spy thriller, we switched to a small car that sped through an underground tunnel that led into the bowels of the stadium. We packed into one elevator, with the detail trying not to crowd Lucia. The presidential box itself is not fancy, rather like a conference room, and Lucia worked on several screens while also watching the game. Through the tinted windows the fans cannot see whether the president is in attendance or not.

Everyone was jealous of me. It was impossible to get tickets, since most were allocated through eco brigades. Keon had almost once gotten some, but then he was a few points short. People mostly sit with their brigades. Eon stadium is built and maintained on the principles of the return economy. The fans have gotten used to eating off edible plates, the exterior walls have enormous hanging gardens planted in the team's colors that function like living air-conditioning. The whole bit. The game took place in the spring after the inauguration, so quite a while after the controversy erupted over the discovery that the DNC had bought all advertising slots after each goal for America. I had watched all the games, of course, but it was very different to be there.

We scored twelve minutes into it with a beautiful header by Raphael Bemgia. *"GOOOOOOOOAAAAALL!"* the stadium erupted, and the chants: *"U-S-A! U-S-A! U-S-A!"* And all on cue, when the side banners flashed her name, they roared: *"Lu-ci-a! Lu-ci-a!"* In the box, we *felt* the chants. The box was thumping up and down with each syllable of Lu-ci-a. At Eon, the fans sit "drum style" in bleachers that are built in tiers, which go up at a fairly steep angle rather than widening toward the top. When the fans stomped and chanted, the glasses in the box shook on the tabletop. It was physical. Lucia was cheering, too. Screaming, really. We beat Mexico 2–0 that day, which some people hadn't expected. Not me! Never doubt the US Eleven!

The words "Lucia Jackson" had appeared for an instant as a quick stroke of red, white, and blue lightning that ran along the panels around the field. Then: "Planet Justice! Lucia Jackson!" The fans have started to expect it. "*GOOOOOOOOAAAAALL!*" then "*U-S-A,*" and then "*Lu-ci-a*" when her name races around the field's perimeter. Screamed and stomped by thousands in the bleachers, whenever one of our strikers locks it in.

Every time the national team wins an international match, Lucia visits the team in the locker room. When she comes in, the players chant *Lu-ci-a, Lu-ci-a*. She hugs all of them and chats with Coach Donovan, who is a friend. The media feed shows that Team USA appears to win each time the president is in attendance. As if she is their good luck charm. When our guys lose, she disappears immediately through the garage without stopping by the locker room. And since nobody could see her in the tinted box, it's like she wasn't in the stadium at all.

The players love Lucia's visits. Since it only happens when they win, they are in a great mood. Lucia loves it, too. She grew up with soccer, before it became so big in our country. After the Mexico game, she practically skipped into the locker room, high-fived and hugged bare-chested players everywhere, and caused such a ruckus that her detail looked seriously concerned. Then she discussed the game for a few minutes with the players, blow-by-blow, and congratulated Raphael on his goal and Josh Pisoni on his saves. She left to the guys' chanting:

"Lu-ci-a! Lu-ci-a!"

Within thirty minutes we were back at the White House.

Did they chant "Lu-ci-a" today? Did she stop by the locker room? What's the fucking score? I cannot believe that no one working in this place had watched the game.

Aunt Christine

Billie Holiday woke me up. I must have fallen asleep in the middle of the afternoon. It's the song we listened to on the last day with Keon's grandparents, and it happened also to be one of Aunt Christine's favorites. Christine was the first person I knew, aside from Keon's grandparents, who took the deliberate-departure route.

I forced myself to do my exercises, and then compiled a list of Lucia's victories and the things we have yet left to do. But the song won't leave my head. It's sad, but Holiday's voice pulls the sadness up, like someone drawing water out of a deep well. Aunt Christine would play it a lot, when she was still well. As if she knew. She would have liked the fact that I work in the White House, fighting for people to have more options for living in a healthier, safer world. Aunt Christine didn't want to die like her father died.

Grandpa had died in great pain even though he had an end-of-life agreement to prevent suffering. There had been several nearly-last-minute trips to the hospital, and anxious, hushed discussions between Mom and Christine about finding care. There wasn't enough money for both insurance and an attendant, and they opted for the former.

Aunt Christine took a leave and moved to Boston to take Grandpa to his tests. They detected all sorts of hidden things that triggered more treatments, more weight loss, more discussions with more doctors, more pain. Each scan showed something that required more tests, and every result led to more problems. There was also an immune issue that they could not figure out. It required blood transfusions, which undid a lot of the work done by the medication he was on.

One night we drove him to a hospital where they refused his insurance, even though that was against the law since it was the only emergency room within a fifty-mile radius. Grandpa sat doubled over in a wheelchair, whimpering like a child, while Mom and I pleaded with a receptionist. Then, without so much as a glance at the woman who kept professing her regret at having to follow the rules, a nurse appeared, smiled at us, and took the wheelchair's handles. "Just follow me," he said, and wheeled Grandpa out of the hospital's doors, past a guard to whom he waved with two fingers as if signaling something in a game, and through a service door that had swung open when he swiped his card.

"I don't have insurance," Grandpa whispered.

"Not to worry," the nurse replied while he helped Grandpa out of the chair and onto a cot in a hallway. He readied some equipment. "Not to worry. You will feel better, and then you will be able to go home to rest. There's nothing for you to worry about."

"Anything we can do?" Mom said, but in a small voice.

"It's going to take a bit," the nurse said. He briefly smiled at her but then turned back to Grandpa. "You just try to relax, maybe sleep a bit. We'll keep you here. It's quiet, and no one is going to disturb you."

I had turned away a moment too late, just before the nurse had adjusted the catheter, and was embarrassed to have glimpsed my grandfather, this proud and elegant man, naked and shivering.

"High time," the nurse said while he pulled up the sheet so Grandpa would not be exposed. Grandpa's lids were fluttering, like those of a small animal resting after a narrow escape, but he wasn't asleep. A grimace of pain. Mom could hardly speak.

"If you'd waited a bit longer, he would have gone into shock," said the nurse quietly. "You have to bring him earlier when he cannot pee. Urine is toxic when it stays in our body."

We stayed in the hallway for another hour or so while Grandpa's bladder emptied out. Some color returned to his cheeks. The nurse checked on him a few times, and brought us coffee and, I remember this well, homemade cinnamon rolls.

At four or five in the morning we checked out through the service entrance to avoid an official discharge. Grandpa hadn't received a chip bracelet, and had gotten only sample medications, so we wouldn't be billed. The handsome nurse hugged Mom, and formally shook Grandpa's hand when we left. He said, "You're a good grandson," as if he were much older, and I, a little kid. We understood that Grandpa would have died that night if we hadn't taken him to that hospital, and if the nurse hadn't helped us out.

Another night, Grandpa slipped and fell, headfirst, into the tub next to the toilet. It was a soaking tub that had been installed years ago when Grandma had still been alive. I found him almost upside down in the empty tub, with one leg hooked over the side, which had probably saved him from breaking his neck. For a moment I thought he had died. Then he moaned quietly, and it took me a minute to extricate him from the tub. I half-carried, half-guided him to his room. His underwear had slipped down and, once I had settled him, I had to lift him a bit off the bed to pull them up. Blood trickled from a small gash on one elbow. The whole time he hadn't spoken, and I avoided catching his eye. I put a Band-Aid on, made sure there were no other cuts, and covered him with a blanket. He pressed my hand for a moment, but turned his head away.

I wish I had clips of Grandpa being happy and without pain. When he rushed into a room, waved his tablet because he disagreed with something in the news, or when he built a bench or a table, or a little wooden stand, in the yard, long past dusk.

"There's no guarantee of progress," he often said. "But humans are restless, and sometimes accidentally move things in the right direction."

I wish I had clips of the times when one of Grandpa's former students messaged him to chat. Then, he looked a good twenty years younger and spoke fast, like a graduate student discussing his thesis. I wish I had a clip of him eating oatmeal for breakfast, with the tablet balanced on the table to read the news, and sipping an espresso he had made for himself with his fancy Italian machine.

Grandpa had written the script for a documentary on wildlife migration that first got me interested in conservation. I loved hearing about his fights with the producers, who wanted only to feature charismatic megafauna and end on an inspiring note.

"The damage done by nature films can't be overestimated," Grandpa would say. "We care about animals that we see in movies, especially if they are nice to look at. But conservation is not about protecting only the plants and animals we want to survive. It's not ours to pick and choose."

A few of Grandpa's storyboards hang framed in our living room. But I don't have clips of Grandpa explaining his decision to include invasive species. "The migrants of the animal kingdom," he would say. "The undocumented aliens, the fish and snakes and bugs and vines that weren't supposed to be here. Who are we, who have invaded everywhere, to decide which animals belong and which should be killed?"

It's hard to recall his good moments because I can't put the depressing images out of my mind. I see Grandpa naked on the drive home, sitting ramrod-straight in the front seat with the urine bag taped to his side, in total silence and with his lips pressed together. His pain wafted through the car like a bad smell.

He died in a hospital, surrounded by nurses, technicians, and machines. Mom and Aunt Christine were also there.

From what they told me, he was in a coma all night, attached to a drip and lots of monitors.

In the morning, a nurse quietly told Mom and Aunt Christine that even though he looked like he was in a deep sleep, he was in pain. She made a point of getting their assent before turning up the morphine drip. Grandpa died a few minutes later. I found out about those last moments only afterward, after the messages, after my rushed trip to the airport, the time standing around the hospital offices to get the paperwork done, and the funeral.

"Is that legal?" I asked Mom when we were back home. "Was that legal to up the morphine?"

She shrugged her shoulders. "It was a medical decision not to let him suffer any longer. We had the end-of-life papers, and Christine had talked to the doctors. But then, early in the morning, with him lying there so small, in those horrible, stiff white sheets, and hardly breathing . . . I didn't know whether he was going to pull through, recover a bit, only to go through more of this. It was time."

Mom cried. I cried.

Not long after, Aunt Christine was diagnosed with an autoimmune syndrome. Mom was devastated, but Christine wouldn't have any of it.

She lost her sight in one eye, and with it, her sense of balance. There was no clear or obvious cause. They put her on medication, poked around, did scans, tried diets and alternative medicine. Aunt Christine met with attorneys, real estate people, wrote a lot of cards by hand and sent them out via courier.

I visited her a few times. She insisted on opening the door instead of buzzing me in from her bed. She walked into the kitchen, steadying herself along the hallway walls with one hand, and then carefully, slowly, made me a coffee.

Morgan and Kendra were perfectly horrible. They argued in front of Aunt Christine over whether all of the expensive doctors were really necessary, asked for money, and just bickered. Morgan was training for a bodybuilding competition and spent most of the time ordering protein supplements on his mom's accounts, and preparing huge shakes with egg whites in her kitchen without cleaning up. He checked his reflection in the living room mirror constantly, with his arms and thighs wrapped in workout tape. Kendra put her energy into fighting with her brother. Once they were literally yelling at each other at the foot of their mom's bed.

Finally, Aunt Christine checked herself into a hospice in Michigan. Things were in a legal gray zone then with some states not enforcing federal guidelines. For Mom, it was hard. Aunt Christine had instructed her not to tell anyone. So Mom had to pretend that Aunt Christine had booked herself on a health cruise with tech blackouts. Kendra didn't know; Morgan didn't know. Only Mom and I knew.

Mom spent a week with Christine at the place while everyone thought she was on her "healing cruise." Later Mom told me that the place had been full of people of Aunt Christine's and her own age. Everyone just close to sixty. "Like a fancy country club that's also a rehab clinic, with people playing tennis, swimming, and also getting treatments. A pretty serious security system to keep the crazies from coming in. But not like a cult," Mom said, "though you definitely felt that you didn't really belong if you were an outsider."

Aunt Christine had bought out her life insurance earlier because of the company's refusal to honor the policies of people who had chosen to end their lives. She spent a good amount on that clinic, and later I heard from Mom that Morgan had been furious that there was less money than he had expected. Kendra was angry that her mother had checked herself in without telling her, and that Mom knew. Neither of them have spoken to us since the funeral.

Then the evangelicals attacked. Mom had posted a few things about Aunt Christine's passing, and some people decided to make her death into their cause. They posted everything they could find on Aunt Christine's death. It got bad.

Since Mom's company requires employees to have a clean media profile, she had to respond to these lunatics that she had inherited nothing, no money, that she had not pushed her sister into giving up. So while she was mourning her sister's death, and dealing with Kendra and Morgan, she had to post her bank statements and all of Christine's estate, including her will, to refute the charges that she had benefited personally from her sister's death.

"These people will stop at nothing, Aleks," Chiara from Asturias's team said to me at work when I told her what was happening. "They are like my family, who put the sanctity of life above everything else. Your mom being there while her sister took her own life: that makes her a target in their view."

"My aunt faced terrible options, and we all know from people with immune syndromes that there was very little chance of improvement."

"Suffering is a sign of virtue," Chiara said. "A station of the cross. You have to understand that for people like my parents, taking your life is outrageous because it interferes with God's plan for each of us."

"You think that as well? Do you think it's wrong for people to end their lives when all the right conditions for that choice are met? When their lives don't feel like life anymore?"

"Aleks, I can't really say. Believe me, I know that it's possible to change one's attitude about certain things. I have benefitted from such changes, to be sure. Look at me! A vegan Asian girl with a disability, and I've been able to go to all the schools I wanted to, play sports, and have a career. Fifty years ago I would've been locked away, or people would have moved when my family came to the neighborhood." She was silent for a moment. "But killing yourself because life is hopeless, and causing everyone pain?"

"That's not why most people do it."

"You know what I mean, Aleks. We'll never understand death; so why take it into our own hands? I'm not saying the religious fanatics are right. But while I get the intellectual arguments — and I'm not saying anything about your aunt — it still feels somehow wrong, like the arguments not to try to save handicapped babies because their lives may not be like those of completely healthy people."

"That's a horrible analogy," I said. "Infants are helpless. Here we are talking — I mean, my mom is fighting for the right for adults to make their own choice regarding death — about a thing that science and technology have long controlled. And insurance companies, and big pharma! There's almost no one today who dies a so-called natural death. Perhaps this is closer to what some God had intended, if that's what people want to believe."

Chiara looked at me.

"I think it's a personal matter, Aleks. I am sorry for your loss, with both your grandfather and your aunt this year. It's really terrible. But just as we don't decide to be born, I don't know whether I think we have the right to decide to die."

For my part, I don't see why laws should force a person to live out a life they don't want.

Google News

Jackson's Father's Death, Revisited

New Picture Reignites Debate from '20 Campaign
Posted February 14, 2021, 6:42pm EST

A photo of President Jackson's late father's corpse prompted an angry response from the White House and reignited a debate over assisted suicide, or "deliberate-departure" practices, which are legal in several states. On Monday, two photographs of Guzmán Morales, Jackson's late father, surfaced online. They show a white-clad body lying facedown near a creek in a muddy area, bordered by tall trees. Mr. Morales died a year ago, shortly before President Jackson's nomination as the Democratic presidential candidate. His death occurred in a clinic in Montana that permits physician-assisted suicides. During her campaign, Jackson was criticized by religious leaders for her outspoken support of assisted suicide, which many faith-based organizations condemn. The controversy over her father's decision to end his life was put to rest for a while when President Jackson's mother revealed that her ex-husband had been suffering from ICS, Immune Collapse Syndrome.

The White House denounced Monday's publication of the two photographs as "upsetting," and "disrespectful." It was not clear who leaked the images, or whether they were drone-captured or man-made. President Jackson took time during a state ceremony in Washington to express her anger.

"My father's death was a terrible loss for me and my family," she said.

"He was a courageous person who put his relatives first. It is shameful that people attack the many families who face agonizing decisions when their loved ones decide on their time to depart." Religious leaders and other opponents of assisted suicide criticized President Jackson's statement.

"Death is not something we have the right to administer," Sean Anscott, a founder of the Right to Life Ministries Movement, said in a press release. "President Jackson's father's death is a private matter, but the physicians that provided him with the drug to kill himself should be tried as accomplices to murder."

Activists like Sophie Lewin, director of *God Giveth God Taketh Away*, a pro-life organization based in Indiana, have seized upon the pictures to argue that Mr. Morales changed his mind at the last minute. There is speculation that after he took his final dose of medication, he changed his mind and tried to return to the clinic to get help from the staff there.

Opponents of assisted suicide claim that patients may experience a change of heart once they have taken medication. Advocacy groups point out that medical professionals have effectively set the moment of death for patients for a long time, especially with the increase in the number of people with impaired cognitive functioning.

Assisted medical end-of-life care is legal in 32 states. Over the past two years, there have been clashes outside clinics and at funerals, where bereaved family members were confronted and, in some cases, attacked, by religious protestors. Erica Bastics, the director of a large senior citizens' organization in Philadelphia, explained. "Frankly, the success of *Joanie Goes Home*, the Academy Award–winning film about a woman's fight to control her life in old age, changed many people's minds. But it also galvanized the protesters, who have resorted to increasingly violent tactics as the population's views shift on the issue." In some cases, protesters have been jailed for threatening funeral congregations and assaulting medical and support staff employed by senior citizen centers.

"This issue is our generation's abortion wars," Lamar Nelson said recently. "It pits the dignity of death against deeply held religious and cultural beliefs."

"We will not stop defending people, especially the elderly, from being pressured to end their own lives," Sean Anscott said in his press release. "It goes against God, and it goes against the values of our country."

President Jackson's administration has requested several injunctions against the news outlets that have posted the images of her father's corpse. The controversy shows that in spite of the relatively high acceptance rates for assisted suicide among the voting population, the issue remains a political problem for elected officials.

Melbourne Bushfires

I've made a fire. It's roaring hot. Of course it's a hologram, but the screen gets so hot that I can't sit close to it. When I try to touch it, or get too close, it disappears instantly, and then it takes a good twenty minutes of fiddling with the holo-kindle and matches until I can get it going again. It took me nearly three full days to discover the fireplace in the wall panels.

If this, too, was Seth's idea, good on him, as the Australians say. Figuring this out, feeling that this panel was slightly different from the rest of the wall, finding the tiny lever to open it, locating the hologram kindle and matches — it made me feel, if only for a moment, like I accomplished something.

I used to lounge in front of Bev's fireplace for long evenings when Keon worked late. We would order take-out and make the fire really big. But then the bushfires in Melbourne happened. After that, Bev had her fireplace bricked up, threw out all of her candles, had her huge gas range replaced by an electric stove. She even got rid of her grill, which is pretty much like asking a teenager, or anyone for that matter, to throw out their phone.

I had visited Bev's family in Australia that year, right after Christmas. Australia was not on the White House calendar for official visits. Australian prime minister Lunt had refused to participate in the Hawai'i meeting, and after hundreds of thousands of people had drowned during Typhoon Michio he said, on camera, "Those island people should have built on higher ground in the first place."

"Storms happen," he said during his apology. "I am sorry for the people who died. But storms have happened in the past, and they will happen in the future. The fact that this one was of such devastating magnitude doesn't mean that we've caused the weather to change."

"He's stupid and knows better," Lucia said. "But his position is not only wrong, it's dangerous."

"President Jackson will be good for America, where they have had their share of disasters," the Aussie prime minister said right after Lucia's election. "But this here is Australia, this is the lucky country. Down under we don't live in fear and worry. That's something Americans do, probably because they don't understand any longer what it means to be part of the land. We know from growing up on this vast continent that human beings are too small to unleash storms."

That took Australia off the table for state visits. For me, even with the brutally long flight, it was a rare opportunity to get away from politics for a few days.

"We will go to New Zealand," Lucia said, "and we will hold APAC there this year. And if Lunt doesn't come, we'll vote them off the Council."

I remember telling Bev about this, all purely confidential, of course.

"He's a bit of a jerk," she said about her prime minister. "But Australia *is* lucky in terms of what happens there. And Australia cannot afford not to be part of APAC; so, he'll probably calm down and show up at the last minute. He just wants to look strong with his party back home."

A few days later, on New Year's Day, when Keon was still counting down the last hours of the last year with his parents in California, I sat with Bev's brothers and sisters and their kids in a huge air-conditioned living room. It was unbearably hot outside, and on a big screen above a stone fireplace, the news showed non-stop footage of bushfires to the north of Melbourne.

"This is the worst I've ever seen," Bev's dad said when he walked in from the garden, bringing a blast of humid air with him. "This morning the courts were covered in ash that's blowing our way."

"How can you play tennis in this heat?" his wife said. She wiped her forehead with a small white towel. Everyone, even the kids, was wearing some kind of exercise outfit. It made the whole scene look a bit like a commercial. For New Year's Day, Bev's family had planned a barbeque after an afternoon swim.

"It'll be on for young and old," Bev said to me with a conspiratorial smile when we went shopping for the event. They still ate meat in Australia when I visited, the way people used to eat meat back home before Kansas happened. Big steaks on the barbie. Burgers. A sausage sizzle. I didn't go into the butcher shop with Bev, and just unloading the bulging bags of meat from the car later made me queasy. I remember a Fourth of July barbeque at some friends of Dad's in Jenkintown, when I was very young. That was when everyone still ate meat, even the old people and the little kids. Nobody had heard of the health risks at that point. Or what they really did to the animals. Or maybe people just didn't believe it. Bev's family in Melbourne was just as nonchalant as those people in Jenkintown had been. Innocent, really, convinced that local meat was safe. But part of me also thinks that the barbeque, or any such meal, harks back to some primal ritual. The tribe gets together to feast collectively on the dead beast, with even little children gnawing on the bones, so that no single person would be responsible for the animal's death.

Bev's family had moved the barbeque to the kitchen because of the heat. Most of the family hung out in the living room and parlor, and everyone was a bit cranky from being inside for too long.

"Mix it up, Aleksie," one of Bev's brothers said, and put two full glasses before me. He filled one with champagne, the other one with beer. "Bev tells me you work in the White House. I'm sure they don't serve good Aussie beer there. And surely not this great French champagne. You'll be pie-eyed in no time."

We just hung out, waiting for dinner, watching the news. I must have nodded off; the night before we hadn't gone to sleep till four in the morning. Just before sunset, there were people at the door — about eight or ten adults, all of whom were cousins or otherwise related, and at least as many kids. I walked over to the windows but couldn't see the street. Everyone was in the large front hallway, but nobody paid attention to me, so I squeezed past the people to get outside. As soon as I'd left the air-conditioned hallway, it felt like the inside of a car that's been in the sun all day. There were cars parked all along the driveway and also on the grass next to the road, between the signs that said that all landscaping was done with run-off rainwater. Next to the cars were two or three adults with several dogs on leashes that were lapping water from a bucket, someone holding a crate with a cat, and I could see on the backseat of one of the cars, there were several cages with parakeets and finches. A small boy with dark curly hair walked past me into the house, carrying a box with two black-and-white guinea pigs amongst wilted lettuce leaves. I went to the edge of the road. On the bed of a pickup truck I saw a crate containing a miniature pig, and a small llama tied down with wide ropes so he couldn't stand up.

I went back inside. The people had left the house as quickly as they had entered, and I realized that this had only been a bathroom stop. They clutched plastic bottles, wet towels, and bags of food that Bev's siblings had given to them.

"They've cleared Nillumbik, and everything in the Yarra Ranges," one of the guys said to Bev's sister. "The fires have reached Banyule. We had to leave. They came with soldiers, police, whatever. Guys with guns jumped over the fence, burst into our house. 'Out! Out!' They yelled. 'Two minutes! Get out!' I thought someone was coming to rob us, but they were ordering us to evacuate. They use some kind of amplifiers. It's so fucking loud that you have to get away. It damages your ears. It totally freaked out the kids. And the dogs."

I felt like an idiot, standing there in shorts and a T-shirt, still a bit drowsy from my nap, and holding my blue sunglasses. Like an idiot who had walked onto the set of a disaster movie.

"If the wind keeps up, this neighborhood is going to be gone by Friday," one of the guys said to the brother who had been plying me with drinks.

"C'mon, now, the fire is miles and miles away," he responded. "You're welcome to stay of course. We'll find a place to put you up."

The woman next to the guy shook her head.

"Not staying here. No frickin' way. This fire is unstoppable, and we want to get as far away as possible. We tried everything — sprinklers, water-bombed the hills, we flooded our street with the hydrants. Look, all of our houses are supposed to be fireproof. But I saw our neighbors' place explode in flames."

She wore a white dress shirt soaked with sweat over shorts. Her hair was plastered to her forehead, even though she wore most of it pulled back into a ponytail.

"On the way here we drove along a wall of flames taller than your trees," she said gesturing at the majestic oaks in front of the house. "I ran over a dog, and the highway was littered with dead rabbits and other animals trying to escape."

"Mommy," a little kid pulled on her hand. "You killed a dog?"

The woman picked up the kid. "We gotta move," she said to the guy who was apparently the husband. "Did you pee?" She had turned to her son. "We need to get out of here," she said to her husband again, and left the house.

"Where is the dog?" the kid said again, but she did not respond. "Did you run over a dog?"

"We're not staying," another tall, lanky woman in shorts and a tank top said. "Sue's right. The kids got a break; so, let's go. Everyone's been to the bathroom?"

Suddenly she screamed: "Let's go!"

Two or three kids quickly got out and scrambled into the cars.

"Let's go! Now! Let's fucking go!" The woman screamed again, and slammed her car door. Then they were gone.

I was embarrassed to be a guest, useless, getting in everyone's way. Especially because I was plastered. We stood around the living room to watch the news. Phone service was bad. We compared different media to find out what was really going on. I didn't know the names of the towns near Melbourne and couldn't make sense of what areas had already been evacuated, how close the fires were. Bev's brothers were on their phones, cursing when they couldn't get reception. The kids had retreated to their rooms. Nobody poured any more drinks. The food had been put on a big table, with plates and silverware, but nobody was eating. I went into the kitchen to help clean up. Gradually, people went to their rooms to sleep.

The next morning, the street was a complete zoo. Very early most of Bev's family was already downstairs, checking the news, or setting up things outside. I stepped onto the patio, and it was as if someone had turned on a huge, hot fan. Bev was outside, by the pool, chatting over the fence with a neighbor who was hosing his yard. Her brother walked over and dropped a garden hose into the pool. I helped him position a pump on the patio that was attached to a sprinkler he had rigged to the roof. Some guys were sealing the windows with heavy, black boards.

It was daytime already but the sky was a dark, dirty gray, and it was windy. I helped Bev's brothers run hoses from the garden faucets to the garage, where we set up more sprinklers.

Shortly after seven a.m., police cars with flashing lights lined the street. One of Bev's brothers, like a few of his neighbors from what I could pick up, didn't want to leave.

"Stay the fuck out," he yelled from behind the ornate gates. Then everything happened fast. Two or three cops in full-body armor leaped over the fancy wall and hedges, trampled exquisite flower beds, and while Bev's brother screamed at them, they broke down his gate from the inside. More cops ran in.

They turned on an amplifier that scared everyone straight.

"Out! Out!" They screamed into tiny mics on their armored vests, and the noise was so painful that you had to run. Then it was just a siren that kind of swept the area in front of the police who were wearing big black headphones. It was deafening and painful, and people didn't know where to turn. The soldiers, or cops, or whatever they were, moved in a line toward us. Their commands blasted from the amplifier with such force that it felt like a punch to the stomach. We scrambled out of the driveway and into our cars.

In the streets, people were carrying their kids while trying to cover their ears. Everyone moved in one direction down the street, while the police marched behind them in a line. Bev had her hands over her ears, screaming at the headphoned cops to stop. Bev's brother was yelling something at his wife, but it was like watching a silent movie — except that instead of a tinkling piano soundtrack, the deafening police commands and sirens made everyone appear mute.

We piled two of Bev's nieces into the car and took off.

Bev had scooped a few framed family pictures from a table in the hallway into a bag that now sat between my feet. I had grabbed my passport and phone but nothing else. People drove in one direction down the suburban streets toward the highway. There it was bumper to bumper, but at least traffic moved. Bev tried to reach her sisters on the cell but couldn't get through.

"Where the fuck are we going?" she said over and over. "What the fuck?"

After a while, the kids started watching something on their tablets and quieted down. All the cars in every lane on both sides of the highway moved in the same direction.

The radio instructed people to head east. Every car was crammed full, with some people practically buried under heaps of stuff. For a while traffic moved slowly, and we didn't speak. The glass in a few of the picture frames had broken and I had cut myself pretty deep on my left hand when I had reached into the bag for my phone. I pressed the hand into the pocket of my shorts, trying to stem the bleeding and ignore the problem.

Finally, we got reception.

"We're all driving south," Bev said. "Like there's anywhere else to go. Call us when there's a chance to get off the highway."

On the screen we saw where the fires spread, but I didn't really understand the map.

"The north of Melbourne is being evacuated," a pretty newscaster said, standing on a smoke-filled lawn in front of a helicopter with spinning blades. "Canberra has declared the situation an emergency and is evacuating all townships north of Melbourne. This morning, the fires trapped a group of one hundred twenty high school students in a runner's camp. . . ."

The picture cut to a crowd of people pushing in front of a ranger standing in a small forest of mics. Behind him, people held up signs: "Jamie call us." "Looking for Sara Busworth." "Kids and Mummy are safe."

"Those poor people," Bev said. "Turn off your screens!" she snapped at the kids in the back. I shut down the news as well.

For a while we drove in silence. Every few hundred feet, army or police vehicles were stationed along the highway. Things were orderly now, almost calm. The sky had changed from the dirty gray to blue, and the air, which even the air conditioner had not been able to filter earlier, no longer tasted of burnt wood. When I opened the window I could feel that it was still very hot, but more like a regular summer day. The kids were asleep in the back. The sudden order was unsettling. I felt jittery, like after an all-nighter on Adderall, but also very tired. My eyes wanted to stay open and fall shut at the same time. Then Bev asked me drive so she could sleep, and I perked up a bit.

We spent the next two days in a motel near the beach. We were lucky. They had blocked the roads back to Melbourne and other people were put up in schools and hospitals, in shipping containers, on army cots. On the news, we watched whole streets in yellow and red flames. The houses billowed thick clouds of dark smoke, and occasionally there were shots of huge structures imploding, with showers of sparks and fumes shooting up. Bev cried a lot.

We were safe. We silently followed the news, or wandered up the road to where a blinking police cruiser blocked access to the highway ramp. We had food, shelter, and information that everyone in Bev's family was safe. There wasn't much to do.

"We're fine," I told Keon on the phone. "Everyone is fine. We're all safe."

"I've been watching the news," he said. "I was really worried."

"It's terrible for everyone else," I said. "They don't know whether their houses are all right, and they're not allowed to return yet."

"But are you okay?" he asked. "Is Bev okay?"

"I'm okay, really," I said. "We're trying to get a flight so she can get home to her kids. And I want to see you."

Lucia had sent a message to ask how I was, and whether my friends were okay. I had planned to be gone for five days, and it was now going on eight.

But Bev's brothers and their families had nowhere to go back to. On Google Earth they had seen only smoke for two days. Then, on a news site, they discovered that one of them had lost his home.

"We'll rebuild," he said, but he did not sound convinced.

"Of course," another brother said.

"Let's be grateful that we got away," the first brother's wife said. "Let's thank God that all we lost are things. We all made it. Mom and Dad made it. If it hadn't been for the police, who knows what would have happened? Just think of those people with their kids in that running camp."

"No one could have known the fires would reach that place," the older brother said. "But you're right that we are the lucky ones."

"Luck doesn't begin to describe it," Bev said. "I cannot even imagine what those parents are going through."

Everyone was silent. The news said that most of the students at the running camp had died when their vans were engulfed by flames after the camp leaders made a wrong turn on a road to the highway.

The lucky country, I remember thinking. *The country that knows how to live with nature.* I had never heard this innocuous phrase about Australia in that way before, as a taunt, as tempting fate. It was devastating to see what happened to Bev's family and everyone in Oz. They had been yanked from their dream so violently.

Finally, Keon was able to book Bev and me on a flight via Bangkok and Seoul, leaving from a small airport halfway to Adelaide. I waited in the car while Bev said goodbye to her family. Some of the roads were open again, and her brothers and sister-in-law were returning to stay with relatives closer to Melbourne. I looked at them, tall and strong people now bowed down after a disaster struck their homes. They gathered around their cars with all of their possessions packed in the boot or on the roofs. "We are fortunate," Bev's sister had cut off one of her kids who complained about missing something. "We have each other."

In the airport in Seoul, while we waited for our third connecting flight, I watched Lucia on the news while she announced the US aid package for Australia. We were about to board when she appeared next to the Australian prime minister.

"Our hearts go out to the Australian families who have lost loved ones in the fires near Melbourne," Lucia said. "The United States has dispatched aid to help Australia battle the fires." The Australian prime minister looked small next to Lucia, even though I knew he was on another continent, and on another screen.

Keon picked us up, and we took Bev home.

"I just want to see the kids," she said in response to his questions about her family. "Thank God everyone is fine. Thank God we got out of that house in time."

The kids told us stories about skiing, the food in New Hampshire, getting stuck in a snowdrift on the drive back, that they had missed two days of school. It was cold in D.C., cold and snowy. Unusually cold, and unusually snowy. And absolutely normal. We made sure Bev had everything, and went home. I told Keon about Melbourne, about the New Year's Day barbecue, about the noise used by the police to drive us out of the house.

I took a shower, slept for a few hours, had one of Keon's shakes, and went to work.

At the White House, they were debating whether a visit to Australia would be appropriate for Lucia.

"Lunt still has not asked for it," Domineek said. "We have no intention of imposing ourselves, especially now that we have offered aid, and Canberra has still not extended an invitation."

By the time we reached a decision, a trip had become moot.

I have the article from *The Sydney Morning Herald* on my tablet, "Lunt Fiddled While Melbourne Burned." Looking at it now, I realize that this was the moment Australia swung the other way — from the swagger of being the "lucky country," to what they are today: steadfast partners in our environmental projects.

The Sydney Morning Herald

Lunt Fiddled While Melbourne Burned

January 3, 2022
Nicholas Mincher

The family of Rowan Bell still cannot grasp that their 16-year old son, a star athlete on his high school's track team and a chess champion, died along with 116 other schoolchildren when the fires cut off their training camp's escape route back to Melbourne. But in classified communications obtained by the *Herald*, the national government had refused several appeals by local authorities for military assistance during the fires. That decision may have cost the 117 children and 14 teachers their lives.

"Prime Minister Lunt's government failed to recognize the danger posed by bushfires for years. The tragic events of last weekend are a result of reckless overdevelopment, the gutting of the forestry department, and Lunt's failure to see the extent of his policies' impact on our environment," said Susie Lanser, leader of the opposition Green Party.

"We are devastated by the loss of lives in Melbourne and are investigating failures in the response," Tom Whittle, a government spokesperson, said.

"We don't blame the firefighters," Rowan's mother, Gayatri Bell, said. "But our son died because the government let natural forests be managed by timber companies, and then didn't send military help fast enough when the fire started."

The Green Party has argued for years that unchecked development and timber plantations have increased the risk of uncontrollable fires. The Lunt administration has defended its decision not to declare a regional emergency until Sunday, when roads to the student track camp were already impassable.

"They played politics with the governor of Queensland [Green Party member] Nat 'Jerry' Trane. They tried to prove that Jerry's low-impact development plan was unnecessary, and that fires were just another seasonal occurrence," said Rowan's father, Luke Bell, an engineer from Malvern. "If we had listened to the Green Party's warnings over the past few years, maybe our son would still be alive."

The Sydney Morning Herald

Lunt Not Welcome at Students' Memorial

January 4, 2022
Bella Sands

Prime Minister Andrew Lunt planned to attend a memorial service held at St. Patrick's Cathedral in Melbourne Tuesday, but was not welcome. When the prime minister's official vehicle pulled up outside of the cathedral, a group of protesters rushed his car waving signs that said: "Burn in Hell," "Your Policies Our Doom," and "Failure to Respond." The last refers to a radio message intercepted by the *Herald* during last weekend's fires in which a Lunt official instructed military officers not to elevate the warning level to that of a regional emergency. A group of parents with yellow-and-blue armbands to commemorate the students locked arms, forcing Lunt to returns to his car.

"We grieve with the families of the students of Camp Ansas," a visibly shaken prime minister said to reporters at the Melbourne Airport before flying back to Canberra. "We will do anything we can to fix the system that failed them during these terrible fires."

The incident was an embarrassing setback for Lunt in his effort to regain the public's trust after several dismissals of the fires' seriousness when they first broke out.

Bev

Tonight, after dinner and the check-up, I was too tired to look at more stuff on the tablet. I turned on the holo-fire, and am thinking about Bev. She's always indulged my political rambling, bought a ticket for every fundraiser for green NGO's, always had my back. She had encouraged me to speak directly to Lucia about my job, right after we had won and when there was a mad scramble to get a post in the administration. That conversation is probably the only reason I ended up at the White House.

After the Melbourne fires, Bev and I had our first and only real disagreement. We've made up, and things are pretty much back to normal. But it was a fight, and it hurt.

Right after our return from Melbourne, Bev went full-on locavore, ate raw, lost quite a bit of weight. No more meat. She gave away a lot of things, got rid of the car, replaced her appliances, paid her carbon tax for every airline ticket. She started using electricity only in the rooms she actually was in, so, even during dinner parties her house became a shadowy maze except for the dining room and a part of the foyer lit by a few bulbs. She kept the air conditioner, but mostly so the remaining furniture wouldn't get damaged with the temperature changes, and it often felt a good ten degrees above anyone's comfort zone. Cut her hair short. *Very* short. Nunnishly short. It seemed that she had realized on a whole other level what I had been working on for years, and we connected even more. After the Melbourne bushfires, she made the environment the central issue of her life. But maybe all that activity was a kind of penance to make up for the fact that she couldn't be in Australia to help her brothers and sisters rebuild their lives. To pay for the fact that she had escaped.

The Melbourne fires had been a terrible coincidence of strong winds, a long, dry winter into October, and then blazing heat for all of December. Land management had something to do with it, of course, but in the way engineers who design a highway are responsible for a pileup during heavy fog.

When we had landed in Dulles none of this was clear yet.

"Aleks, good to have you back," Lucia said when I saw her. "You're okay? Your friend's family, okay?"

I nodded.

She turned to Domineek. "I want to keep a close watch on the prime minister."

While Bev and I had been flying over the clouds above Australia and Asia and the Pacific and Canada and finally Washington, Lucia had put her arm around the Aussie prime minister in the satellite meet-up that I had caught in Seoul. By the time we had landed, Australian media had already turned against him. The families of the teenagers who had died in the runner's camp, including one half-American girl, had started a campaign about his failure to respond in time to the fires. A big scandal.

People in Washington were divided.

"He's a reliable ally for trade and military," the Asia Desk at State insisted, urging the White House to show more support for the Aussie prime minister.

On the other side was Australia's Green Party leader, Sudeera Mits. She and Lucia had been at Oxford together, long before they entered politics. Sudeera was not pleased that Lucia had expressed support for the prime minister.

"PM is opposed to all we fight for," Mits messaged to Lucia.

"Australian public is outraged by PM's refusal to take fires seriously until too late for our children."

Then Mits took that message public.

"They are exploiting this tragedy to gain traction for the environmental cause," Lucia said while we followed Mits's attack on her prime minister.

"We're getting a lot of pressure to condemn the Aussie government's actions," Domineek reported to Lucia. "Polls are showing that 80 percent say the Aussie government and their refusal to adopt green policies is to blame for the deaths of these kids."

"There is no connection between the fires and any policies they could have adopted," Seth said. I wanted to correct him and point out that Australia had not implemented some measures recommended to everyone by forest experts, but Domineek jumped in.

"What I know is that something terrible happened, and that an American mother has been on every web show for the last three days with footage from the camp where her daughter died."

"The mother is gonna be on *Minute with Michelle* tomorrow," Seth said.

"What is Michelle's position?" Lucia asked.

"Mrs. Obama said she will not discuss politics," Domineek said. "But I'm still worried that the public will link Australia's prime minister — "

Lucia cut her off. "Get me on media with the Aussie prime minister tonight. Does that work, Aleks? Timewise, I mean?"

I had become the expert on Australia.

"Yes, it will work, Madam President," I said. "It'll be mid-morning in Canberra when it's evening for us here."

"Keep the mother on *Minute with Michelle*, obviously," Lucia said to Domineek. "And I want a full brief on the major issues we have with Australia in an hour."

I trailed Domineek to her office to try to be part of the group that would prepare the briefing.

"Don't worry, Aleks," she said. "We'll put the environment as our number-one issue. You should go get some sleep!" Then she shut the door.

I watched Lucia's conference with the Australian prime minister from home. I'd fallen asleep on the couch while Keon and Bev had put some food in the steamer. They woke me up to see the meeting.

Lucia first expressed her condolences for the families who lost children in the fires and to the people who had lost their homes. I glanced at Bev, but she was just watching attentively.

"America and HEPP are committed to the pressing issues of our era: clean and safe water, safe food, our forests, and the environment. We especially worry about things that will affect our children — those most vulnerable to changes in the environment. Children who trust us to take care of the planet. They cannot be asked to pay for the crimes we commit today due to shortsightedness and greed."

The Aussie prime minister winced as if Lucia had punched him in the nose.

"That poor guy," Keon said. "Did he think she was gonna help him?"

Lucia went on. She all but blamed the teenagers' deaths on local policies. By the end of the conference, the prime minister had accepted Lucia's invitation to join the APEC Climate Summit in New Zealand. He'd also agreed to rethink water policies, put mining regulation up for vote in Parliament, put in "fire prevention measures," and "use Australia's riches to secure the lucky country's future."

"How can she tell him what to do in his own government?" Bev turned to me and put the screen on mute. "What the hell? Why would Lucia treat Lunt like that after what we've gone through? Is she running Australia now? Aleks?"

"I didn't draft those remarks, Bev. All I know is that the White House is concerned because the American mother who lost her daughter is blaming the Australian government. So Lucia wanted to go on the air with him directly."

"You're exploiting this to force Australia into compliance with your rules." Bev stood up. "I'm sorry to say it, Aleks, but it's disgusting. This, right after her perfunctory condolences."

"Bev, Bev," Keon said. "Yes, they are playing politics. But Jackson is forcing Australia to do the right thing. I'm sure she feels terrible: she has kids herself. But a lot of people think that the fires got so bad because Australia has been ignoring basic forestry rules for too long."

"Let's eat," I said. "I don't think it's good for us to watch this stuff right now."

"I'm sorry, Aleks," Bev said. "But I have to go. You were there. You know what happened. I can't believe Jackson is turning this into a political move."

"Bev, please stay," Keon said.

"I'll be fine," Bev said. "But I'll go. Let's do something when this is over. I just can't watch the American president treat Australia like that."

"You guys will be all right," Keon said, emphasizing the last words. "This is all very upsetting, and Bev has a point."

"Bev," I said, "I didn't know . . ."

"I'll walk you home," Keon said, and caught up with Bev at the door.

"I . . ."

"Aleks does not set international policies," he said to Bev. "He's as surprised as you are."

I kissed Bev good-bye, and then just sat and stared at the mute screen. The news had moved on already, and there was something about the United States limiting imports of gas-powered cars.

"She'll be fine," Keon said when he returned. "But she is offended how Lucia is using the tragedy for political ends."

"It's to force Australia to do the right thing."

"Aleks! Aleks! This is what got Bev so upset. You need to stop for a moment and not see everything in political terms. She is traumatized. You were there! A lot of people died."

"You're right."

"And you need to make it clear to her that you can't influence Lucia's statements the way people think." He looked at me.

"I don't do that!" I said defensively. "I told Bev I didn't know about the statement!"

"But you come off as if you're part of every decision, sweetheart," Keon said. "It's . . . Just make sure you talk to Bev and tell her that you agree with her, that the United States should not influence Australian politics."

I didn't see Bev for a few days. We messaged, "are you ok?" "yes, fine, just need a bit of time, busy with the kids." We both needed space. I thought about what Keon had said. I hadn't been involved in Lucia's decisions – way above my pay grade – but when I was completely honest with myself, I also thought that Lucia had been right. This was a moment of bringing Australia into the fold. And if the fires were the reason to do it, so be it. At least something good would have come out of that tragedy. I tried hard to see Bev's point of view.

"Bev is your best friend, Aleks," Keon said. "You don't have to toe some party line with her. You need to tell her that you understand her anger, and that you're sorry that Lucia made this move. And you don't need to add that you think it has some political merit, which, honestly, isn't even clear to me."

Domineek showed me a copy of the briefing about Australia. "Make sure that the Aussie Green Party knows about this before we release it," she said.

Mits reacted with fury when we got her on the call.

"How can Jackson go online with Lunt? He's gotten a boost like you won't believe from what looks like an endorsement by her!" she screamed.

The Aussie Green Party had hoped for what happened for us with Canada: a public outcry over the government's mishandling of an environmental issue, which would bring down the prime minister. Mits practically jumped through the screen.

"He's been denying the environmental costs of his policies for years!" she exclaimed in her sharp accent. "And now Lucia is handing him the chance at redemption!"

"The president's policy is not to take sides on domestic issues, but to focus on challenges that affect the greater region," I explained.

"Tell Lucia that her actions look like support to Lunt over here," Mits said.

"Fucking wankers," Bev said when we finally met for coffee.

"I'm really sorry," I said. "I had nothing to do with that statement, and I understand why you're upset."

For a bit we just sat and had our coffees. I then told Bev, cautiously, about the Green Party's attempt to get Lucia to criticize Lunt and endorse them instead.

"The Green Party wouldn't even know how to put out a bonfire," Bev spat out. "My brother hates that woman, the one who's friends with Lucia. She doesn't know how to run anything. Lunt's an asshole, but he didn't start those fires. It's despicable how everyone's using a tragedy for political gain. I don't know how you do it." She shook her head and looked out into the street.

"I see your point. But at the White House, they see this as an opportunity to change things for the better in Australia. Lucia sees a chance here to get Australia to join our fight."

"It's just so . . . distasteful," Bev said. "I guess it's for the right cause. At least you must believe that. I just know that I couldn't do it."

Five days later Australia had a new prime minster. His party had staged a coup and put the person he'd mentored in place. It wasn't Mits, but Lunt was gone.

My real worry was Bev.

"Let's put this behind us, Aleks," she said when I saw her next.

"It leaves a bad taste in my mouth, the fact that the American president basically helped to get the Aussie prime minister out of office. I believe you when you say you didn't know about it, and I know it's not your job to make those decisions. But I'd rather not talk about it again."

I wanted to remind Bev that this was for the greater good, that she herself had never liked Lunt. The environmental regulations ready to be signed were more important than any single country's concerns, and Australia, with its vast coastline, simply had to accept rules written for everyone.

"Don't!" Keon had warned me. "Don't lecture her. It's her country; she surely knows more about it than you do. And it's still a political outrage for Australians, the idea that Jackson's statements brought down their prime minister."

I didn't mention it, and after we finished our coffees, Bev and I hugged, and I could feel that we had made up.

At the APEC meeting in Auckland, Australia signed every agreement put in front of them. Lunt's party went insane and blamed the United States for advancing China's interests in the region. Lucia declined to answer any question to that effect. She made a point of being seated with the new Aussie prime minister to one side, and China's leaders on the other. She also invited the grieving mother to the White House, and Asturias made sure their "private meeting" was leaked.

Unless something has changed in the last three days, the Oval Office is still, effectively, shaping Australian policy.

The Associated Press

Dame Zaha Hadid Posthumously Wins Competition to Design "Life-Pods" for Quarantine

May 29, 2021, 8:03AM EST

Quarantine Pod to Go into Production with IKEA on Monday

The late Dame Zaha Hadid, the celebrated architect and designer of iconic museum buildings, sports stadiums, and luxury high-rises around the world, was posthumously honored in a windowless conference room inside the Pentagon as the winner of HEPP's design competition for a portable quarantine ward. The shell-shaped, lightweight, fiberglass design can accommodate individual patients placed under quarantine for dangerous communicable diseases with pandemic potential (DCDPP's), such as Ebola, H1N1, or the recently identified Petrier flu strain.

Hadid's collapsible design can be mass-produced and easily transported to disease hotspots. In an unusual collaboration of the blue-chip architect and IKEA, the global furniture giant, the "Hadid Pod" has already entered production, and the first 20,000 units were shipped to Bangladesh earlier this year. The pod is "designed to protect both the patient under observation, the medical teams, and the population at large. It creates an in-between space that maximizes a potential carrier's comfort but allows for the medical observation and care needed to protect everyone."

The pod resembles a large seed-pod or undulating egg, with several protrusions and concealed hatches to permit patient care.

"We designed this critical space to be life-affirming and nurturing, while accommodating the medical teams' and greater population's needs for complete protection from infectious disease," explained Sopher Ashton from Team Hadid.

The design competition attracted worldwide attention after an outcry stopped the use of military-issued quarantine tents in parts of Southeast Asia. They had been nicknamed "death tents" by the public after a slew of medical personnel fell ill.

Hadid's firm has announced that its design and consulting services will be donated to HEPP. IKEA has agreed to produce the first 200,000 of the curvaceous pods as a donation to HEPP, and produce more pods as needed at cost.

"Most hospital designs privilege function over form," Team Hadid said in a statement on their web feed. "Research shows that life-affirming design improves health outcomes, and that people fare better during quarantine in organically inspired spaces with no sharp edges or angles. The pod is an entry into life."

HEPP officials did not release information on policies of usage for the pod. It is assumed that patients under observation will be sealed into the pod for the full duration of the quarantine period, with medical personnel servicing through air-lock hatches.

Elephants

A tiny parade of engraved elephants marches along the edge of my tablet. They're hardly visible but I can feel them. They signal that the tablet is expensive and nearly indestructible, which is why it's still working after they dumped it into disinfectant when I was checked in. I run my fingers over the elephants, touching the small ridges in the smooth, cool metal like they're signs of life. It's pretty ironic that Apple added an elephant icon to its top-shelf products after they were sold to a Chinese company.

There's Lucia's speech in Johannesburg after they had determined that the population of wild elephants in sub-Saharan Africa had fallen below sustainable levels. There were quite a few world leaders, most of them African, and a phalanx of media.

"This is not a tragedy," Lucia said. "This is a man-made catastrophe, and an indictment of all of us as willfully blind. We knew about the dodo, the passenger pigeon, the Cape lion, the black rhino. We have studied extinctions and vowed to save the elephants from that fate. We have known about the danger to elephants since I was a child. We have known that our love for ivory meant death for one of the most majestic species on earth, that our infatuation with trinkets and fast money would be the doom of the greatest mammal to walk the planet. This is not the fault of one country, not one people's mistake. This is not an African story. We are all, all of us on this planet, to blame."

I pull up the graphics of the elephant population's decline, and clips where Chelsea Clinton, with Lotte and Aidan in tow, and Prince Harry plead with the world to ban the ivory trade to ensure the survival of a genetically diverse elephant population. But it's tedious. The ban on ivory in China didn't work, since ivory carving had been practiced for centuries as an art form as sophisticated as violin-making in Europe. We couldn't stop poaching in Africa, where two tusks could pay a kid's school fees for several years, and where small farmers experienced elephants, if they were so unlucky as to encounter one or even several, as very destructive, dangerous, and sometimes deadly beasts. Everyone tried to change that situation, end ivory trade, empower local communities to benefit from the presence of wild elephants.

"This is not an African story," Lucia repeated at the UN General Assembly. "One continent or nation cannot ensure their survival. We all need to save them."

While everyone put in resources to fund an armed, agile anti-poaching task force, the elephants were dying. Being slaughtered, to be precise. People came together. They showed goodwill, learned to change their ways, saw the greater good. But elephants reproduce at a slower rate than people. Sometimes, simple stories are like that. All the right ingredients for it to end well, except for a kernel of selfishness that sprouts into a noxious weed. The uneasy feeling I can't shake? That all of the good intentions, all of that obsessive focus on the plight of the last elephants, all of the media hoopla made the weed grow.

There are clips of Chelsea and Prince Harry at their global task force meetings, where they devised a plan to pay ivory offsets to a range of African countries with Chinese and US funds. There are clips of Yao Ming, in his trademark robes, before a temple surrounded by devout disciples, expounding on the folly of ivory.

There is a clip of Yu Fe, who has nearly a billion followers, speaking out against ivory, and of Capetown Cubed at a charity concert in Hyde Park playing funk-me to motivate millions around the globe.

At the Beijing Earth Day concert, Mei Mei donned a giant coat made of panda fur to make her point. Shrieks of horror from the thousands of fans nearly drowned her out when the Jumbotron behind her showed two people skin a giant panda tied to a large metal table. Mei Mei finished her song, twirled in her coat like a princess at the ball, and then spoke with the audience. She compared wearing this panda coat to putting an ivory trinket in your home. Meanwhile, on the screen behind her, a panda cub tried to crawl away while a man smacked it almost casually with a huge metal spade. When the little panda stopped moving, the man hurled its limp body on a truck.

"Just as they shoot elephants for ivory," Mei Mei said when the next clip showed an elephant lying in its blood with the tusks removed. The images flickered on her huge black-and-white coat. Her coat was fake, of course, as were the clips of clubbing pandas. Mei Mei made that clear. But the shots of the elephants were real, and she made that clear to her countless devoted fans, as well.

When the elephant population dropped to near-extinction level, a few African nations instituted the death penalty on anyone who killed an elephant for tusks, just like the killing of a giant panda leads to a poacher's execution in China. But almost hourly, you could pull up fresh clips of elephants somewhere in the Namibian savannah or the jungles of Gabon, laying on their side, with the tusks gouged out along with parts of the head. And no poacher in sight.

Prince Harry and Chelsea, Yao Ming, Mei Mei in her coat. Yu Fe and Capetown Cubed. President Lucia Jackson and the US Departments of Wildlife Protection and of State, the UN Species Survival Commission, the politburo in Beijing. The Pan-African Congress, and its special Task Force chaired by the Prime Ministers of South Africa, Namibia, and Kenya. Courageous wardens and customs and port officials from Somalia to Ghana who risked their lives to catch smugglers. Millions around the world who donated to rescue and protection efforts, tipped the police off about ivory sales, and lobbied their governments. So many worked so hard to put the right things in place. But while people's awareness, commitment, and actions inched up, the timeline of the elephants, when graphed on paper, was pointing down as if pulled by gravity.

Keon introduced me to a media feed where your avatar was a real flesh-and-blood game warden wearing a couple of bodycams. We followed a professional who fought poachers with a very serious gun, high-tech equipment, and the right to shoot. Like millions of others, we paid money to see exactly what our warden saw.

Sometimes we spent a bit of money to live chat with the warden and find out about tracking elephants, checking for signs of poachers, how to protect the pachyderms. Keon had been introduced to the game by his brigade. It became really big as a subscription for elementary schools, where savannah elephants became nearly as popular as dinosaurs had been when I was little. The cameras go dark when the warden removes his gun from the holster. But people can hack the system for a live feed of shoot-outs between poachers and wardens. That's the reason, rather than the school subscriptions, why the game makes real money.

"The elephants are our chance to focus on the bigger picture," Lucia said on clips that played when you logged on. "The elephants remind us that life is greater than our daily concerns: that it is majestic, beautiful, and yet fragile in the extreme. The elephants remind us that we can and must work together for change."

Elephants were going to survive in game parks in Gabon, behind the EcoSafe fences in South Africa and Zimbabwe, and of course in zoos. There were going to be breeding programs in place from Sydney to Seattle, some stocked with elephants only recently liberated from their dreary lives in a circus, and databanks to keep those zoo populations diverse. But there was not enough of a genetically diverse population in the wild to sustain itself.

“This is Africa’s century,” Lucia said many times. “This is the century of Africa’s growth,” and she pointed at the peaceful political transitions in the ten sub-Saharan nations that made up 80 percent of economic growth on the continent.

There were breeding programs around the world, and China had made much progress in this area. But none of these efforts would restore elephants to the wild.

“Why are we on this planet?” Lucia asked during the UN General Assembly. “What are we meant to do? These majestic animals are one of the answers staring us in the face. We are here to restore the balance to live as one species among many, and to suppress our worst instincts so that we may live as one with the planet. The problem regarding elephants is our chance to get it right.”

Progress washed over Africa, like a powerful tide that ultimately lifted everyone. Students went to school: young people became doctors, programmers, nurses, teachers, pharmacists, businessmen, bankers, lawyers, engineers. People had enough to lift their gaze beyond their daily needs, and took advantage of education and solid institutions. But progress also brought more trucks for poachers, more guns, more GPS tracking of big game, more gadgets and distractions. Progress brought more wine, women, and song, and the need to pay for that. It was progress all right — more money, better infrastructure, education and healthcare. There were even high-quality artificial substitutes for ivory made from seashells that could not be told apart from the real thing by touch or sight.

Keon and I followed a massive bull, Mbtembo, in an online program that interfaced with the video game. I told Asturias about the show, excited to draw his attention to something new.

“Aleks, we back that show from the White House,” he said after making sure nobody else was around. “It’s also backed by South Africa. I’m about to recruit the guy who designed the game.” That was Malang Diop, who joined Asturias’s team a while ago.

“I don’t really care all that much for elephants,” Malang said when I asked him about the game. “But I care about fail-proof IT systems for Africa, and this one put us on the map."

When I pulled up the screen shots, I wondered whether having the world's attention was good for the elephants, whether buying airtime with avatar wardens in the parks and watching Mbtembo's every move was good in the end.

The money was as critical as the draconian penalties, the worldwide enforcement of a trade ban, the gradual change of heart of Chinese and Japanese consumers. But all that wasn't enough. By the time anti-poaching policies had been enforced and Chinese consumers had aged out of the market, with younger people opting for watches, travel, and real estate instead of ivory trinkets, there were a good number of elephants left in Namibia and Gabon. But their numbers plunged when even the limited poaching outpaced their ability to reproduce.

"Awareness is a key part of conservation," the South African premier insisted in his clip for the reality show. True enough. But didn't people click on the Mbtembo show because they found some kind of thrill in seeing the "last" elephants? The "last" big herd, the "last" big bull in Tanzania, the "last" in Botswana, in Kenya? Didn't they watch it live because when the last of a species was gone, wasn't that something . . . historic?

When they finally found Mbtembo in a pool of blood, his huge head gashed open and already feasted on by vultures and hyenas, people were distraught. With Mbtembo, a lot of people's capacity for hope died a little bit, too. Online vigils around the world, millions of sites turned dark for days. But I can't shake the feeling that all of this attention on the elephants' fight for survival had sent bad energy. Bad karma. To pay such close attention to any living being only in terms of the fragile divide from its death seems wrong. That kind of awe and fascination of watching an entire species fighting its last, desperate battle against man? It's like hunting, or like the Colosseum, in a way.

There were demonstrations in front of the Chinese embassy in D.C. and the consulates on the West Coast. Lucia issued a strong statement on that immediately, and with unaccustomed force. She was upset, disheartened, enraged.

"We live in a world of salivating thugs who will club everything to death until it's too late," she sighed when she heard about Mbtembo. "But to blame the Chinese? To blame the guys who want to make a living after we got our chess sets, piano keys, and tchotchkes? What, exactly, gives us a pass in this tragedy?"

By the time she went on her livestream, her anger was more controlled.

"Let this great animal whose life filled our hearts with joy fuel action," Lucia said into the feed. "Let our knowledge of him and our grief over his death, turn into a strategy for change."

"Ivory prices through the roof," Seth whispered on the way out of the briefing room. "We will flood the markets with artificial." I stayed at work that day, preparing more media bits for Lucia.

"There is a rally at the zoo," Keon messaged later. "My whole brigade is going, even the Republicans. You should try to come." But I could not leave and followed the rally via Keon's camera.

I run my fingers along the troop of engraved elephants on the tablet.

My fingertip hovers above the icon of Mbtembo and the great elephant rumbles toward me, big ears flapping, eyes alert, and his amazing, fatal tusks slicing the air before him as if trying to keep the future at bay.

Mbtembo

I must have dozed off. I'm on the floor, my back pressed against the ridges. The ceiling is off-white and curved. The inside of a giant egg. Or a belly. I move my head to the left. I see Mbtembo rumbling toward me. He approaches, a hulking presence knocking trees and bushes out of the way, like a train that's jumped its tracks. Mbtembo advances as if drawn toward me by force.

He is all swaying movement, all mass. He plants his massive feet and forges toward what lies out of his sight, in the bushes, in the space where the cameras will track him. Where there is a potential threat. He rushes forward, ears out, picking up sounds from the place where a drone camera has zoomed back to keep his mass in the center of my screen. He raises his trunk to pick out the foul stench of a lion, the fumes of a jeep, the rank sweat of man.

The video loops back and the wall is filled again with Mbtembo's massive forehead and the two black eyes, his trunk swaying side to side between white tusks. Strong. Nimble. The curved tusks are rich white ivory against Mbtembo's thundering gray and dusty bulk. Two raised sabers leading into battle. The video loops and Mbtembo starts over, ready to charge again into the spot where the cameras were hidden. Where I now lie in wait.

Mbtembo's reality show, although for probably all but a few minutes every day exceedingly boring, caught the attention of millions of viewers, including Keon and me. It ran as the screen saver on our screens as it did on countless tablets at people's workplaces and in airports, transit stations, checkpoints, and hotels.

"I like that it's slow, and I like that Mbtembo is not only strong but also funny," Keon said. He'd spray water at crocodiles that came too close in a watering hole — behavior that experts on the program considered atypical. Or he'd shake a tree until small branches and leaves fell on his head, only to stomp his feet in what looked like annoyance. And then do it again. On the program you could learn more than you ever wanted to know about all things elephant-related. Occasionally they spliced in more exciting material of herd behavior, which probably occurred thousands of miles from where Mbtembo spent his solitary days and nights. He was a loner, a survivor, and a trophy bull whose life was threatened by the glorious tusks that everyone had their eyes on.

"He's a protector," Keon said. "Like a big brother who will look out for you. He's strong; he's stubborn; and he doesn't give a shit about anything."

At his enormous size and age, Mbtembo did not have to fear animals. His bulk and probably his tusks scared off even packs of lions, which, when he encountered any on the livestream, crashed the site for a while due to overwhelming traffic. But his great tusks ultimately put him face-to-face with a crew of masked poachers in a dusty black Jeep wielding AK-47s.

Keon messaged me at work. I was walking into a meeting in the West Wing conference room, and my tablet was just about to go dark.

"M in trouble turn on blocked feed," he wrote. "Can they send help!??"

I searched frantically for a live feed that some hacker had kept open, while the system had shut down the cameras. Finally, I got one, and Mbtembo was on screen.

Lucia was not there yet, and everyone was on their tablets.

"We're staying online," Chiara whispered to me. "It's something with that elephant."

I messaged Keon, but he didn't respond.

"I found a better feed," someone said, and propped a tablet on the table. "There are poachers, but they are sending wardens right now."

Keon still did not respond.

"Are we sending anyone?" someone asked.

"What can we do? Would that be State?"

I stared at the screen. A helicopter hovered above Mbtembo. The bull charged at it, like a great and gracious heavyweight dancing back and forth in the ring. His trunk was high in the air, his tusks jutting out.

"Is help on the way?" Chiara asked loudly.

People looked around but no one responded.

"POTUS," someone said quietly, and Lucia entered. She joined us at the table to look at the screen.

"The wardens are almost there," Asturias said and propped a second tablet up on the table.

"Can u do something??!" Keon messaged.

"Trying," I messaged back.

But there was nothing we could do, not even Pentagon, which can launch drones within seconds from just about anywhere. The poachers were already on Mbtembo, in full view of the whole world. One guy was leaning out of the chopper with a machine gun aimed at the bull. Another one leaned out of the other side and seemed to wave at the camera, a big grin under mirrored sunglasses.

"Fuck them!" That was Lucia.

I watch a loop of Mbtembo running toward that Jeep again and again, his bulky frame and massive head rushing until the wall of my pod is filled with nothing but gray skin.

"He can't die," Keon messaged while we all watched, in shocked silence, the pirate feeds of the great elephant's end.

I cried but tried to be quiet.

"POTUS on camera," flashed on everyone's screen.

I left the conference room and called Keon. He picked up.

I could not speak. I held the phone to my ear and stared at my tablet. They replayed the moment Mbtembo had first crashed to his front knees, then on his side. People in the room had yelled out. They were silent now. Keon and I were also silent on the phone, but we knew we were both staring at the same scene. I could hear Keon draw in a breath then exhale. I took a deep breath. I had to let the air out slowly so I would not sob.

I managed to say, "It's awful."

Then I said, "I'm sorry."

"I'm so sorry, baby."

They caught the poachers, tracked the helicopter. They are still awaiting their trial. But Mbtembo — fearless, magnificent, awesome Mbtembo — is dead.

I remember the Brooklyn elephant Topsy, who was electrocuted around 1900 in Coney Island in front of running cameras to teach the public about the dangers of electric currents. His handler, a drunk, had been forced to attach the wires to Topsy's legs so that he could get his last paycheck. Mbtembo had no trusted handlers who put chains on him to lead him to his death. He had teams of wardens with high-tech guns committed to protecting him. He had the world's attention on his life to teach us something. But it is as if we've learned nothing. With Mbtembo's death, we witnessed our collective failure.

I see his big and long trunk, massive legs, great hulking body, gently flapping ears. His great white ivory tusks. Mbtembo, the elephant.

Was elephant. Is dead.

Is gone.

The New York Times

SCIENCE

In China, Last Ivory Is Sold to the Highest Bidder

By SUMEEN BOSWORTH

Sep. 4, 2021

The entrance to the antiques shop is right next to the parking garage of one of Chongqing's luxury shopping malls, where sales during peak weekends reach upward of $1 billion. It takes some persistent asking and a friend's recommendation for the shopkeeper to unlock a deep metal drawer filled with the store's most expensive items. Wrapped in heavy velvet are 22 large ivory tusks, carved from tip to sanded bottom, where they will be attached to a wooden base. China's ivory ban, as well as the sheer scarcity of it, have been driving up demand for ivory products. The fact that selling and buying ivory is illegal spurs some buyers on. The only wild elephants in Africa are the few herds living in heavily guarded enclosures in South Africa, Namibia, Tanzania, Kenya, and in the forest parks in Gabon. Conservationists estimate that poachers have slaughtered the majority of the elephants outside of the park. The killing of a large African bull by militia poachers was transmitted live on a popular reality media show in August, prompting global outrage.

Yingzhou King, the shop owner offering the 22 tusks, shows little concern for the fate of the elephants in the wild.

"I love elephants, too," he says, as he cradles a tennis-ball sized ivory carving of three tumbling elephants in his hand. "And they will survive in zoos. But people have carved ivory for thousands of years." China has sentenced traders to long prison terms to deter trade, but these efforts, in addition to sharpshooting game rangers, drone camera surveillance, the Turner-financed global enforcement, and a global awareness campaign led by Chelsea Clinton and Prince Harry of England, may come too late for the elephants.

"The surviving herds are too small to reproduce a genetically diverse population," said Priscilla Goh, chair of the elephant task force at the United Nations Environmental Agency. "The elephant will become extinct just like the African rhino, the American bison, the black lion, the river dolphin. A few animals will remain locked up in zoos. They will not survive in the wild."

Outside of the antiques store, shoppers carry bags from luxury brands to chauffeured cars. Across the driveway is a waiting area with rides for children. On the carousel turns a parade of large big-eared plastic elephants clutching their mates' tails with their trunks. The real ivory tusks fetch upward of US $30,000 on the black market, and often more if the carving is considered high quality. The Chinese government, under pressure from the UN and various NGOs, has increased penalties for trade in ivory to reach life sentences for vendors. But there is still brisk trade going on, and the shopkeeper quickly locks the drawer to prepare for more serious buyers when it becomes clear that there will not be a sale. "We are the end point in a process that's started a long time ago," a spokesperson for the Chinese government explains. "Whatever we do here will not affect the fate of elephants in the wild."

Abad and *Samar*

I'm trying not to let Seth get the better of me. Trying not to think about his annoying "Dude, you gotta inflect this thought" remarks, and the way Lucia tolerates his presence even in meetings where non-staff should be excluded. Trying not to actively search for the gimmicks he's hidden in the pod, for my daily dose of dopamine. But there isn't much else to do. Today I found one. It's pretty ingenious. I figured it out by accident. As I kneeled in front of the bed doing my stretches, the pod turned into the inside of a giant cathedral.

It's possibly St. Peter's in Rome, although there is no single point of view from which to identify it easily. Brunelleschi must be spinning in his grave, on a perfectly aligned axis. There's a procession going on with a long train of priests and nuns from around the world. I can't tell whether the procession is very long, or whether the clip loops back to its beginning. I have watched probably a good forty minutes of it, candles flickering, light slowly changing with the angle of the rays streaming through the stained glass, and a successions of priests reciting Latin phrases which are then repeated by the congregation, like a deep echo emanating from the body of the cathedral itself. Sometimes they sing a phrase or two, and not just *Amen*. Beautiful and moving. I have to stay on both knees to keep the show going. If I so much as shift my weight from one leg to the other, the whole cathedral fades out.

Lucia doesn't only have high tolerance for religion; she loves being inside a big church. During the campaign, we visited a lot of megachurches in convention centers, stadiums, and sometimes movie theaters, with preachers from everywhere, though many of them had Southern accents.

"Come join up front, brother," these preachers would say to me during the altar call, with their wide grins and expensive suits that, to me, still looked cheap. Colorful suits, big suits: suits befitting the Second Great Awakening. I knew they would consider a few central ways of my life sinful and wrong, maybe with the exception of the fact that I called Mom every day. My love for Keon: a sin. Each time, I politely lowered my head and declined to join them up front.

For Lucia, it was natural.

Noah, yes, *that* Noah, became a leading figure in the movement. An angry steward of the earth. A misunderstood prophet telling everyone that bad times were coming unless they changed their ways.

"The Lord has given us the planet to cherish and protect, to safeguard and treasure," a minister would intone, and Lucia would respond with "Amen" along with the tens of thousands in the bleachers. After one of the big churches adopted environmentalism as an issue, we had invitations from every pulpit in America.

"God put man in the Garden of Eden, gave him dominion, and asked him to cultivate and save the earth."

The Flood became a symbol for environmental degradation, and the construction of the ark served as the symbol for our responsibility to act now.

"*Abad* and *samar*—provide and protect." I remember the Hebrew that was used in so many of the sermons.

"Creation care," "to worship and obey," "to have dominion."

"We shall bring creation into freedom and the glory of the Lord," some pastor would shout out, and the congregation, including Lucia, would respond: "Glory!"

She always looked radiant. Positively beatific. I lowered my head a bit while the *glories* and the *amens* washed over me. They'd unleash those floods to drown the likes of Keon and me in a nanosecond.

"It's our God-given task to protect and steward this planet He has given to us," a common line would go. "As Christians, we know that Jesus Christ blessed the animals and plants. They are God's creation, and as such deserve our care and protection."

"Do you feel despair at the immensity of our problems?" Lucia would ask these large congregations in an arena outside of Dallas, or Atlanta, or L.A. "Do you think that the fate of our rivers and our forests, our lakes and even the sea, is beyond your control? God has given us the challenge to save the planet so we remember that He is greater than us! Look out at His creation and see this time we live in as a blessing! It is an opportunity given by God for us to join together as one."

"This is not a Godless universe," the megachurch people started every meeting. That was after the short prayer in the conference room where everyone looked down at the floor, and Lucia was probably one of very few folks from Washington who really reflected on what was being said. The rest of us staffers and security — Protestants, Jews, Buddhists, atheists, Catholics, Muslims, a few Mormons, whatever — wondered how she could put up with that, aside from the political advantage that was obvious to all.

"I grew up praying for money, for work, for the car to start in the morning," she told the good people at church. "I grew up with my father's prayers for a good crop, for rainfall that would not come, for hail to stop. I prayed for my mom to get well. And, since I was a little American girl, I prayed also for nice sneakers." The line got a laugh of relief, after the mention of Lucia's mom. "I know that prayer works. I was taught by nuns at school. Now I pray for creation to be saved."

While Lucia spoke, Domineek fervently prayed in the back. She prayed not for redemption but for the tens of thousands of worshipers to check the box next to Lucia's name on election day, and maybe even send a tithe. We went to quite a few churches, especially in Texas and California, during Dust Bowl II. That was before HEPP and Mexico, of course. When big poultry and pork tanked in those states, the megachurches ran retraining programs for farmworkers.

Lucia's affinity for all things spiritual, and her father's religion, surely made a difference. Occasionally, she would attend a church without putting it on the news. We'd keep the camera hovering outside in a parking lot and take her feed offline. Asturias never filled those gaps with canned footage. A blank screen on the feed meant: candidate Jackson, and later President Jackson, is spiritually refueling. Our message was clear and simple. Soon, alongside workshops and prayer meetings on *Saving Your Marriage*, *Pray Away the Debt*, and *Spiritual Support in Tough Times*, there were *Planet Awareness* and *Stewards of the Earth* workshops. The other side blew that one pretty nicely. They said that harvesting from the earth was our God-given right. For people who saw their fields and gardens dry up, their swimming holes disappear, and their meat getting unsafe, that was out of touch. They needed extraordinary help, and they prayed for it. The fact that Lucia prayed alongside them did the trick.

Still Waters

The food is tolerable, but I can't get used to the electrolytes in the water. It tastes slightly salty, like minerals. The fluoride debates had caused my parents to start buying only "true-pure" water, after some studies claimed that fluoride led to memory loss. None of this was proven, but with memory illnesses becoming so pervasive, people got worried. I mostly stuck with "true-pure," at least at home, and bought water even when Keon got filters for all of the faucets in the apartment.

Soon after the election, Lucia had appointed a water czar. She was a wealthy woman from outside of politics, who had managed a huge food conglomerate. Lucia thought that this global experience would help her to manage the water issues with Mexico. But right after her confirmation, a few governors up for reelection decided to push an anti-fluoride campaign, to win points with fifty-plus voters. They blamed federal overreach for "spiking the water," and threatened to cut off water mains with neighboring states unless federal guidelines about what constituted healthy drinking water were tightened. The governors were grandstanding and nobody really believed, initially, that this would become a real issue. But the water czar got dragged into it.

The czar tried to fight the governors' posturing with reason. She appointed a panel of scientists to study the fluoride-leads-to-Alzheimer's claims. Then she quietly encouraged several of the Big Water companies to file injunctions against a bunch of websites that had made that claim. It backfired. People rallied around their webcasters, as they always will, and the debate about their right to report the news gave the claim that fluoride causes memory loss more airtime. Fear is powerful, and it does not always paralyze. Fear can motivate you. So when the water czar tried to reason with fear, and dispel fear with evidence, it all blew up.

Many people had seen a parent or a relative or a neighbor gradually lose their mind. Everyone knew about homes for the elderly where dozens of people walked around aimlessly, like zombies without the cravings, or a really, really sad version of one of those geezer road movies. These kinds of memory loss were weird, inexplicable, scary. Water seemed like a viable culprit — how else to explain the pervasive increase in memory loss? So when the water czar disputed the possibility of the fluoride in water making us sick, people felt as if she were denying the existence of a strange illness. They looked for a theory to hold on to: something to blame and solve before the illness touched them. The czar faced the press daily and even endured Congressional hearings where people brought in confused relatives who suffered from hydro diseases. She resigned a week later. I wonder whether she drinks "true-pure" at home.

Lucia didn't appoint another water czar, but instead assigned State to look at water, and moved the fluoride issue back to Health alone. She blamed the Republicans for blocking her choices of another water czar, but of course they had nothing to do with that appointment. Sometimes it's better in politics not to address an issue. I take another sip of water that I hope isn't laced with more than just electrolytes.

When I look at this spill-proof pitcher full of clear water, I can recount at least one victory. The water czar had to resign because water was one of Lucia's big concerns. The lack thereof, of course, in California and Texas, and the flow of that Texan and Californian water on Mexican strawberry and avocado fields. The water that had seeped into basements, swirled through living rooms and eroded roads on the Atlantic Coast from Jersey all the way down to the Keys. The water that ate much of the coastline of Louisiana, turned forests into salty swamps studded with dead trees. The water that turned the island-dwelling people of Kiribati into climate refugees. The water that had rushed through Yokohama and lifted up ships and warehouses as large as football fields like scraps of Styrofoam bobbing in a pool. The water that washed successive rows of fancy mansions from their fortified plots onto the beaches of Malibu and Santa Barbara, and the water that had licked and lapped around the tip of Manhattan prompting another New York mayor to get religion about the environment and rush to Washington with wet shoes and socks demanding that finally, now that New York real estate had been soaked again, something ought to be done.

In the White House we started calling it BWN, Bad Water News: floods, tsunamis, erosion, displacement, destruction, crime, toxins, droughts. But there's also "Still Waters."

"Still Waters" was the originally classified name for Lucia's project in the Middle East. "He leads me beside still waters," was the quote from Psalms 23 that the previous administration had cited all the time, and Lucia did not want to change it. We had inherited the project, the whole kit and caboodle, from them. Their ideas hadn't been half bad. His administration had set up shell companies to build a network of desalinization plants on the coastline from Egypt to Jordan. All financed by the United States, out of the media's eye, even while fighting continued. It was more advanced technology than anything we had used in HEPP at that point. The water these plants produced was then shipped via pipelines as far away as Sudan and southern Libya.

"Good water yields good politics," our predecessor had liked to say, but most of the data from the project, when we first learned about it in our transition meetings, was so scrambled that we never knew what was part of actual planning and what was fake. I suspect there was a lot more strong-arming involved than they ever admitted. All presidents hand over projects without outlining all the messy details. This keeps the next president clean, in a way, by offering the possibility of plausible deniability. It can also haunt you, of course, since a few months into it, a new administration will be held accountable for everything that had been signed by the previous one.

Lucia appreciated the leverage gained by providing clean water to the region from a system operated by the United States, as a neutral outsider in the middle of fighting. So when it was time to turn on the largest desalinization plant off the shore of Israel, as a neutral outsider she could not appear to support one country over another. Instead of attending the ceremony, she followed Teddy Roosevelt's example when he opened the Panama Canal with a telegram, and opened the pipelines by text message. We all stood around her in the Oval and watched as she texted "insha'Allah" and "behatzlacha" to the head office of the plant. On the monitors we watched water rushing into pipes, and workers cheering.

The plants sit offshore like oil platforms. They have protection from our navy, and the pipelines are guarded around the clock. And so far, it works. For almost a hundred years the Israelis and the Arabs had been fighting. Now, with their water controlled by an international force which is really just an extension of the HEPP, they come to the table twice a year. Israel has made small concessions; so has the Palestinian Authority. Jordan has been critical, and Egypt, and Lebanon. A lot remains unresolved. But with the great drought, when tankers had to bring in water from Europe, they had to face a shared problem. There were mobs who stormed desalinization plants, thinking that water could actually be found there. But once the wells ran dry and even people in Tel Aviv and Haifa depended on water trucks, and desalinization couldn't keep up, everything changed. There is little besides air and water that people really can't do without, pretty quickly. Food you can do without for a long time, and shelter can almost seem a luxury in times of crisis. Not so with water.

People stopped listening to their leaders when there hadn't been running water in weeks. At first there was a lot of finger pointing. "They stole our water!" You could hear on every side. But then people figured out that no one, or maybe everyone, was to blame. Every day's headlines, in webcasts throughout the region, listed the worst drought cases. It didn't hurt that most of the news in the region is owned by a couple of folks in Silicon Valley, who were, by then, fully supportive of our plans. They fanned the panic. Clips of herds of cattle that had to be shot lest they die of thirst, of mobs attacking and turning over water trucks, of people beating one another over a container that inevitably ended up broken on the pavement, with two bloodied fathers aghast at the water they had wanted for their children spilling into the dust.

"Let them run dry," Seth had said after another round of peace talks ended with walkouts. "Let them run completely dry. Let's see how long they can fight one another when their soldiers don't have anything to drink." Sanctions had not worked. One or two or three small wars hadn't worked. The lack of water brought them back to the table.

"With the aid of the United States, it will be possible for the entire region, led by Egypt, Israel, and Jordan, to share in ocean-generated freshwater," Lucia explained. "This water will be produced under HEPP authority and be distributed in co-financed pipelines."

There have been hiccups, of course, setbacks and small spots of corruption. But on the whole, the project has worked. There's been water in the Middle East for over a year now, and as ugly as the fights over holy sites and border areas have remained, the desalinization plants, those high-tech fortresses floating in the sea, have not been touched.

Beijing

I just did an exercise routine I found on the tablet. Lunges, jumps, and upper body stuff for tennis players. I figured out how to make the entire bathroom recede by pushing a button under the showerhead. I can also flip the bed and table up so they are flush against the wall. Enough space for a tennis pro to do the exercises.

I got my heart rate up to 172. That's when the medics banged on the door, made all sorts of signs for me to stop. But they wouldn't enter. I continued to jump around a bit more, just to piss them off.

I don't think I'll see results after a few days, but who knows how many calories they put in the food. Keon would be happy to know I am working out.

"You don't think only with your brain, you know," he often says. And then he laughs. "And not only with your tablet. Not with your dick, either. We think with our entire bodies, and many of our decisions are based on what we physically sense rather than know. With all of our senses, not just the five that we're taught about in school. And that's not just some bullshit new age stuff. That's actual science."

Keon is right. I'm sure he's read up on everything related to my situation. He probably knows the rules of quarantine better than the people in the committees who designed them.

I believe that everything is connected, too. Mind, body, heart, and soul. Sense and mind. Brain and dick. My back. Sometimes, though, I think we are all connected to tablets even when we switch them off. Who has time to work out? Especially in Washington.

While I exercised I was able to clear my head for a bit. I've had a few bad moments today. I banged on the wall for a while, screamed for the medics, yelled for them get me out, or at least online. Nobody responded, and after a while I stopped. But it's hard to turn off my thoughts. I worry about Lucia, about what's going on at the White House, about the briefing in Congress on HEPP, about the carbon trade-off bill, about the storm funds being managed by — whom? Who's covering for me? Probably someone from State or FDA? Maybe the tall Asian girl with the attitude, the one who lectured me once after a briefing on natural negotiation that all shoreline stuff is part of State, since it's national security. Sheila. Yes, probably her. It's probably "Sorry, you're not Madam Secretary" Sheila. That Sheila. I feel powerless, useless. The only thing I'm not worried about is actually being sick. I've been symptom-free for three days.

Of course, things at the White House can go on without me, but there are matters that need my attention.

"You're an advisor, Aleks, remember that," Domineek points out to me regularly. "Lucia wants you around for the environmental stuff, and even if you've been on Air Force One a few times, you're not in Briefings; you don't have full clearance; you don't go to the Situation Room."

Briefings! I know I am not in Briefings, obviously. And I know that I don't have clearance for the Situation Room. But it's actually better to be just an advisor. All these idiots jostling for position around Lucia, feeling important when they brush past you on their way to Briefings, or to the Oval, and all they do is tell Lucia what they think she wants to hear, so they look good.

"Your role is to position me on environmental issues on the global stage," Lucia told me right after the election. "We have a huge team, plus the whole DNC, plus the Chiefs of Staff, to drive the domestic agenda. It's critical that we don't work on environmental issues only as a domestic problem. You're here to keep the environment on every portfolio, domestic and State. And to turn our stance on the environment into a plus, while State sees everything as a potential crisis and a threat."

India remains a huge concern for me, and some of the issues in the Pacific. Plastics, mostly. We have another meeting with India scheduled for later this month. Water in North Africa, of course. The shore projects . . .

Stop!

It does not help anything to worry about what I'm missing. For a few minutes this morning, while working out, I was able to do that. I just focused on the exercise, and could turn off my mind. It's no different than when Lucia is on Nantucket in August or goes on an undisclosed trip, like Rio last year, when everyone slows down and we feed the media canned stories that were taped weeks before.

Focus. Just gather the info on how Lucia fared internationally so we can leverage that in the next campaign. Do what I can right now, locked in this goddamn box, and get my mind from spinning out of control about what's happening outside.

Take stock of Beijing, when Lucia's face became an icon.

An image of Keon interrupts my train of thought. "It's only world politics, baby," he sometimes jokes when we spend hours discussing work stuff. "It's only the future of the planet at stake!" And then he takes the tablet out of my hands and carries it with outstretched arms and slow steps with straight knees, as if he's leading a funeral procession or military parade, into the other room. He drops it ceremoniously on the couch or on a chair. Or on the floor. Ouch. I know better than to go after him and pick it up right then. God, I miss him.

To work, then.

We need to convince voters that all international victories are really victories for America. The biggest challenge had been China, and that's not quite settled yet. American voters have been taught for generations to distrust the Chinese, even if over half of the

American stock market, including most of the retirement accounts, makes its money there. Hell, Americans have been taught that the Chinese are a threat and not to be trusted since the nineteenth century. It became official policy in 1882, and that policy, which the Act was repealed in 1943, technically lasted till 1965. But even after 1965 there's been fearmongering about the Chinese who steal our jobs, pollute the world.

The things people get away with saying about China! As if nobody else in the world had ever burned a lump of coal, built a factory, dumped toxins in a river. As if Europe had not cut down its forests to read the news printed every single day on actual paper, delivered to tens of millions of people each morning for over a century, only to burn that paper afterwards. It's the chopsticks! It's fossil fuels! China's great roaring furnaces! That's what people say who live in houses chilled some 30 degrees below the outside temperature, and drive cars alone to work and back each day. As if Americans didn't still use water-flushing toilets, and as if America had not overfished the oceans, and dumped the sludge from hog farms into wetlands and bayous from Minnesota to Texas.

"The Chinese buy all of our pork!" Uncle Wynn said. "They eat over a million pigs a year!" That was only after he'd given up most meat, like myself, after the Kansas outbreaks. But he had grown up just like me, meat for every meal, big steaks to celebrate big occasions, hot dogs even for kids. Even small kids. Hard to imagine now.

I picture Uncle Wynn, in his air-conditioned living room overlooking the Gulf. "The Chinese hunt whales! And they have engineered monster fruits, and rice, that'll poison us all."

"The Chinese don't hunt whales; we are the leading producers of GMOs, and all of their factories produce things like the tools in your shed," I responded.

"Whatever! They are still creating big problems for us all!"

"He won't listen to you," Aunt Sophia said.

"We can't blame the Chinese for heating up the planet and then buy the stuff they manufacture," I said.

"I buy American-made," Uncle Wynn said.

"We are focused on the voting public," Lucia said in our conversations on China. "That means that we are not focused on rational beings who weigh all the options. Or rather, we are focused on rational beings when they vote, which is in many cases not a rational moment."

"It's a big job to re-educate the American public," Keon says. "All they understand is that China and India are the problem — at least in terms of the environment."

"Americans need to have an enemy, Aleks," Domineek explained to me when we started discussing Lucia's visit to Beijing. "All people need enemies. And it's better for us to have that enemy abroad. Look at Churchill's immense popularity during World War II, when the Brits hated the Nazis. And what happened to him once the Nazis had been defeated? They threw him out of office. When the Soviets were our enemies, we had one of our best runs in history, from Kennedy to Reagan. When the Arabs became our enemy, our economy grew like never before. I don't care whether we hate the Chinese or the Martians. No offense to anyone in particular. It just lets people have something that unifies them as Americans."

"China is our most important ally in changing what's going wrong with the environment," I responded. "We have to work with China if we want to keep our shores clean."

"Good to know, Aleks," Domineek said. "I'm happy Lucia gets along with China. I just want to be sure that you, as her advisor on the environment, understand the *political* environment we live in here, in these United States of America. I need votes in the Senate, and I need to worry about midterms. Without those votes, you can kiss the trees and oceans and your carbon offsets and hydro cars good-bye. You may be able to take over Canada and Mexico, but you cannot occupy the American Senate! If we cozy up to China too much, we're likely to lose seats. And *we* cannot afford that."

"I'll make sure that the Beijing visit looks like a victory for America," I said.

"You do that, Aleks," Domineek said, already turning her attention to her screen. "You better make it look like the president's trip to China is a victory for *us*."

I have a lot of footage from Beijing. Air Force One with the major automakers, Domineek, Commerce, Energy, EPA. A full court press. For the next campaign, that trip needs to become a sound bite, like *Jackson Subdues China.*

US Compels China to Comply.

Maybe that's what we did?

A Victory for American Automakers.

"It helps to have the truth on your side," as Lucia likes to say.

"But it's not essential," Domineek usually adds.

Even before Air Force One had taken off, the Republicans had attacked Lucia for getting in bed with China. The Democrats had criticized her, too, for not pushing hard enough. Nobody trusted Beijing.

"President Jackson lets China off the hook," we heard everywhere on the Hill.

"How can you honor a Chinese company that's known to pollute whole rivers?" One of the senators asked Lucia directly in a planning meeting. The question was aimed at me. "How can we honor a Chinese company that has built automated factories everywhere in Africa, instead of putting people there to work?"

"The UN is giving Apple China its Green Award," I said as if he didn't know that. "The secretary general personally invited President Jackson to give the award on behalf of the UN."

After the meeting, Lucia took me aside. "Both parties disagree with our trip to Beijing. I just love creating consensus. It's such a good feeling to have both parties unite behind one thing," she said.

For a moment, I didn't know whether she was joking.

"This is your moment, Aleks," she continued. "We have a window before midterms. Don't let Domineek or our senators make you crazy with their domestic worries. They are not happy we're going to Beijing. But elections are almost two years away, so there's not a lot of campaigning for another eight months. This is our moment to do something for the planet without costing us votes."

I was summoned by Domineek before I had made it back to my desk.

"Lucia's presence at the Chinese Green Summit is a huge boost to young American voters," I said when I walked into her office. "Over forty percent of them are under thirty and care more about the environment than about education."

"Don't lecture me on our demographics, Aleks," she cut me off.

"I didn't mean to lecture, Domineek," I said quickly. "I'm sorry about that. But this is the moment to capitalize on Beijing's willingness to let the Chinese environmental movement get big. It doesn't threaten them politically, and they see it as a big win in terms of international politics."

"I only care about people who can vote in this country. You may have noticed that POTUS gets elected here, and not in China. So let's hope you're right that this China trip will play well with the base," Domineek said.

A lot of things happened very quickly. The DNC thought we needed a stronger American showing so it wouldn't look like Lucia was doing the Chinese a favor with her visit. There was some discussion about overdoing it, making it look like we were kowtowing to the Chinese. In the end, it was decided that we invite American carmakers along.

SAIC had nearly eclipsed General Motors, Toyota, and Ford as the world's carmaker. While the Americans, Koreans, and Japanese had built up electric and solar, SAIC had rolled out a new generation of hydro cars. It's almost funny to think that at that time people had doubted hydros, as they had once doubted headlights, windshield wipers, or chip-adjusted glasses. *Loud and Dirty,* as one of SAIC's first hydro ads had put it famously, and with bad grammar: "Why Drive Loud, Wasteful and Dirty?"

China hadn't allowed drivers to use their headlights in city traffic until Beijing's mayor visited New York in the 1970s and saw that it's safer to drive with the lights on. But that era, when Americans dominated the auto market, is history now. Today China sets the trends.

Except for VW, in Keon's opinion. "Still the best cars around," he insisted when he leased his baby-blue VW Typhoon last year. "Efficient, smart, and above all, sexy."

"And kind of dishonest," my mom added.

But even the Typhoon has been outsold by SAIC models in Europe and Asia. The American carmakers fought the entry of SAIC into the HEPP market like hell, of course. They demanded tariffs and trade embargoes, and commissioned an avalanche of studies to assert that electric beat hydrogen in green impact numbers and safety, and that all foreign companies cheated on emissions numbers.

"All environmental studies give hydros lower numbers," Lucia explained flatly in a meeting with US automakers in Seattle. "We know that people under forty prefer hydros."

"People under forty don't buy cars anymore," the Ford guy responded.

"Mr. Chairman," Lucia interrupted him. "With all due respect — which does not seem to be something you have in plentiful supply — your focus groups throughout the past administration have been telling you what you want to hear. The studies you have commissioned have said the same thing for decades based on computer models, and without any real-life data to back them up. The fact is that the world is still populated by people, not machines, and those people make individual and often arbitrary choices. I'm a politician; so, I know how arbitrary those choices can be. But when it comes to hydro, consumers are voting with their wallets, and they are right."

The Ford guy stared at Lucia as if she had just insulted his mother.

"I remember something Henry Ford said, and it's something you're surely familiar with," Lucia continued brightly. "My father used to say it a lot when we were little, and I've always taken it to heart. 'Anyone who stops learning is old, whether at twenty or eighty. Anyone who keeps learning stays young.'"

I smiled to myself since I had sent the Ford quote to Lucia just that morning. No one else was smiling.

"Hydro cars sell and perform better," Lucia said. "Green technologies must be shared, and countries must work together to make a change for the better. HEPP will not impose tariffs on a technology that is the most beneficial option for our environment right here in America, and also for the planet. I have no intention in barring a type of car that US consumers want. Competition is healthy!"

Lucia smiled broadly at the executives who had all supported her opponents in the last election.

"I invite you and your esteemed colleagues to accompany me to Beijing for the Global Environmental Summit. In Beijing you will be able to see, firsthand, a great number of hydro consumers who take the environment seriously."

Ouch, I thought.

"Our carmakers are stuck in amber," she pointed out during our postmortem. "China has allowed the environmental movement because it relieves pressure on their political system, and it'll turn Chinese brands into global leaders in the world markets."

"SAIC hydros have reached forty percent market share in Southeast Asia, with 10% ten percent annual growth," I said. For an instant, I thought about Keon's preference for VWs, but added, "And I can say for myself that riding in an SAIC is not only great fun but also the coolest thing around."

"A third of the world's population lives in Asia," Lucia said. "The environmental movement in China is the largest citizens' movement in the world. They have pressured Beijing to adopt strict environmental regulations for all the major industries. SAIC has signed their green pledge, making hydros the top-selling vehicles in the world. That is something we expect to happen here."

We had a few conference calls to plan for the trip to Beijing after our meetings with the auto execs. They were angry that HEPP would not protect their markets here. Lucia pressed on as if unaware of the tension.

"We are going to see a massive display of the movement's strength in Beijing this Saturday," Lucia said on one such call.

"Is it going to be safe to be at this rally?" the head of KIA G.M. asked. She was an impressive woman, in black slacks and a red blouse that had surely been expensive but reminded me of a waitress uniform. "Why are Chinese leaders allowing these crazies to demonstrate?"

"Domineek will take it from here," Lucia said instead of responding.

With a click she ended her participation in the call. I quickly jumped off, too.

Beijing was boiling hot. We spent the first day cooped up in a hotel where a parade of officials was scheduled to meet with Lucia. Practically the entire politburo had wanted their audience with her, one person at a time. I left it to State to sieve through who mattered at the moment. These individual meetings were the price we had to pay for Lucia to address the greatest gathering of young Chinese in a decade. Probably one of the greatest mass events in history, period. While I left Lucia in the care of State, I met with Apple officials, as the major sponsor for the Summit. Their media push was a main reason why I had wanted Lucia to be here.

"With Apple, it's best if they insert our stuff into their streams from their base," Asturias said when we discussed our media strategy. "Apple is tricky about seeding direct messages on their platforms."

"Tricky about hacking, you mean," Chiara said.

"'No hacking at the White House,'" he responded in a deep, mock-serious tone, and they burst out laughing as if they had made a very clever joke.

"Letting Apple do the work means less work for me," Chiara said.

I took both Asturias and Chiara to my meeting with the Apple folks. The Apple rep, named Guotin, was a fairly young, handsome guy with a razor-sharp crew cut. A straight shooter. And one of us. I liked him right away. Four beautiful, tall women in suits hovered near him like pilot fish around a shark.

"President Jackson appeals to younger Asians," Guotin said. "They relate to her environmental message. And what Americans like still shapes the taste of the world. I love the States, but personally, I don't get it." He raised his eyebrows. "In any case, we are pleased to sponsor the Summit with President Jackson as the speaker."

"A third of the world's consumers are Asian," one of the women said. The guy nodded in agreement, and I realized that they weren't assistants after all — they were the real sharks, and he was a tiger shark, at best. "And unlike Americans, Chinese people actually pay attention to what happens elsewhere." She looked at us as if accusing us of a deep failure. "This is why Apple China is sponsoring the Earth Summit as a global event. It's not a national thing but something that will engage Apple's community in one hundred forty countries on our platforms. Because we care what happens anywhere in the world."

She had emphasized the word "we," and there was a brief silence.

"It's a win-win," I said and smiled at everyone, American-style. "President Jackson also believes that environmental work must be done internationally, across borders. And you get her participation in the Summit."

"There can be no logos visible behind the president when she's on full camera," Chiara said. "We also use our own drones, and we control the main feed."

"Of course no logos!" Guotin said. "Apple is a sponsor but this is not a commercial venture. This is not about selling products. This is about global engagement."

I gave him a smile, which he acknowledged.

"They're using us as much as we are using them," Chiara said when we had barely left the room. "Just look at this!"

Outside the hotel windows, traffic was blocked on one of Beijing's multi-lane avenues. As far as we could see there were tall posts ablaze with green flags. There were huge banners with portraits of Lucia and "Welcome President Jackson" in English and Chinese above the road. Apple holograms were slowly spinning atop the flagpoles, which gave the display a festive flair.

"No logos my ass!" Chiara said and pointed at the holograms. "We can't keep the pres-cams locked on POTUS without putting all those little apples on the feed, too."

Thousands of people streamed along the avenue in a single direction, while others sat on small plastic stools, gathered around stalls that sold food and drinks, even flew kites. Many were dressed in matching metallic pastels like those worn by Apple employees around the world. It looked like a Qingming scroll, except metallicized and come to life. The younger people wore white and green metallic face paint. Many people carried puffy silver bags.

"You'll have to keep your drones very close to POTUS, Chiara," Asturias said. "Just don't get them caught in her hair."

Chiara laughed. Once, when Lucia was boarding Marine One, a tiny drone camera had gotten entangled in her hair. You could still find the viral clip of buzzing dark strands that the media had instantly dubbed "News from Inside President Jackson's Head."

"And ask Apple for the frequency of their holos so that we can edit them out," Asturias said.

"Aye, aye, sir," Chiara said, and focused on her tablet.

For a little while we waited in a special room near the hotel lobby with the auto CEOs. They were tense, unsure what to expect. When

Lucia and her detail finally showed up, we were taken to the hotel garage and then driven on golf carts through a long underground tunnel. We climbed up a flight of stairs past security. Finally, we emerged back into daylight. We were on a big glass stage that floated in the middle of Tiananmen Square. An ocean of people extended in all directions and spilled into the streets leading away from the square. Long rows of potted trees sectioned the crowd into a vast star-like pattern centered by the stage.

"No water restrictions here, I guess," Seth said with a grimace. "Look at this! Real plants everywhere!"

"Look how many people are here," I said. "And look at the screens! There must be hundreds of thousands here alone!"

"If you please come here," a Chinese official said while Lucia was taken to another part of the stage.

"Check these out!" One of the CEOs pointed at a series of large silver globes that hovered above the crowds.

"Displays," Guotin said. I hadn't noticed that he had joined our group. "That way everyone can see what's happening here on stage. There are drone cameras above the crowd."

He came over and stood next to me.

The globes pulsed in a shade of pale blue that made them look transparent against the hazy sky.

The crowd grew quiet when the stage changed colors to a deep emerald green. The Chinese premier and Lucia walked to the center, and their faces showed up on the floating globes. The pres-cams hovered next to Lucia's head.

"It is humbling to stand here today, to look out at all of you gathered here, and to speak to you and so many more gathered around the world." Lucia beamed when she spoke and looked out over the crowd. "You are an inspiration! You are what the world needs! You know that what we need is action!"

Only the crowd near the stage looked in our direction. Underneath the globes, the people looked up at where Lucia's face was displayed with eerie clarity.

"Gotta hand it to them for sound," Asturias whispered to me. "There's virtually no echoing."

"We are here today to honor those of you who are changing our world right now." Lucia's voice boomed across the sea of people. "We are here to honor those of you who protect the sanctity of your homeland. We are here to honor those of you who take action, who care about preserving the planet."

The crowd cheered wildly and the screen showed crowds before iconic sites in Paris, Cairo, Rio, Cape Town, Sydney, Mumbai.

"And hello to our friends in Washington." The globes flashed to the Mall where a huge crowd was gathered under a night sky, with the same fluorescent green flags but without Apple's spinning globes.

The crowd in Washington cheered loudly and waved green lightsticks and neon American flags in the air. The crowd before us waved their flags and cheered as well.

"Never before have so many people in every country of the world joined together for one cause. Change is coming."

Washington went wild. For a moment, the crowd in Tiananmen roared back at the Americans on the Mall, and then the globes flashed on large crowds also in San Francisco, in New York's Central Park, in Toronto, and on the Zócalo in Mexico City.

"I have come here today inspired by you!" Lucia called out and raised both arms like a conductor for the grand finale. "I have come here to be guided by you!"

People waved and shouted. The Chinese premier looked on from the side. Behind him, the celebrity speakers were cheering while their faces appeared on the globes.

"Today is a big day," Lucia called out. "Today is the day when we, as governments, commit to actions inspired by you — people who want to preserve and protect the planet."

The globes switched to aerial shots of forests and oceans.

"What is this bullshit?" one of the auto CEOs said when the glass stage beneath us turned to roiling waves. I actually reached for the railing.

The CEO pointed his chin up over the crowd and past the silver balloons. In the air above streamed Chinese characters in red.

The globes displayed the faces of groups of people in identical shirts and caps.

"A healthy planet means clean air, clean water, healthy people. You are teaching everyone to live in harmony."

The red characters boosted Lucia's words as if she was speaking into the sky, and the sky responded.

Now the Chinese premier spoke.

"You have restored the natural shoreline of the Heilongjiang River," it flashed across the sky, in English, while the globes displayed the beaming face of a young woman surrounded by others in green shirts. With shouldered spades, they looked straight out of a Mao-era propaganda poster except for their earpieces and shades. Applause thundered but new figures already flashed up.

"You have turned Shanghai's garbage dumps into a park," declared a ribbon of words carried by the wind. "The garbage from our cities now lights and heats the homes for hundreds of millions!"

The globes showed a large park next to a gleaming white power plant emitting ribbons of white smoke. Those images then switched to rows of sleek apartment towers lining the boulevards of Pudong.

"You have planted a thousand miles of beach grass to fight erosion in Zhejiang and Fuijian Provinces," the premier's next message raced across the sky. Grass swayed on the screens and everywhere on the glass stage.

A young man walked to its center and waved.

"We have reintroduced the small panda into Shaanxi Province."

The crowd cheered wildly at pictures of the red panda. Many of them wore matching shirts and were grouped along the rows of potted trees.

A scene of workers in hard hats with interlocked arms appeared on the round screens. "We restored the shoreline of the port of Tokyo," they called out in Japanese while English and Chinese appeared in the sky around them. There was less applause while people waited for what would come next. "It's the Japanese premier," one of our guys said. "I can't believe he showed up for this!" A man in a suit and tie stepped next to Lucia and the Chinese premier and bowed to the crowd. He raised both arms and congratulated his team in Japanese.

The video zoomed back, and we saw thousands upon thousands of other workers standing on docks amidst towering cranes and machinery, all topped by huge green flags. People were cheering again.

"We developed the hydro," another group of workers declared. "We have built the car that will save the planet!"

The crowd went wild at that, and even the Chinese premier raised one arm.

The flashing characters above, the huge images of workers and activists on the spinning globes and Jumbotrons, and the sounds of crashing waves, wind, birdcalls, and clanking metal drowned out everything but the crowd's cheers.

"Don't tell me they're gonna feature a car ad for SAIC here," one of the CEOs said behind me.

"We didn't come for that," another one added and snorted.

Lucia raised one hand, again looking like a conductor directing a huge orchestra.

"You are the solution that will lead us to the future," she called out. "Solutions are within reach. Apple is leading the way, SAIC is leading the way, but it is you, you above all, who have made this change. It is a great day for the planet."

"How dare she?" one of the auto execs said behind me.

The Chinese premier stepped forward. He wore an open-collared shirt, no tie, and a small green braided flag on his lapel.

"I serve this great nation with humility and gratitude," he said. "I am lucky to have been born Chinese, the son of a country that puts her people at the center. I am lucky to have you, my fellow citizens, to ensure a clean and healthy future for the planet. I am lucky that

China has the world's greatest companies to lead the way."

The CEOs' reaction was delayed by a split second until the Chinese premier's words came up in English in the sky. They groaned.

"You are pointing the way!" the premier called out. Wild cheers. "As the world's leading economy, China is proud to host this Summit."

"This is ridiculous," one of the CEOs said, and twisted his face. "Insulting."

"We're on camera," another one said and flashed a grin. "Let's not make this worse."

"Motherfuckers," another one said through clenched teeth.

The CEOs had grown up in a world where the greatest country was the United States, and all of the world's consumers had wanted a piece of America in their hands, in their homes, on their bodies, and even in their fridge. They were products of the greatest tech generation in history. That had ended when Apple was bought by a Chinese trust.

"I am lucky to lead a nation that has produced Zheng He, who saw that the world is larger than his hometown," the premier continued. "You are the proper heirs of Zheng He's vision. You have come here to secure the planet's future. You have come here to look beyond your daily concerns, beyond your regional worries, and find solutions that benefit us all. Today we listen to you."

The Jumbotrons and globes showed a long dam separating a huge lake from a valley below.

"Sun Yat-sen had a vision for China to harness the power of water to fuel our growth," the premier said.

On the screens, Sun's face gently turned from side to side with a smile to match the Mona Lisa's.

"Is that Mao?" one of the CEOs behind me said. I didn't even respond.

"The Three Gorges Dam has produced more electricity than any other project in the history of mankind," a man on the screen said while his words floated in the sky above.

"But we took this power and created new problems," a woman said.

The picture went back to the Chinese premier.

"This year, we restore the flow of the Yangtze River by twenty percent," he said. "Every year we open the dam a bit more, and in five years the Yangtze River will water the land of the Hubei Province as it had for many thousands of years. Through green technologies, we have reduced our energy needs by forty percent. By reopening Three Gorges, we will reduce the unintended upstream effects of the dam."

The screens showed water rushing from the bottom of the structure into the valley below.

"Isn't this their great energy source?" said one of the Americans behind me in a hushed voice. "How can they just open up this dam again? Isn't that going to flood the region below?"

"The environmental damage and pollution became more expensive than the energy." I was surprised to hear Asturias's soft voice. He almost always kept out of conversations with people he didn't know.

"The Three Gorges Lake has basically become a big stinking cesspool," Asturias continued. "And below the dam, the land has become polluted with artificial fertilizer since the water stopped flooding it each spring. They've lost a huge amount of agriculture. And with automated factories, people have no work. Don't believe that China is opening the dam out of the goodness of their hearts."

As if on cue, Lucia's voice boomed across the square. I glanced at Asturias, but his face was already buried in his tablet. I knew he was making sure that, at this moment, clips of Lucia zoomed across the globe on hundreds of millions of little screens, like blossoms floating off a flowering tree in spring.

"We applaud China for restoring harmony with the planet," Lucia called out. "We all gain more when nature is a partner, a force to align with rather than to exploit. You have opened the floodgates to a brighter future. You have looked beyond the horizon: you see a China and a world that can be better for everyone."

"The Yangtze reopened," I said to myself.

"What the hell is this?" one of the auto execs said. "Why are we applauding the Chinese opening a dam?"

"Because all these people are your customers, and because SAIC has taken ninety percent of your market share in Asia," I responded.

"You saw them celebrate the hydro earlier," another one of the CEOs said. "This Summit is basically a huge marketing push for their vehicles."

"With a worldwide audience," Asturias said. "Estimated feed is over two billion people right now."

"This is far greater than 'the Chinese,'" I added. "The Chinese leaders rely on President Jackson's voice, her face, because the people understand that she really cares about the environment. It's a major chance for the planet. It's probably our last chance to keep some kind of market share."

I turned toward the crowd to hide my flushed face, but there was no response from the CEOs.

"America is proud to join Chinese efforts to help the world," Lucia said only a few feet away from us. But her voice came from everywhere, and her face beamed from countless orbs above us.

"Our car manufacturers will meet green standards around the world," Lucia announced to the world while our small group was splashed on the globes.

I vaguely smiled while I looked at myself and the CEOs appearing on the globes.

"What the hell," one of the CEOs hissed through his smile.

"SAIC has led the world in hydros," Lucia said. "It is time we all adopt those high standards."

"Motherfucker."

"We were not told about this!" he hissed again, when the cameras were back on Lucia. "She's committing us to meeting European standards?"

"Motherfucker," the woman in the fast-food suit repeated.

"That's a matter for Congress," I said. "But we all know that European market share depends entirely on meeting green standards."

"To drag us here without looping us in . . ." the head of KIA G.M. said. "Is this supposed to be a joke?"

I heard the unmistakable opening chords of "Earth Anthem" and looked around to spot Mei Mei Bieber. People were already moving with the music, but Lucia remained on stage. To my great surprise, she took a handheld mic and, with the help of two tall security guys, stepped up on a small platform. And then Lucia spoke, but almost sang the first few words of "Earth Anthem" in a hushed voice. People roared and cheered, and even the Chinese premier moved a bit to the beat. Mei Mei appeared on another platform, and then she sang "Earth Anthem" up to the chorus, when the rest of the celebrities joined them.

I thought I could feel the CEOs behind me gasp, but I didn't turn around. I loved this song, and I was awed.

"What is the timeline on the opening of the Three Gorges Dam?" were Lucia's first words when we got off the stage. "Does this align with HEPP sustainability principles? Will the other APEC leaders be at dinner tonight?"

The CEOs rushed Lucia like college guys at a flag football game. The pres-cams were on, and she smiled and shook hands without uttering a word. The presence of the tiny cameras kept the CEOs in check.

"Make sure we have Japan next to China at tonight's dinner," Lucia whispered to someone from State. "China opening the Three Gorges Dam could prompt Japan to also abandon hydropower. How was the tune-in in Japan?"

"Brought down the servers," Asturias smiled without glancing up from his screen.

"I want to meet the Yangtze River organizers," Lucia said when we passed the security bots.

We walked fast, and Lucia was talking to at least five people at once. In the lobby, the president stopped near a small gathering before her detail could usher her into the elevator. They wore green lapel pins, which identified them as part of some environmental group.

"You are returning the Yangtze to the world!" she addressed the people, and shook hands. "You are an inspiration for all of us who want to reverse course." Her interpreter worked fast, and the people nodded. "By changing our thinking, you are changing the world. The Three Gorges Dam had been the biggest man-made change in the history of China. But your courage, your resilience, your vision have proven to be bigger!"

The activists smiled and clapped, unsure of what to do.

Lucia grabbed one of the presidential cams out of the air.

"This calls for a clip." She beamed and backed into the group of activists. Her detail moved in but she waved them off. The activists squeezed together to fit into the old-fashioned picture that Lucia now took panorama style. Chiara had steered the other drone away to make this moment somewhat unique, except for the lens cameras worn by security, the hotel staff, and probably most of the civilians in the room. Lucia handed the drone to another staffer and laughed.

"I remember standing on the Three Gorges Dam and seeing a lake on one side, drought on the other. Today we embark on a path of harmony."

Dinner that night was a long, boring affair, with speeches and toasts. The auto execs were still fuming.

"Buying a green car empowers people," Lucia explained to them. "It's one of the few personal choices people can make to change the world. Your companies have to serve consumers, or you will lose. That's key to keeping your market in Europe and China. I brought you here to see for yourselves the size of those markets."

"We were blindsided," the Ford CEO said.

"The US government has no intention of forcing you to do anything," Lucia said. "You realize that the message here reaches a good third of the world's population, and probably sixty percent of the world's consumers. We presented you to the world in a favorable light. But we cannot keep SAIC out of America when our citizens want clean cars."

I managed to get a seat at a table with Guotin, away from the CEOs.

Lucia had to stand up every few minutes to acknowledge another toast.

"Some things will never change," she murmured and winked at me when I passed her table later.

"But some things will," she messaged me when we watched a film of the Three Gorges Dam being taken out of commission, with holograms of Sun Yat-sen and Mao Tze Dong next to the current premier on the stage.

Much of the evening was backed by ambient sounds of water rushing; I went to the bathroom at least three times.

On the flight home, Lucia slept in her cabin. The CEOs had settled down a bit after they had their meetings with Chinese trade officials in the morning. They had hatched some deal to combine their American brand with Chinese technology. Asturias's team looked like they had wrestled a bear.

I stared out the window at the vast Russian tundra below. It stretched milky white under the clouds like shredded gauze. Some things had changed in China. The Yangtze River would flow again, and the greatest engineering feat in the history of China would become another relic from the industrial age.

You're Welcome

On my screen saver are clips from Bev's and my trip to Ladakh. Temples, mountains, the old lady with whom Bev traded bags in a dusty village with windows shuttered against the heat, the Rinpoche's Tibetan school where we visited every single grade, from the little kids who all wanted to shake our hands to the teenagers who spoke fluent English but were too self-conscious to use it, while Sareen and Rajiv, who had come along on the trip to have a taste of adventure and not to listen to schoolkids sing to us, waited outside. Many of the clips contain a tiny picture of Lucia. They sold these small icons, held in flimsy shiny frames, in convenience stores alongside photos of the Tibetan leaders, Bollywood stars, and countless gods and saints. We saw them in small temples placed around altars, in restaurants glued to registers, and in quite a few cars dangling from the mirrors. "American? You are American! See there is Lucia Jackson," our driver greeted us at the airport and waved a key ring with at least six pictures of Lucia. Bev chose her to drive us around.

It had been the impact of Beijing. That's when Lucia became a rock star even in countries whose populations had been largely hostile to the United States. After Beijing, she had the name recognition of an athlete or media celebrity. It was mostly women who bought Lucia's picture. They related to her. Women worried about their family's health, women bought the groceries, and women followed the news. Lucia fought for children's health, for food safety, against the big drug companies. Especially in poorer countries women cared that Lucia had lost her husband young. In India I was told that women include Lucia in their prayers for their families, and in parts of Europe people light candles for her at mass.

"People like what other people like," Keon said when I returned from Beijing. "The strange thing about desire is that we often don't really know what we like for ourselves. More often we like something because other people like it, too."

On the flight home from Beijing, Lucia had emerged after a few hours to face the CEOs. They had been chatting and enjoying the edibles on board. They were tired, dozing off. Fatigued. Lucia pounced. "I understand the people in Beijing— the environmental activists you like to refer to as crazies—and you should as well," she said. "You just witnessed a historic moment."

I hit Record on the tablet.

"You are probably aware that I grew up hungry during the drought, working nonstop for harvests. We prayed for rain, but then it was mostly torrential floods that swept through. They tried to tame the weather by seeding clouds. They tried to breed crops that withstand droughts. They tried to subjugate the planet. It was a futile struggle. As you know much of California's water was stolen; the fields dried up. We had been in a war with Mexico, and we didn't know it."

"With all due respect, Madam President," one of the men said. "That's exactly the point with China! They are destroying our industries."

"The point is that we can only succeed by working with China!" Lucia said. "Just as we are working with Mexico now, and not against it. China will not back down unless they have domestic problems. So either we hope for a revolution down here"—Lucia pointed at the window— "or we work with them."

"What do you think working with them will look like?" asked

Terris. “We are ready to enter their market, but their government props up their carmakers. It’s not an even playing field.”

“I believe in free markets,” Lucia said. “I don’t much believe in governments helping anyone to sell things.”

The CEOs stared at her. They were trying to blink away their high, and quickly.

“Our best bet is the Chinese green movement,” Lucia continued. “You have gotten this backwards. The green movement, globally speaking, is your only chance. And the Chinese politburo is scared shitless by this movement.”

Lucia took a glass of champagne from the cart.

“We should toast them! They are our opening into China. The only access we have, since Beijing will have to placate those ‘crazies,’ as you call them, if they start demanding American cars. If you can get a model on the market quick. You get to sell more cars. And in the long run that helps everyone. It helps the planet. That’s the whole point.”

She emptied the flute of champagne and put on her headphones.

“By the way,” she said, pulling one earpiece off. “Since you are so eager to have the government help, I just did. I just fought for you. And you’re welcome.”

The CEOs in the cabin looked chastised, but their buzz kept them from responding. I was impressed with Lucia. She had turned toward China but also put pressure on our carmakers to step it up. Without China, they wouldn’t survive in the long run, but without them, she wouldn’t, either. As much as I hated the expression of a win-win, the trip to Beijing had been it.

Eco Brigades I

On the display it says Saturday morning, though of course there's no change here. Same banging noises, same medical checkup, same gradual change in lighting to make me feel like it's dawn.

Keon must have been up and at it for a few hours already, as on every weekend. He is more serious about his brigade than me. We met at an eco brigade, like everyone else we know, but now we belong to different ones. On Saturdays Keon usually has big projects: digging a canal in some wetland or drainage area, with a Bobcat or a real bulldozer, or helping with actual construction near some river or other. "I love big machines," he says with a wide grin, and sends me clips of him on top of some tractor or truck.

I love to see Keon leave early on Saturdays, bouncing with energy, even though he's wearing heavy work boots and carrying his kit bag of tools, safety helmet, gloves. He's super excited, and I love meeting him afterward, in the afternoon, when he comes back caked in mud, or dripping with sweat, his uniform green and sticky with tree sap, and so very happy.

"Like the National Guard and the church rolled into one," Keon likes to say when he tries to convince me to join his higher-level brigades. "But without the preaching!" The first ones I knew about were kind of alternative, even renegade, mostly college kids with a cause, which we emulated in our high school. They planted empty lots and turned strips of grass in mall parking lots into vegetable beds. Disruptive planting. Edible weeds — "invasive food crops," as we're supposed to say — on the roofs of garages and schools. That kind of stuff. I love going out early and turning the well-groomed, bland strips of land next to a public building or in a private development into a vegetable plot. We worked fast, carefully, and in secret, and often people didn't notice for a few days. We had contacts with contractors who left our beds alone until stuff had taken root. It was all mapped on everyone's tablets by the same team that posted updates on where people could harvest free stuff. But it was well hidden, so they didn't find out until the time lettuce had sprouted, and by then there were people who would actively fight for the plot-turned-garden. Nobody wants to be the neighborhood tough who uproots a garden. It's really bad press. Some kids at schools ran campaigns to shame developers and towns who let land lie fallow. A lot of places now designate part of their open spaces for community planting.

My little gang of seed bombers and stealth planters is a brigade, but it's a bit more renegade that Keon's. Most kids first got involved in community service as a school requirement, but then many stayed with it, since everyone else did it. Where else were you going to meet people? It was as much a social thing as an act of doing good.

The brigades did more than compensate for slashed budgets. They took hold because people got together, got *engaged,* around a shared cause. Colleges started giving credit for brigade work. That shifted it from a voluntary thing for green-minded folks to a matter of pride, and of belonging. Eco travel had been big before, I think. In college, it was the only kind of trip people went on: work brigades to help the world. If you didn't go on some kind of brigade trip, you'd simply miss out. I met my first two boyfriends and my first girlfriend on college brigades, and Keon met his ex-girlfriend there. Most people like to go out and meet up on Saturdays (that's how it started: *Save Saturdays*), or whatever day they have off.

"It makes people feel good," Mom said when she first joined a group of people who organized, first over drinks, later in an office, and finally in city hall, to reduce water consumption and plant native crops in our neighborhood. "It's like what my grandparents had with Tupperware parties and country clubs."

Mom met James there, I think, or she met someone who knew James and brought him along, which changed her life for the better at least in some ways, after she and Dad separated. Me and Keon: what can I say?

Even Uncle Wynn, who hates anything organized by "those foolish hippies," is part of a brigade. He works with a crew of guys with their own uniforms, big trucks, and tools, who go out and fix whatever problem the city doesn't get to.

"I love those guys!" he says, winking at me. "Not the way you love guys, but I love these guys."

"And you get a tax break," Mom said to him when he showed off all of his shiny new equipment in his garage, with the brigade logos on it.

"That's not the point," he said. "The point is that my crew is out there finding the problems, and instead of waiting for some idiot in Washington or Tallahassee to tell us what to do, we just do it! And you can be sure that most of it wouldn't get fixed without us."

"And it lets you ride around in a big truck with your friends all weekend," Aunt Sophia said. "And not pay taxes on the truck."

Other people join simply because they have time and they believe in it. Many of them grew up right after the turn of the millennium, when the country was adrift. Things got bad. Government budgets got slashed and services began to dwindle.

"People were anxious in ways you can't imagine," Keon's grandmother told me once. "A lot of things seemed to spin out of their control, even while new technologies promised to fix a lot of problems."

"We were just sick of seeing problems everywhere without a way of fixing anything," Keon's grandfather had added. "We just went out and *did* stuff. The whole brigade thing, that organizing aspect, came later."

"Church was a big factor for us," Keon's grandmother said. "We knew that we could make a change. And all of our friends were doing it."

"For me, my work organized it," one of their friends said. "My mom had gotten sick, and I really wanted to do something about landfills."

"Landfills," a few people echoed her as if we were in a church. "Ah yes. Landfills."

"Did your brigade really work at landfills?" Keon's grandfather asked.

"We actually did," the woman said. "But then I got involved in shared living arrangements. Lower-impact housing, greening existing buildings. The stuff that started with ride sharing. A lot of outreach and behavior training. I worked for a foundation to set up housing for poor people. Maximizing existing homes rather than building new ones."

"Office brigade," Keon's grandmother said. "Same as me. I couldn't get excited about urban farming, cleaning wetlands, picking up trash, raising chickens. But my brigade changed the way run-off water was used in New Orleans."

"Church and state," Keon's grandfather said. "The unholy alliance. Your brigade sure was the hottest ticket in town."

"Sure *is* the hottest ticket," she said. "Sure is. We have a waiting list for volunteers, and they now have chapters everywhere."

None of the retired people at that dinner talked about their former jobs, or their careers. People described what they were doing now in an eco brigade, who they had met there, what they had been able to achieve. What they were doing today. It ranged from the urban farmers — the kind of people I mostly hung with on Saturdays — to Keon's grandmother's type, whose eco brigade was a political force in New Orleans, a premier social club, and an unspoken must for anyone who wanted to matter in town.

When Keon and I meet on Saturday afternoons for late brunch, after I've worked all morning in one of the smaller urban plots my brigade has set up and maintains, and he jumps out of his brigade truck beaming with pride, full of stories and mud, I am happy. I plant flowers in our lots, though nothing that looks too flashy, too cultivated. Mostly edible, though, to meet out group's requirements: dandelion, hardy kiwi, honeysuckle, hops, sunflowers, nasturtium. We don't harvest all of it, and I sneak in clematis, peonies, and roses. But I mostly like invasive species for urban settings. Where are they going to invade, in any case? Dupont Circle? Break up the concrete side walk? The parking lot?

Japanese honeysuckle, bamboo, variegated kudzus, orange dandelion. I've had a lot of success with a new Japanese hybrid of dandelion, and, with another kid from my brigade, we've seed bombed a lot of spaces especially around schools, where there isn't enough money for regular landscaping, in Maryland. Two weeks later: strips bursting with yellow and orange, like screenshots of the sunset framed by concrete, before they explode in small orbits of feathery seeds that will spread fast.

Bamboo has been a hit. I've planted whole groves where people harvest shoots and cut it for bamboo mats. It's certainly made the place look nicer. Keon's brigade is for the big boys and girls — they drive out to the shoreline and help restore roads to the habitat, with jackhammers and all. Or they construct green shelters for commuters along main bus routes, with planted roofs that my teams then take over.

Keon and I don't have to worry about points, but others do.

"It's not supposed to matter, obviously, but everyone knows that more points with your brigade make you look better," one guy in my group told me. "My brother's kids were accepted to a good preschool because they had so many points."

He is worried. He works in IT and is really good with setting up timed hoses, and keeps track of our plots online.

"They haven't accepted any kid whose parents didn't score at least above forty," his wife explained to me one Saturday while I dug up bamboo runners to plant next to a Dunkin' Donuts down the street.

"We're doing pretty well." She raised her arm to show me her wristband, which showed two points for that month. "And with spring planting we should be fine."

"I'll need some help next week with transplanting the kiwi. And I would love to take more of this bamboo to some other spots," I offered. "If you want me to log you in for all of that, I'm happy to."

"That would be fantastic," she said quickly, in a way that made it obvious she'd been hoping I'd offer. "Thanks so much."

"No worries," I said and turned back to the bamboo. I glanced at my wristband and imagined the points building up.

I can usually get out once or twice a week before work to help my brigade, but we have a lot of projects. So her help is welcome. Some people at work asked me to join their brigades, but I like to keep work and brigade stuff separate. Of course, we run a lot of the White House messaging through the brigades. And obviously Lucia goes out and visits brigades on the weekends, and all the politicians sponsor all sorts of competitions for brigades. But I like the renegade types, the brigades that aren't so slick with sponsors and their live feeds.

"You're a radical at heart," Keon's grandmother would say when people discovered by accident what my brigade has done.

Keon said, "Aleks likes people who fight a cause that others haven't fought yet. And he loves to plant stuff that will take over your house."

It's true that I prefer the disorganized brigades — the eco guerillas that we get upset about in the White House, the ones who start boycotts and sabotage things. I admire their courage, not just their fuck-you attitude toward the police. I admire their courage in being outside of the system, not worried about points or social status.

"How many points do we have?" I sometimes ask Keon, who keeps track of our points online. I never look.

"I'm absolutely certain your points helped me in my job," he claims.

"I doubt it. Why would they care if your partner is in a brigade or not?"

"Because if you weren't, it would just be . . . weird. Like you don't care."

"I care every day at work. But I plant bamboo because I like it, and because it makes me happy. I'm not even sure it does very much to save the planet."

"It makes a difference," Keon says with a grin. "You make a difference."

I miss him a lot right now. I think about how worried he must be, and I hope his brigade is keeping him busy today. I hope that he is out, fixing a huge run-off drainpipe or taking apart old seawalls.

More Than Hippies On the Team

I felt high on the return from China even though I hadn't taken any edibles. I kept quiet, feeling a bit smug about the way we had pressured the American CEOs into coming along to Beijing. We had achieved something huge.

But I also tried listen to what Americans outside the Beltway think about Lucia's global role. Most CEOs, including my traveling companions on that flight, are as average as any other voter, only with a lot more money. For all Americans, Asturias's team was spinning the news, of course. We didn't plant false items, but selected certain moments for what Asturias called "media treatment." Cecily and Victor, who I don't see all that much since he's often doing IT work for Asturias "in the field," whatever that means, picked clips in which Lucia seemed to challenge the Chinese, even if those scenes were from different contexts. They planted those clips on social media of our "mules"—people who had clicked on a political ad of either party in the last year. The mules never got to see what they carried, including their friends' comments. But each time someone responded, the clip migrated from their feed to another equally blind, equally compliant mule.

"It's like viral but invisible," Victor explained to me in his California drawl. "Like, absolutely undetectable to those who carry it. Think of a piece of tape stuck on your back, right between your shoulders. You just can't see it. We get most uptick from Republicans, of course, whose friends think they are posting anti-Lucia stuff. But we've learned that as long as people see items about the president, the content does not matter. You know, Aleks, dude. Nobody reads on social media. People only follow."

I wasn't entirely convinced. The CEOs were not happy with Lucia's performance. "We better find a way to make real Americans care about the planet. People who think that the environment is an issue for hippies and Democrats," said Domineek after I debriefed her on the trip.

Hence, Halo Michelle.

White House Strategy Memo

To: Interested Parties
From: Jeff Ríaz-Beale
Date: November 20, 2020
Re: Demographics of the Environmental Voters

Issue: The past election victory of President-elect Jackson has proven once and for all that environmental justice has become a key voter issue in American politics. The successive devastations of Hurricanes Erika and Fernando, on the eastern Atlantic coast and Washington, D.C., in fall of 2019, not only altered the physical environment of our capital and ravaged miles of shore; they changed voter attitudes about environmental issues. The preelection narrative, that this election was going to be about protecting American interests against foreign takeovers, misses the mark. According to surveys fielded on election nights, conducted by two independent firms, it was equally important that a candidate "prepare the nation for the impact of environmental disasters." The hurricanes did their part in swaying voters, as did a series of contamination scandals around staple foods (E. coli outbreak in Kansas) that especially affected children and the elderly.

But the reach of this issue has not been as deep for a crucial part of the population: voters of Latino or African descent or affiliation. We won the election on environmental issues ultimately because we were strongly backed by white female voters. Given demographic trends and the fact that the environment is the one single issue that unites us all, we need a new strategy to connect an especially critical part of our base, black and Latino voters, with the most critical issue of our and our children's lifetime.

Proposal: I believe we need a new approach to winning over votes on the environmental platform. This approach involves shifting away from the alarmist, moralistic, and condescending rhetoric of the Green Party and including voters in all socioeconomic groups as potential solutions to the problem. We need to run a campaign that presents the bigger picture not as an overwhelming threat but as a cause that unites us all. We need to link everyday voter issues with the environmental movement.

Key Strategy: This issue of making environmental issues resonate with the majority of voters, i.e., people of black, Latino, and Asian ancestry or affiliation, is of critical importance for the success of our candidate. I propose including Michelle Obama, the grande dame of the movement, as our key spokesperson and strategist. Mrs. Obama's unrivaled popularity, her stellar role promoting health-conscious eating, and last but not least the ubiquity of her halo-of-hair silhouette as a sign of environmental awareness makes her an indispensable ally. In extensive voter surveys, we have found Mrs. Obama to rank higher in respect and likeability than any incumbent or former politician or candidate. Given that Mrs. Obama has never run for office and will not do so in our campaign, her support will give us much needed neutral lift.

Key Points and Takeaways:

1. The federal government's second and third-highest expenditures after Homeland Security are shore and storm

protection, and water management. We need to convince Congress and voters that "Restore the Shore," "Controlled Collapse," and "Natural Negotiation" (allowing nature to reclaim high-risk inhabited areas rather than fighting nature on its ground), and water reuse policies are feasible and necessary measures. Anything else will break the bank.

Worst case scenario: A major weather event bankrupts state and federal relief efforts, providing little, if any, political benefit. Hurricanes Erika and Fernando cost the opposition the election. We cannot afford to have that happen to us.

2. Unless black and Latino voters get behind the environmental issue, we will not be able to win midterms. Black and Latino families have been disproportionately affected by food security issues, unequal availability of pandemic-issued drugs, and grid problems with water, electricity, and IT. The environmental activism in the United States has many genealogies: it originates with primarily Latino farmhands' protests over toxic pesticides and fertilizers, and the eco consumption movement became a widespread youth phenomenon for all demographic groups via the hip-hop entertainment industry. By celebrating these origin stories of environmental awareness, we can dispel the myth that American environmentalism is a deep ecology, country-club mindset that aims to restore the wilderness, concerns only white populations, and tells poor people how to live. The helpful fact is that truth is on our side: Environmental issues have always affected the majority of Americans, and the majority means — it warrants emphasis — people of African, Latino, and Asian descent. Mrs. Obama's reach with this segment of the voting population, through her web show and rallies, can bring this group over to our side.

After assessing this proposal against core elements of our strategy, my recommendation is to appoint Mrs. Obama to a newly created position of presidential environmental advisor.

Mrs. Obama will handle much of the in-nation contact with community projects, with Congress (especially the House Subcommittee on Storm Control), and with industry.

I believe that the recent devastations of two hurricanes, plus the food scandals, make Mrs. Obama's function critical for our success.

Cost: Mrs. Obama's salary will be funded entirely out of green point budgets of our own campaigns.

Action Items if We Choose to Proceed: POTUS grants Mrs. Obama authority over community activists and food safety.

Media Strategy: Mrs. Obama will share 12 percent of Jackson-feed airtime on the web. Our cyber stream aligns POTUS's live feed with Mrs. Obama's proven media presence on Minute with Michelle programs, and incorporates the profile halo icon into all environmental-related communication.

Mrs. Obama will head a green mentoring program with long-term sustainability grants for underrepresented groups in key electoral states. We have funding for such projects from designated green trade programs. Mrs. Obama joining our teams is a win-win. She has consistent above-80-percent pull with black and Latino voters who will soon constitute 50+ percent of the voting public (34+ percent of population).

Our tent is held up by the shared concerns of all Americans. It is green, and that means it is inclusive enough to accommodate all voters. Environmentalism is an ecumenical issue that transcends partisan politics. With the expertise, reputation, and leadership of Michelle Obama, we will make good on President Jackson's promise to protect the environment, which benefits everyone, including all Americans.

Artforum

A Monthly Blast Devoted to the Arts

Mold, "Valley Art"

Site-specific piece in Touron-en-Rhiis, France, European Union
Date Stamped September 4, 2021, EST
Jasmine M. Haley

When driving to the artist Mold's recent and largest-ever work in the French Valley of Touron-en-Rhiis, the road weaves through picturesque villages filled with preserved thatched-roofed farms with carved oak gables overlooked by five-hundred-year-old church steeples. The two-lane country road ambles past a patchwork of wheat and sunflower fields and pastures dotted with brown horses and white cows, and through dense beech forests where the speckled light resembles that on the ocean floor.

"None of this is natural," said Mold— whose given name is Kalaf Pit—with a dismissive sweep of his hand when we drove through the cool, dark forest on a recent June morning.

"People have changed this valley for thousands of years. It's long past the point where we can call it natural," he explained. "There isn't one wild thing left here. People planted the trees in those patches of forest, and not even the streams run in a way that nature intended. All the birds are sick from insecticides, or they are species that have taken over when some other type of bird got hunted to extinction. They feed on beetles imported accidentally from Asia, and the foxes feed on garbage."

It's a good four-hour drive from Paris to Touron-en-Rhiis, and Mold's acerbic deconstruction of this UNESCO-protected landscape doesn't leave even one proverbial stone in the bucolic scene unturned. Mold, whose artist's name refers both to the way he regards humans as a "toxic, fungus-like encumbrance on the planet," and to his work of "molding" landscapes, rejects the labels "public art" and "earth art." Born in Portugal of Angolan parents, he has been awarded some of the art world's most prestigious accolades and has been honored with a career retrospective at age forty-two at New York's MOMA and the Doha Pavilions. The sketches for his projects command top prices.

It is mid-morning by the time we arrive at one of twelve marked vista points that constitute Mold's long-term project. His mood visibly softens as we overlook the valley. A small river runs among the fields and the patches of forest, slim and silvery like the contrails of a plane. A reddish-brown falcon circles in the pale blue sky.

"From this spot right here, you cannot see any man-made structures," Mold explains, and points me to a spot marked by some rocks sunk into the ground. "Look exactly above that wooden post there. All you're now seeing in the valley below is organic. It's not natural, but it's organic growth."

For sixteen years, since 2005, Mold has worked with local communities and private landowners to move or lower the rooflines of buildings, reroute roads, and plant and care for trees and shrubs so that from this and eleven other vista points like it, you see only organic growth.

"There are whole villages down there, a hospital, two schools, and lots of roads," Mold explains. "There are power lines, a railroad track, supermarkets. You name it."

None of it is visible from where we stand. The valley looks green, peaceful, and untouched.

"The point is not to make this look 'natural,' like a valley in one of your protected parks," Mold says. "The point is to show that we can live with the environment even today. This isn't 'earth art.' Those macho guys bulldozed huge amounts of rock and soil into patterns to be viewed from drones, military-style. Or they piled up stones and tortured trees into pretty patterns like a bunch of mad gardeners. They wanted to build the pyramids all over. Another form of environmental violence. I'm tired of it."

The twelve vista points are found only on old-fashioned printed maps, but not via GPS. The maps can be obtained by asking local residents for them, but they must not be bought or sold. Mold is never without his tablet, however. He jams the GPS systems daily so viewers cannot post his project's locations.

I've seen my share of earth art. I started with Christo's *The Gates* in New York's Central Park as a kid, visited Robert Smithson's *Spiral Jetty* and De Maria's Texas lightning fields as a teenager, have seen Turrell's *Roden Crater* in Arizona from a plane, and spent three months as an intern at Michael Heizer's *City* in Nevada. I've also seen picture-perfect European valleys before, and once spent a long summer in a Tuscan hillside town writing a book. But the knowledge that the soothingly green landscape I am looking at is really a densely populated valley first farmed and settled one thousand years ago changes what I see.

Looking at this landscape is like guessing someone's hidden thoughts while studying their open face. The experience of looking at Mold's work is also strangely solitary. I know that in the valley below people go about their day while I stand here without being able to see them. Time seems to slow. I begin to understand Mold's tattoos on his arms: "Five years have passed/five summers, with the length/Of five long winters." This piece is as much about hiding the man-made parts of the landscape as it is about the way our perception changes with time. Mold's *Valley* seeps slowly into my consciousness, the way great art is supposed to happen.

"It's not about restoring a lost state of nature," Mold says. "I am not an eco-artist and don't believe in turning back the clock."

Below us, the only movement is the birds flying in and out of fields.

"*Valley* is a reminder that we live on the planet as guests," Mold says.

"Sixteen years is not a long time in human history," explains Evelyn VanVeulen, professor of environment and media at the Sorbonne in Paris. "It's taken Mold that long to make the valley look uninhabited from these twelve points. But in terms of environmental history, sixteen years is nothing—a mere speck on the timeline of the planet's four and a half billion year history."

Yet sixteen years of lobbying local residents, raising money, paying people and villages for air rights and root rights have left their mark on Mold.

"To undo what we have done to the planet will take centuries," Mold says. "My work is about thinking in larger periods, and acknowledging that a lot of things can't be undone."

We spend the next few hours looking at the valley from various angles. It's like a treasure hunt with the reward of seeing nothing, like staring into a page in the book of nature, with all man-made signs erased.

It is nearly dusk when we reach the twelfth and final location from which to view the valley.

"Just in time," Mold explains. "The project is for day viewing only."

The sun-sensitive map fades away before my eyes when the last rays of sunlight vanish for the day. There is still enough light to see, and I notice Mold's famous profile, with the little crown of dreadlocks springing from the otherwise shaved head. Mold is jumpy now, anxious to leave.

"Show's over," he declares and gets into our Solar. "Don't wear it out with your eyes."

It's getting dark, and the valley extends under a velvet sky with a few early stars.

At some distance, probably a good twenty kilometers from our viewing site, I can make out a faint glow. The valley does not participate in opt-outs ("bullshit games for rich towns, like vegan luxury resorts," according to Mold). I now understand why Mold wants to leave. *Valley* only works during daytime, since electric lights reveal human habitation.

As if he can read my mind, Mold groans.

"There are people living there after all. And they like to be on the map," he says, referring to the valley's inhabitants. "They were awarded last year's Ted Turner Green Prize, as the first non-artists to win it. But at the end of the day," he chuckles at his joke, "at the end of the day, they remain the same selfish bastards like the rest of us. Only during the day, they're hidden from view."

Or maybe not, I think while casting a last look at the smudge of light disturbing the weirdly peaceful scene. Maybe they are not quite as selfish as us, having upended their lives for over a decade to allow this project to happen.

Mold's *Valley* cleverly avoids the machismo of massive earth art. *Valley* clears our view the way ginger clears the palate, or a rainstorm clears the skies. It affords us a new perspective on our planet, and to see our role as a participant rather than main actor.

Valley

From Wikipedia, the free encyclopedia

[This article refers to the artwork by the artist Mold. For the geological feature see valleys; for the rock opera see Leontyne Kessers.]

Valley is a site-specific long-term work of environmental art created by Portuguese-Angolan artist and activist Mold (born name Kalaf Pit)[1] in Touron-en-Rhis (variously spelled Touron-en-Rhiis), Republic of France, the European Union.[2] The work consists of 12 viewing sites, or "harmony spots," from which the valley of Touron-en-Rhis, about 250 km from the city of Chartres, can be viewed during daylight hours in May–September. *Valley* also refers to the interactive site managed by Mold on which viewers can follow the work's planning and progress.[3]

Description [edit]

Valley extends for an area of about 42 square kilometers around the village of Touron-en-Rhiis. It consists of the environment found in that region, made up of fields, patches of forest, farms, small workshops, houses, roads, and rail lines. The work constrains the visitors' view of that environment to only natural growth by screening from view all man-made activity or structures (except fields and planted forest).[4]

Visibility [edit]

Valley is visible only during daytime in the European summer months, from roughly middle of May until late September. At night and in the winter, *Valley* is not visible since the lack of foliage makes the man-made structures visible. Mold envisioned the work to last for only one summer, or until tree growth would block the viewing platforms. He has extended its duration to the present.[5] *Valley* is visible only when viewed from one of the twelve viewing sites. The sites are marked on daylight-sensitive, non-photographable paper maps. Because of concealed scramblers located throughout the valley, the vista points cannot be located via GPS.[6]

Construction [edit]

Over a period of sixteen years, Mold has altered or moved man-made structures, rerouted streets, installed ground-level street lights, removed electric wires and poles, and planted trees and shrubs to obscure all human traces from view from any of the twelve viewing stations.

Controversy [edit]

Some critics have described Mold's *Valley* as part of the tradition of earth and land art of the 1960s and 1970s such as Robert Smithson's *Spiral Jetty,*[7] Michael Heizer's *City,* Andrew Goldsworthy's works, and Christo and Jean-Claude's projects. A most prominent example of EEA, or environmentally engaged art, *Valley* belongs in the category of performance of great magnitude such as James Turrell's *Roden Crater,* or Tehching Hsieh's durational performances.

Mold has strongly rejected comparisons with these precursors, whom he considers artists of eco-violence and the "hidden militarism of American postmodernity."[8] Mold made those comments in 2021 when *Valley* was awarded the Turner Green Prize for Environmental Justice. In 2021, *Valley* was also voted one of the top five most important artworks by users of Weibo.

Financing [edit]

Valley was financed by the European Commission through a special fund designated for environmental activism, and through private donations. The estimated cost of the project is believed to be between 200 and 600M Euros. [9] With the sale of blueprints, drawings, postcards, and the light-sensitive maps, Mold has raised money for projects in Ecuador, Doha, Senegal, and Australia to be unveiled throughout the next decade.

Rock Star

It's 4:30 a.m. on what is my fourth day here. Can't go back to sleep. I had my açai, checked into the medical panel, and searched my tablet for clips before the medics came by. I wasn't feeling very well. I decided to try them again to let me go online.

They had nothing useful to say to me through their stupid protective screen. Might as well be robots.

"Yes, Aleks."

"No, Aleks."

"We're monitoring it."

"No, there's no connectivity in here."

"Even if we tried, we couldn't get you online."

"We've updated your next of kin."

I gave them a list on the first day.

"What's the update?" I asked. "What update did you give them? Who did you give it to?"

"That your status remains unchanged," they responded.

"Please! I need to get a message out!" I banged on the door.

They walked away.

I didn't want to go back to sleep, though I had a headache. I've requested, several times, not to be given sleeping aids and drugs. But who knows what's pumped into the room. When I think how many times in the past four years I had wished for nothing more than a quiet room, to be offline, totally disconnected, with nothing to do but sleep . . .

I drifted off, then woke again and got up to watch a few clips of Lucia to fend off the fatigue. I don't think I'd sat through a whole speech of hers as an actual audience member, once she had taken office. Watching a full oration the way other people see her is amazing. I nearly forgot that sense of belonging to something bigger. It makes me feel inspired, motivated to work, and like a slouch for wanting to nap.

Lucia spoke about the growth trap, one of her favorite topics. She's so well-rehearsed that you wouldn't expect much beyond political boilerplate. There were no notes, no teleprompter. But at her fingertips she had the relevant figures: how salaries fared during the second chip revolution, proof that when consumption rises, environmental costs also go up, effectively wiping out the gains made by growth. The environment is a common good, rather than something to be managed by private or national interests, and the United States is singularly equipped to lead a coalition toward this end. But before Lucia reached that point, she'd talked about her father's struggle to make a living during the drought. I clicked on different angles when she spoke about the efforts to find water, from drone-seeding clouds to people waving wands. There was audience laughter when she spoke of doing a rain dance, in all earnestness, until her parents called a doctor because they thought she was sick. Her words rippled across the audience's faces like sunlight on a lake. People nodded when she talked about the fact that some of the medical problems, particularly those that afflict the very young and old, came from an unhealthy environment. Furrowed brows followed when she described how her father's last months were spent in terrible suffering, how the nights in a hospital taught her about unconditional love, and how she agonized over the decision to let him go on his own terms. She choked up at that moment, and it wasn't theater.

She called out to the audience to raise a hand if they were

worried about a parent's or loved one's health. She listed the bills that had died in Congress but that would have raised the standards for food and water safety. Then she asked who would approve stricter standards to make our food and water safer. As though she was conducting a huge and heaving symphony, a sea of fists flew up.

The crowd fell silent when Lucia talked about losing her husband to an undiagnosed illness just before Election Day. She tried to resuscitate him while the doctors told her to stay away, for fear of contagion, and her children were not allowed to say goodbye to their father. Just to think of Isabella and Marisol with a fever, and Lucia risking everything to tend to her husband chokes me up — and I have heard the story many times.

She recalled her fight with the big insurance companies to recognize autoimmune syndromes, and how she replaced the whole US Department of Health and Human Services after taking office.

"We Americans do not want to live in fear of getting sick from our food," she said. "We don't want to live in fear of breathing air, of swimming in lakes, of drinking water. We count on our government to keep these things clean and safe for all."

She singled out people in the crowd by name without looking at a prompter. They were activists but also teachers, food inspectors, farmers, tech workers, who had to worry about radiation and such.

Her refrain was simple and powerful.

"*You* can make a difference." "*You* are the person the world needs." "*You* matter to this woman standing here."

"Your president believes that America needs to be the leader in this fight to protect the commons and to guide private, as well as other nations' interests to keep the planet livable."

Watching the speeches made me feel better. It's worth working for her, even though the pay is shit, and the hours are impossible. There is hope. I am going to come out of this goddamn pod with a blueprint to win the next election.

"We can put POTUS online from the get-go," Asturias had said right after the election. "Or we can constantly update our firewalls, take down the bullshit and doctored pics other people will put up, and hope that any leak or hack won't be too big."

"Is there no chance of keeping our systems secure?" Lucia had asked. "Can't people be stopped from using unauthorized images of me in their feeds?"

"Nope," Asturias had replied. "That's not possible. We will be hacked: we will be leaked; our stuff will be all over the place. The only option is to encrypt and re-encrypt constantly, hide our stuff, put up false leaks, and hope to be ahead of the hackers always by a step. That's why we hired the best team I could find."

Asturias grinned while his guys looked at newly elected President Lucia Jackson without showing much emotion.

"Unless . . ." Chiara said.

Lucia nodded for her to continue.

"Unless we go all out transparent on those wankers," Chiara continued. "Feed all the information we produce, and I mean *all* of it. And of course spice it up with a bunch of info that's misleading. Let those things distract them, but put up our own authorized feed so that people have to compete with it."

"Instead of hiding what we do, bury them with info," Malang said.

"So I'll be online constantly," Lucia said. "Campaign mode never stops."

"Think campaign mode times a thousand," Asturias said. "And the First Family, too. The children, your mother."

That's how we decided on the livestream. The kids were easier than Lucia to get on board. Soon they didn't mind the drones when they came downstairs.

Asturias has nicknamed the drone cams Marilyn and Monica, since they're on the president like bees on honey, but of course we never told Lucia that.

The speech was filmed with several drones. You can zoom in on individuals, or you can watch a continuous shot of the crowd's responses. I know how it's done. I know it's theater. I've peeked behind the curtain.

And yet I feel inspired.

And yet I am awed.

Google News

Ha'areti Water Bigger than Panama Canal

New US-Backed Desalinization Plants to Provide Clean Water for Fractured Middle East

One hundred and twenty years ago US president Theodore Roosevelt sent a Morse signal to open the gates of the Panama Canal, linking the Atlantic and the Pacific Oceans to inaugurate a century of highly profitable shipping for the United States. Yesterday, US President Lucia Jackson texted *Insh'Allah* and *Behatzlacha* to a network of offshore desalinization plants along the Mediterranean coast. Jackson's message opened the pipelines that will provide clean water to a region larger than Texas and California that has been riven with political strife since the British turned a former colony into a state for the Jews.

Jackson's ambitious project is a multinational network of desalinization plants that is jointly managed by American, Israeli, Egyptian, and Jordanian companies, but defended by navy ships solely under US and HEPP control.

"The Good Water Project enables us to put aside differences for our common good," Jackson said in the Oval Office while screens displayed dispensing stations from Cairo to Amman, Jerusalem, and as far south as Khartoum.

The project is not unprecedented, since there have been jointly managed oil platforms and pipelines in conflict regions for years. But Good Water dwarfs these projects. Once the entire network is operational, the volume of water dispensed will exceed that produced by all existing water treatment plants in Europe. Jackson announced the project as a multinational "environmentally sound project" partly funded by the UN's Global Green Fund. There has been criticism within and outside of the States.

"This is Jackson spending US tax dollars to help people hostile to our country," said Majority Leader Senator Frantzen, from Kentucky.

"This project does little besides justifying a permanent US naval presence in the region," said Olesya Kodchenkova, Russia's envoy to the Middle East Peace Quartet, an independent body of national envoys tasked to broker peace in the region. "Water should not be controlled by one nation or political body."

The prime minister of Israel, Ruti Leitel, describes the Good Water Project as a way to peace. "After decades of stalled talks, we need a shared goal. After the devastating drought of the past few years, Good Water has become an urgently needed solution to a problem that transcends politics and religion."

With or without opposition, the water is already transforming lives. Villages have returned to the mountain slopes of Jordan and Lebanon that were abandoned during the drought. At border crossings, guards from separate countries stand shoulder to shoulder to protect the pipelines that traverse the region like the veins and arteries of a single body. One hundred and twenty years ago the United States opened the Panama Canal to ease trade between East and West, and to help the development of the western part of the United States. Today the Panama Canal generates over $2 billion each year for Panama. It remains to be seen whether the Clean Water, or Ha'areti, project will remain under US control for as long as the Panama Canal had been. At this point, Good Water is expected to break even, and create goodwill which runs in short supply in the region.

Beef

The food isn't that bad here, for a hospital. The only problem is that everything arrives in small, off-white packets that contain healthful enzymes. "The packets are to be eaten prior to any other food," it says in bold print on them. "Significantly boosts immune responses." So I don't throw them out; that's not how I've been raised. Even though they taste like overcooked pasta, and I think they leave a weird aftertaste. The protein inside of the packs arrives in whatever form I request: steak, burger, filet, chicken cubes, sausages, ribs. My favorite is the ribs.

None of it, of course, is actual meat. Not that I would eat meat, but they've banned it in hospitals and schools since the E. coli outbreak in England.

I remember that before that time, a long while ago, when we'd order paper-thin slices of filet or a few cubes of chicken on a stick as a special treat, the way people order fancy wine. The last beef burger I ate was before Brazil and Argentina joined HEPP, and there was not yet much control, or consumer interest, on what country beef came from.

The summer right after that last hamburger, I took my first required college class: a pasture-to-table course in sustainability. I was excited to take the pre-frosh requirement off-campus instead of hauling furniture for the moving company, which I had done the two summers before that. I picked a program at a small college in Virginia so that I could stay at Uncle Wynn and Aunt Sophia's place on the weekends. I wanted to know what I was eating. The instructor encouraged our different points of view, but it was clear that her agenda was to get us off meat entirely. For our class, they had raised a couple of pullets that had just gotten big enough for slaughter. The hens were more like pets than farm animals. They ran around the place and even into the dorms to look for food, while the instructor explained the principles of sustainable and free-range farming to us under a grove of sycamore trees. The hens settled in our rooms at night, sitting on top of dressers or bedframes, and one of them loved getting into the shower with me. We were taught the history of different types of slaughter, from ancient times to today, and how these methods developed into religious rules to protect humans from disease rather than out of respect for the animals. We also read every food guru's treatise on responsible eating, and listened to several post-humanist philosophers who couldn't find a logical justification for slaughtering animals without also agreeing to end the lives of severely handicapped or injured human beings. "But that's not philosophy," one of my classmates said. "This is just sophistry, when you push any given argument to an extreme."

We were required to feed and care for our hens. Mine had been named Lincoln before I got there. Lincoln was a Cornish cross pullet, white with a speck of brown on the wings when I arrived, which faded away over the summer. When I placed my hand on her back, she became totally quiet and wouldn't move, and I could carry her around like a lap dog or a bunny. We had to make sure they were inside when the hawks were circling at midday, chase them indoors again at dusk when the foxes came out. Mix their feed, pick worms from the worm box, clean up. We practiced on bamboo shoots how to slice a chicken's neck. For days, we stood at long wooden tables and chopped. "With gusto!" our instructor cried out, while we slashed and hacked away.

Lincoln sat on the table next to my tablet and books, scratched a bit on the wood, and then settled down so close to me that I couldn't see all of my readings. Like a cat. I would push a bit but she would slide right back to be as close to me as possible. Weird bird. On the big day, we all had to catch our hens. After weeks of reading and arguing, and feeding and protecting, we were instructed to put our hens in upside-down large metal cones with their heads sticking out the bottom. As soon as they were upside down, they froze in place. No movement, just the beady eyes looking at us, as if to ask, why upside down? Why this now? Then, slice! I didn't do it right. I had to hack away at Lincoln's neck while blood sprayed at me as if from a fire sprinkler for what felt like a minute or two. Finally, the head came off. I almost puked. After that, I've eaten meat exactly three times.

Freshmen year, Sharmenie, who has probably become Keon and my best friend with the exception of Bev, and I made friends with a girl from Los Angeles who'd taken a similar class in her high school. We all were down on meat, me because of my memory of Lincoln and everyone else because of the risks. But we also looked down a bit on the militant vegans for being so sanctimonious and for trying to shock people into better behavior. Like most kids in our dorm, we were officially vegetarian but once Sharmenie, the L.A. girl, and I sneaked off to get a club sandwich with turkey bacon, just so we didn't feel bullied. We didn't really eat it, but we had ordered meat, which felt like we had broken our vows.

The three of us also went to a protest in D.C. during our first semester to demonstrate at the EPA. The focus there was beef. I had grown up with the idea that locally grown and slaughtered cattle was acceptable and safe from mass-farm outbreaks. I assumed that it was possible to raise cattle responsibly by farmers who cared about their herds and about the land, and that the size of a herd, the stuff they ate, the way they had been bred mattered in terms of our health. We all thought that in college. Responsible farming. Conscious cattle. Certified beef. Crossbred resistance. Sustainable meats. Back then, I had no idea how the government worked, and certainly had no clue that a protest at a federal agency was the one surefire way to be ignored by everyone from Congress to the White House to the media. It would have been more effective to stand in the middle of a farm in Kansas or wave some flags and project stuff onto the walls of a Walmart.

Looking back at those two days, which were really my introduction to politics, the protest was such an unholy alliance. We chanted alongside big, sweaty union workers, who had long ago lost most of their jobs in hog farming and trucking to automation, and a good many regular folks who carried professional-looking signs in Spanish and English demanding "farmer's rights." We tried talking with them, but there was little interest. Even then Sharmenie and I suspected that these defenders of "sustainable beef," "green growth," and "responsible farming" were on the payroll of Big Cattle. We listened to them rage about government overreach because "Washington," to which they referred as if it were Sudan or a satellite above the South Pacific, had ordered the destruction of whole herds, including those raised by small farmers in sustainable ways. They had videos of brown-and-white cows on green pastures being herded onto "killing trucks," where they claimed federal agents shot them all and dumped them in trenches to be destroyed. That was awful, of course, but where had those cows been headed in a few months anyway, if the disease hadn't gotten to them? And there had been huge protests at supermarkets, fast-food joints, and restaurants. Several truck drivers had been dragged from the cabs of large refrigerated trucks and nearly beaten to death by enraged parents. A few burger joints had been set on fire, and several chains were successfully boycotted. Whole school districts stopped serving meat.

Our college protest, which consisted of marching in circles in front of the departments of health and trade, and even in front of the White House fence for our allocated twenty minutes, was not as dramatic. Through the police barricade I spoke with a reporter, who kept glancing at her wristband, to explain in as few words as possible that everyone had a right to eat "safe beef," that cattle could be raised in "sustainable ways," and that "our generation" was ready to "demand real change." It was terribly obvious to me that things could be improved. I thought that the problem was the way cattle had been bred and raised in factories only for slaughter, rather than in herds where individual animals took on more natural roles, and farmers culled herds with an understanding of these roles.

"You've learned something important about your part in an animal's death," my teacher in Virginia had said when Lincoln's blood had sprayed my face and chest while I hacked away at the chicken's neck. "The point is to make you aware of what happens before food arrives on your plate and make your own choices with that knowledge."

Sharmenie and I locked arms, and chanted with the other protesters in the street and on social media. We were genuinely excited to participate. It wasn't exactly Dr. King on the Mall, but we very much felt it was our generation's moral cause. I admit that Sharmenie and I had felt a twinge of pride and self-righteousness for bussing to D.C. on a beautiful fall Saturday to change the way we eat, instead of jumping in my roommates' SUV for the season's last run to the beach. We did not delude ourselves in believing our actions would change the world overnight, and maybe not even in the long run. "But people can change," I said to Sharmenie while we looked at the White House through the intimidating fence. "They will do the right thing, if they have the right information."

What I didn't know about myself then was that I was looking for leadership as well, that although we had read and listened to a lot of ideas, we were searching for someone to channel and amplify, but more importantly, to give real content to our voice. We had a complaint, an issue, something that we cared deeply about. Something that was greater than ourselves: the survival of our species, and the moral duty we had toward all the other species on earth. We worried about the degradation of the environment, and the way our food system created health risks for everyone.

But we didn't yet know how to transform our complaint into something to inspire others to change. The problem was not that we suspected the others in those protests of being on Big Cattle's payroll, although it was quite possible. The problem was that everyone saw the same problem, but that their solutions did not converge in a common goal. For me, for America, and for the world, I didn't yet know that we needed Lucia.

"Progress is not inevitable," Sharmenie said. "People won't do the right thing, unless it benefits them. The only way they'll care about the planet is when they get sick."

"I know," I responded. "Unfortunately the arc of our moral universe does not inevitably bend toward justice. But that's exactly why we are out here!" The arc of humanity winds its way like a weed fed by rainstorms and manure toward a source of light. It may be the sun. But Klieg lights will also do. An inspiring leader can also bend the arc of humanity toward doom. Change, both good and bad, is possible, and politics — the right kind of politics — are necessary.

My summer class with Lincoln had involved a lot of reading. We studied Socrates' and Plato's question of whether there is any inherent reason for people to be good. Socrates' answer that being good means being more in harmony with oneself appeared to me, for the longest time, as if he had just posited the reason for being good as its outcome. We read Sappho, about the way desire functions as the engine of the world, and how satisfaction is so difficult to achieve since, as humans, we want not this or that, not one shiny object that puts an end to our craving or to be with this particular person, but we want to *want:* we want the thrill of desiring for the sake of feeling that urge, of falling in love over and over again, or getting something new as a goal in itself. We want desire to go on, not for it to be sated. Getting what we want aligns us with new needs, and then we want more and different things. We want to live, but the only way we know how to do that is to consume life itself. It was the summer before college, and while I didn't really understand much about philosophy, I *knew* what that meant, always wanting something or someone else. It meant being awake to the world and living for the future. I hadn't dated anybody in high school, but I had had my share of crushes: on several boys and on one or two girls. And I had always surprised myself when, suddenly, my interest in that person was gone, like a flame that had been blown out, even though nothing had happened, and I soon found myself obsessing about someone else. And how wanting someone led to wanting someone else.

In class, we jumped to Dante as the first great humanist, to understand how our post-religious, modern age started with someone who employed reason to examine and deepen, rather than abandon, faith. I developed my first and only crush on a teacher, the philosopher with the blond curls and rows of tiny silver chains with small charms flowing down her chest over her indigo shirts. She argued that the Enlightenment did not end superstition and belief, but smuggled these ideas into our modern age as our steadfast belief in progress, and a better future.

While we collected worms from the compost and cleaned chicken poop, we debated Hume and Rousseau, trying to figure out if humans are inherently good or bad, and whether social conventions serve to enchain or liberate our true nature. I read a lot of Leopardi that summer, too, which challenged the idea that the world will inevitably improve. I can't imagine reading Rousseau in any other setting than a farm, when he describes how man first staked a little plot, told everyone else that they couldn't step on it, and how this small move got us all, or at least those of us whose governments let us own land, all the way to today's world order. Rousseau seemed sentimental and wrongheaded about all sorts of things and, as our teacher didn't tire of explaining, about most people in the world who were not European males. But when you had to clear your small patch of land from poison ivy, which gave me a rash that required shots after the natural remedies only made it worse, the idea about fencing in your field and telling everyone to walk around rather than through it sounded pretty solid. And

Rousseau's idea that one would set up rules and laws and legitimize the threat of violence to keep it that way also seemed reasonable. I wrote an impassioned defense of Rousseau's unrealized and radical idea that animals ought to have a share in natural rights, and that men are bound by a "certain form of duty" toward them. My only A+ in all of college, and it had been my very first assignment. We read Robespierre's famous speech in which he extols his unshakeable faith in the future in the exact language of the religion he had just overthrown. And we debated how the Founding Fathers injected a particular notion of inevitable progress into America's self-understanding, like a slow-burning fuse that everyone from Washington to Dr. King tapped into, but that nobody thought to adjust until it got us into our current state of environmental disaster.

I also can't imagine reading Jefferson anywhere but in Virginia. Most of these authors must sound terribly stilted and detached when read elsewhere, or deceitful and clueless. Our teacher was brilliant. She helped us to identify these ideas of progress as naïve and sentimental, and guided us to develop a moral system that did not depend on an assumption about human nature as being inherently good. She left it to us to find a position, with regard to the idea of progress as a good engine or the unstoppable force that compromised everything, while we worked the farm, kept our charges safe from hawks, foxes, and disease, and got ready for the big day of slaughtering and eating our hens.

Her idea of progress was veganism. But she created enough space so we could defend our ideas with the same seriousness with which I made sure nobody pinched any worms from my bucket after I'd spent the afternoon digging though the compost.

We read Marx and Engels on marriage, of course, as proof that our cherished moral conventions, and most social institutions, had been set up to protect property and male dominance. We looked at the introduction of matrilineal law, *partus sequitur ventrem*, in 1662 Virginia, which ensured that an enslaved woman's offspring inherited her and not the father's status, to understand how a society adjusts presumably inalterable assumptions to fit a new, and in this case, pernicious, plan. If America could give up patrilineal law to accommodate the evil of slavery, it could surely adjust contemporary assumptions to change things for the better. And Darwin. Our teacher hammered into us that Darwin says nowhere that progress is inevitable, or that evolution inevitably leads to better outcomes.

"How we choose to live is one option among several," she said, "and it's up to us to determine the better alternative."

It's close to what Lucia has said in so many speeches, minus the references to European philosophy. While Lincoln put on the pounds that would get her to slaughtering size, in total oblivion that my affection and care for her had the goal of eating her later, it brought us full circle to Socrates, with a detour via species' rights. "Better alternatives" meant living in a manner more in harmony with ourselves, but no longer as philosopher kings, but as one kind of animal among others.

Our teacher, as orthodox as she surely was about veganism as mankind's proper calling, also advocated that we ought to love our food, which meant, for non-vegans, raising with care the animals you'd ultimately eat.

It was a great, long American summer, which I spent working and reading in the mornings on the farm, and chilling with my buddies on lawn chairs placed in the shallow end of a reed-lined pond until the daily thunderstorms rolled in, when I rushed into the chicken coop to sit with the pullets to keep them calm. This seemed completely sane to me at the time. There was a little flirtation, and a bit more one humid evening with a thoughtful guy from Mayotte who worked at a local store and had the most amazing golden eyes. Keon and I have seen him once since then, in Paris, and he's invited me and "le boyfriend" to visit him in Réunion, where he works as a media host.

It must have been when I was already working in Washington and had almost entirely given up meat, when the Kansas school thing happened. Another friend from freshmen year who'd moved there, Sandra Glesson, with whom I had been in a global human rights course and who had sort of dated Sharmenie for a few weeks, lost her two-year-old son to E. coli. It was devastating, and it became a big story. I had kept in touch with Sandra only on social media, and I was shocked when she shared with me that her son had died because he ate certified but clearly unsafe beef in his daycare.

In her grief, Sandra started sharing clips of sick children. It was hard to look at those pictures but equally hard to ignore her. These were kids who had eaten certified safe and organic hot dogs, or a supermarket meat labeled as organic turkey that had apparently contained traces of beef. It was enraging to watch how everyone from the daycare center to the hospital had at first refused to acknowledge that he had died because of bad meat. Sandra's media profile became hard-hitting. She arranged pictures of her son next to leaked footage from cattle factories, clips that so many people had gotten sued over because of ag-gag laws, so many times. She posted all of her hospital bills, plus documents showing congressional funding for big cattle, trade exemptions for beef, claims that beef was safe from various suppliers in which people sound stupid, if it were not so serious. Some of the big aggregators picked it up, so of course Big Cattle immediately threw all sorts of injunctions at her. She posted those, too, probably indifferent to the legal threat to her after her little boy had died. Then the web host shut down her site. She went a little mad then. I remember a web show in which the host said to Sandra, "You seem understandably upset and emotional over all of this," and Sandra responded, looking not at the woman but directly into the camera, "Oh no, I'm not emotional. I am dangerous."

Antigone for our times. A public relations disaster for Big Cattle, for sustainable farming, for parts of the medical community, and above all, for the EPA.

On the big web shows, Sandra read her son's death certificate, where the cause of death was listed as "adverse reaction to unknown toxin," and then the legal letters threatening her with all sorts of things unless she stopped blaming beef. The Big Cattle lawyers had made a strategic error in that letter when they linked the kid's death and beef, which the hospital, surely on advice from better lawyers, had refused to state as a possible cause.

People rallied around Sandra. To deny a mother's right to post pictures of her dead son online: that touches a nerve. People began to worry about eating meat. It made people feel self-conscious when they ordered it, the way folks were at some point made to feel about buying coats made from the fur of rare animals. It seemed extravagant and immoral, since it supported an industry that refused any responsibility for dead kids and attacked a grieving mother.

My decision to go vegan was influenced by Sandra, but it did not come overnight, the way some vegans mythologize their awakening. And it wasn't only Lincoln who changed my mind. For me it was more of a realization that I could do fine without meat. The loss in pleasure was not so significant as to make me long for something that could endanger my health, and to support an industry that bullied parents and treated animals horribly. I kind of just stopped eating meat and then gradually lost interest, the way most people grow out of dirt bikes, long hair, and hookups.

"It's because you're an Aquarius," Keon said, when I passed on the meat even at one of Bev's sausage sizzles in her garden. "That's why it's easy for you to give up things. But it would be nice if you had some compassion for those of us for whom it isn't so easy."

Today, beef is out of the question for most people, except on very special occasions. It is the insane prices, for one thing. And I don't really know anyone who lets their kids eat beef. Way too risky, also for the elderly. A few people I know are really into horse meat now, Korean-style, or like the French, but that's not for me. Maybe at some point we'll forget the taste of beef, the way we forgot what passenger pigeons tasted like, or whale meat, or emu.

Mata Ganga

I have no food options here — all part of the program to keep people in quarantine engaged and stimulated. Mystery dinner? Check. Dopamine? Check. Food additives to keep me calm? Most likely, check. Random study that links people's immune response to guess work and pleasant surprises? Check. Seth gets his way again? Check.

Today's lunch is a kind of cheese-less saag paneer, rice, and gluten-free naan. The flavors brought to mind the excellent Indian meal I had with Michelle Obama in Texas.

"Nearly half of the world's population lives in Asia," Lucia said when Delhi sent an invitation during our first May in Washington. "We need to engage more with the places on the planet where solutions are urgently needed. Their motivation to find answers exceeds ours, in fact."

Domineek had not liked the idea of another trip to India.

"A second state visit in such a short amount of time," she sighed. "It just looks weird, no matter how many people there are in India. Don't tell me that this trip means cancelling Texas."

"It's not my decision," I started to say, but decided right then, while standing in front of Domineek's desk like a schoolboy in the principal's office, that I should take credit for it. Bad idea.

"Actually, India is buying a lot of our technology these days. So we can package this as a trade visit. Commerce can come along.

I'll find a way to send Mrs. Obama to Texas."

"I don't like it, Aleks," Domineek said. "Not a bit. Not even if Commerce and State agree to go. And you do not determine Mrs. Obama's schedule. And most of all, I don't need a lecture from you on the economy."

Domineek's phone buzzed. I mumbled something and left. There was no time to call Keon to process. I messaged State to see whether they could push for India, for defense or security. They messaged back; I had to go over there. The next few days were not easy. Domineek did not message me once, and looked right through me in meetings.

"'If you want to ignore me, let me help you,'" Keon said when I told him about it that night. "That's what my grandma says. And I know that you have to work with Domineek, and that she controls access to the president. But really, Aleks, if you let her get to you, she'll win her petty little war."

I stopped pushing India; I stayed away from a few meetings, and I did not message Domineek.

"But don't hide!" Keon said.

When the India trip was announced, Lucia posted about it on social media.

"America and Europe have been the planet's biggest polluters for two centuries. We transformed two continents in the process and changed habitats around the globe. But we have learned that we live in a global century. We need the help and leadership of India and the countries of Asia to achieve significant change."

Domineek was not happy, but of course she couldn't let Lucia know that, once the decision had been made.

"I still think the India trip is a mistake, Aleks," she hissed at the end of a briefing that week.

"Ignore her!" Keon said when I told him about it. "She's just angry that Lucia likes an idea that wasn't hers. Find a way to make it look as if it had been her idea."

As usual, Keon was right. It helped that I ended up going with

Mrs. Obama to visit Big Garbage in Texas instead of on the India trip. I turned over the planning for India, including the pre-trip press, to Domineek.

Since Texas had become the country's largest buyer of garbage from the other states, we depended on a few big foundries for our PACs. They incinerated so much trash in their facilities that Texas could export energy and the obsidian-like glast thus produced. And, probably by relying on the networks, and the kickbacks and payoffs set up for the old oil and gas companies, they made a fortune doing it. Part of the kitchen in our apartment is built with glast, which Keon's landlord installed before we moved in together, along with brand-new appliances, because of the subsidies. We liked it so much that I recommended glast to Mom for her bathrooms and kitchens, and she used man-made obsidian tiles for her patio, too, and loves it.

In Texas, Michelle and I spent a day at one of the trash tycoon's estates.

"All of this is made from trash," the guy said while he walked us to his living room, past a huge galley kitchen and windows overlooking a vast, sparkling blue pool surrounded by oversized midnight-blue planters. "Even the tiles in the bathrooms are glast."

"We can see that trash has been good to you," Michelle said. "So let's find a way to pay that back."

Michelle was direct, charming, and persuasive. Like a super-nice, super-efficient, super-elegant tank. She was determined to involve local communities in the garbage business, without creating an underclass of rag pickers, through training programs for local kids, for all parts of the logistics of trash, including hauling, processing, and engineering new products and energy.

We sat in the huge living room with the three-story-high natural stone fireplace. "This was also built from trash, but the kind we converted into money," the guy said.

I smiled but didn't know what to say. The house was impressive, indeed, even if a lot of things in it seemed a bit off-scale: too big, or too smooth.

Michelle was in her element. She accepted a whiskey, chatted with the guy's wife for a bit, and then we ate a big Indian meal served on big obsidian plates, on the big obsidian table. The guy's two adult sons, who ran the family foundation, joined us. Michelle did her pitch. Job training, environmental giveback, local engagement, local energy grids.

I kept quiet and listened to Michelle, while keeping peripheral watch on Lucia on one of the screens. She was in India, and a large screen near the kitchen was set to the presidential feed.

Halo Michelle worked her magic on those Texan guys. They lounged in the big, denim-covered couches as in a homemade movie. "Don't fall in love with a Texan," Keon had messaged that morning, but there was no fear of that. They were good-looking, with dark hair and bright green eyes, but they stared at Halo Michelle like two prize-winning oxen paraded out for sale.

I switched seats so I could follow the screens a bit better. Michelle was finished with her presentation, but the rapt audience of the two Texans and their dad asked questions to continue basking in her attention. For a few minutes, the guys' mother, a beautiful woman with spiky black hair, sparkling chin to waist in diamonds, chatted quietly with me. While we talked, we both watched the screen with the news. On the feed, Lucia entered a vast atrium filled with orchids arranged under tall, arched windows. It was a formal reception filled with India's elite in resplendent clothes. The other screen had a clip of Lucia in a dark blue sari. No bindi, but with her hair held back by a large silver comb. I wondered whether she was trying too hard, and whether Gabi had come along on Air Force One to do her hair and wardrobe before they deplaned.

I have clips of Lucia at the environmental march in Delhi, in front of an enormous crowd of mostly young people. To her right is the Indian prime minister and to her left, next to Domineek, a prominent activist.

I scroll ahead to the scene everyone remembers. Michelle had the Texan guys in stitches over something she said about barbeques and men who cook. They were literally slapping their knees, while Michelle smiled at them with her eyebrows raised. I turned back to the screen. Something on the screens had caught their attention as well. Michelle, the three Texan guys, and the mother, who was now standing near one of the couches, all turned to look.

At first, it was a regular Indian street scene, with cars, trucks, vans, buses, carts, scooters, dogs, an occasional camel, hawkers selling things. Then there were motorcycles and official-looking cars with flashing lights that cleared the road, and then stopped alongside it. Below is the River Ganges, vast, slow-moving, and brown. There were lots of people, most of them in white saris, walking up and down stone steps leading to the river. Lucia has stepped out of one of the official cars and now passed through the throng, surrounded by a bunch of white-uniformed security guys with wraparound glasses and helmet-like contraptions, which made them look like astronauts or half-bots.

The people parted for Lucia, and she and the bots descended the stairs.

"Where's our security?" Michelle asked nobody in particular while we stared at the screen. "Where's the President's detail?"

At the bottom of the steps, a throng of people in green had gathered. They held signs and banners, but we could not make out what they said. The clip was unsteady, and I wondered who was responsible for programming the drones.

Lucia kept moving down toward the crowd in green while people cheered and waved. The half-bots closed rank on both sides of the steps to block off the crowd. When she reached the bottom of the stairs, without so much as a moment's hesitation, she took the next step that was just below the water, and then continued down the stairs straight into the river. There were small groups of people around her in the water, standing and watching her while their robes flowed around them. Small floats drifted by covered with what looked like flowers, heaps of plants, or bunched-up bags.

"Fantastic!" Michelle said as she jumped up and applauded in the air-conditioned Texas living room. Other people had joined to look at our commander-in-chief wading into the River Ganges.

The Texan brothers were standing up now, as was I. Lucia was in the water up to her waist.

Marilyn and Monica must have hovered right above Lucia, for the next thing transmitted to the world's screens was the president of the United States floating in the brownish Ganges, face tilted up and surrounded by the soft wave of her dark hair, her blue sari billowing gently all around her. The bot-like guards were next to her now, submerged in the water up to their bulky chests and extending their arms above the surface at shoulder height, probably to keep some weapons in their sleeves dry. Lucia looked regal, but the blue fabric wafting around her made her seem like a princess in a Disney movie.

"Good for the president!" our hosts exclaimed and laughed. "Take a dip and let the world watch you!"

"Fantastic," Michelle just repeated. "That's the coolest thing she's done. And she ditched her detail."

We lost the connection for a few moments, and the screens cut to a pre-recorded segment on India. Then Lucia was back and everyone in the living room spontaneously cheered. Lucia was either wading or swimming in the river, with the phalanx of officers floating in a circle around her.

That's probably the best-known picture of Lucia, her swimming in Mata Ganga. It hadn't been planned on the official itinerary, and we learned quickly it was the only official image of an American president ever swimming in non-US waters. My phone went mad at that moment, buzzing with staff alert messages and Keon calling. I put Keon on ScreenCall and kept watching.

People in India went wild.

"Mother Lucia Dips in Mata Ganga," *The Times of India* proclaimed, and the prime minister used it as a proof that his government was cleaning up the river.

"I sense why this river, this awesome, wonderful river, matters so much to people," Lucia said in her newsfeed a few days later. "In those waters felt the greatness of this river, and the greatness of the country which it feeds. The fact that the Ganges is swimmable again is a reason for hope."

Someone had turned on the sound, but the clips from India were not yet dubbed. The mood in the Texas house was festive, as if Lucia had won another election.

"'Mother Lucia?'" I messaged Asturias and Domineek incredulously when the comments started. "We cannot let 'Mother Lucia' stick. Can you filter that out and replace with President Jackson??!" But the clip became so iconic that Asturias's team let the "Mother Lucia" moniker live on. It's one of those images you see everywhere in India now, on the backs of cars, on T-shirts, on food stalls. We're not totally comfortable with all the reasons for its popularity, and we've tried to stop the ultra-nationalists from using it in campaigning. But the Green Party uses it as well. Lucia visited a school in the south of India afterward, which — coincidentally or because Domineek had wanted to tie in with our efforts in Texas — was made entirely of glast. It was a gorgeous, midnight-blue building with big windows and translucent levers, and planted roofs and walls.

"In India, we see some creative solutions to our pressing problems," Lucia said in front of the school. "With new engineering, especially high-grade incineration and glassification, we can turn waste into wonders."

Next to Lucia stood Sonya Narayan. The building glowed softly, as if it was quietly breathing in the afternoon light. Our Texas trash tycoons loved that footage even more than the Mata Ganga pics. "We helped the Indians develop these plants," Texas Dad said. "They adopted our technologies some time ago. Now we are ready to use glast for road construction and buildings in this country as well."

After more whiskey, Michelle and I left the trash tycoons, who turned out to be really nice and who've been to the White House a few times since then, with a commitment for training programs, and a lot more money for our PAC.

I look at Lucia swimming in the Ganges and can't help but smile. I wish I could claim that clip as my brilliant idea, as a clever photo-op to appeal to a population of more than a billion who had thought environmentalism was basically Yankee imperialism waving a green flag. But I can't take credit for it.

The White House head of security had been furious at Domineek, who they blamed for putting a visit to the Ganges on the India agenda. Domineek? She wouldn't swim in a five-star hotel pool without first running a test on the water. She surely hadn't come up with the idea of letting POTUS dip into India's holy river.

The opposition went crazy. They called Lucia all sorts of names, and tried to make a national security issue out of the fact that she had ditched her detail and allowed the Indian bots to guard her in the water. Even some of our folks worried about a picture of the American president afloat, adrift, vulnerable.

I asked Lucia about it when she was back in Washington and we had a few seconds alone.

"Why did you decide to walk into the river at that moment, without telling anyone, instead of just standing at the shore to give your speech?" I said.

"It was unbearably hot, Aleks," she responded. "Unbearably hot. And I had to pee."

The Guardian

US President Lucia Jackson Takes Dip in India's Holy River

Monday, 21 June, 2021, 11AM GMT
theguardian.co.uk

DELHI, INDIA - US leader visits environmental summit in Delhi to show support for embattled Indian Prime Minister Nanda.

US President Lucia Jackson delivered a rousing speech on the need for international cooperation at an environmental summit in Delhi but not before taking an unexpected and controversial dip in the River Ganges, considered holy by India's Hindu population of approximately 1 billion.

The US president stepped into the river that has been a flashpoint in Prime Minister Nanda's environmental policies.

In India, the reaction was largely positive. "She's shown that India's challenges and our solutions to those challenges matter to the rest of the world," said Sonya Narayan, one of India's leading writers and a forceful voice in the environmental movement that has been critical of Prime Minister Nanda's policies.

"President Jackson's dip in Mother Ganges proves that our policies to clean up India are working," Prime Minister Nanda said.

In the United States, the unscheduled swim made waves when Jackson's political opponents condemned the presidential dip.

"It was inappropriate behavior on an official state visit," Senator Michuns of Kentucky said. "President Jackson presented an image that was anything but presidential."

At the summit in Delhi, President Jackson stressed America's role in tackling what she described as "jointly caused challenges that require jointly created solutions."

India has been lagging behind other nations, especially China, in moving away from fossil fuels, and it has struggled to balance industrial growth with environmental stewardship.

The presidential dip has prompted countless activists around the globe to post pictures of themselves alone, or in groups of up to several hundred people, all wearing indigo robes and wading into rivers and lakes that require cleaning up. Asked about this global trend, a White House spokesman said that President Jackson believes that "small gestures can lead to big change."

India's prime minister, saying he had been surprised by the commander-in-chief's action, added, "Next time, I hope she'll take me along for a swim!"

Big Nanda

In college, I took kung fu classes for a while in a tiny studio above a laundromat from a guy who spoke almost no English, could jump into full splits, crush bricks with his head, and really made you work.

"You work like cow in room," he would say.

After a few lessons, and after silently bristling at what I thought was an insult, I got what he meant. You can practice martial arts in a space no bigger than a cow's stable. Well here I am, locked into this stable-sized pod. At least two more days to go, so I might as well work out.

I did my exercises and halfheartedly searched for more hidden levers. I want the surprise, but I don't want Seth's ideas in my head.

I still had India on my mind. We had never developed a clear strategy. Our first visit there was a disaster, politically speaking. We had hours of meetings with Indian officials from that visit, everyone sitting on big, fabric-covered chairs in a windowless room along tables with long-stemmed flowers arranged in long, flat vases at the center.

"Our American industries have shown that green profits are possible," Lucia said. "Our tech transfer programs can bring this technology to Indian counterparts."

The Indians erupted in Hindi. We had brought an interpreter, but they had given us only four hours' notice that the conference proceedings would be switched to Hindi, even though they all spoke perfect English. Our interpreter was a young Princeton graduate with a degree in bioethics. She sat right next to Lucia.

"We want to help you achieve your goals," Lucia said before the Indian prime minister could speak.

"Madam President," he said formally but quickly. "India is not looking to the United States for help. Our nation has become an independent and strong country on its own. Our workforce is among the youngest and best trained in the world. We are the oldest, yet youngest country on the planet." He paused and looked around the room.

"India does not wish to be held back by Western regulations. Our country still needs to grow—just like your country was allowed to grow, unfettered by restrictions for two hundred years. Indira Gandhi and Jawaharlal Nehru fought for India's right to self-determination. We have no intention of letting others tell us now, when we will soon celebrate the centenary of India's independence from the yoke of colonialism, on how to grow."

"Burden," the interpreter said, correcting herself.

"No, 'yoke' is quite right," the prime minister said, switching to English. "The yoke of regulations!" He went back to Hindi. "We have no intention of letting others tell us how to grow, even if it is in the name of protecting the environment."

"India is America's partner," Lucia responded. She looked around the room. "We have supported your efforts, in all areas from Ladakh in the Himalayas to your border with Pakistan in the west, for a very long time." She paused. "The bases at Leh are of strategic importance to the United States, as you know. America intends to continue this support in the future, and especially during the colder months."

The prime minister stood up. The reference to the Christmas Conflict of 2018 was difficult to miss: when American troops had stopped a Pakistani offensive into Jammu and Kashmir, which had nearly overwhelmed the Indian forces in Srinagar, who were busy digging out of a snowstorm. That's when American troops had set up the security cordon that now bordered most of northern India and all of Kashmir.

"We will also continue to help in India's coastal regions," Lucia said.

Two other members of the Indian delegation stood up. This was a reference to the US Navy's help during Typhoon Kalele, when Indian coastlines had been devastated and US warships had brought in supplies and food. "We will continue to help India prosper in a world that is safe and secure for everyone. Indian ingenuity has helped Americans consume less energy in their homes. Many of the bright young Indians you mention are at the helm of the greatest American companies. But just as America has helped India, we expect India to help us achieve our goals in protecting our shared environment."

The Indian prime minister remained standing. Lucia stood, and they faced each other while two other members of the Indian delegation stood as if at attention, and the rest of us remained seated. This exchange had not been scheduled. *Off-script, off-script,* I thought, and tried unsuccessfully to steal a glimpse of Domineek's face. But Lucia was clearly enjoying herself.

"Our cap-and-trade program has reduced particulates to levels well below those of our neighbor states," the Indian prime minister said. "Over the past twenty years we have cleaned up Mother Ganga, and this success has inspired many other states to clean their rivers."

Seth nudged me.

"World Bank money," he whispered. "India has made a fortune off cleaning the Ganges."

I knew about the charges against the previous Indian government's use of World Bank environmental loans.

"And we have taken control of major polluters to protect our beautiful country for the next generation."

"Mr. Prime Minister," Lucia used his brief pause to interject.

"India can be a model for other countries. I have seen firsthand how much progress has been made here, and how much the shift to alternative power has accomplished. I have been inspired and impressed! We also think that the private sector can develop green practices in tandem with the government. That is why we would like to consider a trade agreement in the first place, to help the planet."

The dinner was a bust. The prime minister wouldn't budge on his plan to regulate some "polluters," even if the list of those companies did not contain one Indian conglomerate but only US-based companies. It was a ploy to nationalize foreign-owned entities.

We debriefed in Lucia's suite. We had a few senators with us, among them the three Indian-Americans in Congress, as well as the American ambassador in Delhi and her wife.

"They're going to end up in so much legal trouble that the World Bank won't loan them money," Lucia said. "Collectivization had been tried by Nehru, and then by Indira Gandhi, and it didn't work then. It never works. Taking over companies is the surest way to destroy an economy. It isn't going to work now."

I was jetlagged, and my eyes kept closing against my will. I had a huge amount of work ahead in gathering the data on companies that the Indians claimed were out of compliance with standards they had just invented. Suddenly, or perhaps I had missed a brief exchange, the ambassador and her wife got up. Lucia also got up and put on her jacket. An hour later our motorcade turned into a very long bougainvillea-bordered brick driveway. There were several black cars parked outside. The house was a stack of enormous concrete cubes that seemed to float on thin supports above a few square pools where pale pink flowers swayed on slender stalks.

We walked up a few steps on a wooden staircase. In the center of the long and tall foyer was what our host described as a "harras of horses" — except only the taxidermic hoofs and the massive bottom parts of several horses' legs were mounted atop a smooth slab of ebony. It felt to me as if the bodies of the missing horses occupied the vast room with their absent bulk. In the hallways were Chuck Close–like mosaics of Hindu deities, Bollywood stars, and religious figures. The shimmering portraits were made of thousands of minuscule screens, each one too small to make out with the naked eye. The ambassador's wife whispered to me, "All tiny shots of pornography," and kept walking.

The tables and shelves in the house were covered with what seemed like thousands upon thousands of jasmine blossoms — including around a screen on a desk that looked like a polished cube of copper, and even on the serving tables around the plates of appetizers, the main dishes, and the glasses and drinks.

I spent the next hour or so in a soft antigravity chair dreamed up by one of Delhi's hip designers, with my eyes closed but too tired to fall asleep, nobody paying me any mind. Lucia was meeting with the prime minister in another part of the house. At some point I got hungry and loaded up a plate with appetizers. The ambassador's wife touched my arm, told me to put down my plate and follow her through a side door down some narrow stairs. We arrived in a large, white-tiled kitchen. Three or four people were sleeping on the floor to one side, and a woman dressed in white was cleaning dishes at a huge steel sink. The ambassador's wife told me to sit down, and proceeded to speak in Hindi with one of the cooks. I stared though screened windows into a courtyard filled with several large piles of garbage and ringed by beautifully decorated walls topped with bougainvillea. After a while, we were served two plates of saag paneer, and two boxes of ice-cold Coke. I hesitated, thought about it, then relented. The creamy spinach, buttery cheese, and soft rice worked together beautifully. A whole season arranged on a plate. It was like eating spring itself. I felt at home and also transported, comforted by the dish before me.

"This is why I love being in India," the ambassador's wife said. "It's not that," she gestured toward the ceiling, above which was the big house with the mounted hoofs in the long hallway, the precious, dirty art, the jasmine blossoms strewn around the fancy plates and glasses on the beautifully carved tables, and the well-dressed guests and polite attendants.

"It's moments like these, right here," she said softly. She had short brown hair, but only now did I notice how it was carefully sculpted into small, shiny ringlets around her face.

There were now five people sleeping on the floor next to us while others prepared trays to send upstairs. We ate in silence.

"What about our environmental agenda?" I asked, gesturing at the silhouette of a middle-aged woman picking through the garbage heaps outside.

"President Jackson is getting it right," the ambassador's wife said. "It's not about the environment as separate from us. It's about the awareness that we are part of the environment, and the environment is part of us."

I raised my eyebrows and nodded for her to continue.

"Look at the petrochemicals you ingested just yesterday: drinking water trucked to the hotel in plastic jugs," she said. "The microparts you put on your skin, the ones you ingest when you brush your teeth. I switched to chewing betel, and look." She flashed her absurdly white teeth at me. "India has forced Big Water to sell only boxed water. Not ideal, still garbage, but — " she paused for a moment and pointed at the garbage heaps outside. "At least it's degradable and doesn't make people sick. Jackson's point that this is 'not about choices *between* us and the planet but about us *and* the planet' is exactly right. India is far too big and too complicated to choose one over the other."

She ate a few spoonful of saag paneer.

"Eat, eat," she said, and gestured at my dish. "POTUS is handling Nanda exactly the right way." I finished my plate and now dug into a sweet concoction served in a tall-stemmed glass. I had asked whether it was vegan, and the woman who served us our food nodded vigorously. I wasn't entirely sure.

A phone beeped and, after thanking the woman who had served us, we quickly returned via the service staircase to the big rooms.

“We’re leaving,” Lucia’s security guy said sharply as if I had kept them waiting, even though POTUS wasn’t here yet. Minutes later, we pulled out of the driveway. The sun had not yet risen, but there was already a lot of traffic on the road. Lucia was in a good mood.

“We might be able to make some headway with India after all,” she said to Domineek before pulling down her sleeping mask. “This was a good idea, to visit this house.” She slept all the way back to Delhi while I tried to focus on something on the horizon not to get carsick. When we pulled into the hotel’s underground garage, it was already day. I staggered to my room.

For the rest of the trip’s itinerary, I partnered with the house owner’s chief of staff, a cool guy named Jamal, who had studied at UCLA.

Lucia was completely upbeat for the next few days.

“We got concessions for all of the American companies,” she announced after our visit to the Red Fort in Delhi. “Not one of them will be forced under Indian control. And Delhi will sign on to APAC accords on cap-and-trade.”

I have pictures from that trip on the tablet, uploaded directly from Lucia’s live feed. There is “The Big Nanda,” India’s prime minister, in a blindingly white lungi and billowy pants, walking toward us in a long and high hall decorated with dioramas of tigers and peacocks. It must have been another hotel or perhaps a government building.

“Lucia!”

The next clip is of a state dinner. It was a huge affair, with hundreds of people in attendance. The women were dripping with jewelry and wore beautiful outfits and had expensive faces, and the men wore white lungis or were in black tie. The Big Nanda is addressing Lucia as “President Jackson” and “Madam President.”

During Lucia’s short speech he fixes his eyes on her.

“India is on a path to lead the world in many areas,” Lucia said. “It is a friendship forged by mutual respect and admiration between the United States and the Republic of India, the world’s youngest and one of the world's oldest nations. Today we celebrate the beginning of a partnership that will benefit more than a billion people and the planet, and will protect the water and air that we all share."

Over the course of several visits to India in the next two years, Nanda has worked hard on Lucia's plan to admit Pakistan and Bangladesh into APAC, which he chaired. But I'm stuck on the clip where the Nanda, the Big Man of India, exclaims: "Lucia! Lucia!" and breaks into that big toothy smile, raises his arms, and looks as if he's going to skip.

The Times of India

Is Lucia Jackson Another Green Imperialist? What the US Election Means for India

Op-Ed by NAVEENA KARIS
5:00AM Indian Standard Time, morning edition, November 5, 2020

This week's surprise victory of Senator Lucia Jackson to become the forty-sixth president of the United States by defeating Craig Weston, whose campaign was rocked by a series of financial scandals, is a good thing for India. To understand how Jackson's "ecumenical environmentalism" platform benefits our nation of 1.3 billion people who have long suffered from US green imperialism, one needs to understand how radical Jackson's position is. US voters swept in Jackson out of rage over the scandals that brought down Weston. Sometimes anger, as we know from the myth of Kali, yields good things. Jackson's proposals of controlled collapse, restoring the shore, her commitment to renewables and food security, and especially opening the US market to tariff-free imports of UN-certified green technology benefit India. Her move away from global carbon taxes and trades will greatly reduce our unfair financial obligations to the UN.

The US market for certified green technologies remains vast. Three hundred million American households are expected to replace existing electronic equipment with solar-based products. India is the global leader in solar manufacturing, except for vehicles, and the leader in green living software design. When Jackson's administration implements new regulations, India's share of tech equipment is expected to rise by 228 percent in the next four years.

I have fought for over two decades against Western-based green imperialism that holds emerging countries down in low-impact cycles of disenfranchisement. Green imperialism and green racism have deep roots in a White myth of the wilderness perpetuated by the likes of Queen Victoria and Rudyard Kipling, Herman Melville and Al Gore. The idea that Americans ought to serve as green stewards of the earth is a mockery in light of the fact that the American continent is more scarred by eco-violence than anywhere else on the planet.

Jackson's platform is truly global and inclusive. (A) She understands that fighting for the planet's survival is not the struggle of an ill-behaved but now reformed adolescent against a stern and disappointed parent. Water, air, and even soil do not belong to nations where these resources are found. (B) Jackson supported an unlikely coalition of local residents, radical environmentalists, and Native American groups who successfully blocked the state of Minnesota from granting mining rights to Rio Tinto, who have destroyed much of the land on which India's poor live. (C) She gained entry to the White House by a "fluke" (as many describe it). This election might signal an urgently needed turn toward real concerns for the health of the planet.

Naveena Karis, 64, is a Nobel Prize–winning novelist and political activist. Her treatise, Ecocide, *has sold over 10 million copies worldwide.*

Red, White, and Blue

The clips of "Mother Lucia Visits Mother Ganga" make me want to go swimming. It's another two days until I will be cleared and released. Two mornings, noons, afternoons, early evenings, and two long nights. No symptoms.

Lucia cared greatly about India, even more so after that visit.

"It's not only the population of India that makes it critical for the planet," she explained in a meeting with the secretary of state. "With Russia's turn to anti-Western tradition, and her efforts to pressure other countries into a no-win game of environment versus consumption, we have to support India. India has had great success in the past two decades in reducing child mortality, lowering birthrates, and lifting people out of poverty. They have also shown real commitment to cleaning up its rivers and shoreline — and I do not mean only the Ganges River," she added with a smile.

"We have tremendous opportunities for turning trash into energy," one of the guys from Trade said.

"If India enacts new regulations on energy production — which we have reason to believe they will — our trash industry can take off there."

The "reason to believe" was Asturias's skill in hacking confidential Indian data. We never quite knew, of course, whether the data was deliberately planted for us to hack, since every government releases fake data to lead hackers down a rabbit hole.

"I am not terribly interested in expanding our trash empire," someone from State said.

"We are more concerned that India might join Russia in an alliance of pronounced anti-Western attitudes. If India were to join that alliance, we will have little influence in the region."

"We are no longer fighting the Cold War," Lucia cut him off. "India has realized that it can benefit from partnering with us. And the anti-consumption movement out of Russia plays as anti-Indian for most Indian voters."

"The next election in India is a while off, and we know how much Russia is doing to shape the outcome."

Again, that is information from Asturias, even though State supposedly had better cyber guys than any other part of government, including the CIA.

"And we are not counting on a picture of me floating down the Ganges to do our work." Lucia waited for a moment, and then laughed. Everyone joined in.

"The great question of our time is the question of resources," she said, cutting through the mirth. "We over-consume, overeat, overproduce, overwater, over-fertilize, overfish, overheat, and over-cool. Our solution is not to stop all of these things. We may as well try to turn back time. But we can create a zero-waste economy. Many people want to reverse course altogether and stop consumption of goods. We know that even in the HEPP, and around here, some people think the Russian model of wholesale opt-outs is the solution."

"But those folks don't know how Russia really keeps its energy addiction going!" one guy from State interjected. Lucia ignored him.

"I am not interested in a fight between right and wrong. We hold these meetings," she paused briefly to look around the room at the guys from State, Treasury, EPA, and International Trade, plus our staffers and the oddballs on Asturias's team, "to focus on the greater good of the planet — the Russian way or our way. At some point we may see which direction leads to a better future."

The guys from State shook their heads, and Asturias stared at the screen in front of him.

"I also think behavior modification that limits consumption, and using renewables, is the better option. Our solutions are chosen based on solid science, but the data are thin."

The guys from EPA stared hard. They all held fancy PhDs from MIT, Caltech, Stanford, in new fields that recombined the sciences like strands of DNA. They were data-driven, metric-obsessed.

"We have to avoid pitting one solution against others," Lucia said. "That starts in this room, where I will not tolerate turf disputes or pissing contests. The best idea wins, but the person who came up with the idea will have to look for love and medals elsewhere."

We were all silent. I thought about the amount of time I usually had left over to find and keep love: roughly four hours at night, once I subtracted bathroom breaks, food, and showers. I wondered how earnest Keon was when he assured me almost nightly, when I'd fallen asleep on the couch, that he totally supported my work and loved me for my political passion.

"America's leadership in these decades is to teach people to think beyond their immediate concerns, beyond the lifeboat they happen to sit in, and about the fact that the water, the air, the sky do not know political boundaries."

Lucia paused to regain their attention. "I will not shy away from assuming a global leadership role," Lucia said. "But I will put America's interest first at every turn because we have recognized those interests to be the preservation, protection, and restoration of the earth. Which brings me to India and our supposed conflict with Russia."

The people from State didn't lift their eyes from the table.

"We are not partnering with India to keep the Russian influence out of South Asia," Lucia said. "That may be a positive side effect, and State will continue to assess the need and strategy for such containment. We are partnering with India because more than an ideological difference is at stake here. What is at stake is a massive impact on the oceans and the ozone layer, and that affects us all. I want you to remember this point in all of your decisions, in every meeting, every negotiation, every draft of every agreement." Lucia looked around the room, at everyone.

"And if we contain Russia in the process, all the better," the Secretary added.

"And if we can push our clean trash technologies, all the better," the Trade guys said.

Lucia got up and to everyone's surprise slowly clapped while turning once around to look everyone in the eyes. A few people briefly joined, a bit hesitantly.

"I told you that you better not look for love or medals of distinction here," she said and clapped one more time, hard. "So consider this, right now, all the praise you'll get. And every time you enjoy the luxury of drawing a breath of unpolluted air, of taking a sip of unpolluted water, of looking at a bright, blue sky, consider that your reward."

I can flip through pages and pages of trade agreements with India, position papers on our policies on Russia, more draft bills on trash regulation and interstate trash-hauling contracts than anyone could read in a lifetime. These documents are matched with fake information for potential hackers, courtesy of Asturias. "Pigs in a blanket," he calls his specialty of burying real documents inside fake files.

But my favorite clip is the shot of Lucia stepping out of Mata Ganga, her sari and indigo shawl trailing behind her. People are cheering wildly behind a phalanx of officers standing waist-deep in water as if posing in a Zhang Huan image.

The clip might be doctored, since the river behind Lucia now turns into a glorious and weird magenta. The cameras flash like stars at Lucia wrapped in blue in front of the iridescent reddish water. The clip becomes blurry, and instead of the American president emerging from India's holy river dripping wet, we see red, white, and blue.

File Accessed: Sandstorm

Voice Message to: Aleks Verdan, February 1, 2021, EST 9:42 a.m.
From: Li Yanfen, Beijing, PRC
Private Communication/Channel Open

Hi Aleks,
Hope all's well.

Things are okay with me. Work the same, play nonexistent – haha, well almost. The Dutch girl I was seeing, Lena, had to go back to her hometown several weeks ago since her mom got sick. We video chat but something has changed. I thought I'd send you a few lines so you know what's up with me.

How are you? Exciting times in the White House? How's Keon? Please say hi from me. I saw some pictures of you guys on a beach, but I don't know whether that was a vacation. Hope you two have some time for a break. Here we see a lot of footage of your president and how much she's interested in China. I always look for you, but I don't think I see you in her live feed. Do you think it's true that she cares for China? Do you think she is really in support of what we do?

I've been pretty active in my environmental group here. I kept going to meetings even after Lena left. There are some cool people there, and we kind of became friends. We held some demonstrations two weeks ago — I sent you some links, not sure you got them. But the problem with the demonstrations was what everyone's problem is here.

I know you've heard about the sandstorms. It's true that the storms have never been this bad before. For almost two weeks now, there has been no school, and everyone who works in an office has been forced to telecommute. There are so few people in the streets, it's eerie. And whoever is out makes sure their head is completely covered with a scarf and glasses and a mask. It's been so bad that the government sends heavy food trucks so you can get food in the basement or garage of big apartment buildings without going outside. I had to go help Lena pack her things and find a ride for her to go to the airport. Most flights were grounded already, but she insisted on going and trying her luck getting on a plane. I wrapped myself in the hoods they hand out now, and wore a face mask, goggles, gloves, etc. I secured everywhere with thick rubber bands and tape, the way they've given instructions, so you look like a sausage. But by the time I got to her house I was still covered in dust everywhere. I mean everywhere: eyelids, in my ears, between my teeth, fingernails, my toes, inside my underwear. It sticks to everything. It's completely impossible to use tablets or phones outside — the sand eats into them and you can throw it out afterward. My friend lost his phone that way, and it's hard to buy replacements right now. But people like us can manage. The biggest problem is for older people and babies. I have two colleagues who have left for Hong Kong who are hoping they will be able to work from there for a while. They have babies at home, and one of them coughed so much that he cried all the time and wouldn't eat anymore. Thank heavens my parents are in Guangzhou.

You remember the new super-tall mall across the street from your old language school, near the 3rd Ring road? The one with a hotel on top? Well you cannot even see it from across the street. I can't send you pictures. All you see is this dirty red color. It's hard to describe but imagine a really bad snowstorm except the sand hurts when it hits your face and it sticks to your clothes.

They've distributed goggles and masks but you have to get inside somewhere and clean the goggles and put on a fresh mask every twenty minutes or so.

Some people say that a lot of soldiers went blind during the first days of the storm because their masks didn't seal right. In my group, they've somehow gotten the numbers from local hospitals. Someone leaks them the data every day. Don't know if it's official, but they're posting it; you know how it is. It's like thousands of people who are sick, and many children are taken out of Beijing. Whole elementary schools in some of the outer districts, trains full of kids with their parents, trying to find out where their kids are headed and scrambling to find a way to get to those places, if you believe these reports. The people in my group are obsessed with getting the correct data. Jessamie, the girl who stayed with you and Keon last summer, posts those numbers every day online. She has a huge number of followers now, even though she posts nothing but numbers. I kind of see the point of putting all this online.

But Jessamie seems almost excited about the sand. She sends messages all the time with new data. She hasn't left the office, and the fact that we suddenly have all these people interested in the environment makes her and most of the group feel really gratified. Like they think that people will wake up to stuff that we have been talking about for a long time, the way the government needs to regulate industry for pollution, etc. Except that these storms have probably, for once, nothing to do with the government, or any factories.

I think it's bad in a different way. All of us get updates constantly, but I don't see this as an exciting opportunity to get more people to join the group.

What is the government gonna do? They've planted something like hundreds of millions of trees between here and the Gobi desert, and they've even constructed these huge fans in some neighborhoods to blow the wind in another direction. They've declared states of emergency, and now they claim that they can bring down the rain but when it finally rained last week, things got a lot worse, with the sand clogging up the drains and some of the controls in trains, which then got stuck.

This sand is so tiny, so fine and so sticky that what great big project is going to stop it?

It's just getting me down, while the environmental group is all excited and working overtime like a stupid college hack-a-thon. I know you have enough stress and don't need to hear about mine. And maybe it's just the fact that Lena had to leave. It felt a little bit like she was fleeing from Beijing. I know her mom needs her at home but with the deserted streets and my colleagues going to HK and just sitting inside all day staring at the computer or out the window at a wall of red, it doesn't feel good. She just left. It's depressing. I know it will stop — the storms always come in winter, and this year it's just going to be a bit longer. But this also feels different. Like someone threw a dirty wet blanket over Beijing and is holding it down to suffocate us all.

When I was little, I often visited my grandparents in their hometown near Guangzhou. They had been moved to a huge apartment building when their village was razed for the train line. My grandmother had three cats that lived on the small balcony of their apartment. They scared me a little — I think they were freaked out to be in the small space after village life, and I never went to the balcony by myself. It was covered with a net so the cats could not jump down.

One summer, when I stayed with my grandparents, one of the cats got injured somehow. We came home and heard it shrieking on the balcony. It cowered in a corner and the side of its head was torn open — I never understood what happened. There were some drying racks and tools on the balcony, and a washing machine that drained in the bathroom through a long rubber hose that ran through the living room.

The injured cat would not stop shrieking, and my grandmother yelled at my grandfather to help it, to do something. He went out to the balcony, and I think he tried to catch it to bring it to the vet. But when he got a hold of it, the shrieking got worse, and the other two cats went crazy. They jumped into the netting, swayed there, hissing, and tried to scramble up to the top of the balcony away from the other cat. My grandmother was crying now, just standing in the doorway looking through the glass door, but we heard this horrible shrieking. The other two cats tried to get out through the netting, but we were on a high floor, so my grandmother now yelled through the glass door for them to come down, to stop this somehow.

My grandfather had used a red towel to catch the injured cat. He twisted the cat into a bundle and held it tight. The bundle moved and shook, and my grandmother grabbed my arm while we stood at the glass door and watched. The cat's shrieks got muffled and then grew weaker. The other two cats had calmed down, and were now just hanging on to the net that kept them safe on the balcony. My grandmother stared through the window and said nothing. My grandfather's face was twisted with effort but he looked not at the bundle in his hands but straight at my grandmother. After a few minutes the bundle was still. It was silent now. My grandmother opened the glass door from the inside, and my grandfather carried the bundle through the living room, the hallway, and out of the front door and down the stairs. Maybe that's what we are here in Beijing, a sick cat and this damn sand is going to suffocate us.

Aleks — I'm sorry to be so down today. I'll be better soon, I'm sure, and I'll send you something fun. Enjoy the blue sky in Washington (I saw it on the news last night), and breathe in the fresh air for me. When you visit Beijing next, it will be spring or summer, and the sand will have blown away. I'm not gonna listen to this, or hit transcribe, since I'm sure I would it erase it all then. I actually really loved my grandfather — please don't think he was a cruel man. He had no choice on that day, really.

Take good care, have a drink (or two or three) on me, tell me how Keon is doing, how it is in the White House (unless you'll have to kill me then ☺).

Ciao,

Yanfen

Sand Brigades

Livechat, February 16, 2021, China Standard Time, 11:32 p.m.

To: Aleks
From: Li Yanfen, Beijing
Hey Aleks,

Sorry I haven't responded to your New Year's message. Things have gotten worse here. It's been so difficult to go outside these few days, and then the government started work brigades. They message you individually and you have to report to a team. Weibo has blown up over this — the return to Mao Tze Dong? What are their plans? But nobody's feed got shut down. After a while I stopped following the feed and just went downstairs. What else to do? They said dress warmly and bring enough masks for the day. There were a bunch of people from my building, mostly younger people like me, but also some older guys in shiny sneakers and long scarves wrapped around their heads. Some guys were waiting in the garage below my building, where the food trucks have been making deliveries for a few weeks. They were young, pretty nice. I couldn't figure out whether they were army or volunteers.

We went out in a truck, me and a bunch of people. We had shovels and brooms on the truck, and boxes with gloves and more face masks. For six hours every day I've cleared intersections, tram tracks, subway station stairs, traffic lights, street signs. We wipe, brush and shovel the sand into big piles, and then garbage trucks come by and suck it up.

It's really hard work, and at first I just signed on for the exercise. What else was I gonna do? I don't think the government is enforcing these calls for service, but if you don't go there's nothing to do at all, and it feels weird to go downstairs and stand in line for food next to your neighbors when they know you're a slacker. You get an armband with the date stamped on it to wear after each day, so everyone knows who has worked. But in terms of the actual work, it's wet and cold, you can't use a phone since they'll break, and there's no way to get back home without that truck. It looks like the pictures of China from last century, especially since the fucking sand makes everything look washed out, like there's no color in the world: yellow-brown work brigades, like dirty snowmen with shovels and brooms, lined up along a street or train line as far as you can see (which isn't far).

But for the first time in a long while, I think the eco-movement is doing something useful. The guys who organized my unit have come down from Harbin to help out. They have a green organization up there, kind of like our group. Jessamie is super excited about people joining our lists. I've been hanging with her some, but she is too giddy about the whole situation for my taste. All she sees is an opportunity to recruit more people. The Harbin guys don't seem to care about media so much — they didn't even ask me to sign their lists.

I'm not sure if any of this is helping, this shoveling and bagging of the sand. More blows in constantly. But at least we are *doing* something. When we return to the garage at night, we all sit on makeshift benches our crew built out of old furniture, and empty our boots and clothes from the sand. Then we get blasted with air guns. Taking a shower just makes the sand stick. Imagine a lot of guys in a garage holding on to poles while they are being blasted by big air guns that make their hair and dicks flop around. It would be funny but it's actually a bit painful. Then I usually patrol the walkways with another person to check on some neighbors. You know how big my building is, and we've knocked on the doors of neighbors who didn't even know about the trucks that deliver food directly to the garage.

You know how they say about Beijing, "It's a city where you have to find your way in"? I created a system for these people to get their orders in. Without that, I'm not sure what some of them would do for food. It's a bit strange, shoveling sand and going door to door every night to be sure the older people are okay, while the government has huge wind-blower machines, and the army is out in force to keep the airports clear.

Aleks, gonna sign off—send me a message sometime? Do you actually see the president a lot? Is she really serious about China policies? Are you traveling? Please message back soon.

It must be nice to see a blue sky and breathe without a mask.

Take good care,
Yanfen

China Daily

Beijing Work Brigades Fight Invading Sand

China/Society
Updated 17-2-20, 5:35 A.M. China Standard Time
Morning Edition
By Elizabeth Sozi (*China Daily*)

The recent extreme weather in Beijing has left many of the municipality's 12 million registered residents locked in their homes. For over a week, public schools and universities have been closed, with classes delivered remotely online. After three subway trains were stalled by sand, stranding thousands of commuters for the night, many businesses suspended onsite operations. The fine-grained sand brought in by winter storms from the Gobi Desert has damaged or shut down countless switching stations, and is creating problems for the operation of mechanized garage doors for the buildings that house plowing equipment. The government has employed high-level turbines to remove the sand from airport runways and critical intersections, but many smaller streets have become impassable with stuck vehicles. This week, the municipality recruited tens of thousands of volunteers to clear sand from transportation hubs.

The work brigades are led by municipal employees to clear mostly subway and train stations. The volunteers are issued masks and tools by the municipality's public works department. They do not receive compensation, but "day passes," that many businesses and all public employers will recognize for vacation days later in the year.

The effort may turn out to be the largest volunteer project in the Beijing-Tianjin-Hebei area ever, with the involvement of up to 12 million people daily.

I Have Been Moved

I have been moved. Woke up today — day five, it is — in a room with actual windows. The windows look out on a parking lot planted with bamboo, so I could be anywhere. All I remember is falling asleep while watching Yanfen's video messages from Beijing when they had the sandstorms. And now I've woken up in this room, which is a little bigger than the pod. More like a regular hospital room, but with a desk and a bed that can be flipped up like a Murphy bed, as in the pod. Same door as the pod, and the mesh membrane contraption. But a big, wide window. I've spent a while banging on the door to get someone to talk to me. Then I just looked out the window. Banged on that, too, pretty hard, but it's clear that the glass is strong as a plate of steel.

How was I moved? Why?

"You're still under observation," the med said when they finally showed up.

"Where am I?" I asked. "Why have I been moved?"

The weirdest thing is that I miss the pod. I like the window, but there's little but the bamboo and a patch of sky to see, and that only when I crouch on the floor and press my face to the glass. It's clear that the parking lot hasn't been used in a while. Bamboo shoots are breaking up the asphalt. What's weird is that after only four days, I had gotten used to the pod, and I had started to wait for the random screen programmings on the walls, and the piped-in sound. . .

Even though I don't know how I was moved here, I'm okay. I'm sure there's something in the food that made me feel this calm, but I don't know.

I don't want to discover what gimmicks they have hidden in this room, what contraptions I can discover. I don't want to play Seth's and Suad's game anymore.

Connectivity!

I got connected!

I should write that word in sparkly type, with fireworks and whistles.

Connected!

I was doing my tennis pro routine while watching clips of Lucia's "We Are But a Moment" speech. Watching the speech in so many locations is a bit like a time machine: Lucia with various hairdos, in pearls and gowns, a rainbow of suits, saris, bundled in parkas, a woven poncho, even, but still during the campaign, barefoot once. I wrote parts of that speech and then Lucia tweaked it after it had gone through vetting at State for the overseas events. No matter where she gives the speech, at some point Lucia paces along the front edge of the stage, facing the crowd.

"If along the edge of this stage we map the entire history of our planet, then the history of all of humanity is no longer than maybe an inch. We are but a moment!"

Then the tablet froze. I couldn't get back to the speech. Batches of files were downloading.

A huge pile of emails, messages, clips, and other stuff that tags my name or face somewhere. Lots of them are old, just things I was copied on and knew about — things that Asturias would put on my drive regularly. But also — and this is weird — countless clips and messages that I haven't seen, but that have my name highlighted or face tagged. I am positive that I had not seen these before. Why did they suddenly download? There's no sender, no message as far as I can see. No fucking clue. Still can't get my actual updated messages, and still can't go online. I've tried going to just any random site, assuming that the firewall is down. Waited and waited. But no dice. Just this data dump. Still no current news.

Here, in one of the new clips, is Lucia, in a room with a bunch of suited-up guys, and Seth and Domineek.

"We have made great progress in reducing our impact on the environment," Lucia says. "But the numbers work against us."

Behind her is a world map.

"The red areas are OPRs, overpopulated regions." The map changes colors and the red regions switch to purple. "You now see the great success stories of the past quarter century. The purple areas show overpopulated areas where infant mortality, poverty, and disease have decreased, and access to education, food, and water have drastically improved. Those are the poster areas for the UN, for our development goals, for all the big NGOs. But this success is producing new problems." Lucia turns to a woman at her side. "This is Geenie Carduff."

Geenie gets up.

"As President Jackson said, we have reversed dangerous trends. We have reduced carbon emissions, hit our targets for reducing water pollution. But studies show that all of our gains are offset by the shift of low-impact into high-impact populations. I am not a Malthusian, and what we have determined, based on years of data collection and models by teams around the globe, is not a simplistic claim that populations outgrow food supply."

"Which gets us to the reason we are here today." Lucia moves her along.

"The fact is that once these populations live the way we do, even when we have lowered our high-impact behaviors, the planet cannot be protected. The way we got to this point, through high-yield food production, is also the way we will get out."

"Our concern with the planet is as an interdependent environment," Lucia says. "All of our policies have to address that reality. What we are deciding here today is not merely what is critical for America, but nothing less than the future of the planet."

"We have convened a panel of ethics experts to advise us on these policies," Geenie says.

The screen behind her now shows a conference table lined with about a dozen academic-looking types who surround a woman with long, flowing hair, like the apostles and a female, blond Messiah.

"These experts have advised us that a humane way to control populations in over-populated nations and over-populated regions, OPNs and OPRs, is by way of monitored, careful, and deliberate use of certain GMOs. These crops have helped the world's populations to become healthier and grow. The same crops will help maintain a population level that won't outpace the planet's capacity to sustain us."

A lot of scientific data gets displayed. Lucia sits through all of it — something she rarely does in briefings. When she stands up, the twelve apostles pop up on the screen again. I recognize two of them: a big media ethics guy who is on all of the web shows, and the other person, the blond woman . . . is she the head of Human Rights Watch? She who is one of our archenemies, the thorn in Lucia's side who has not stopped calling our policies anti-humane? She gazes calmly from the screen. Lucia is thanking them.

Eugenics. The Nazis. Tuskegee. Tuberculosis blankets for Native Americans. Breeding out the black in Australia.

Lucia's face is a mask. I feel queasy.

"The United States will lend all possible support to fund and distribute these GMOs in OPNs. Our environmental team, led by Aleks Verdan, is leading the efforts to push sustainable farming practices, especially in India, Indonesia, and key regions of sub-Saharan Africa. To date, we have been able to lower the birth rate in several test regions to 2.1 children per family."

I stop the clip. Led by me? What efforts?

The file somehow downloaded to my computer, I realize at this point, because I am mentioned by name. My name, with a project I've never heard of. What I am sure of is that I was not there, was not briefed on any of that.

I rewind the file to look at that part again.

But what was this group? Why did Lucia mention me when I was not there, although the topic squarely falls within my purview? The clip was clearly made for internal archiving since it's not edited for media use. A rough cut, with my electronic watermark, and Lucia mentioning my name.

I feel numb, exhausted.

Maybe it's a clip I was sent from the White House for comment and approval?

But there's no message. I'm not really online—what downloaded, like a truck that fell from the sky, is this batch of files. And each single clip, heavy like a cinder block, with my name etched in it.

After Connectivity

I rack my brain, trying to remember meetings in which we discussed the issues in those clips that just downloaded. Of course human population was always in the background of our discussions. But usually, it came up in Lucia's terms of the great potential people have when properly motivated.

"Today what matters for people is to see themselves in the process," Lucia said during the campaign. "What matters is that they turn something into an issue, that they see others like themselves participate. That they see others doing the same thing."

Our strategy: to empower people so they become part of the solution; not to make us more resilient but to enter into regenerative processes that build a shared future. It was not a matter of appealing to their better nature. It was a matter of realizing that putting people at the center of every solution was the only way forward. The eco brigades had effectively engaged people in the US. In other countries, we had spent a hell of a lot of money on local outfits, from indigenous collectives to townships to whole environmental movements.

"Activists are our allies," Lucia said. "They are a source of strength, and without them nothing will change. If one doesn't see people like oneself behind an issue, one doesn't trust it. The failure to let people shape and run the message directed at them is the biggest mistake we can make."

"But these people want to stop progress," we heard from Congress, from corporate lobbies, from everyone. I heard it from Uncle Wynn. "They want to turn back the clock, live like farmers. Regeneration really means turning back time. They want to get rid of vaccines, get rid of fertilizer, get rid of electricity."

"They are the people who will create new demand and new markets," Lucia said. "They are the ones who force American companies to improve their products for a global market. They want clean energy, clean water, clean and healthy food. Americans are best at inventing those things."

Our local partnerships worked because there was new technology to support change. Retrofit existing structures or put in more efficient new ones. Trash into fuel. Give land back to nature. Restore the shore. Health before wealth. And people remained at the center. Local organizations, local activism, local efforts.

"People understand that the environment impacts their lives," Lucia said. "They know that their kids' health is impacted by water, air, and food. They also know intuitively that the health of the planet is essential to their own health."

We included people of all stripes: union, faith-based, greenies. Even people the party often shied away from: radicals, occupiers, opt-outers, boycotters.

"The kind of folk who want to burn this city down," Domineek often said, "and turn Washington back into a swamp."

"It's already a swamp," someone inevitably responded.

I've worked with a lot of them. Sometimes it's tricky, since some of them refuse official meetings, official recognition, any semblance that the US government supports them. Occasionally, there has been the surreal moment in which the White House "expresses concern" over some disruptive action that we — which is to say the same White House — funded. Politics. And their goals are our goals. Saving the planet before it's too late.

Even before the inauguration, when we had not yet gotten

support from Silicon Valley, we created a special fund to support groups who refused to officially accept our money. Today their funding is run through two NGOs that are aboveboard. Our legal team worked hard to set this up in the right way so that they could keep their funding after we won the election, without creating liability for anyone. They didn't want to be supported by government, and we could not be seen to fund a nonprofit. But they figured something out. Keon worked for one of them a few years ago, when we were just out of college and before their business took off. They believe in people changing the way things are done, and, even if sometimes they do things in pretty outrageous ways to get attention, we share the same values.

I return to the new files that have shown up on my tablet. They have my signature, my approval stamped on them, my name. They are official policy.

Eco Brigades II

There is a clip of Lucia addressing some people on the role of militias. She refers to me in her opening remarks.

"The White House environmental advisor, Aleks Verdan, known to many of you, has largely shaped our strategy for outreach and engagement. The objective is to reverse some of the damaging trends we've allowed for too long — trends that threaten the survival of our species. Without a healthy planet, there is no point in improving education, providing health care, food, shelter, or clean water. Without a healthy planet, there is no point in working for peace or improving trade. Without a healthy planet, there is no point in making money."

Lucia paused.

"This is not another salvo in the science wars, or about belief."

Behind Lucia, a globe with one of the earliest environmental logos slowly rotated. The logo seemed as if it was from a long time ago, when our environmental budget had been tight. Back when our staff was so small that I both booked her lectures and carried her changes of clothes. I remember being teased about it by other staffers. I didn't care. I always liked those moments right before Lucia stepped into the light, when we sat together for a moment so she could slip on her shoes. We laughed during those times: Lucia would stretch out her foot, vamping it up like a screen legend, and

I'd say, invariably, "Great legs!" like the cobbler to the stars. We loved those moments getting her ready to win people over. There was a bit of a conspiratorial feeling in us when I handed her the shoes, because it was all part of the political charade. But there was also a core of understanding and closeness that felt pure, that was not about manipulating or putting anybody on. The recognition that we both played a part, and that we knew it, but that we played that part for a greater good. That was when I would still say "Go get 'em," or "Good luck." Today she has other handlers, of course, and there is Gabi, but occasionally we still huddle right before a meeting when she needs some info about the folks in attendance.

There were crowds on the screen behind her: rallies in various cities, shots of the Beijing visit, Lucia's first big speech on the Zócalo, of Calgary.

"It is their message that matters," Lucia said, and turned halfway toward the screen where a group of people in matching green windbreakers marched toward what looked like a village. The shot panned out to reveal a windswept plateau, and then cut to the people on top of the Three Gorges Dam. I thought I spotted Li Guanzheng, the community organizer for whom I had organized a brief media moment with Lucia. Indeed, there they were now: Lucia and Li in matching caps. There was even a glimpse of my shadow on Li's face since I had been standing right next to the drone camera when this was taken.

Someone else stood up and joined Lucia at the end of the table. I didn't recognize him. A trim guy with a taut, Calvinist face. Surely the result of lots of exercise and a strict diet.

"We have enabled local green groups to enforce policies. We have empowered people on a local level, at the grassroots level, so to speak." He looked as if he was going to smile but only his eyes flashed, without mirth. "To serve as enforcers of environmental rules."

The pictures behind Lucia and the guy changed to rows and rows of paramilitary units, with green helmets.

"These citizen groups enforce local ordinances and environmental laws. We've found citizen brigades far more effective than police enforcement to achieve compliance."

"These are people committed to the planet's well-being," Lucia said.

There were quick glimpses of opt-out enforcers in Germany and of guys at a makeshift roadblock on an expressway in what could have been any large city in northern Africa or the Middle East.

"These groups have proven more effective in changing behavior on the ground than any of our policies," Lucia said.

"What about vigilante mobs shutting down factories? What about Seoul?" The question came from somewhere offscreen, and on the display behind Lucia there appeared shots of the Seoul protests at the KIA factories. They were the familiar images of people rushing in all directions away from drones spraying tear gas, and of others frantically using long sticks to whack at the drones and crash them into the police. "A lot of people died in those riots over pollution, and now we want to encourage that kind of thing? We want to support and arm local militias?"

"These local groups function like antibodies, if you will," Lucia said. "They have to be guided from within, of course. We have had success in getting local leaders involved."

Li Guanzheng appeared again behind Lucia on the screen. "The Seoul protests, the Daka riots, the shutdown of the Nicaragua Canal site were all controlled riots to focus political attention away from other issues."

"Did the KIA people agree to this?" the same voice asked from offscreen. "Did the Chinese approve shutting down of the Nicaragua Canal?"

"In fact, they did," Lucia said. "Like all of us in this room, and like the eco-forces organized by people on the ground, even the people at KIA and our partners in Beijing, realize that the planet takes precedence. And we have reserves to cover actual losses when these distractions become necessary."

"We have used KIA and Nicaragua as decoys?" the same voice said.

"You're still not seeing the bigger picture," Lucia responded. "These leaders have realized that if we don't defend the planet, life will be untenable for us all."

"President Jackson's broad appeal has permitted us to galvanize local movements in many places," Domineek said in what sounded like the session's summary.

"Indeed," Lucia said. "We have used my media presence to identify local groups that carry out and enforce policies. It is a way of diffusing and outsourcing enforcement, especially in OPRs, without reliable leadership or governments."

"We've had great success in Japan after Typhoon Michio, where local eco militias prevented the resettlement of sensitive shore regions. Canada just after Banff was also a success, where a minimum of actual troops is supported by local organized groups. Also, in Cambodia during H1N12, where we had tried forced quarantine for the first time. It worked because of local civilian enforcement."

Lucia had left the room, but Domineek stayed behind.

The White House. But what room? What group is this? I go back to the moment where she mentions my name. She mentions me casually, the way you refer to someone who's missing due to scheduling, and she praises me for making the environmental message a central plank in our policy.

The clip with Li Guanzheng, and with the militias in Germany, Cambodia, or is it Egypt? People in eco-militias attacking their neighbors for the cause?

I have a sudden, sharp headache, right behind my eyes, but when I lower my head for a moment, it almost makes me throw up. I don't want to ask for any medicine, because it will just put me to sleep. I sit up, try to breathe for a few moments. I don't know what I'm feeling. Like something has opened up inside of me, a hole that's getting bigger, but that's just empty. Empty. Numb.

Fear and Love

Many of the new clips have my initials, and others are memos on which I am only one of several recipients. It makes it look as though I've signed off on these docs and attended all the meetings.

But I haven't.

We had so many debates on how best to get people on board with our eco agenda. They always fell into one of two camps: fear and love. Lucia was good at using the love approach: no matter if I knew how a speech or statement had been edited and packaged, how every modulation of her voice, every clip and elongation and pause had been synthesized for effect — political kitsch, of course, ersatz emotions — I was moved nonetheless.

Managing fear was more often my province, using real-life events. The flu pandemic of 2019 and our decision to disseminate uncensored footage from wards in Hong Kong. People had crawled on the floors in their own waste and over dead bodies after the staff had abandoned the hospital; corpses were bunched high against glass doors that had automatically sealed when pathogens were detected. Reluctantly, we had released footage of families drowned in flash floods, and clips of thousands upon thousands of cattle being foamed to death to snuff out a disease. Well-timed doses of fear had been effective in getting people to accept travel restrictions, food inspections, home checks, quarantine, the rationing of medication. We took every measure we could short of risking getting thrown out on our ears in the next election. We managed fear and provided continued assurance that we were protecting people from the worst ravages the planet would muster, and that our policies could appease a world out of control.

Our chief goal — the one that informs all our actions — is to save and protect the planet. It's what I believe in: it's probably the only thing I really, truly believe in. Maybe — when I don't feel insecure — maybe sometimes I also believe in the astonishing possibility that someone as beautiful and intelligent and wise as Keon truly loves me back. But that belief, the belief in love, is like anadromous fish during a river run — constantly moving, tremblingly alive, and working constantly even just to stay in the same spot. My belief that the planet must be our first priority, by contrast, is a rock.

Our political agenda encourages people to live better, healthier, more responsible, and peaceful lives that don't exploit nature until nature has run out. We believe that there is still time to reverse course and keep the planet not just habitable but healthy.

"Sophistry," Lucia would cut us off when discussions went on for too long, with someone arguing that without people there won't be a need for politics.

"Without people, the fate of the planet, whether it lives or dies, will occur in the vast indifference of the universe," Lucia said. "After people, other species would survive, even if it's likely to be rats and roaches. But without people, there would be no one to *love* the planet, and to think that its existence matters for its own sake."

I cannot find the clips of those discussions. Instead: confidential memos, clips of meetings and directives for issues that are supposed to be in my bailiwick but that are utterly strange to me.

The Guardian

EcoSafe Funds Green Artist's Projects

4:23AM GMT
Miranda Goh

PORTUGAL - Tuesday, 2 December, 2021—Several documents recently released by WikiLeaks contain images of bank transactions showing that the prize-winning Portuguese artist Mold has received funding from EcoSafe for several projects. EcoSafe is the manufacturer of environmental safety equipment. The company has been accused of fostering anti-foreigner violence in several regions. The revelation came on the heels of Mold winning the Ted Turner Green Prize awarded by the UN, set at 1 million bit points (approximately US$1.7M). The prize is awarded annually for "ecologically sound and sustainable acts that contribute to the survival of our planet."

EcoSafe is a US-Canadian company that provides eco barriers to countries seeking to limit the movement of populations that carry diseases and could potentially overwhelm existing infrastructure or intend to settle in protected environments such as nature preserves, wildlife corridors, and sustainable agricultural zones.

EcoSafe has come under attack for designing eco sensors that track individuals who have crossed borders legally but have previously visited infectious zones. They have also been criticized for marketing "smart" fences that have caused the deaths of people trying to scale them.

"EcoSafe has stoked people's fear of outsiders as the greatest threat to their environment, even if those risks are predominantly domestic," said Kenia Ruiz of Global Human Rights Watch. "Their business model is based on demonizing the sick and the powerless."

It is estimated that EcoSafe supplies "environmental safety equipment" to at least 70 governments in addition to many private entities. EcoSafe installed the eco barrier that seals Turkey from its southern and eastern neighbors and the eco barriers that protect most of the public and private game preserves in South Africa, Botswana, and Zimbabwe. Their products and methods have been criticized as inhumane by human rights organizations in several countries.

"Our products are safe and protect some of the most precious regions on the planet from destruction," Edoardo Pisani, a spokesman for the company said. "We deeply regret any loss of human life due to lawless behavior."

Mold initially defended the fact that he accepted EcoSafe funding since they "provide important means of keeping our environment safe." But when the leak site published images of dead people hanging on a fence that surrounds the pristine coastal regions of Croatia, where Mold is set to unveil another project, he announced that all funding from EcoSafe would be returned.

Pork

It's been nearly a day since I have been moved. I've watched so many clips from that download that my eyes hurt. My headache is a bit better, but I still feel nauseous and agitated, like I've had ten espressos. At dinner I forced myself to turn the tablet off and look out the windows at the bamboo. It makes me think of the shed, and of Saturday mornings, working in one of the urban plots. The food here, in this room, is different. Just now, it was pork ribs — tender, juicy baby back ribs nestled in a small edible tray. I didn't know they made pork substitute that tasty. When I looked at my tablet for stored information on pork, I found a clip about pork in China that I hadn't seen before. It mentions me.

Lucia, WHO staffers, Domineek, Seth, some people I don't know, several senators, Chinese delegates. The clip is tagged as my feed, the watermark saying it was recorded on my tablet, with my fingerprint log. There is no way I was there.

"Beef consumption in the US has declined by 40 percent since the Kansas outbreak," Domineek said to the group. "This reduction is not only healthier for American consumers, but it has also led to the culling of significant numbers of cattle in the US and South America."

"Our industry has been decimated!" one of the Senators from Kansas called out. "Cattle are being wiped out not by disease but by fear and federal directives!"

"What you call federal orders have been last-minute measures to protect human life," Lucia said. "If we had not ordered the destruction of the herds, thousands of people in the US would have died."

Nobody responded. After a moment, she continued. "This is all water under the bridge. We are not here to discuss beef. Today's issue is pork."

I fast forward a bit.

"The only way to limit the pork industry in China is by reducing consumer demand," Domineek said. "An outbreak caused by pork is the only way to do that."

"You are proposing a controlled outbreak?" one of the Chinese guys asked.

"It is the only way to keep the pork industry from destroying much of China's countryside," the woman from the EPA said. "There will be a human cost, to be sure," she explained. "But we know that these outbreaks burn out fairly quickly. People develop immunity. We have an accurate and precise survival rate. The overall gain is that, after the worst has passed, the market for commercially raised pork will all but disappear."

"A simple salmonella strain," Heather said. "It will produce human casualties, but it can be contained. Ultimately, it eliminates overbred, and thus especially vulnerable, stock. It makes the farms safer. And it shifts consumer demand to sustainable hog farming."

"Can human exposure be kept at a minimum?" Lucia asked. "Aleks has been working on education and awareness in China for a while. But can't people be made aware of these risks before an outbreak hits?"

"No, Madam President," Heather said. "Unfortunately, consumers have not responded to awareness campaigns."

"It's like vaccinations," the senator said.

"Like vaccinations," Lucia echoed him and left the room.

I pushed away my plate.

Contaminated meat to teach the public something? Sacrificing a few people for the greater good?

"Aren't you hungry? Are you feeling okay?" I didn't look at the medic when they picked up the tray.

Opt-Out Investigation

October 23, 2021
To: UN Commissioner on the Environment, Her Excellency Raina Al-Islam
Aleks Verdan, environmental advisor, the White House
President Lucia Jackson, the White House
From: Rosamond King, executive director, Human Rights Watch

Our investigation into the deaths of 458 individuals in the city of Timişoara last June has determined that these people were killed by a mob for not adhering to non-official rules about shutting off all electricity in an opt-out event. Most of the 458 individuals resided in a poor section of Timişoara largely populated by recent immigrants from the southern Mediterranean (North Africa).

When the citizens of Timişoara organized an opt-out event to signal their commitment to reduce energy use, the inhabitants of a nearby settlement were either not informed of the "rules" (a code of conduct not officially endorsed but tacitly enforced by local police) or could not understand the Romanian instructions. When several inhabitants of this area refused to turn off all lights, including safety lights along a canal, a mob of citizen enforcers attacked them.

News reports and official government statements from

Romanian authorities have blamed ethnic tensions for the deaths.

Our findings differ sharply from this explanation. An exhaustive review of all available evidence shows that the individuals were targeted and killed for not following opt-out rules. It also showed that local police enforcement did nothing to stop these killings, and that opt-outers have grown increasingly militant. Our agency requests a UN review of our findings so that similar incidents can be prevented in the future. Our agency also requests that the UN assists in monitoring and regulating citizen brigades and opt-outs in Europe, where the European commissioner for environmental security has promoted and funded such citizen-led environmental efforts on a large scale.

Vaccinations

A little while ago they gave me two shots. Boosters of some kind. I just put my shoulder against the membrane and pop! Pop! They put them in.

Then I searched for vaccinations on the tablet and found what's below. All these files must be things that got onto my tablet by accident? When Asturias did a sweep? But then why have I not seen them before? Why did they all come up at once?

— — -

Department of Health and Human Services
Department of Defense
Environmental Advisors to the White House
Department of Homeland Security
Department of Education

Re: Vaccination Requirements for School Attendance, Federal Financial Aid, State and Federal ID, Driver's Licenses, Marriage Licenses

Extensive studies show that the 2018 smallpox pandemic in the Chicago suburb of Oak Park can be traced to a 26-year old schoolteacher who carried the virus back from a honeymoon trip to India. Upon her return, the teacher introduced the virus into a school with a population of some 800 children. It is estimated that nearly 30 percent of these children had not been vaccinated against smallpox, measles, rubella, or mumps, as required by state law for children enrolled in public education.

During the outbreak, 216 children developed symptoms. The school was closed and measures were taken to protect the public (forced quarantine under National Guard supervision). In spite of state-of-the-art medical care, 43 of the infected children died during the outbreak. The WHO and the Department of Health and Human Services have conducted independent and separate studies of this outbreak and jointly implemented mandatory requirements to achieve full vaccination compliance.

1. All children enrolled in accredited schools and educational programs, including religious schools, will be required to be vaccinated. Vaccinations will be provided free of charge during first week of school. All children will be tested on premises for antibodies; only vaccinated children will be admitted to public schools.
2. All students who fail to furnish proof of vaccination before enrollment in an accredited primary education institute are ineligible for Federal and State loan and grant programs, including any Free Lunch programs, After-School Programs, Pell Westons, Federal Work Study, Stafford Loans, and Pence Westons.
3. No schools will be permitted to open without full vaccination compliance.
4. Failure to comply with mandated vaccination requirements precludes the issuance of state IDs, driver's licenses, passports, marriage licenses, or proofs of residency.
5. These requirements apply to all persons residing in the US (including undocumented aliens, legal permanent residents, seasonal agricultural and service workers, long-term visitors

and refugees). All relevant Homeland Security forms (e.g., the application for Resident Alien status, I-485, and so on) include clear statements on the requirement for vaccination.

6. All persons using public or private fee-based transportation (bus, train, boat and ferry, and plane travel) are required to facilitate biometric data checks when using transit.
7. Compliance with vaccination standards is mandatory for anyone receiving state or federal assistance (food stamps, free-lunch programs, transportation vouchers, early childhood programs, Medicare, Medicaid, Social Security, veterans' benefits, travel on public roads, air and train travel, usage of public land or buildings).
8. All individuals employed by state or federal governments (law enforcement, security, federal agencies, public works, education, states and municipal agencies, sanitation, housing, etc.) are required to comply with vaccination requirements. Failure to comply renders anyone ineligible for employment.
9. All participants in eco brigades are required to be vaccinated.

Had this bill been ratified by Congress? I scrolled back. My office is listed as a sponsor, but I don't remember any meetings. There's no date, and when I search the tablet for corresponding files that I would have created, I can't find any.

I've always assumed vaccinations are important, and I probably have an unreasonable faith in the medical profession.

"Not all anti-vaxxers are crazy," Keon said once when we were on the highway, stuck behind a caravan of buses with "anti-vaxxination" signs plastered on the sides. "A lot of the science they cite has been verified outside of the States," he added. We were going from Florida to Louisiana on our way to visit his grandparents, so it must have been before 2018. I remember the asphalt shimmering in the heat, and the trees on both sides choked by kudzu and bitter melon vines.

"It's because of these wackos that smallpox came back," I said to Keon. "And that they now have kids with polio again in Europe."

"But there are side effects for sure," Keon said. "These people are just worried for their children." I looked at the people staring out the back of the bus, their faces framed in the shiny tinted windows. Robert Frank's *The Americans* for our age. They didn't look like insane radicals.

"I don't mean these anti-vaxxers have side effects," Keon said, as if he'd read my mind. "I mean there are probably things we will all get because we've been vaccinated so much. It's a trade-off, like most things."

I remember distinctly that we were going to see his grandparents because of the way Keon said nothing after he mentioned the side effects of vaccinations. His grandfather had signs of dementia, or "the big A," and a lot of people blamed environmental causes for that. Vaccination being one of them, even if all major media disputed it. Antidepressants another. Sleeping pills another. Goddamn daffodils.

After looking at this file, it's clear that the bus caravan was probably organized by people who couldn't get on public transportation because their biometrics didn't scan.

I'm trying to find other files about vaccinations, and there are two things I've discovered on the tablet.

Re: Vaxxers and Non-Compliant Populations

The surgeon general estimates that federal measures to ensure safe numbers of vaccination bring about 80–85 percent of the population into compliance.

About 10 percent of the population is out of compliance for religious or ideological reasons (the "anti-vaxxers," as the anti-health movement is known). Of these 10 percent, a disproportionate number are children of anti-vaxxer parents. A total of over 4.4 million children in the United States and HEPP territories are currently not vaccinated for major diseases, including MMR, smallpox, polio, HIV, tuberculosis, and SARS-2b. These children are at an immense risk. They also pose a threat to the rest of the population.

Five percent of the residents in the United States and HEPP/Canada and 18 percent of residents of HEPP/Mexico are out of compliance because they do not participate in governmental programs (medical care, education, employment).

Proposal: Given the enormous health risk posed for the general public by the unvaccinated population (cf. SARS-2b in Hong Kong, 2016, with 600,000 casualties; smallpox in Chicago, 2018, with 2,700 casualties; return of polio in the UK and northern EU countries), the surgeon general proposes targeting adults in those populations during short processing stays with law enforcement. Local authorities should use all available legal means ("broken taillight policies") to bring non-compliant adults into temporary custody. All parents with non-vaccinated children are to be charged immediately with child endangerment, negligence, and posing high risks to the public.

Police courts are to refuse religious and ideological exemptions in accordance with the *McCarwen vs. United States* ruling that puts the nation's health above freedom to exercise religion. All individuals thus charged will be offered full amnesty when they accept immunization at that point. Police enforcement and presiding judges are instructed to make the choice clear between vaccination or legal consequences. Vaccinate or lose your child ought to be the basic, unequivocal message. Get vaccinated or get locked up.

Children: For obvious reasons, unvaccinated children pose a particular threat to the general public. The surgeon general recommends removal, even temporarily, of unvaccinated children from non-compliant parents so they can be vaccinated. The overall goal is vaccination, not punishment. This will lessen the risk posed to themselves and to the general population.

Public-health squads can vaccinate children effectively and quickly. These on-the-spot vaccinations of children, many of whom are home-schooled, can be performed at shopping malls, concert venues, sports facilities, playgrounds, or other gathering places.

When unvaccinated children are accompanied by guardians, law enforcement should treat them like abducted children.

While individual rights and concerns (particularly civil rights, though not the claim for religious exemption) need to be acknowledged, respect for those rights must not supersede the general public's right to be safe from contagious disease and pandemics. The greater good trumps the individual's concerns; health is a public good that must not be sacrificed or compromised.

I know for certain that I have not seen these directives. An extra-judicial dragnet for non-vaccinated adults? Vaccination by force, via secret agents for anti-vaxxer children in malls and movie theaters?

I remember watching the commotion around two screaming parents in a Maryland mall once. They were held by security officers, while a lot of official police and some mall cops surrounded their preteen girls. One of the girls was in tears, sobbing. The other seemed unconcerned at first, just looking at her phone, but then tried to run. The officers grabbed her and quickly carried her, literally kicking and screaming, through a door next to an ice cream store. It was upsetting, but the whole scene lasted less than a minute. I didn't want to stare, but now I remember.

"Those are anti-vaxxers," my friend Stephanie had said dismissively. "Wackos."

At the time, I'd assumed she was talking about shoplifting or vagrancy or truancy. Now, after reading these memos that bear my name, I realize those two teenagers were probably caught on the mall's biometric scanner and then forcibly vaccinated. Shocked kids, screaming parents, lots of security — the whole thing over in less than a minute.

"America has always been about the proper balance between the individual and the collective," Lucia once said in a meeting. "But the public's health always trumps the individual, especially in our day and age. We cannot afford to return to a time when whole cities were wiped out by some plague. With modern travel, we could lose several cities at once."

No American cities have been lost, as far as I know. Small crises, yes: Chicago smallpox, a few retirement communities in Albuquerque, two high schools in Seattle (or Portland?). And the standoff with the commune of anti-vaxxers in Nevada that ended really badly. I'd always thought it was a raid gone wrong, with all those shot, parents who had set up their kids as human shields, according to the media. On the whole, the fear of massive outbreak is probably exaggerated. I don't understand how they got these memos past anyone in Justice.

The Times

Avian Influenza Outbreak Worst in Dakar History

By ALAÏS DIOP
Last Updated at 10:35 a.m., December 16, 2022

DAKAR, SENEGAL - Three weeks into the worst outbreak of avian influenza in this elegant African city abutting the Atlantic, all roads are closed. Life has come to a standstill. The palm-lined avenues and sun-dappled plazas are deserted. The members of the national assembly have been sent to their home districts, and the presidential palace is surrounded by armed guards. The only people seen in public are health squads in hazmat suits, and a handful of masked family members standing vigil outside one of the many quarantine centers. All schools and workplaces are closed, and food trucks deliver rations to people hiding behind closed doors. If the whole city looks like a scene out of Albert Camus' novel *The Plague*, it is due to the health cordons stationed on access roads. Battalions of armed medical staff block all roads leading to Léopold Sédar Senghor International Airport near Yoff, a residential part of town where people must pass through barbed-wire checkpoints to reach their guarded homes.

"We are imprisoned in our own city," says Yolande N'dour, mayor of Dakar. Although Senegal's president, Daouda Niang, has registered complaints with the World Health Organization and the UN, there is widespread belief in Dakar that he asked the UN to send in militarized guards.

"He's been pressured to shut down Dakar. His complaints are just political theater. He's in on this plan to isolate us, and we're left to rot," said

Lydie Sekai, a designer whose clothes sell in Paris and New York.

There have been several shootings after citizens tried to storm the barricades blocking roads leading out of Dakar.

"The fact that Dakar has been cut off from the outside world by foreign military units without our UN mandate is an outrage," reads a statement signed by several human rights organizations. The influenza outbreak has claimed at least 3,200 lives here, according to WHO officials. Some patients have recovered after treatment with Reflu, a flu treatment. People with compromised immune systems and other complications are at greater risk.

"Letting a disease burn out is the safest option for the greatest number of people," said Dr. Sandra Pressner, a pandemic specialist who has authored several studies on the drawbacks and benefits of 'burn-out' policies. "Exporting the disease poses a risk for potentially hundreds of millions of people. We are doing everything possible to help the sick. But letting the disease run its course in a controlled setting has proven the most effective measure to contain a disease."

The people of Senegal are scared and angry.

"We're left to die here, while the NGOs and the UN wait for this to be over," said a member of Parliament who declined to be identified. "Look at Ngozie's Twitter! Not one mention of a casualty for the past two weeks! I've lost a son and daughter-in-law to this horror. Our children are dying, our elders are dying. And instead of doctors, they sent in soldiers."

When night falls in Dakar there are groups of youths roaming the streets, and "medical security officers" in armored vehicles parked at all roads leading out of town. "We have flown in hundreds of doctors," Dr. Pressner said. "But in many cases, there is not much we can do." Drone cameras from major news stations hover over the city. Occasionally a drone is captured by civilians and smashed to pieces in the street, often to loud cheers.

"The clock is ticking in Dakar," says N'dour in one of the few rooms of the mayor's mansion still open for business. "They're waiting for us to die or the infected to survive. But until they know that the disease has run its course, we'll be here alone."

The White House has been conspicuously silent on the issue, although most of the armed guards cordoning Dakar, including the soldiers guarding the presidential palace, are assumed to be American-trained military personnel.

"Lockdowns and forced quarantines have proven effective means of containing outbreaks," said Senator Jeremy Walcott, Republican of Texas, chair of the National Public Health Committee. "We are very concerned for Senegal, but we are putting the health of hundreds of millions above the mobility of one city, for a brief period."

Clearana

To: President Lucia Jackson
From: US Surgeon General Meghna Bhatsee
Susannah Gottshen, Chairman of the Executive Board, the World Health Organization
Aidan Cabot, The Honorable Senate Committee Leader on Environmental Policy
Rohan Vinja, Environmental Protection Agency
Nyamal Siddig, Envoy of the Economic Common of the West African States
Aleks Verdan, White House Presidential Advisor on the Environment
Re: Clinical Trials of Clearana/Birth Rates in ODNs and ODRs

Safe water is a fundamental human right. Every year more than 840,000 people die due to lack of clean water. For the past five years, since 2014, the governments of several sub-Saharan nations north of Namibia and Botswana have used the purification chemical Clearana for urban water supplies. Clearana is a safe, reliable, and inexpensive method of ensuring water quality for large populations. A number of African countries (with the exception of Eritrea) rely almost exclusively on Clearana to provide safe water in heavily populated areas with decaying or insufficient infrastructure or a dropping groundwater table. Even water contaminated by livestock can be treated with Clearana to meet WHO safety standards. Clearana was approved for use after six years of testing in blind trials. It has been in use in some US states, including Nevada, Texas, and New Mexico, for several years.

While Clearana is considered absolutely safe, recent data on birth rates show a link between the use of Clearana and fertility rates. Previous studies had only considered OPNs (Overpopulated Nations), but now include OPRs (Overpopulated Regions). In OPN studies, fertility rates remain unaffected by use of Clearana. This result is due to a greater sample size, which includes populations with less dependence on treated water (since many people in sub-Saharan Africa outside of the big cities maintain independent water systems). Studies of OPR populations show a significant link between Clearana and a decline in fertility rates.

In meetings with officials from Niger, the Democratic Republic of the Congo, Nigeria, Uganda, North Sudan, and South Sudan, WHO staff learned that this link had been known to local health agencies, and that the use of Clearana (rather than other water-purification methods) was approved with this knowledge by the highest levels of government. In all public statements, the WHO has strongly opposed the use of drugs without informed consent, including especially drugs that affect fertility rates.

Local governments claim that reduced fertility is the only human side effect. They also claim that high birth rates among poor populations constitute a greater health risk than the use of Clearana. The link between high fertility rates and poverty, child mortality rates, communal disease, and economic stagnation has been documented in independent studies. Effectively, Clearana has been used to reduce the fertility rate in some regions of sub-Saharan Africa by two percentage points. (In comparison, the fertility rate in all European nations is below two percent.) The drop in birth rates has resulted in lowered infant mortality, higher literacy rates, and greater overall earning power for the current generations of young African adults. The demographic dividend of using Clearana is undeniable: without the use of Clearana, part of sub-Saharan Africa faces a population bottom-out, where economic gains cannot offset rising costs needed to finance education infrastructure and health care, and where urbanization leads to megacities such as Lagos. Four decades of explosive population growth have resulted in more famines, pressure on Europe due to immigration, and irreversible environmental damage, including loss of biodiversity and agrable land.

With the widespread use of Clearana as a water-purification method, some of these trends have slowed. The results have been beneficial for the affected populations in terms of health and economic status. After careful study and extensive consultation with African counterparts, the WHO recommends continued usage of Clearana as a measure to control population growth in select sub-Saharan African countries.

STRICTLY CONFIDENTIAL CLASSIFIED RED

BSE Briefing
The White House
CLASSIFIED
President Jackson:

After extensive study and based on the work done by the Greenhouse Emissions Committee, the White House environmental advisor, and the UN Climate Report 2016, we view the current BSE (Bovine spongiform encephalopathy) outbreak as an unprecedented opportunity to curtail beef consumption. Cattle farming is the greatest threat to the world's remaining rain forests and open prairies, the planet's "lungs" and the habitat of 31 percent of highly endangered species. Cattle production is driven by demand: in the past decade, beef production in Brazil and China grew by 27 percent. The BSE outbreak is the rare, and possibly once-in-a-lifetime, opportunity to discourage the consumption of beef as a dangerous convention.

We propose to allow the BSE epidemic to run its course in select populations. It is our only hope of curtailing the disastrous impact of the beef industry on health metrics and the environment.

This is not only good planetary stewardship but also sound

science. BSE occurs everywhere in cattle, but the conditions of "high yield farming" tip this occurrence of BSE into a public health hazard. The current outbreak has cost hundreds of human lives and required the destruction of tens of millions of head of cattle. Instead of procuring temporary solutions, the existing outbreak should be allowed to run its course. Fatality rates for BSE are 65 percent, with the remaining patients recovering fully when given adequate treatment. The number of casualties will be outweighed by diminished consumption and, ultimately, production of beef. As public health specialists and medical experts, we know that fear can be marshaled for the greater good.

Megacities

The swamp of files that suddenly appeared on my tablet is greater than I thought. There are clips embedded within clips, confidential stuff that shows decrypted links to random things taken off various media. Not all of it is edited, and some things are subtitled in languages other than English. Maybe Khmer, Thai, and Vietnamese, and definitely also French, Arabic, and Mandarin.

Grafted to the clip where the WHO signs off on population control as part of their "water keepers" pledge is a link to another meeting. In that clip, Lucia stands at a big conference table with a few tiny wooden and metal sculptures levitating a few inches or so above it. Must be some rich tech guy's house.

"Our water policies have resulted in important demographic shifts in OPNs over the past few years," Lucia said. "Where those measures have been in effect, environmental and public health indicators have improved across the board. We have saved lives, and we are restoring the possibility of a future for regions most taxed by overpopulation."

There were about twelve people in the room, plus Seth, Domineek, and two antagonistic senators I know well. Bill Kenton of Kentucky and Shawna Pritzer of Colorado consume probably one quarter of my attention and energy when we send proposals to Congress. They have voted against everything we've put to the floor, have fought for Big Agribusiness and Big Cattle, have refused to join all official meetings in Mexico or Canada even after HEPP was created through an act of Congress, used state power to slow down incentives for hydro and wind power, and resisted things that are apolitical no-brainers, such as replanting garbage dumps with bioengineered plants that break down plastics.

"Don't address your message to them," Keon always says when I vent about these guys, their malice and stupidity. "Craft your message around 'yes,' and 'next.' The more you focus on their obstruction, the more energy you'll send their way." Keon is right, even though I don't really go for that whole chi-energy bit. Although nearly everyone in the Beltway practices meditation, has a breathing coach, and does yoga, these are no Buddhists. Karma returns every election cycle, and mitzvahs are done only when you can bank on them being returned with interest.

And now I'm seeing these two dangerous, obstructionist, and democratically elected idiots in the same room with Lucia. "The challenge we face today is not controlling the rural populations," Lucia addressed the room. "The greatest challenge is the megacities that we have allowed to grow unchecked. To adopt a quote from Winston Churchill, who had overcome adversaries as great as those faced by the planet today, 'We shape our cities; thereafter they shape us.' The enormous problems for the people in these places—disease, pollution, water, energy—pose sometimes even greater risks for people outside of them. Many of the megacities of the world in Indonesia, Kenya, Nigeria, Mexico, Malaysia, and even India and China, are tragically failing."

Lucia paused. Behind her on the screen rolled a series of well-known images of the great slum fires in Delhi in 2019, then of a flooded city with streets like raging rivers carrying cars, houses, and people, and then other images of gun-wielding militias chasing panicked people fleeing across railroad tracks and a highway out of a shantytown and into a river. The White House had used those images frequently to promote sustainable policies, natural negotiation, solar, hydro, urban agriculture, "safe" antibiotics, and water treatment. America had done well with all of these industries.

"These crises are wake-up calls and opportunities," Lucia had said at a memorial for the victims of the big Delhi fires. The event had been carried live by media around the world. She had stood next to The Big Nanda, at the edge of a huge plaza covered with thousands of bodies wrapped in white sheets. The dead had all been treated to seal in disease, but time was of the essence to get them buried in the heat. A vast field of corpses.

"For every life lost in these tragic fires, we will build fireproof housing and provide solar-powered cooking stoves. Your families will be safe." I had seen the draft of that speech, but it quite literally had been underwritten by American manufacturers of fireproof materials and solar-cell stoves. Public-private partnership, it was called. "Charity with a bottom line," Seth likes to say.

On the clip in front of me, Lucia had paused for a moment for the pictures from all these catastrophes to roll by.

"These crises will continue and escalate," she said to the people gathered in the room. We spent an average of $600 on each African who had been hospitalized during the Ebola crisis in 2014. On the American infected with Ebola who had made it to New York in the same year, we spent $800,000. I had prepared those numbers for Domineek, and I knew that Lucia had looked at them. "If the cities of the world are allowed to grow further, more people will die." Lucia looked around the room. "You are the experts in this area," she said. "You have managed some of the greatest problems facing our planet today. You have saved millions of lives with water-treatment plants. You have rescued millions from storms and floods. You have made food safer, housing more secure. You have developed crops that make kids healthy, and you have wiped out diseases that killed millions every year only a short while ago."

Nobody said anything.

"Obviously, the problems presented in megacities cannot be resolved with Band-Aid solutions. Their sheer size taxes the environment irreversibly. They are containers about to burst their seams."

Behind Lucia was heat sensor imagery of some big city. Mexico City? Delhi?

"The only way to address these problems is to downsize the megacities," said one of the men at the table. "We have to halt or severely limit growth."

Lucia looked around the table.

"People will continue to leave rural areas to find work," Seth said.

"So we have to remove these incentives," another guy said.

"That will not do," Lucia said. "We have to actively discourage people. Make them not only *not* want to move to a megacity, but make them want to stay away at all cost. You all know what happened after the Hong Kong outbreak. You know what happened after the riots in Lagos." Lucia paused for a moment.

"People were afraid. The slums emptied out. People returned to the countryside," one of the senators said.

"There are factors beyond our control," Domineek said. "Remember last summer's heat wave in India? We lost tens of thousands of people in a matter of weeks. There were brownouts and not enough backup energy for days. The population had simply outstripped the infrastructure. It would have been possible to retrofit existing buildings to provide relief," he said, "but that would have simply brought in even more people, and ultimately some bigger crisis would have taken an even bigger toll."

"Like culling the herd," one of the guys at the table said.

"It's a matter of making decisions now, as difficult as that is, before similar situations affect tens of millions in the future," Lucia said.

"Culling the herd," the guy repeated.

"Our agencies have a mandate to help, not cause or exacerbate problems. How can we justify instigating a crisis?" a woman in a gray silk blouse and a few strands of expensive-looking beads said. She looked like an NGO'er, but rich, probably a founder.

"It's not a matter of starting anything," Lucia said. "It is a matter of letting things run their course. Megacities grew without planning, without oversight, without direction. We can let them get smaller by simply staying out of the way, adopting a policy of non-intervention. Like any ecosystem, a megacity will collapse once its population reaches a tipping point."

"Self-collapse is the safest way to stop the devastation brought about by megacities," Seth said. "There are fewer political issues since the process is organic, so to speak."

"The riots in Lagos were stopped by police," a distinguished-looking African woman said. She had an American accent and wore an intricately patterned yellow-and-red long scarf wrapped around her shoulders over a black jacket. "The outbreak in Hong Kong was traced to a batch of contaminated chicken in a military cafeteria, which had been inspected by the city's health inspectors."

"A single straw can tip the balance," Lucia said. "In some of those cases, Mme. Garçan, the authorities unintentionally lit the first match, so to speak. But the combustible material was there — an unsustainable burden on the environment. The reason for the outbreaks is the size of these places. The fire, the terrible riots: tragic but ultimately natural ways of resizing. While we mourn the losses in Hong Kong, today the city is healthier, more resilient, and more sustainable than before the outbreak."

"So we are going to stand by while these places burn?" the woman asked. "You want us to be complicit in such a plan? Is that why have we been invited here?"

"You are here to continue your important work," Lucia responded. "You are here because you know more about these areas than any of us, Mme. Garçan. We will not intervene in some of the events unfolding in megacities. We need your organization's expertise and assistance containing these areas to protect the people outside the crisis zone."

"This plan has already been approved in a closed plenary session of the WHO's key members. Our own environmental advisor,

Aleks Verdan, has been in touch with key UN member states," Seth added. "We are here to inform you that the US and HEPP will not intervene and stop a collapse in progress. We will, however, provide assistance to *contain* instances of collapse in megacities. We will help the populations around these areas."

"Let them rot," Mme. Garçan said. "That is going to be our health policy?" She looked around the table. "My mission is to build infrastructure and schools for the poor. What the hell are you asking me to do?"

"It's a delicate balance," Lucia said. "But when we intervene and save megacities, we only delay more serious environmental crises and the inevitable collapse."

"So we do nothing but watch as people die," Mme. Garçan said. Her lips were pressed tight, and she put her hands against the edge of the table as if preparing to get up. But she stayed put.

"We're done here," Lucia said. "As I said, this meeting is informational only. We want you to know that HEPP forces will not intervene."

Lucia got up and walked over to Mme. Garçan to whisper something in her ear. The woman followed Lucia out of the room, followed by Domineek, Seth, and the two awful senators.

I had to put my head between my knees for a moment, so I wouldn't throw up.

The New York Times

Global South America

March 16, 2022

World Briefing

BRAZIL - The Brazilian ministry of health has ordered the destruction of an additional 16 million head of cattle after a strain of BSE (mad cow disease) was discovered on ranches and in Brazilian beef processed in plants in Argentina, Chile, the United States, France, the UK, Australia, and China.

This last order follows the destruction of over 60 million head of cattle over the past two weeks in Brazil after outbreaks of BSE overwhelmed hospitals in Brazil, Argentina, and the European Union. Farmworkers shut down roads in Brasilia and São Paolo to protest the destruction of cattle, which they view as an overreaction prompted by animal rights and environmental activists. The beef industry has grown 20 percent in the last two decades in Brazil, which is the third largest producer of meat after China and the United States. Industry leaders point out that technology has reduced pasture area by 6 percent, while productivity per hectare increased by 25 percent.

The destruction of herds in Brazil occurred in response to the worldwide epidemic that has cost hundreds of lives in Europe and South America. Hospitals in Brazil, Argentina, and several European nations have refused to accept patients suspected of carrying BSE. In France and Germany, the governments have denied the existence of BSE cases, although the WHO has posted those cases on their websites. In the UK and in Poland, patients suspected of being affected by BSE have been transferred to military hospitals. Activists blame beef, but there have been claims that the disease is transmitted via medical equipment. Some experts claim that the BSE strain in Brazil's herds is not fatal to humans.

As a precautionary measure, the US and the EU have instituted a complete ban on Brazilian beef and the destruction of all Brazilian meat currently in US or European processing plants and stores. They have also urged consumers to discard any food products suspected to contain traces of Brazilian beef. The Brazilian Minister of Trade, Cantarelli Terner, has sharply criticized these measures as "irresponsible manipulations of the market based on fear, not facts."

Google News

Climate Refugees Granted Limited Political Status

The United Nations
New York City, USA
April 14, 2022
Access time stamp April 14, 2022 by Aleks Verdan

In a closed session in Brussels, the security chamber of the European Union formally recognized refugees from countries affected by environmental disaster, such as storms, flooding, severe weather, crop failure, toxic spills, pollution, and drought, as political refugees. An important part of this recognition is that refugees must originally be citizens or legal residents in countries that have signed the Johannesburg Compact of Climate Control and implemented measures to protect the environment.

Human rights advocates welcome the new category, which automatically grants political protection to hundreds of thousands of refugees from low-lying areas in Bangladesh. But it leaves out similar numbers from neighboring cities in Bengal, which has been slow to adopt the measures created in Johannesburg.

It is unclear whether the new status grants these individuals access to residency or rights in any region.

The Daily Sun

Protecting Elephants: Townships Resettled

October 14, 2022

By ANLI BEDJA

Access Time Stamp October 14, 2022 by Aleks Verdan

In an effort to protect the dwindling number of wild elephants in South Africa, the government ordered the relocation of several unauthorized townships that have developed near Kruger National Park in recent years. The townships are home to an estimated 300,000 people, many of them migrants and their families from other African nations or parts of Asia, who have found employment in the park's resort hotels, or as game wardens and workers.

"It's not sustainable to have hundreds of thousands of people set up an unauthorized encampment next to a protected park," said William Forsyth, head of South Africa's Department of Development. "These parks are our only hope of ensuring the survival of the wild elephant population in South Africa."

Human rights advocates have criticized the action that destroyed the shantytown and moved most residents to locations as far away as Johannesburg. One hundred twenty-eight people are reported to have died in clashes with police and during the destruction of a storefront church that had not been fully evacuated when bulldozers moved in early Sunday morning. The events that led to the collapse of the building remain under investigation.

The South African government has issued a statement of "sincere regret" over the casualties, but defends the relocation of the shantytown as a necessary step to protect the park. Two years ago, high security "smart" fences were erected around the park to keep out poachers and itinerant farmers. Critics say that under pressure from international agencies the government places the protection of game parks above the needs of its rural population for inhabitable space.

Opening the Dam

I have spent a few hours trying to search the downloaded files systematically. I found footage of the big Earth Day events in China. The clip starts, weirdly enough, with Keon and me in our formal wear (old-school tuxedos, and Keon with Jheri curls that I didn't remember and that make him look like a pop star from the last century) at the American Symphony Orchestra's concert at the People's Hall in Beijing. I remember that Chinese media made a big deal of the fact that America's greatest orchestra had so many musicians of Asian extraction.

"And they all studied in Shanghai," Keon pointed out when I told him about the media focus. "That's why they are so good."

The visit was the first time Keon met Yanfen. They got along well, and we spent a day with him and a German or Dutch girl he was dating, in the Imperial Gardens, drinking white wine and eating fried fish while looking out over the swaying lotus blossoms.

Footage of what looks like villages being flooded that evidently had little or no advance warning is spliced into the middle of the concert clips. There are Chinese subtitles on Lucia's speech in Tiananmen Square about the Three Gorges Dam. Then, shots of flooded houses and people crowded on rooftops and on top of walls. In one scene a wall collapses and at least thirty people in orange life vests tumble into the rushing water below.

There are police and military close by, but they keep their distance from the stranded people. It's not difficult to figure out what is going on: the people wearing vests are not being helped or rescued, but the police are there to keep the media away. The clip shows police rushing toward the camera until it goes dark — it's like a trick sequence. More footage is spliced together without subtitles, but with voiceovers from Lucia's speech.

"Together we can restore the river to its original course," she says. "Together we can find a way to live with nature and not dam it in."

Rushing water carries rooftops, small cars, trees — and also countless people in orange life vests, who are whisked along by the current until they get sucked under. Some of them pop back up like corks. Soldiers are lined up along embankments, bridges, and overpasses. I stop and rewind the clip, it's very jumpy footage, and I worry about losing the whole clip when I rewind. The soldiers hold rifles and use long poles to keep people from reaching the shore. I remember our visit to Tokyo right after Typhoon Michio, and the official who explained that they helped only people who had followed instructions to evacuate. But in this clip from the dam flood, people are wearing government-issued vests, which makes me think they followed the rules.

The New York Times

POLITICS

Changes in Voter Identification in 16 States

By ANDREA GERSHIN

January 6, 2019

Sixteen US states, including the populous states of Texas, California, and New Jersey, have added work brigade identification badges, the ubiquitous "greenies" worn by all members of the brigades, as acceptable forms of identification for local and federal elections. That makes 41 states that accept these eco-IDs. Environmental activists hailed the decision while political watchdog groups criticized the move as keeping people who do not participate in eco brigades from voting. Membership in eco brigades among those 18–35 years of age is at 65 percent of the population. The badges store members' personal, medical, and financial data, serve as driver's licenses, and now also identify the members of eco brigades as registered voters.

Burn-Out Policies

From: Surgeon General, Vice Admiral
Sandini Poddhar, MD, MBA
To: POTUS
Re: Public Health response to L-MRSA epidemic
Background:

The L-strain MRSA outbreak has affected some 30,000 people in Asia and overwhelmed the public health systems of Hong Kong and Southern China. All air travel from Hong Kong has been halted, and travelers from mainland China are individually screened and quarantined upon arrival in suspected cases. This recent outbreak of L-strain MRSA in several Asian regions, including Hong Kong and Shenzen, PRC, mandates a joint response by the government. At the president's request, the surgeon general has carried out studies that combine WHO data with data gathered by the US military in response to major outbreaks over the past 40 years.

L-strain MRSA for untreated patients has a mortality rate of over 85 percent. To our knowledge, there have been 12 confirmed cases in the US. All of them have been fatal; none of them have been made public. It can be assumed that the number of non-registered cases is at least triple that amount.

Given the extreme and only partially understood contagion of L-strain MRSA, the current lack of available treatment, and the suspected number of latent and undocumented carriers in Asia, we recommend the following policies.

Our first line of defense should be the prevention of entry. Economic, social, political, and even humanitarian considerations must be put aside temporarily. All travel from Hong Kong must be banned immediately. People who have visited Hong Kong or mainland China in the past week should not be allowed entry to the United States until the 21-day incubation period passes. Under federal directives, travelers who circumvent these rules are subject to arrest and detention until their health status has been verified.

After extensive analysis of all available medical, public-health, logistical, and political data, and after long-term review of the spread of HIV in the 1990s, and Ebola in 2014, we have concluded that the disease must be allowed to burn itself out. There is currently no known cure for L-MRSA. Treatment includes quarantine/isolation, IV nutrition, and a cleanliness regimen. The public suspects that medical facilities spread L-MRSA in so called "death units." For this reason, patients have escaped from hospitals in several locations in spite of strict security measures.

Given the absence of available treatment, the low survival rate, and the enormous risk posed for the world's population, we recommend the complete isolation of L-MRSA areas through a cordon sanitaire enforced by Chinese, US, and HEPP forces. Survivors develop complete immunity. About 30 percent of the population is immune for reasons not yet understood. With the isolation of L-MRSA in these two hot spots, the disease is expected to run its full course within 84 days.

The economic impact of isolating Shenzen and Hong Kong through a cordon sanitaire is estimated at US$14 B/month.

The costs of L-MRSA spreading to other parts of Asia, Europe, or the US are inestimable.

Inaction will likely lead to the deaths of millions of people in mainland China, other parts of Asia, and the US. The only defensible and compassionate course of action is the temporary isolation of the disease-carrying population until the disease has burned itself out.

Lucia in India

I've asked for pain relievers to get rid of my pounding headache, but then didn't take them for fear that they would make me sleepy. Drinking lots and lots of water, but I'm not feeling so well. I found another clip in which I am mentioned but have never seen before. It's Lucia speaking to a group of about fifty Indian legislators or politicians of some sort in an ornate room with etched crystal walls and a large stone-topped table in its center. Most are in suits, a few men in lungis, and a good number of women in ornate saris. Big Nanda sits next to Lucia.

"It is an honor and a privilege to speak to you today. The United States and India have a special relationship. We are the two greatest democracies in the world, beacons of hope in a world enamored by less open, less free, and less just forms of government. The Republic of India and the United States share more than the commitment to freedom and the democratically created rule of law. Our nations also share the wish to preserve and protect the environment, to keep our planet safe and healthy for generations to come."

The people around the table knock on it for applause.

"I am here today to talk about water. In the United States, we have made some progress in cleaning our rivers and lakes. I believe our government's environmental advisor, Aleks Verdan, is known to some of you. We have won over industries by convincing our voters that healthy rivers mean healthy children, and healthy lives. Well, I need to be accurate — our voters have allowed us to work with the private sector to keep our rivers clean."

Nanda stood up.

"President Jackson is too modest here," he said, and smiled. "It has been her achievement to push through legislation that guarantees a future for America's rivers."

Lucia did not say anything.

"The Republic of India faces some additional challenges," Nanda said. "We have gathered you here today because you have been at the forefront of our country's push for cleaner water." He nodded at a few individuals around the table. "We seek your advice on how to proceed."

"The greatest challenge to Indian waterways is our own people," a man said. He had a closely trimmed white beard and longish hair, and wore a white lungi with blue seams. "No matter how much we restrict polluters and other offenders," he said, "we cannot monitor a population as vast as ours."

"We are here to address this challenge in humane and sustainable ways," said the prime minister. "We are here to applaud you for your work on India's rivers, and above all, to find ways to control our population."

A ripple went through the audience, followed by hushed chatter.

"We know this is a difficult topic," Nanda said loudly to cut through the noise. "But we also know it is a critical issue that needs the attention of our best minds."

"The United States, in cooperation and with full approval of the UN, has successfully developed programs to right-size the populations of several nations," Lucia said. "This has been accomplished in humane and safe ways." More chatter, louder this time.

"China failed with its policies!"

"We won't stand for it!"

"Our greatest concern is the well-being of Indians in this great nation," Nanda cut through the noise. "We want to adopt some of the measures to control the growth of our population without relying on outmoded, draconian birth-restriction policies like other countries."

"What has been effective is a simple additive that through independent studies has proven to be completely safe," Lucia said. "It's a simple compound that leaves treated water safe but limits fertility."

There were even more noisy objections now.

"We are here because we face difficult choices," Nanda said.

"How do we know this substance is safe?" a woman seated at the table said sharply. "Whose studies are we supposed to accept as true?" She looked at Lucia. "Why is the US taking an interest in this matter?"

"We have used this method with success for twenty years now," Lucia responded, without raising her voice. The noise stopped so people could hear. "It's safe. Some of the results are classified, but I can provide aggregate data that show huge improvement for all environmental and public-health indexes in user regions."

"The results are truly impressive," Nanda said. "Increased overall health, decreased infant mortality, higher education attainment, and economic opportunities, especially for girls and women. And a significant improvement in all environmental markers: water, air, pollution, energy, even species protection."

"The United States takes a great interest in finding—and funding—humane solutions because these issues affect us all," Lucia said.

"Water knows no borders," Nanda said. "Neither does pollution or disease." He paused but people were silent now, waiting for him to say more.

"Our proposal is to introduce these fertility measures immediately in all of our states. I urge you to look at the data on your screens and ask questions. But I remind you that we cannot afford to resist action. I also remind you of the terrible loss of life in overpopulated parts of the country due to flooding just last year. If we do not act, nature will exact its toll in less humane ways."

"If we decline to act now we are condemning millions to starvation, suffering, and death," Lucia said.

The clip ends here.

My Job

President Lucia Jackson
The Oval Office
THE WHITE HOUSE
June 12, 2022

Dear Seth:

I am pleased to appoint you to the position of White House special advisor on the environment, effective June 13, 2022. You will report directly to me in any and all matters relating to policy and strategy on environmental issues.

Your contributions to our strategy in securing the planet's future have been invaluable so far, and I look forward to achieving even greater things together.

Sincerely,

Lucia Jackson

Google News

U.N. Expands Width of Cordons Sanitaires

Access Time Stamp May 12, 2022 by Aleks Verdan

After a contentious debate on Wednesday that followed months of expert testimonies and reports from several health and human rights organizations, the UN Security Council granted India the right to patrol with drones and dogs the cordon sanitaire extending two miles from Indian territory into Bengal. The issue of a country's right to patrol a health safety zone outside of its border has been a point of contention. In 2021, Ghana deployed trained dogs to identify humans infected with Ebola into a mile-wide stretch of Togo cleared as a cordon sanitaire. The dogs identified carriers who were then detained in Togo with Ghanaian drones.

In Wednesday's resolution, the Security Council granted countries the right to patrol for infection outside of their borders. The resolution follows similar ones that allow countries to deny permission to airplanes with disease-carrying passengers to enter domestic airspace and land in local airports, even if the plane is in distress. In 2021, French fighter jets shot down a civilian airliner originating in the Central African Republic when the pilot tried to land without permission at an airport near Toulouse. The military action was ruled permissible by the International Court in the Hague.

Officials of the WHO and the White House special advisor on the environment welcomed the resolution. "While we have to honor humanitarian concerns, we have to let countries protect their citizens from an outbreak," said a White House spokeswoman. "The creation of cordons sanitaires has to be approved by all adjoining states and overseen by a UN-led task force. But countries have the right to protect their citizens from pathogens crossing the border, which can happen before an infected person reaches the border itself."

The UN resolution effectively subordinates the rights of a carrier country to those of a healthy region.

"It puts the health of rich nations above those of poor people," said Meri Hassain, professor of epidemiology at Johns Hopkins University's School for Global Public Health.

"It's a question of scale," said Emily Hernan, of the British delegation that strongly lobbied for the resolution. "We make the health of many our main concern. We are adhering to the principles laid out by President Jackson in her address to the UN to protect the planet's health."

Allowing countries to control the cordons sanitaires is viewed by many as a necessary and logical measure in controlling pandemics that have cost tens of thousands of lives in the last decade. The UN resolution does not specify how humanitarian or legal disputes in the cordons sanitaires will be mediated.

Secret Cruise

From: Centers for Disease Control
To: White House
National Security Concern
Planning Document
Scenario: Communicable Disease on Large Passenger Vessel (Cruise Ship)

The Centers for Disease Control puts the likelihood of a communicable disease outbreak on a passenger vessel at moderate risk level. An outbreak is considered an emergency when at least 18 percent of a medium to large ship's total population is infected or suspected of infection. During the 2010s, several scenarios occurred on cruise ships off the coasts of the North American south (Florida to Cuba), and in the eastern Pacific (Southern HEPP/Mexico). In those cases, medical emergency teams were dispatched to the ships and large numbers of infected passengers were airlifted to mainland quarantine units. This exceedingly costly procedure resulted in several casualties of medical and support staff in the quarantine units. In one case, the quarantine units had to be closed and eliminated before the disease could be contained within the affected individuals. The evacuation protocol effectively moored the ship's remaining population for a total of 140 days, since additional previously undetected cases became symptomatic during the subsequent incubation cycle. In several cases, local harbor masters refused entry to vessels, and small flotillas of armed private vessels tried to block access to the harbor entry and the docks. In other cases, all of a cruise ship's passengers were disembarked and transported to quarantine stations dispersed across HEPP. In addition to tremendous costs, this scenario created public-health risks for local populations in several HEPP locations. We have reports of passengers evading quarantine and merging undetected with the local population.

In recent years, we have seen mass outbreaks of drug-resistant flu strains, the Bouvier virus in northern Africa, parts of Europe, and several locations in south Asia. An assessment of these scenarios, and the unresolved case of the Japanese-operated cruise ship Eternity, which sank off the west coast of New Zealand in 2016 in calm seas, led to the following protocol:

If a vessel carries passengers and/or crew infected with, or suspected of being infected with one of the Class O diseases, the vessel will be intercepted and escorted by HEPP and/or US Navy vessels to high seas beyond 160 nautical miles from any shore or port with a population of over 5,000.

In the case of a Class O infection, the vessel's population will be provided with medical and other supplies but sail under HEPP command. Every measure will be taken to support and provide medical care for the vessel's population, regardless of the nationality of individual passengers and the ship's flag. CDC and HEPP will provide medical support, and the public will be assured that all passengers can be monitored and treated on board.

In the case of an illness with high infection rates and long incubation or carrier periods, the vessel will not be permitted to return to shore. Medical assessment will be provided by CDC staff. If the infection rate on board exceeds a tipping point established by the CDC (above .15 as of date of this memo), the vessel's return to shore would pose a significant public health risk. Every effort will be made, via airdrops and locally deployed personnel, airlifted to the moored ship, to help the affected passengers and crew.

US Navy will be ordered by the president of the United States to sink the vessel in a way that leaves all bodies at sea at least 160 nautical miles from the nearest inhabited shore. Measures must be taken to contain the site of sinking, and prevent the movement of infected bodies outside of that area ("drop and drown" methods). Dissemination of any and all information concerning the use of weapons to sink an infected vessel is reserved to the secretary of defense, the secretary of health, and the president of the United States. No communiqué or release of information will be posted without specific prior authority.

Report on Banff National Park Incident

From: Travis Hernández, administrator, EPA
To: President Jackson
Re: Incident at Banff National Park
Accessed: Aleks Verdan, December 12, 2022 [time stamp]

Dear President Jackson,

I herewith present the findings of an investigation conducted jointly by the EPA, Federal Bureau of Reclamation, CIA, FBI, and US Military Command into the assassination of 12 EPA agents in Banff National Park, Canada, on July 12, 2021.

The full report is attached. Our shared and unequivocal conclusion is that the US EPA agents were assassinated by a team of US soldiers acting under sole command of one lieutenant colonel. That individual was court-martialed for an unrelated incident in 2021 and committed suicide as a civilian later that year. Our inquiry uncovered conclusive evidence that the order stopped with this individual. All of the soldiers have been taken off duty and are awaiting their proceedings. They claim that they acted in the belief that their target was a highly dangerous gang of terrorists. The scope of our inquiry was limited strictly to fact-finding.

We feel obligated to stress in the most absolute manner that no information about these findings must be made public lest irreparable reputational damage be done to our military.

This is a highly unusual case of a rogue officer acting recklessly. The chiefs of staff have ordered a full review of the investigation protocols for incidents involving small elite teams deployed in civilian settings.

Respectfully submitted,

Travis Hernández
Administrator, EPA

The Shed

On my tablet I am watching a vast pinkish landscape, rings upon rings of red, pink, and magenta earth piled around deeper brownish holes speckled with white, crystalline spots. Cloud shadows hurl across the landscape, which has been gouged by mining sites that look like huge, fleshy orchid blossoms sprouting out of the valley's floor.

There is no machinery in sight. No yellow earth movers, no silvery trucks crawling along the highways like wood lice scurrying in a damp basement. A few seconds later, we are flying low over woods, above several roads carved into the forest, a deep green soothing to the eye.

The camera descends, and our shed comes into view. I see the feathery bamboo, the hardy cacti I put in to create something like a rock garden, the beds of deer-resistant purple asters that I put in one fall when I got terrible poison ivy on one arm and spread it, stupidly, to my forehead, the thick pillows of white hellebores. The footage is shaky now, and edited quickly, like a trick sequence. There are three people rushing around. One of them is Keon, wearing a black knit cap, puffy vest over a gray sweater, black shorts over running tights, and his red sneakers. The other two people are in suits. Within minutes, boxes, bags, and our suitcases are piled on the small brick patio in front of the shed, where Keon usually sits in the mornings to meditate when we are there. The chairs are pushed to the side, almost into the bed of asters.

It's a big pile, and I recognize my bags and a bundle of coats just tied together with a belt or rope. There are two or three clear plastic bags stuffed with bedding or towels, it seems. Each of the bags is tagged with a bright red sticker and some numbers. The pile grows bigger while the two guys scurry back and forth. Keon arranges the bundles and bags, and now carefully sets the framed set of Grandpa's film stills from our living room on the ground. The stuff looks like most of the movable content of our apartment in the city, minus the furniture. Keon gives no sign that he is aware of a drone or someone filming; this must be edited and sped-up security footage. Now he shakes the hands of the two guys in suits, who look like security and not at all like disheveled movers, although they've just lobbed an entire apartment's worth of stuff out of a . . . chopper? How did Keon get access to a cargo chopper?

The car is parked next to the house near a huge heap of withered sunflower stalks and brush ready for the compost. There's a lot of stuff to do this season. Winter crops need to be put in. I'll do bulbs, of course, and in the spring, the place will explode in clouds of crocuses and snowdrops, then daffodils and hyacinths, and even long, droopy tulips if I'm lucky and can find some on the deep web.

We have to trim the berry patch. The berries run down into a gulch and toward the woods. Every fall we clear branches out of the trees above to keep the berries with enough sunlight. They are all wild species, some of them wonderfully invasive, that produce small, hard berries. Not like those big, plump berries you get at the market, ready to plop on top of a sundae — but these will survive anything.

We didn't find them locally, although they look native enough: gnarled, low to the ground, unfriendly with big thorns. They have been brought back by a collective in Ohio, where people are committed to resilient, edible crops.

But what is going on with this move? What the hell?

The suited guys have vanished from sight. Keon carries Grandpa's pictures into the house. The bamboo, the asters, the hellebores are bent down by sudden gusts of wind — the chopper is taking off. Keon shields his eyes and looks straight into the camera, which must be mounted on the chopper, but he does not wave or smile.

The forest appears again, from above, stitched up by service roads. When Keon bought the shed with his grandparents' money, we could get there only in a four-wheel drive. When we drove there right after they ended their lives, the need to pay close attention to how and where we were physically moving along the surface of the earth, had been soothing. A reminder that the country is vast, and that being in a particular location matters. That we matter, in how we live on this planet in our particularities, in space and time, and not only as data points, sites for decisions to be taken. Keon's grandparents' deaths had left a terrible void, but they had taken this decision, from what I can only imagine, in a very present state. Keon's grief and pain when he was struck by the finality of their absence had been lined with the awareness that they had chosen the time and place. I don't believe we go anywhere once we are gone. I don't believe in heaven, in an afterlife, in a beyond. I don't find solace in the fact that we return to matter, ashes to ashes, dust to dust. Eaten by worms, and fertilizing the fields. But I think that we *matter* as human beings because we existed on *this* particular planet, and that without us, this planet matters not at all. Even if in the rhythms of the universe, humanity's hum will not be missed once our species is gone, it matters that we lived here, on earth, and not just on any planet. It matters that we existed, as individuals, as Keon's grandmother with her pretty wigs and three marriages, and his grandfather with his penchant for Russian literature and whiskey, neat, starting at noon. Earth matters, but only in the sense that it provides us with the possibility of existing in a particular place at a particular time.

The clip banks close to the mining holes dug into the reddish and magenta soil at the forest's edge. Towns and highways come into view.

I watch it over and over, trying to slow the footage, but it's a locked file. The ragged, pinkish holes cut into the brown earth are starkly beautiful, violent like a Frank Stella painting made of shiny scrap metal. The forest is a deep green. I rewind the clip to watch Keon and the suited guys speed-piling our stuff, the swaying asters and the bright green bamboo bowing down when the chopper takes off. It's hard to tell, but Keon looks grateful, or maybe relieved, when the guys say something to him when they're done. They keep their gloves on when they shake hands. Something I notice only now.

Please Let Me Go

I am not proud of what I've done. It'll cost me my security clearance, if not more. This morning when they checked my vitals, I pulled the medic's arm toward me and slammed the reach-through down on it, as far as it would go, at the same time. His arm got stuck, and I didn't let go. He screamed and tried to pull his arm back but not very strongly. It was clear that he was afraid his suit would break. So I held his arm tight in a vise, while he pleaded and whimpered.

"Let me go, please," he moaned. "Aleks, man, just let go of my arm." Like he was afraid that I would bite into it.

"I'll let go when I get some answers," I said. "What's my status? Why was I moved? Why can't I go online? What are these files about? Get me in touch with my partner, and with the White House! I need to get in touch with the outside!"

The medic wriggled his arm a little, but I held on tighter, wedging it between my arm in a way made him scream.

"Let go of my arm! You're breaking it!"

"What's my status? Tell me!"

I knew they were watching me, listening. Through the screen I could see a few shapes moving.

"Aleks, please let him go," another voice said over the intercom. "You're putting everyone at great risk, including yourself."

"Please, let me go," the medic said.

"What is my status? I am entitled to some information! What risk?"

"You are still under observation," the voice said. "Incubation can take up to eight days, so, I cannot tell you yet."

"You said five days. I was told five days! And I have no fucking symptoms."

"You are here, Aleks, so we can take care of you," another medic said who had suddenly appeared in the hallway outside.

"Why was I moved? *How* are you taking care of me? I thought infection is five days? I was told five! I mean incubation? Incubation, not infection! Why can't I go online? Are there drugs in this water? In the air?" I was yelling. Without meaning to I must have jerked or twisted the medic's arm.

"The suit!" he screamed but did not pull his arm back.

I almost let go.

"Aleks, you're exposing him," the other medic said. "Aleks, be reasonable!" A few of them were gathered on the other side of the screen now. I could feel the guy tense his arm, so I held on more tightly.

"Am I contagious? What is my status?"

"Your status is unchanged, Aleks. You are under observation and during that time you may be contagious. We're keeping everyone up to date."

"Why can't I go online? Let me talk with Keon!" I demanded.

"Aleks, you're putting him at risk," one of the medics said again. "You need to let go of him. Then we'll tell you what you need to know."

"Why was I moved? When did you move me?"

They didn't respond. I held fast to the medic's arm.

"You requested the move, Aleks," the medic said, slowly.

"What are you talking about?"

"We moved you yesterday," said the guy whose arm I was holding. He sounded like he couldn't get enough air through his mask. I didn't loosen my grip.

"Everyone gets moved after five days. We discussed this. You said yes to being moved. We are in another facility, in Maryland."

I couldn't see his eyes behind the mask.

"I requested a move or everyone gets moved — which is it?"

"Please let me go," the guy said.

I wasn't going to. I needed answers. I tightened my grip around the guy's arm. My own arm hurt a bit, and my legs started to hurt. I was crouching against the wall and tried to get into a better position without letting go of the arm. For a moment I imagined slipping my body through the opening as the medic pulled back his arm, even though it's only as big as a football.

The other medics huddled around the guy. They whispered something, and I braced myself for them to pull the guy's arm back through the opening. Fourth quarter, fourth down. Aleks down seven. Go!

"Just lemme go, man," the guy pleaded again. "Please. You're gonna rip the suit." His voice was a hoarse whisper now.

"Am I contagious?!"

The medic pulled his arm, yanked and twisted, and I could feel the suit starting to tear. I let go. He quickly retracted this arm. He scrambled backwards on his legs and hands while extending his previously trapped arm in front of him as if it was a dangerous, foreign thing and not a part of his body. The other medics quickly slammed a thick plastic board against the opening.

"Aleks, you have just put everyone at risk," one of the medics said via the intercom. He actually shouted. "You could be contagious, asshole."

He didn't say anything more. They had left.

"Hey!" I called out, but I had very suddenly become conscious of what I had done. "Hey!" I called again.

I had attacked a medic, almost broken his suit, risked exposing him. What if the membrane around his arm had broken? I'd hoped to remind them that I'd crossed the Rubicon, the five-day mark, and that since I don't have any symptoms, I should be released.

But I had nearly crossed a wholly different line — the one when crossed without permission puts everyone at risk. When the medic scrambled back from the opening, I was shocked. I backed down. And fast. They could have sucked the air out of the pod. Blasted me with sedatives. They would've had every right to stop me, in any way, from acting out.

Now I've slept for a few hours, so maybe they pumped something into the room. My forehead feels heavy like there's a weight placed behind my eyes. I start to sweat when I think about the fact that I grabbed the medic's arm.

The hole is fixed, but now I have to put my arm through a different airlock to get tested. They want to scan my skin, which I guess is how you can determine an infection in its earliest stages. My skin feels fine to me. I've looked everywhere, checked for any spots or rashes. I'm trying to think calmly, rationally. I am embarrassed for having attacked the medic. Ashamed. Frustrated. What was I thinking? I've probably been put on some kind of watch. I have asked again to not be given any drugs, but how can I know? Now they don't even come close to the door.

Something has changed.

I sleep a lot. Drink a lot of fluids. The inside of my mouth feel dry. My forehead feels warm.

www.ingramcontent.com/pod-product-compliance
Lightning Source LLC
Chambersburg PA
CBHW020819180626
46814CB00001B/34

9781734735390